About

Kelli Ireland spent corporate America. Unexpectedly sense of humour, she chose to carpe the diem and pursue her passion for writing. A fan of happily-ever-afters, she found she loved being the Puppet Master for the most unlikely couples. Seeing them through the best and worst of each other while helping them survive the joys and disasters of falling in love? Best. Thing. Ever. Visit Kelli's website at kelliireland.com

Cara Colter shares ten acres in British Columbia with her real-life hero Rob, ten horses, a dog, and a cat. She has three grown children and a grandson. Cara is a recipient of the Career Achievement Award in the Love and Laughter category from *Romantic Times Book Reviews*. Cara invites you to visit her on Facebook!

Award-winning author **Jennifer Faye** pens fun contemporary romances. With more than a million books sold, she's internationally published with books translated into more than a dozen languages and her work has been optioned for film. Now living her dream, she resides with her very patient husband and Writer Kitty. When she's not plotting out her next romance, you can find her with a mug of tea and a book. Learn more at jenniferfaye.com

Workplace Romance

Workplace Romance:
The Wedding Planner

KELLI IRELAND

CARA COLTER

JENNIFER FAYE

MILLS & BOON

First Published in Great Britain 2024
by Mills & Boon, an imprint of HarperCollins*Publishers* Ltd,
1 London Bridge Street, London, SE1 9GF

www.harpercollins.co.uk

HarperCollins*Publishers*
Macken House, 39/40 Mayor Street Upper,
Dublin 1, D01 C9W8, Ireland

ISBN: 978-0-263-32334-4

WICKED HEAT

KELLI IRELAND

To all the readers around the world who have found joy in the pages I've written. This one's for you.

CHAPTER ONE

ELLA MONTGOMERY PRESSED her forehead against the plane's small window, her stomach wedged near the top of her throat. She watched as the ground rapidly approached, the pilot executing what felt like a slimly controlled descent through the trade winds. Flying always reminded her just how fragile mortality was. A small mechanical failure. A miscalculated approach. Hell, an unpredicted shift in the wind. Any of it could change her round-trip ticket to a one-way. No refunds. No guarantees.

She held her breath as the tires skipped across the crumbling asphalt runway, the wings flexing far more than anything metal ever should. A flock of feral chickens scattered into the thick brush, necks extended in alarm, the rooster frantic to keep up with his ladies.

The pilot hit the brakes on the twin engines, and the momentum thrust Ella forward in a seat designed to be comfortable for individuals still mastering the fundamentals of addition and subtraction. With her hands gripping the armrests, she gritted her teeth and rode out an arrival more in line with a dirt runway in remote Wyoming rather than her actual destination: Bora Bora, French Polynesia.

The Cessna puttered down the short airstrip before turning sharply and taxiing to the private airport. Two visibly harried baggage handlers tended the luggage. One crouched in the belly of the plane at the next gate over and tossed luggage out the plane's belly button while the other caught said luggage and created a small pile on the tarmac. To the side of it all stood a lone airport representative in a starched white uniform sporting several leis draped over his arm.

The plane was small enough that the pilot didn't use the intercom but instead emerged from the cabin. He opened the front exit at the same time a rolling ladder hit the side of the plane, a metallic clank resonating through the cabin.

Then the pilot stood—as much as he could in the compact space—and addressed the passengers in the eight-seat cabin. "Ladies and gentlemen, welcome to Parkaire Field in beautiful Bora Bora. If you'll gather your personal belongings, your baggage will be available at the foot of the stairs, where you or your driver may retrieve it."

Seated in the second row from the front, Ella decided to wait out the minirush of fellow travelers anxious to be off the puddle jumper. She watched people contort their bodies into amusing shapes in an effort to retrieve their luggage and make their way to the front. A man who'd sat in the row opposite her tugged with ferocious intent on the handle of the large briefcase he'd shoved under the seat in front of him. The handle gave way and the man lunged ass first into the aisle, plowing into another traveler who stood beside Ella's seat.

The assaulted passenger lurched sideways, flailing as he tried to regain his balance...but failed. Not just failed, but *failed*. He tumbled into her lap, all long arms and longer legs. A button from his suit jacket popped free and skipped across Ella's forehead. Paperwork scattered as the stranger's messenger bag was upended and a laptop landed on top of her foot.

"Sorry, sorry, sorry," the assailant repeated as he retrieved his briefcase and clutched it to his chest with one hand, mopping his forehead with the other.

"No worries. It's bound to happen in such cramped quarters."

Without offering to help Ella up, the pardoned man shuffled the few steps to the front of the plane and down the stairs.

"Right," the stranger on her lap mused in a proper British accent, amusement saturating each word. "Because it's certainly de rigueur to hip-check fellow passengers." He twisted around to look down at her, mischief darkening his gaze. "Is it not?"

She shouldn't engage with him—she *knew* she shouldn't—but he was so damned attractive, sitting there in her lap flirting, with the challenge in his eyes so open, that she couldn't stop herself. Tilting her head in a coquettish manner, she met his gaze head-on. "I suppose it depends, really."

"Oh?"

She nodded somberly.

One corner of his mouth twitched. "Pray tell, what does it depend on?"

She sat up a little straighter just as he leaned in. Her lips brushed the shell of his ear as she spoke. "I suppose it all comes down to one thing. Is your ass in the habit of assaulting laps?"

"I'll be honest. I've been considering it as a side job."

"Obviously."

"Obviously?" he said on a choked laugh.

The stranger twisted and turned as he tried to free himself from the narrow alleyway created by the seat in front of her and her upper body. He managed, but not without accidentally brushing the outer edge of her breast.

His touch made her draw in a sharp breath.

The man cleared his throat and eyed his laptop bag, which rested between her legs.

She wasn't going to help him retrieve it. Nope. Not any more than she'd stop him *from* retrieving it.

He considered her for a second before reaching for the bag, twisting a bit more than necessary. The result allowed the back of his free hand to skate down her bared calf.

He might have shivered, but she couldn't be sure given her own reaction.

She looked him over then let her eyes linger on

his face as she answered. "You're clearly in need of additional funds. The charity shops in your neighborhood must have stopped carrying the best quality Hermès socks or Rolex watches like they used to." Her gaze landed on his, and eyes the color of dark chocolate stared back with unerring intensity.

If I were a strawberry, I'd totally dip that.

The thought made her grin.

The stranger grinned back. "Penny for your—"

"Not even for a hundred thousand pennies, but thanks." She barely managed to stifle a sigh. Of course, he had a British accent. Her personal kryptonite.

Ella smoothed her hair, fighting the urge to fan her face. "You know, if you told me this was your first lap dance, I'd have said you were doing pretty well…right up until you broke that no-touch rule."

"My first? Ha." He pushed a lock of errant hair back into place. "You're perfectly aware that this is precisely how these things go. I impress you with my moves on the first dance. The first is always gratis, by the way. Then you're enticed to pay for the second dance, wherein I employ my signature moves and render you speechless. And trust me, my lady," he all but purred, "I'm highly skilled at keeping things professional. Everything is part of a job, even pleasure."

She chuffed out a laugh, gathering her own things. "Signature moves. You think pretty highly of yourself, Oxford." Man, he smelled good—cologne that smelled like windblown shores laid over the warm wool of his suit and heat from his skin that carried the essence of *him*. Drawing a deep breath, she briefly closed her eyes before glancing up to meet his gaze. "I would imagine you've had ample opportunities to perfect those moves. Particularly the keep-it-professional routine."

He tilted his chin down and leaned forward, closing the distance between them. "Pay up and find out," he said in a soft but unquestionably suggestive tone. "For your convenience, I take all major credit cards— even Diner's Club. Cash as well. Lady's preference."

Her mouth twitched, and she blinked with slow suggestiveness. "I save my bills for tipping."

"Lucky me," he murmured.

From the front of the plane, the pilot cleared his throat, clearly fighting laughter.

Ella shot the stranger a sly look. "It seems we're causing a scene."

"This is hardly a scene."

"No? You're an expert, then?"

He leaned close enough that, this time, it was his lips a whisper from her ear. "A bona fide professional."

A moment of sheer hysteria ensued. What if this guy actually *was* a gigolo? Wouldn't that be the icing on the wedding cake she had yet to design.

Patting the man's outer thigh in dismissal, she shook her head. "Unfortunately, I'm scene averse. Time to go."

"Pity, that." He gave a short nod toward the small messenger bag in the overhead bin. "Yours?"

"Yep." She straightened her skirt and moved to

stand only to find he'd retrieved the bag and held it for her.

He looked at her then, no pretense. No artifice. No sexy banter. It was *that* look, hunter to hunted. "I'll see you to the bottom of the stairs. It is, after all, the least I can do."

"Thanks," she managed, the sheer sexual pull of his person making her fight the urge to rub her thighs together. Nothing like starting the most critical job she'd ever had by engaging in seriously unprofessional behavior with a gorgeous man.

And she *was* here for a job. No, not *a* job. *The* job—the one that would revive a career that had been on life support ever since her business partner, Rob Darlain, had bailed on her.

Rob had taken *their* pitch for a TV show to a local cable network. They'd offered him the gig, which catapulted him to regional fame. Then the national network had come calling. Ella had been left to plan children's birthday parties and bar mitzvahs instead of the exclusive, high-end events for which she and Rob had become recognized. And it didn't help that he'd claimed to be the exclusive coordinator/designer while labeling Ella the help. The contract she had in her bag was her shot to not only prove her ex-partner wrong but to really, truly make a comeback. This event would park her business, her *name*, at the top of the list of event planners favored by society's upper echelon.

Ella preceded the stranger to the exit, hunched over due to the low ceiling made lower by her heels' height. Every woman had a list of things she refused to cut corners on, from the brand of her coffee to the skin care line she used to the gym membership she ate noodles to afford. For Ella, her shoes were near the very top of that list. The heels she'd worn today had been a careful choice. They were her only pair of Louboutins, and she'd saved for months to buy them when times had been good. They were her power shoes, her I-can-do-anything-I-set-my-mind-to shoes. They were ass-kicking, name-taking shoes. She saw them as her personal totem, her symbol of power and control. Some might find her foolish. But those people didn't fuel the voice in her head, the voice that demanded she be the best at what she did.

Ella sighed.

If she could pull this job off… No. *When* she pulled this job off, it would mean no more choosing between groceries or gas, electricity or water.

With the Los Angeles elite being what they were, the culture being what it was, she'd been required to sign a confidentiality clause. She wouldn't even know who the bride and groom were until the day before the rehearsal. So instead of dealing with the bride, Ella had agreed to work with the bride's personally appointed representative. She, or he, would have the final say in approving the plans and could, per contractual agreement, make suggestions and changes as she saw fit. If Ella hadn't been desperate to relaunch her career, and if she wasn't sick and tired of eating noodle packs to survive, she'd have balked at that stipulation. But she needed this. More than the bride needed an "unrecognized" event planner no one would suspect had been hired to coordinate the wedding of the year.

Whatever. It would work.

It had to.

Ella was prepared to realign the heavens if it meant making this wedding go off without a hitch. She'd worked too hard and for too long to settle for anything less. If she failed?

"Not going to happen," she said to herself.

The resort's shuttle pulled up near the plane. Stepping around several chickens that had wandered back onto the tarmac, she hoisted her messenger bag onto her shoulder, extended her suitcase handle and headed toward the vehicle.

She had seven days to pull off the social event of the year—the event that would put money in her account, restore her professional reputation and maybe, just maybe, give her back the most valuable thing she'd lost over the last couple of years.

Self-respect.

Liam Baggett made his way from the plane much slower than the woman he'd crashed into. Pity he'd failed to charm her. Had he possessed an ounce of the infamous Baggett charisma, he'd at least have procured her number. No reason this whole trip had to test his moxie. Especially not when there was a gorgeous distraction within easy reach.

He glanced her way again and watched as she dodged a rather large rooster. The woman was stunning in a nontraditional way. Mouth a tad too wide but lips decidedly lush, eyes a devastating green, her hair varying shades of brown that said someone with talent had taken what nature gave her and enhanced it to suit that pale complexion. She possessed a lovely figure he'd briefly—*far* too briefly—had his hands on. He hadn't noticed her legs until she'd made for the plane's front exit. In truth, he'd been so distracted as he admired their toned length that he'd nearly knocked his skull on the door.

Blinking rapidly, he chastised himself for allowing the distraction, no matter how fine. He had one life to save and another to destroy before he returned to London and resumed the helm of his late father's empire.

Trade winds blew with predictable unpredictability, tousling his hair.

Should have cut the damn mop before flying out. "If there'd been time, I *would* have," he groused to no one save the hen who'd taken a liking to the shine of his shoes. "Bloody bird. You're a barnyard animal, not a magpie." He scooted her away with his foot, but she returned post haste to continue the burgeoning love affair.

The one benefit to the breeze was that it kept the temperatures tolerable. For an Englishman who saw the sun roughly every third day, and only if he was able to leave the office before dark, it was bloody warm.

Searching the tarmac, he found the shuttle to the resort waiting, both side and rear doors open and the driver posted at the back to load passengers' bags. Liam gathered his bags and briefcase, strode to the van and delivered all but his briefcase into the driver's care. He rounded the passenger doors, set one foot on the running board and stopped. The woman who'd fascinated him only minutes before was in the far seat and rapidly entering notes on her iPad.

He wordlessly moved into his seat, all the while keeping watch on his travel companion.

The driver shut the doors with authority before clambering into his seat. Putting the van in gear, he took off down the road. Less than one hundred yards later, he was looking in the rearview mirror instead of out the windshield and talking to the woman with an easy demeanor. "The roads between here and the resort can be a bit trying, miss, so you may want to forgo typing until arrival." Then he hit the gas and they shot away at breakneck speed…right through a massive pothole.

The woman fumbled her iPad, recovered it before it hit the floor and caught the driver's stare. "A bit trying, huh?"

He laughed. "Wait until we hit traffic. Here in Bora Bora, traffic includes cars, motorcycles, scooters, and even the occasional cart and donkey."

She stuffed her iPad into her bag without further comment, yet Liam couldn't help but notice the way her shoulders didn't move with the bus's motion. The muscles in her neck were visible and appeared rigid. And despite her sunglasses, there were faint lines that radiated from the corner of each eye. Lines that clearly represented both stress and worry.

He was about to speak, to restart the banter they'd shared on the plane, but she turned away, reaching in to her bag and retrieving a travel pack of ibuprofen. She ripped the package open, retrieved two pills and tossed them into her mouth. Without water available, she struggled to get them down but managed.

What could be so bad a woman lands in paradise and has to take something for a headache? And why am I obsessing? I have my own issues with this godforsaken trip.

Still…

The gentleman's code Liam lived by demanded he do something to distract her. Leaning toward her, he said, "My travel agent assured me the resort was a guaranteed headache-free zone."

The woman whipped her entire upper body toward him, eyes wide as she pushed at a strand of hair that had worked its way out of her chignon. Recognition dawned, and her eyes warmed. "You," she said, smiling.

"And you as well."

"What are you doing…" She shook her head. "Never mind."

"You have impeccable taste in locale as well as accommodation." He nodded at the driver as the man wove between slower moving traffic as if the ten-seat bus were an IndyCar, their route Le Mans. "The Royal Crescent is a lush resort. If you didn't reserve a cabana over the water, you should consider upgrading."

"I actually have a room in the resort proper." When he said nothing, only watched her, she shrugged. "It suits my needs."

"Sometimes simply meeting one's needs should be abandoned in favor of obtaining one's desires, don't you think?"

She stared at an indeterminate point over his shoulder, tapping her forefinger against her lower lip as she considered his question. It was only seconds before she shifted her gaze to meet his. The wicked gleam in those impossibly green eyes told him she'd give as well as she got. "Actually, no. I'm of the opinion that a woman shouldn't leave desire on her wish list. A smart woman places her desires, whatever...*whomever*...they might be, near the very top of her list of necessities. Wouldn't *you* agree?" She arched a dark brow, the wordless gesture a direct challenge.

He had intended to bait her. Clearly, she knew it. What Liam had never expected, though, was that she'd take the bait. The image of reeling her in had his heart beating a bit faster, breath coming a bit shorter. He liked it, liked *her*, and found himself hungering for the thrill of the chase.

He traced his fingers over the tanned skin on her shoulder.

She drew in a deep breath.

He smiled, knowing full well that the look he gave her was leonine. How often had he been accused of letting that particular look loose in both boardroom and bedroom when he discovered exactly what he wanted? Today, this second, what he wanted was this woman.

"Touché," he murmured, shifting slightly to accommodate his rising desire.

She laughed then, the sound as sultry and evocative in its richness and depth as the first sip of the finest scotch rolling across the palate. Her laughter whipped through him, muddying his thoughts and fogging his awareness of everything but her.

"You're staring," she murmured.

"So I am."

The woman's brows rose slightly. "So...stop?"

"I will."

"When?"

Liam lifted one shoulder in a partial shrug. "When I'm done looking."

Turning in her seat, she glanced out the window. "The scenery is beautiful."

"It certainly is," Liam murmured. She twisted back around and drew a breath, certainly to deliver a sharp rebuttal, but Liam wasn't looking at her—he was staring at the lush jungle landscape outside.

The faint flush that spread across her exposed décolletage and crept up her neck was quite adorable, though he doubted she'd agree with his assessment. In his experience, few women were keen on being considered cute, and those that favored the more juvenile assessment weren't the type he desired. But this woman—with her singular focus, quick wit and physical appeal—was exactly the type to pique his interests.

With her staying at the same resort, their paths were certain to cross.

Liam smiled.

Perhaps this trip wouldn't be such a chore after all.

CHAPTER TWO

THE DRIVER SPED up to the resort's elegant porte cochere and stopped with enough force that the van bounced back and forth on its shocks like a child's rocking horse. When Ella could convince herself they had truly stopped, she mentally logged the travel time in case the wedding guests wanted to know...or take a cab. She peeled her fingers from her armrests. Her muscles suffered mild rigor as she attempted to move toward the open door. That meant she had to accept the hand offered to help her down. Only it wasn't the driver. Her fellow passenger, the stranger she found all too alluring, had quickly and quietly exited and then, quite unexpectedly, rounded the shuttle and waited by her door. She paused.

He waited.

Chastising herself for hesitating, she took his hand and stepped out of the vehicle. After all, the gesture was nothing but a courtesy. Yes, he'd clearly been flirting earlier, but it had been innocent. Or innocent enough. The problem was that she'd wanted to flirt back. And flirty banter led to things she'd forbidden herself this trip, things like a tryst that could call her professionalism into question. It was just…

She glanced at him and found him staring at her unabashedly.

Damn it.

She turned her back on him, reaffirming her decision to avoid personal entertainment. Men like him were few and far between, and thank God for it. He was the exact type of distraction she couldn't afford. Not on this trip. Not when her future hinged on the success of this job.

Stepping forward, she returned the doorman's smile as he ushered her into the air-conditioned lobby. "Welcome to the Royal Crescent. Your luggage has been tagged. Once you've checked in, a valet will deliver your bags to your room."

"Thank you," she said.

Ella sighed as cool air swept over her bare arms and legs. Thank God for air-conditioning.

The resort seemed classy and sophisticated, giving an impression of subtle but irrefutable wealth and luxuries both small and large. A gentleman wearing all white and bearing a tray of champagne approached, offering her a glass. A single strawberry churned up bubbles as it gently bounced about the glass bottom.

She sipped and sighed again. Chilled to perfection, the dry bite was ideal with the fruit's sweet tartness.

This place was going to be the perfect backdrop for the wedding Ella had planned.

Scanning the lobby, her gaze landed on the concierge desk and the three people staffing it. The obvious leader of the group, a uniformed man who appeared to be in his fifties, rose and headed her way with a grin. He stopped and said something in the ear of the waiter bearing the champagne. The younger man nodded and stepped to Ella's left, proffering a glass to the person behind her, a person she didn't need to see in order to identify.

Heat—*his* heat—spread across her back and chased away the air's artificial chill. Her muscles, finally relaxing after the harried trip, became fluid, languid even. The urge to close the distance between them, to move back into what she knew was a solid torso, to feel the strength in the hands and arms that had effectively pinned her to her seat, had her instinctively shifting her weight onto her heels.

What the hell?

Sure, she believed in instant and undeniable attraction. Some called it chemistry. But her reaction to this total stranger was far beyond anything she'd ever experienced, and she didn't like it. At all. It pushed against her self-control with the wildly rapid, incessantly repetitive tap-tap-tap of a crack-addled woodpecker.

Lust, untamed and unchecked. There was no other name for it.

The word wound through her senses and made her more aware of the earthy undertones of his cologne, the smell of hot leather from his briefcase and the susurrus of silk against wool as he moved.

"Madam?"

Ella blinked rapidly and brought the man she had assumed was the concierge into focus. "I'm sorry. Would you repeat that? I was lost in thought for a moment, I'm afraid."

"I said my name is Arvin. I'm the resort's head event coordinator. And a woman soon to be wed certainly cannot be blamed if her mind wanders a bit." He grinned wider. "Particularly in an environment so conducive to romance, yes?"

Ella's brow wrinkled as her brows squinched together. It was her typical reaction to stress, one her mother swore had begun at age three and would have Ella bearing deep, undesirable ridges in her forehead before she was forty. She absently pressed her fingertips against the ridges in an attempt to smooth her skin. "I'm sorry, but…who's going to be newly wed?"

The coordinator's smile faltered as he glanced between her and the stranger she knew still stood within earshot. "I…well…*you* are, madam." He raised a clipboard that held several sheets of paper with printed information and handwritten notes in the margins. "My staff and I have worked diligently on the preparations for the ceremony, just as you requested." He looked at the list and began ticking off items. "We've made arrangements for cake tasting, set up appointments with three florists, have a string quartet that will play in the lobby this evening so you might hear the quality of their performance. Then there's the—"

"I'm not getting married," she said. "I'm *coordinating* the wedding."

"No." The denial, issued in that decidedly upper-crust British accent, was ripe with disbelief. "Not you."

Ella slowly turned to face the handsome stranger, working to keep her composure. "I'm not sure what you mean by that."

"You're the one my sister hired to pull together this...this..." He dropped his briefcase and waved both hands wildly, the gesture encompassing the entire lobby. *"This."*

"Do *not* tell me that you're the family member my unnamed bride has chosen as her surrogate decision maker."

"Oh, bloody hell. You *are* her. The event coordinator." The last few words were enunciated with whip-like consonants and gunshot vowels.

"Yes, I am."

The stranger downed his champagne in two long swallows then held the empty glass out with one hand while the waiter retrieved it. "You're Ella Montgomery."

"Again, yes, I am. You are?"

He watched her through narrowed eyes. "Liam Baggett. The bride's brother."

"Baggett." Her mind raced through the list of starlets she'd compiled as possible brides, but none was named Baggett. In fact, the name didn't ring any bells at all.

Confusion must have decorated her face, because

Liam finally offered, "Half brother. Same father, different mothers. My mother died when I was very young, and my father remarried roughly five years later. My sister was born from that union."

"Still, Baggett isn't ringing any bells." Closing her eyes, she drew in a deep breath, held it for a count of ten and then let it go to a second count of ten. What had she done? How had she let herself invest everything she had, from money to the last of her reputation, in an event she was expected to plan without contact with the bride? Had she been set up to fail? The thought made her stomach lurch, the motion as nauseating as it was violent. "Tell me I'm not being punked. Tell me I haven't flown more than halfway around the world to be made a fool of. Tell me—"

"What I'll tell you is that my sister used a different name for the screen to keep some type of separation between her private life and her public persona. It's a closely guarded secret, hence the reason you'll be dealing with me, not her."

The event coordinator had watched the verbal volley with interest. "So you're arranging your wedding while here, yes?"

"We're not getting married," they both said at the same time.

"I'm sorry. I don't understand," he said, small beads of sweat dotting his hairline as he glanced from his clipboard to Ella and finally to Liam.

"I'm not the bride," Ella said through gritted teeth. "I'm the wedding planner for Mr. Baggett's half sister and her fiancé."

Arvin's hands shook as he flipped through the paperwork on his clipboard, crossing out certain things and adding notes to others. "I see." He looked up, pupils dark in wide eyes. "As I said before, my name is Arvin, and I am—"

"The resort's event coordinator." Ella shook Arvin's hand by rote. "It's nice to meet you, Arvin. I need to make sure that you understand that I am absolutely *not* the bride."

"I'm clear, Ms. Montgomery, and I sincerely apologize for the misunderstanding. My staff took to heart your admonition that all must be perfect. We have two team members plus myself at your disposal around the clock." He glanced at the last page and paled radically. "Oh, sweet and merciful…"

"Arvin?"

"As a show of our appreciation for choosing the Royal Crescent, your room was upgraded to the honeymoon suite bungalow."

"I appreciate the gesture, but it certainly wasn't necessary." Ella felt her brow furrow and let it do as it would, wrinkles be damned. "But the change doesn't seem like something that would warrant panic."

"Normally, it wouldn't." Arvin dragged his arm across his forehead to wipe away sweat that only popped right back up. "But there was, as I also previously indicated, the belief that you were the bride." He began to fan himself with the clipboard. "And that…that…Mr. Baggett was your…"

"Groom," Ella whispered, throat so tight the word emerged as a strangled wheeze.

Behind her, Liam made a choking sound.

Ella didn't bother turning around. Surely he couldn't be any more dumbfounded than she was. "I can't, Arvin." And she couldn't. Proximity to that man would destroy every good intention she had. If she didn't succumb to his flirtation, he'd likely succumb to hers. What happened after that was precisely what the honeymoon suite had been created for.

This was bad.

The event coordinator touched his earpiece and gave a fractional nod. "Your bags have been tagged and will be delivered within the half hour."

"I can't do this," she whispered. "Rooming with Mr. Baggett is *not* an option."

"I… I…" Arvin stood very straight.

Ella closed her eyes. This couldn't be a portent of what lay ahead. It just…it couldn't be. "If you'll simply assign us separate rooms, I'll retrieve my luggage and get to work on the wedding."

Arvin tugged at his shirt collar, his face flushing a horrid fuchsia. "I'm so sorry, Ms. Montgomery, but the resort is booked solid. When we upgraded you and Mr. Baggett to the suite, the rooms that you each originally booked were assigned to guests on our waiting list."

Ella took a second glass of champagne and threw it back, eyes watering with the bubbles' bite. "Waiting list? How can there be a waiting list when this is supposed to be the beginning of the off-season?"

Arvin shrugged. "It's our annual carnival."

"That wasn't advertised on the resort's website."

Panic clawed its way up the back of her throat and threatened to choke off her air supply.

"I am sorry, Ms. Montgomery. Our website has been undergoing a complete redesign, and—"

"Surely there's a neighboring resort. I could get a room there and commute back and forth to the Royal Crescent. A rental house. A house with a room for rent. A yurt. Something," she muttered, looking around the crowded lobby. "Anything."

The Brit behind her leaned in close, and the crisp smell of champagne that lay over a hint of tart strawberry wrapped around her as he spoke quietly into her ear. "This is the equivalent of the French Polynesian Mardi Gras, Ms. Montgomery. There won't be rooms available anywhere on the island for a solid ten days. I'd have thought you, as a professional wedding planner, would have known as much."

He was right. She should have known. But even her embarrassment wasn't enough to stop his whispered breath from skating along her jaw and caressing the shape of her ear. Shivers threatened to shatter her composure. Things low in her belly tightened, and she stepped closer to the other man. "I can't stay with him," she said, the words tumbling over one another. "I can't."

"As I said, miss, the resort is booked to capacity. I'm certain we can find a…rollaway bed…perhaps?" There was a sense of undisguised pleading in his entire persona, from his nearly vibrating frame to the pitch of every word. "I cannot afford this type of mistake on my employment record, Ms. Montgomery. At the very least, I could be demoted. At worst?" He shook his head as he swallowed, the gulp loud enough to be heard over the hum of the crowded lobby. "And my wife—it would reflect poorly on her as well. Please, allow me to do whatever I may to make this right."

Ella took a deep breath, held it for a count of ten and then let it out slowly. Squaring her shoulders, she faced Liam and offered a small approximation of a smile. "Surely we're adult enough to make this work? I'll take the rollaway; you take the bed. We're going to be working together so much, this might even work to our benefit."

Liam's eyes narrowed farther. "What do you hope to gain?"

"Nothing." She looked back at Arvin. "It's what I don't want him to lose."

Liam was quiet long enough Ella was certain she'd have to plead with him to go along with it. Then he spoke, his voice rich with implied debauchery. "Surely, as two grown adults in command of their faculties and capable of informed decision making, we can share a room for a few days."

Ella swallowed hard and nodded. "It's just for a few days."

CHAPTER THREE

DESPITE HIS IRRITATION with the situation, Liam had to admit he admired the woman in front of him. She obviously didn't want to room with him, and, while that stung his damnable pride as much as it piqued his equally damnable interest, he found a solid sense of respect blooming alongside his lust. No matter who'd made the mistake, she wouldn't let this hotel employee suffer for the error.

The singular good thing that came from this debacle? Proximity to Ella would make manipulating the situation much, much easier. A few well-placed comments, a nudge here, a suggestion there and voilà. The unrealistically short engagement following an even shorter committed relationship would *not* result in the worst possible outcome: a wedding. No, the event would be canceled, and Liam could go back to his day-to-day operations in London while his sister, Jenna, came to her senses about the type of man her fiancé truly was: gold digger, fame seeker, all-around narcissistic bastard and someone whose short-fused temper didn't suit Jenna's go-with-the-flow demeanor. Sure, she'd be livid at first. And likely a bit heartbroken. But when she realized the future Liam had saved her from? She'd be grateful. He could weather the emotional storm until that understanding dawned. She was an exceptionally bright woman. It wouldn't take long.

He nodded to the other gentleman. "I've been a guest here before, so I'll show Ms. Montgomery to the appropriate over-the-water bungalow if you'll provide general directions." Arvin began to speak, offering to take them himself, but Liam gently interrupted. "Ms. Montgomery would likely benefit from a chance to quietly settle into her living quarters before she begins her work. My sister, the bride, is a bit, hmm. Let's call her exacting."

Ella stood tall, strong, as she drew in a sharp breath and her spine went a fraction more rigid. A fraction was all she had to spare, though, without outright shattering from the afternoon's stress. He felt a bit bad for her, but his primary objective was postponing the wedding if not outright stopping it. For good.

Directions were provided without hesitation, and Liam offered Ella his arm. "I suppose calling you 'darling' at this point wouldn't go over so well. Shall we?"

Ignoring the gentlemanly gesture, Ella rolled her eyes and bit her lip. He watched as she licked her lower lip with slow, smooth sensuality. "Well, this is about as bad as it can get." She looked up through thick lashes. "Right? Tell me this is as bad as it can get."

Liam blinked a couple of times and rolled his shoulders in an attempt to dislodge the guilt draped around his neck like a heavy stole. "It can always get worse."

She shook her head. "Just once, I wish someone would lie to me when I ask them to instead of lying to me when I don't expect it."

The guilt wound around his neck like a garrote, strangling his response. "Bungalows are this way." He gestured to the nearest door and, taking her messenger bag for her before cupping her elbow, gently steered her toward the exit. The nagging voice in his head, the part that made him good at reading people in the boardroom, wouldn't hush. He had to know what she'd meant. "People lie to you often?"

"I'm a wedding planner." She shot him a short look and snorted with incredible derision. "I see people lie to me, their parents, their significant others all the time. People tend to lie the most when it matters the most."

"Are you always so cynical?"

"Practical." Gently pulling her elbow from his grip, she held out her hand and waggled her fingers. When he didn't respond, she plucked her bag from his shoulder. "And I can manage."

"No doubt." Still, he opened the door for her. He'd do what he had to do to spare his sister, but he'd still treat Ella Montgomery like the lady she was. Until he couldn't, for Jenna's sake. If Ella had siblings, she'd understand. Surely. "How, exactly, do people manage to lie the most when it matters the most?"

"Honestly? Lies always matter." She navigated the narrow bridge that led away from the sand and out to the bungalows.

"To the right, here," Liam said, pointing toward a bungalow set away from the others. "I suppose they wanted to provide us some privacy, being newly-weds and all."

She laughed softly. "Sound carries more effi-ciently over water than it does land."

An image of her, hair out of its neat twist and spread around her, linen sheets rumpled and draped across her naked body, one breast bared, a long leg exposed to the hip… Sweet Mary, save him from his suddenly overactive imagination. Heat burned through him like fuel exposed to a lightning strike. He had to focus, to remember what they'd been talk-ing about and remind himself she'd failed to answer his question. "For clarity's sake…" Irritated at the tightness in his throat, he reached up and, with rough execution, undid his tie and the top button of his dress shirt. Then he tried again. "For clarity's sake, does a white lie qualify? Particularly if it's meant to spare one's feelings?"

She paused at the door and waited while he re-trieved one of the two keys in the little envelope and swiped it across the electronic door lock. He handed her the spare key and then pushed the door open to a spacious, elegant bungalow complete with a small infinity-edge pool, glass-paneled floor in the living room, small kitchen and, through the open French doors, a mosquito-netted king bed with an abundance of pillows.

"Go on then," he said as he moved into the bedroom and dropped his briefcase on the desk. An enormous fresh flower arrangement was situated on one nightstand and scented the ocean breeze with the smell of freesia, roses and something utterly wild. He paused to trace a finger along a single rose petal before calling out, "I'm all ears."

"Just forget it." Her voice was muffled, as if she were in the bathroom.

"Can't. Sorry. Nature of the beast."

"Look, bottom line is that I've come to believe there's not a time when being lied to *doesn't* matter. If it's important enough to lie about, it's important." She leaned around the corner, inhaling as if to say something else, but her eyes widened and she gasped. "This is the honeymoon suite?" She walked through the room and headed straight out the second set of French doors that led to the expansive deck and the view of the crystalline waters and colorful reefs teeming with sea life. "This is incredible!"

"Almost makes it worth being married."

She shot him a sharp look. "Consider our marriage annulled."

"Such short wedded bliss," he said on a sigh. "I didn't even get to kiss the bride."

She laughed, the sound soft but reserved. "You wish."

"I do."

This time, she truly laughed. Liam found himself caught between wanting to watch versus taking her mouth with his and swallowing the sexy, sultry sound. He hadn't realized he'd been waiting to hear her laughter, but he had. She had the kind of laugh that would turn men's heads, would compel them to seek out the siren responsible. And though he wasn't one to wager, Liam was absolutely willing to bet Ella was a fun lover, one who laughed when she loved—right up to the point that teasing and laughter were consumed by passion that would be as avaricious as it was unreserved.

Her laughter trailed off, but Liam continued to stare. He couldn't look away. Never had a woman enchanted him like this, and she'd done it unintentionally and without an ounce of pretension. And suddenly, he had to know—had to fill in a blank his imagination had created.

"What would our kiss have been like?"

Her gaze darted to his, her lips parted and the tip of her tongue swept out and touched the edge of her cupid's bow. Different emotions ranging from surprise to curiosity flashed across her face, but Liam was most interested in the emotional revelation that struck.

Desire.

He stepped closer and paused, giving her every chance to tell him to bugger off. Instead, she shifted so their hips lined up, her body acknowledging what she verbally denied. "There wouldn't have been a kiss."

"You won't kiss your groom? Rather odd, don't you think?"

"You're not my groom." Her voice was raspy, husky and told him everything he needed to know.

"And you're not my bride, yet I still can't stop myself from wondering."

"Stop putting ideas in my head."

"Where would you rather I put them?" he teased.

"Oh, God," she whispered, moving fractionally toward him. "You're temptation incarnate."

He leaned forward, bracing a hand on the railing on either side of her. "And what's your position on temptation?"

"Never turn it down."

"Why?"

She moved into him, closing that final distance so their bodies touched. One slender hand rested on his chest; the other wound through his hair, gripping just tight enough to exert control. Eyes locked with his, she pulled him toward her at the same time she rose on her toes. "You never know when it might come around again."

Liam groaned as their mouths came together in a rush of heat and hurry and hunger. There was nothing tentative about the kiss. It would burn hot and then hotter until it became a supernova that consumed them both.

Her body was pliant, yielding to his, pushing back against him in every critical place. Liam wondered that their clothes didn't turn to ash at every point of contact.

And he wanted more of her, then and there, than he'd ever wanted of another woman.

He hesitated a split second, but it was enough.

Ella broke the kiss, slipped under his arm and took several long strides toward the bedroom. Pausing, she reached down and slipped her heels off. Liam watched as she curled her bare feet into the fluffy rug and then uncurled them.

He couldn't believe that this woman, this siren, would have toenails painted the faintest seashell pink. It seemed like a secret that he alone knew, and he had the strangest urge to keep anyone else from knowing this tiny private thing about her.

This had to stop.

He hadn't come here to engage in a tryst. The only reason compelling enough to take him away from the office mid–corporate takeover was his little sister's well-being. When she'd told him she needed help planning the perfect wedding, he'd met her and her fiancé in London for dinner. The man, semi-professional baseball player Mike Feigenbaum, had been attentive at first. That had quickly devolved following a phone call the man had taken midmeal—answering without apology and leaving the table without excusing himself. He'd missed most of the main course and had snapped at Jenna when she went to check on him. She'd been upset, and her proposed groom had done nothing to console her. Instead, he'd shown signs of a temper Liam wouldn't allow Jenna to become tied to.

So he'd flown halfway round the world to stop his sister from marrying a domineering asshole following a whirlwind romance that had been documented by all the gossip rags.

Rolling up his sleeves and strolling with feigned casualness to the hammock, Liam lay down and locked his hands behind his head. He watched Ella from under half-lowered eyelids. She was temptation incarnate. Her body was in lush profile to him, her unapologetic stare locked on his.

"So that's what our kiss would have been like?" He rubbed his chin between thumb and forefinger. "Sufficient."

She chuffed out a sound of indignation laced with disbelief. "If that driving wood behind your zipper is *any* indication, that kiss was far more than sufficient." Bending, she scooped up her shoes. "And seeing as I've been more than clear on my lack of appreciation for liars, I'd suggest you cut the crap."

"Testy." Liam gently set the hammock to rocking and continued to watch Ella. "Tell me, have you always had this aversion to fibbers, or is this something new?"

"I've never been a fan of lying. What's the point?"

"To get what one wants, I assume."

Her face closed up, any and all emotion under lock and key. "No matter whom you hurt?"

"Who hurt you?" The question wasn't meant to

be as weighty as it sounded, but Liam found himself desperately wanting to resolve the problem for this fiery woman. It would cost him little and potentially relieve her of some personal baggage.

She looked at him askance, worrying her bottom lip.

"Tell me."

"Ask nicely," she retorted.

He waited.

So did she.

Liam rolled his eyes. "Please."

"You've heard of *Two Turtle Doves*?"

He shook his head.

"It's a prime-time TV show. I was supposed to be half of it. My business partner sold me out, took our idea to the network and they bought it…without me as a cohost."

Liam set his foot on the deck and stopped the hammock's rocking. "Threw you under the bus, did she?"

"He, and yes. Clients followed the fame, and that left me coordinating children's birthday parties and bar mitzvahs to make ends meet. No one wanted the event planner who hadn't been good enough for the network to pick up."

"But you were excluded. It wasn't a matter of being good enough," he countered.

"That part didn't make the network news. All people knew was that I was cut out of the deal. They assumed."

"So your partner lied…"

"And everyone believed him. He ruined my life with a single lie." She shrugged. "That pretty much made me a stickler for the truth. And now your sister's wedding is going to put me back on the map and reestablish my reputation as the premier event coordinator for the upper echelon of Los Angeles."

The truth pricked the little guilt he allowed himself, but he couldn't let that sway him from his course of action, no matter how deliciously tempting he found Ella, nor how heartbreaking her story was. Jenna's happiness and well-being *had* to come before all else, including Ella's business. After all, she would have a multitude of opportunities to reclaim her place in the who's who of society planners. But Jenna? She had one real shot at a happily-ever-after, and it was *not* going to happen with some semiprofessional baseball player from Wisconsin.

Settling deeper into the hammock, Liam set the swing into motion once more. He closed his eyes and forced his breathing into a rhythmic pattern—in, two, three, four, five…hold…out, two, three, four, five, six, seven, eight. His heart rate slowed. The churning in his stomach eased. And he was able to address Ella, who'd moved to stand at the foot of the hammock.

"I can't speak to the reputation you once had, but I've no doubt you're perfectly capable. My sister wouldn't have hired you if you weren't." He opened his eyes. "Seeing as we're going to be spending the next seven days together, how do you propose we best handle our close proximity?"

She tilted her head toward the bedroom before flicking open the top button of her blouse. She grinned, backing away from him. "I can handle the… proximity issue…if you can. First thing I'm going to do is put my dive suit on and check out the resort's dive excursion. Your sister and her fiancé wanted some fun prewedding activities for their guests, so I'm planning a group dive. But I want to check out the instructors myself and make sure the experience not only meets but exceeds the hype. Sunken ship, hammerhead sharks, colorful reefs with abundant life—all that jazz."

Liam stood and moved toward her, closing the distance with measured steps until he stood mere inches from her. He looked down and stared into light green eyes rimmed with ebony lashes. Reaching out, he tucked a stray hair behind her ear.

"I, uh…"

He leaned toward her, quietly amused at the way she responded, instinctively moving closer to him before she caught herself. Undoubtedly, it was her need for control that forced her to pause midmotion. But she didn't retreat, didn't recover the steps she'd taken toward him.

Good to know.

"I thought we'd cleared this up," she said. "Business before pleasure."

"Oh, we did." He deftly removed the earring that had been about to fall free of her ear, handing it over. "I didn't want you to lose this. It looks like the real deal."

She took it from him, closing her fingers around the earring and stepping back. "Thank you."

He began to unbutton his shirt, thrilling as her eyes followed each button until he hit his waist and pulled his shirttails free. Then she looked up, eyes wide.

Someone knocked at the door.

His mouth kicked up in a small smile, though his eyes never left hers. "I'll get that, as it's likely our luggage."

"Sure."

He started for the door. Several steps away, he glanced back and found her rooted in the same spot, her eyes locked on his backside.

"I'll have our bags put in here. If you'll give me five minutes, I've a mind to grab my suit and head out with you."

"You dive?" she blurted out.

"I do."

"Is your future brother-in-law certified, do you know?"

He tried not to scowl and, by the worried look on Ella's face, achieved far less than even 50 percent success. "I'm not certain. But I suppose he's like anyone else—he'll either dive or drown."

Her brow furrowed at the comment, but she didn't reply.

He shrugged out of his shirt and tossed it on the bed. "Be right back."

He rounded the corner but still managed to hear her reply.

"Please, God, let them be trunks. But if You're listening, it would be fine if they're small."

Long before they reached the dive center, Ella was certain she'd been cosmically destined to face death by drowning. Why? If Liam Baggett was a menace in a power suit, then he was lethal in swim trunks. Yes, *small* swim trunks, at that. God's existence had been verified the moment Liam walked out of their bungalow, towel slung over one broad...broad...shoulder, his lips still slightly swollen from their kiss.

Their kiss. What had she been *thinking*? The answer was simple: nothing. She'd been living on the sheer influx of desire that had clouded her brain and determined conservative thinking—and living—to be a crime given proximity to *him*.

She sneaked another look, this one longer. And she wasn't any sorrier this time than she had been when she'd stolen the first, second or third looks.

His upper body had the professionally chiseled look that came from long hours in the gym and, for good measure, a little physical work on the side. His thighs were lean but corded with muscle. If she touched his calves, they'd be solid. But his arms were the most arresting part of him. They were nothing less than sculpted perfection, a wordless covenant that protection could be found within their embrace.

Ella shook her head. *Covenant? Protection? You're thinking Henry Cavill as Superman, not British surrogate wedding decision maker.*

They passed the bar, and she eyed it longingly. If she stopped for a drink, just one, they'd miss this excursion but could still catch the last outing today. Watching the bartender muddle the mint as he put together a mojito almost made the decision for her... "Ella?"

Instinct had her rubbing her furrowed brow and forcing herself to take a deep breath. "Yes?"

Liam waited several feet ahead of her, a knowing look in his eyes. "If you want another..."

Kiss. Say kiss.

"...drink that badly, I'm sure we can make the next excursion. We've plenty of time before the wedding party's arrival."

Wedding party. Job. Stay focused.

"No." The word registered clear and sharper than she'd intended. "No," she said again, this time more pleasantly. "I need to... *We* need to use every minute to our advantage to ensure your sister's wedding comes together without a hitch. No cutting corners, and certainly no making do."

That same shadow she'd seen earlier passed over his face. "Of course."

"Wait. What's that look? Is there something I should know?"

He glanced away, his gaze fixed on some unseen spot in the water. "What, specifically, are you referring to?"

"I'm referring to the wedding. I mentioned it being perfect and your face went totally blank. Is there something you aren't telling me? Something

I should know?" She hesitated. "Is it something between the bride and groom?"

"I assure you, Ella, that my interests lie solely in securing my sister's well-being. Nothing more, and certainly nothing less. Understand that I will do whatever I must to ensure her happiness is secured. She's the priority here, not me."

"Of course." Ella gripped her shoulder and pulled, stretching, before repeating the same with the other side. She was wound so tight she couldn't tell up from down, left from right, or brotherly concern from familial dissatisfaction. His answer struck her as a bit odd, though. Aggression created a solid foundation for every word he spoke. What was he willfully omitting?

The answer wasn't right there for the plucking, but she'd figure it out. One thing was certain, however. He loved his sister and, like he said, she was the priority. At least they agreed on that much.

"About that drink?"

A shake of her head before she resumed the trek to the beachfront dive hut. "It's best I don't give in to temptation before hitting the water."

The wind carried his response to her, soft and so sexually charged it seemed lightning should have struck. "On that, Ella, we very much disagree."

Fighting to keep from visibly clenching her thighs at the impact of his words, she focused on retying the sarong around her waist. Her dive suit wasn't skimpy, but it fit tight, and the thin neoprene did nothing but enhance every movement. So she'd suffer a little discomfort. It wouldn't kill her.

Liam remained silent the rest of the walk, lagging behind just far enough that she felt his eyes caressing every line of her body, every inch of her bare skin.

CHAPTER FOUR

WAVES ROCKED THE 109-foot catamaran, the slap of water against the fiberglass hull soft. Rhythmic. Every now and then, the breeze would gather enough momentum that the sails swelled and billowed. The fabric would snap taut only to fall back to its lethargic default when the winds quieted. Clouds were sparse—brilliant white against the endless azure sky. If the Garden of Eden had been anything like this particular slice of paradise, Adam had been a fool to risk it all over a mediocre piece of fruit. For Eve, though? Particularly if she'd looked anything like Ella...

"I'd have eaten brussels sprouts if she'd offered," he murmured.

Ella had started the trip by grilling the dive instructors, asking for everything from credentials to referrals. The poor men had been overwhelmed, though she hadn't understood why. And wasn't that just like her. She was everything brilliant and strong and professional...yet kind...and wearing a bikini. The poor dive instructors had been tripping over themselves to satisfy her every request. If they knew how the woman kissed? They'd be lost—land or sea, it wouldn't matter.

As for himself? Well, he'd simply watched with avaricious appreciation as she took off the short dive suit and revealed the little number beneath. Thankfully, she hadn't required anything of him. Even so, they hadn't cleared the outermost harbor buoys before he'd lost the little bit of temper he'd packed for the afternoon.

"For God's sake, Ella," he bit out. "Leave the men to their jobs. I'm certain your questions will be answered in due course, either by the instructors or through the experience."

Ella's chin had set, and she'd shot him a sharp look. "I get your point, Liam. I'm annoying him by *doing* my *job*. Let me make something perfectly clear now, before we go any farther. You seem like you'd be the type who's more comfortable dealing with women as accessories. That's fine if it's okay with the women in question. But I'm absolutely *not* that woman. I don't require a man to intervene, to handle the difficult tasks—the proverbial heavy lifting. Thanks for feeling the need here, but I'm good. If you think I should retire to the deck and lie back, get a little sun and let the men do their jobs, think again." She smiled sweetly at Liam. "Unless you're willing to join me."

"Well, shit," he muttered. "Insult my manhood when I'm just trying to help you relax. What's the old saying? 'Out of the frying pan—'"

"Oh, you have no idea the fire you've just waltzed

into," she murmured, retrieving a glass of punch offered by the boat's deckhand. "See, if you had grown up in the United States, Smokey the Bear would have taught you not to play with fire unless you were prepared to get burned. But after that interruption? You better hope there's a first aid kit onboard, because I'm about to blister your ass."

"Foreplay in such a public manner?" Liam teased. "I'll take my chances."

She grinned into her cup. "You're just that type, aren't you?"

"What type is that?"

Shaking her head, she wandered over to an unclaimed space on the deck and lay down before shooting him a quick, devilish look. "You know— the type to make things a little public."

He sank down beside her, propped himself up on one arm and leaned over her, seeing his reflection in her sunglasses a split second before his subconscious made the decision his conscious mind would've eventually landed on. He kissed her. Quick. All heat and passion, without apology and certainly without regret. He'd only had the one taste of her, but he craved more. She was an instant addiction.

Breaking away, he smiled down at her. The stunned look on her face sent a thrill through him. Seducing her, or being seduced by her, would be worth every effort. Or almost any compromise. So she was clear, however, he leaned closer and said, "I don't mind public displays of affection."

"Apparently not." She cleared her throat and

shifted so his lips could easily find her neck. "Liam…" Her gaze slid to his and then away. "While I don't know who your sister is and, yes, that irritates me like you wouldn't believe, I do know she's high profile. Seriously high profile. And people— everyone from guests to trade magazines to gossip rags—will name me as the event coordinator. You're obviously the bride's family. Do you really think it's wise to be seen cavorting with the hired help?"

He buried his nose in the crook of her neck and nibbled his way across the expanse of skin to her collarbone. A quick nip elicited a gasp and he pushed up to lean on one elbow again, thrilling at the sight of her nipples pearled beneath her bikini top. "Don't be confused here, Ella. *I* didn't hire you."

"True, but—"

He cupped her jaw and rested his thumb over her lips. "Don't borrow trouble. Wherever this goes, we're two consenting adults. No one need worry about anything else."

A small grin tugged at one corner of her mouth. "Do you really believe you know what's best for everyone—what they should think or how they should behave…"

He arched a brow. "Darling, when people want to be right the first time around, they seek out my opinion. So, in a nutshell, yes." Something whispered through his consciousness, something as uncomfortable as it was unintelligible. Ella, in taking his advice, was going to be dead wrong. He smothered the feeling as he waited out her response.

She laughed and shook her head. Instead of replying, she shifted her gaze and stared out at the seemingly endless expanse of water behind him. The rapid tap-tap-tap of one bare foot against the deck created an anxious rhythm in the conversational void.

Liam grew twitchy as the silence continued. He wanted Ella to say something that would stop him from examining his response too closely, something that might soothe the discomfort left by the vague thought he'd taken a misstep. He'd always been at the conversational helm, directing people wherever he wanted them to go. Now, to have Ella stop like this left Liam out of sorts. Suddenly *he* was the one tapping his foot, and *he* struggled against the urge to say something, *do* something.

He moved to take her hand, wanting the physical contact, hoping it would assuage the unpleasant pressure on his conscience.

She picked up her punch, shutting down his attempt.

"Like that, is it?"

"For now."

"And why, exactly, should that be the case 'for now'?"

She sat up, crossing her legs and spinning to face him. The move put her at arm's length. "You're clearly suffering delusions of grandeur, believing you know what's best for everyone." She took a demure sip of the punch. "What's best for *me* is to finish this, suit up and get in the water as soon as possible."

"And why, pray tell, do you believe that?"

She tipped her glasses down her nose and looked up at him, sun already bronzing her skin to reveal a smattering of faint freckles over her nose. "You'll follow, and that means you'll either have to shut up and breathe or chastise me...and drown."

Laughter erupted from him in a rush. No one—*no one*—talked to him like this. Ella Montgomery must have a set of stainless steel balls *and* a spine to match. He liked that about her. Far more than he should, in truth. She was compassionate, professional, quick thinking... And she was starting to become more than a short-term distraction.

She'd never be a potential bride, despite his earlier joke, because Liam didn't do forever. He leased his car. He leased his plane. He leased his flat. Hell, he had term versus whole life insurance. Everything in his life had an end date, even his career. Thanks to sound financial planning, he would retire in sixteen years at age fifty.

So that mythical woman, the one capable of enticing Liam to rethink a forever type of commitment? She didn't exist. Not for him and, given what he'd witnessed within his peer group, within the business world and, God knew, within his family, not for anyone.

It struck him that if Ella had him shoring up his emotional boundaries and personal beliefs, he should be careful.

Standing, he moved to the front of the catamaran, leaned against one of the masts and quickly outlined his plan.

Seduction would necessarily come first. His. Hers. Theirs. It mattered little so long as it occurred.

Second, mutual physical pleasure—always a fine goal.

Third, he'd get her out of his system, thus removing any craving he might have for her.

Fourth, and finally, he'd ensure there were no strings.

That gave him roughly forty-eight hours to complete his plan before he got back to business as usual.

He'd worked with less.

The dive had been a complete success, and Ella signed the paperwork that made the excursion an official group activity for the wedding guests.

Headed back to the bungalow with Liam, she laid a hand on his arm, hoping the physical contact would smooth the way to her next task. "I know you don't want to give me guests' names in order to protect your sister's identity. I get that. I do," she emphasized when he looked down at her, face entirely deadpan. "I'm not asking for names. I don't need them. I just need the guest preferences from your spreadsheet. I can't do my job, can't represent your sister's best interests, without them."

His arm stiffened beneath her hand before he broke contact, stepping away. "Ella, I understand you need the spreadsheet, and I'll get it to you as soon as I have a chance to amend it and remove names. You'll have it in plenty of time to do what my sister hired you to do."

Irritation brought a hot flush to her cheeks. A fallen coconut lay in the middle of the path, and for a brief moment she envisioned braining him with the shell before stealing his computer and running off to print the mysterious list. Sighing, she toed the coconut off the path and continued walking beside him. "This isn't a want, Liam. It's a need. No matter what you may think of my profession, that's precisely what it is. A profession. I'm a professional. It's a business, not some fun little hostess-styled sideline thing I do to break the daily ennui of living as a high-society wife."

"My mother might take offense to that assessment of her monthly luncheons."

"Then I'll issue an apology. *To your mother.*" She shoved her hands through the mass of hair she'd unbraided and let dry in the sea breeze. "If you'll just give me—"

He wrapped an arm around her waist and led her into the dense tropical foliage that lined the path. It was cultivated but had grown up, taken on a wild feel.

She let out a small squeak of surprise when he took her hips and backed her into a palm tree. Looking over his shoulder, he found the greenery had closed behind them. For all intents and purposes, they were well off the beaten path, not steps off a cultivated one.

Perfect.

"Let's talk about want versus need." Shifting, he pressed against her. The fabric of their swimwear did nothing to hide his full, throbbing erection.

"Let's," she murmured. Her hands went to his

hips. He arched a brow, and she knew she'd surprised him. "Seize every moment or there might not be another, remember?"

"I guarantee there will be another."

"Then perhaps…" She made as if to step away, and he took one hand gently, firmly.

"I wanted you earlier, Ella. Now?" He swallowed and looked askance, and she wasn't sure if it was his confession or the sun that deepened the color of his cheeks. "Now, this is sheer, unadulterated need."

"I understand."

He cupped her chin and lifted her face to his. "Do you? I'm not playing around, Ella. I hunger for you in a way that defies logic and explanation."

"Feeling's mutual," she murmured.

A group of young adults passed by only feet from where they stood. The teens never paused, never glanced their way.

Ella adjusted her stance so that the length of his cock pressed along the soft, bare skin of her belly. The fabric of his swim trunks was stretched beyond manufacturer recommendations, no doubt.

His hips thrust forward as he sucked in a breath. His heat branded her skin. "Please, Ella. I'll get down on one knee and— Holy *shit*."

She dropped to *her* knees and freed him from the constrictive fabric. He was much larger than she'd thought, and she'd guessed he was big. She had a moment of doubt. Could she manage him?

One way to find out.

She slid the tip of her tongue up his pulsing length

and then slipped her lips over his broad crown. The palm tree trunk at her back scraped across her skin. That strange dichotomy of sensations—smooth, silky skin on her tongue and rasping bark against her back—heightened Ella's every sensation. She lowered herself down his length, the tang of salt water and man saturating her awareness. He ran his hands through her hair, his fingers spasming as she lifted herself off his length and found a sensitive spot just beneath the corona. She paused, thrilling at the command she wielded over the powerful man who stood before her. He shook so that his legs seemed to almost fail him. His breaths were so harsh he sounded like a racehorse nearing the finish line. And the way he had to remove one hand from her head to prop himself up on the palm tree at her back? She ruled his body just then, and she relished every second.

Reaching up, Ella cupped Liam's sac, gently rolling it in her palm at the same time she sank down his length. The tip of his cock brushed the back of her throat, and she hummed her approval.

He groaned, knees bending so she had to adjust her position.

"Ella," he ground out. "I can't…"

She worked him harder, feeling the subtle change as his testicles drew tight just seconds before he lost control. It was all Ella could do to keep from touching herself, bringing herself over that beautiful edge and joining him in the fall, but this was about him, about her command of him, her control, his pleasure.

Next time, and there would be a next time, she'd see to it that he gave as well as he received.

Releasing him, she found him staring down at her, his forearm propped on the tree, his forehead resting on his arm. The sated look in his eyes was sexy as hell, but it couldn't compare to the slightly swollen bottom lip—he must have bitten down on it to keep quiet. She'd done that to him, driven him to the point he'd nearly cried out.

And she suddenly wanted nothing more than to drive him so far beyond rational thought that he lost all reason and simply let go.

Next time.

Liam offered her a hand, and she rose with his help. He nuzzled her neck, her sensitive skin erupting in goose bumps. She wanted him, more than she'd ever wanted anyone. Even a short affair would be enough. Enjoy him while she was here, removed as they were from everyday life stress, and take the memory with her when she left. That would do.

It would have to.

She sagged against him, something akin to disappointment sneaking in and leaving a dark smudge on what had been a bright moment. Reality was always such a quick way to go from thrilled to simply breathing in and out. The only option was to live in the moment and enjoy what little free time she had between work and related obligations.

"Ella?"

Her name, a soft question on his lips, had her lifting her face to his. "Hmm?"

"Thank you."

She grinned. "Not what I expected, but I suppose you're welcome."

He smiled and then surprised her by bursting out laughing. "Well, 'you're welcome' wasn't what I expected, either. No matter. What I meant was, that was absolutely incredible. And generous." He kissed her, soft and swift. "And you'll get your own back soon enough."

One eyebrow shot up. "Is that so?"

"It is." He ran a thumb over her eyebrow. "Have dinner with me."

"Agreed. But you have to do one thing for me."

"And that is?"

Irritation prickled along her spine. "You won't agree out of gratitude?"

Liam blinked slowly. "Darling, I learned early on to never make blind promises to old friends or new lovers. It tends to sully the relationship."

Relationship. Not the word she would use for a tryst, but he could call it whatever he wanted.

He hooked a finger under her chin and drew her attention back to him. "What is it you want from me?"

"The revised list." The request was flat, even to her ears.

"Have dinner with me, Ella, and I'll bring the list. The event coordinator texted me on our way back from the dive. He's coordinated a banquet on the beach with local performers, and you'll make your final menu choices then as well. The goal, I believe, is to have you consider the same or similar event for the post-ceremonial reception. He and his staff have contracted quite a few entertainers, and they want you to pick your favorites."

"Why did he text you?"

"I'm not sure. He did ask me to pass the information along to you. I would speculate he simply assumed we'd attend together."

"Why don't you let me have the list. I'll attend the dinner and then bring back suggestions based on what they've put together. There's no need for you to come with me. It's really a simple event. No need to…" She took his hand and squeezed it before letting go. "I can do this more quickly and efficiently if you're not there to distract me."

"First, I'm here on behalf of my sister and her groom. It only makes sense that I see what's being proposed. Second, dining alone is never as entertaining as dining with a partner." He traced the line of her jaw, a smile playing at each corner of his mouth. "Distractions aren't necessarily a bad thing, Ella."

"Clearly you've never tried dating in Los Angeles."

He arched a brow, inquiry unspoken.

"My dates usually wrap up with me trying to avoid the awkward good-night kiss while wishing I'd told the guy no when he asked, picked up Chinese takeout and brought it home to watch *The Big Bang Theory* reruns…*alone*."

Liam shook his head, the look on his face one of disappointment. "You are, without a doubt, choosing the wrong men."

She tapped a finger against her pursed lips and

pretended to consider his words. "You know, you might be on to something."

He studied her with an intensity that left her shifting her weight from foot to foot, and then he spoke, each word registering low but clear. "Have dinner with me, and I'll show you how the men who've taken you out should have done it."

She considered him, truly curious as to what he'd do differently. Before she could respond, he pulled her close, pressed a kiss to her temple and said softly, "Those are my terms, Ella. Accept them and I'll provide the list of amended guest preferences as well as a night you won't forget."

"Deal."

He tucked a wayward strand of hair behind her ear. "I'd say I'll pick you up at seven, but to make things easier, why don't we meet in the living room?"

"Again, deal."

He kissed her then, kissed her like he meant it. Stepping back, he set himself to rights before offering a hand and leading them back onto the path. An approaching couple smiled and looked away.

Ella blushed.

"That color looks good on your cheeks," Liam murmured. "I've a favor, if you don't mind."

"What's that?"

"Would you allow me to shower first? It will give me a few extra minutes to revise the list and print it for you."

Visions of him in the shower, wet and soaped up,

rendered her mute. An answer was necessary, but words eluded her. All she could do was nod.

Her mind flashed over dinner and went straight to the point when they would head back to the bungalow, where Liam Baggett had promised to show her how a date *should* end.

Even her imagination knew there were things he'd be able to show her, things she'd never considered. But come morning, she'd know.

Firsthand.

CHAPTER FIVE

LIAM DID AS PROMISED, showering first and then retrieving and printing the list. What he hadn't told
Ella was that the list had already been modified.
Well before his arrival at this tropical paradise, Liam
had created several versions of the list, unsure which
would be necessary. So while Ella had showered,
he'd found the list with no names but guest char-
acteristics, some accurate and others, well... He'd
switched guest preferences, omitting some items and
outright changing others.

He hadn't once hesitated, had never questioned
the outcome because he'd been so clear in his focus,
had known what he needed to do to unravel the wedding at its very seams. He'd done all this well before
he'd met Ella. Long before he'd even considered he
might suffer some form of remorse for setting the
wedding planner's career back. Not destroying it,
certainly. That hadn't been the plan. But even now,
as drawn to Ella as he was, he would do whatever
he deemed necessary for his sister, Jenna, to emerge
happy and whole. He'd just be sure to help Ella re-

cover from whatever societal storm resulted from his sister's dissolved nuptials.

Printout in hand, he wandered through the bungalow's living room and stood on the deck. The sun had settled low on the horizon. Everything was cast in broad, rich strokes of pinks and purples and oranges. Night would follow quickly, and the stars would dominate the night sky.

Soft footfalls drew his attention, and he turned. The barefoot woman in the doorway dulled the sunset's brilliance. His thoughts swung from planning a seduction to being seduced.

"Ella," he said, his voice saturated with something akin to reverence.

She wore a dress that, at first glance, appeared to be a full-length, sleeveless number in predictable black. But the simple sheath enhanced her silhouette. Every curve seemed like a fantasy yet unfulfilled, hidden by a touch of shadow here and a hint of promise there.

His mind was so jumbled that his entire vocabulary disappeared in a blink. He couldn't do more than stare like an obsessed idiot who wouldn't have been able to reply had he been at gunpoint.

She was flitting about and, thank God, didn't seem to notice the effect she had on him.

"I'm not wearing shoes since dinner's on the beach. Voluntary sand between the toes is one thing. Sand in the shoes? Entirely different sitch." She cleared her throat and, on a small smile, turned back into the room. "Two seconds. I forgot my earrings."

The move revealed the other side of the dress. Liam's ability to form coherent thoughts went the way of his vocabulary, leaving him staring wide-eyed and slack jawed. How many years would he spend dreaming about the soft, exposed skin of her back or the faint suntan lines earned this afternoon? He saw it all, more even, because the dress's back wasn't just open, it was *open*. Nothing but a maze of thin crisscrossing straps that dipped so low it was millimeters from that scandalous point where her back and her back*side* met.

Adjusting the front of his trousers, he spun away and walked to the balcony railing, gripping it with strength fueled half by fury, half by desire. Fury at his inability to control his reaction to the woman he'd planned to seduce. As for the desire? That was self-explanatory. He glanced over his shoulder and watched her approach him with such grace and composure he had to remind himself to breathe. Yes, this was desire of the most destructive kind. A single glance and she rendered him mute. Senseless. *Common*.

"Ready?"

There were a thousand things he wanted to say, and not a single damn word came out. Instead of stumbling through some inane compliment and embarrassing himself, he wordlessly proffered his arm, squashing the small thrill that coursed through him when she laid her hand across the exposed skin of his forearm. Never before had he thanked God he'd rolled his sleeves up.

First time for everything, I suppose.

A shake of his head to clear it, and then he was guiding Ella down the steps to the walkway and toward the beachfront. He watched her from the corner of his eye, this woman who threatened to undermine his plans. And she seemed completely unaware she had derailed him, turned him inside out, tied him in knots.

"You're quiet."

Her softly spoken comment drew him out of his musings. Looking down at her, his breath caught all over again, and he had to smile. He'd always prided himself on laying out intelligent plans and executing them with logic paired with practicality. It was, for all intents and purposes, his modus operandi.

But with her backless black dress and bare feet and shell-pink toes, Ella Montgomery had shattered that MO as if it were an illusion. Part of him wondered if he shouldn't be irritated. The larger part of him couldn't bring himself to care. Falling slave to her siren's call sounded like an ideal plan. He would come to her call, allow her to draw him down to the depths of dark passion, where he would willingly drown.

"Liam?"

His gaze met hers, inwardly thrilling at the sharp catch of her breath, the involuntary widening of her pupils, the slight tightening of her fingers on his forearm.

"Apologies. Woolgathering at an inopportune moment. What did you say?"

"I said I'm sure you have a lot on your mind with your sister's impending marriage, and I hope you'll tell me about her so that I get this right."

"Of course." She would instinctually assume he was at a loss over the wedding details. He wouldn't correct her. Not yet.

Guilt's sharp fingers clawed their way up his back, caressing his nape before scraping along his scalp. His skin crawled in response. He was going to ruin this woman's career—at least superficially…temporarily—and he knew it. Of course, he fully planned to use his connections to help her rebuild. Hell, he'd buy Ella's way into society's good graces if he had to. But Ella would have to trust him to help reestablish her reputation when all seemed lost. For that to happen, he had to first earn that trust. *While lying to her about the wedding plans. And seducing her.*

Guilt's weighted talons sank so deep they scraped bone.

It was a new feeling, this particular level of guilt. He'd dismantled businesses, sold pieces and dissolved personnel departments with less apprehension than he experienced just then. Frankly? He didn't understand this sensation any more than he liked it.

So master the moment and deal with tomorrow, tomorrow.

Right. Time to take control, to set aside the unfamiliar apprehension where Ella was concerned, to focus on her as a woman—one he found disconcertingly appealing. Show her that the men she'd dated in Los Angeles were just overgrown boys who hadn't been equipped to satisfy a woman of her caliber.

He'd deal with the fallout when it came.

Ella was hyperaware of the man at her side. The slight abrasion of his skin against her palm. His spicy cologne, faint but distinct enough to tease her senses. The way the breeze mussed his otherwise perfect hair. He'd been suspiciously quiet despite her attempts to draw him into conversation, his responses short and without elucidation.

Irritating man.

He hadn't been so quiet this afternoon.

It seemed that she'd needlessly worked herself into a minor frenzy over this evening. He was absolutely calm. Of course, he had the list she needed. He didn't have a client showing up in a few days who expected a perfect wedding, much of it based on revisions she wasn't yet privy to.

God, that *list*. It was her invisible nemesis. She needed it now. Particularly if it was an updated version of what she'd been provided by the bride's personal assistant. Without up-to-date information, Ella was effectively working blind. So she'd have dinner, tease Liam about the way dating *should* go, flirt and play a little, and then she would get down to business. First thing she'd do was coordinate the hell out of this wedding and, immediately after that, she'd ensure that her reputation was back in working order.

Arm in arm, they stepped off the cultivated path, feet sinking into the white-sand beach.

Ella gasped.

Arvin and his staff had taken the plan she'd given them and outdone themselves. It was as if they'd crawled into her mind and plucked images, bringing thoughts and feelings together to create the perfect montage, from the big picture to the finest details. They'd hit every mark.

Pale blue porcelain fire pots lit the path to the lone dining table, small clusters of seashells encircling the base of each pot. All around the entertaining area, tiki torches had been placed in seemingly random places in the sand, their flames swaying in the breeze.

The table had been set up with low ottoman-style pouf chairs done in clean, unembellished linen. It was adorned with a white linen tablecloth, and a burlap runner ran the length, anchoring a fresh flower arrangement done in a long, low style that would allow guests to easily converse over it. From the place settings to the crystal to the candlelight, the presentation was immaculate. Every color was precisely what Ella had ordered, right down to the shade of navy blue in the accents, the bright white hydrangea, the pale ivory of the calla lilies and the rich colors of local flora.

"This is amazing," she breathed, her fingers tightening on Liam's arm as she sought to slow her breathing. It was going to be okay. Everything was going to be beyond okay if the resort's planning crew could pull off something like this. "Absolutely amazing."

The bride's taste was disturbingly similar to Ella's, and, seeing it all come together, she had the briefest flash of what her own wedding would be like. Someday. Far, far away. Probably around the same time she became eligible to collect retirement.

Forcing herself to let go of Liam's arm, Ella strode forward to check the silver pattern. She was almost to the table when Arvin, the event coordinator, intercepted her.

He gave a small bow and, just beyond the firelight's glow, musicians began to play softly. The classical piece drifted across the air. Arvin rose and met her gaze head-on. "It is my sincerest hope you will find everything to your approval. My staff and I worked straight from the specifications and sketches you provided prior to your arrival."

He wrung his hands as he spoke, his wide, bright eyes searching her face. She took his hands in hers and squeezed gently. "It's positively the most beautiful setup I've ever seen, Arvin. I mean it. The entire presentation is stunning. It's like you crawled inside my head and looked at my imagination's snapshots. I'm certain the bride and her future husband will be thrilled. You and your staff should be commended on doing such a spectacular job. In fact, I'd like the name of your supervisor. She, or he, needs to know what incredible talent this resort possesses in you, your leadership and your people."

He closed his eyes for a brief second before replying. "Thank you, Ms. Montgomery. I want to apologize once more for the misunderstanding regarding whose wedding had brought you to the resort. I spent the afternoon calling all over the island trying to secure another room, but there isn't a single vacancy. I even tried a couple of homes with rooms for rent, but everything is booked. I would willingly offer you the bedroom in my home if you find yourself strongly opposed to the current arrangement."

Disappointment spiked through her—a way out of her current situation when, in truth, she no longer wanted one. She hesitated, not sure what to say, when a deep voice drifted through the dark and saved her.

"That's very generous of you, Arvin, but we'll manage the current arrangements without any trouble. And in regards to the current setup, Ms. Montgomery is right in saying that you and your staff have done a beautiful job. We'll only make a few minor changes."

Ella spun, the sand churning under her feet and tipping her off balance. She grabbed Liam's arms to keep from falling. Looking up, she searched his face. "Changes? What changes? This is precisely what your sister asked for. It's her dream setup."

"You're right. It's *her* dream, Ella. But it's certainly not her groom's vision of the perfect wedding. My sister discussed her wishes with her fiancé, and there were a few things in particular he wanted to see changed or added."

"I need that list," she all but growled. "Now."

"As agreed, I'll provide it after dinner." Adjusting her hold on his arm, he gently turned her toward the table. "Where would you have us sit, Arvin?"

"You may choose whichever seat you prefer, but I had planned for you and Ms. Montgomery to sit in the seats reserved for the bride and groom. The northern seat places the bride closest to the water with a slightly better view of the performers." He pulled out one of the two ottoman-style seats and gestured in a genteel way. "Once you've been seated, madam, sir, I'll have the meal served. We've adhered to your request for local custom and cuisine. The chef will serve pork, chicken and an optional fresh-caught parrot fish, all locally sourced and cooked in a traditional *himaa*, a pit dug in the ground and heated with volcanic rock. There are marinated plantains for those who prefer a vegetarian or vegan diet. The central proteins will be accompanied by dishes of *po'e*, *fei*, *uru* and *fafa*. The drink served with the meal will be *miti haari*, which is coconut milk diluted with spring water and lime. We will, of course, also provide a variety of beer in the bottle and a selection of white wines. Champagne will be chilled and provided later in the meal for the traditional toasts to the bride and groom."

Ella relaxed fractionally at the realization that the meal was exactly what she'd asked for—local tradition combined with a handful of dishes that would cater to Hollywood's particular, more diet-restrictive tastes. "It sounds divine."

"We'll want to ensure that a bottle of that new sports drink—what's it called? Power something—

is at each place setting." Liam dug out his phone and thumbed through a couple of screens before nodding. "Here it is. Yes, it's PowerBoost. The company is the groom's newest sponsor, and he wants them represented. He's asked that place settings alternate flavors between Manic Melon and Electrified Kiwi."

A faint film that tasted suspiciously like shock seasoned with a hefty dose of denial coated Ella's tongue. "No. That shit is either fluorescent pink or neon green."

Arvin paled.

Liam shrugged. "And?"

"It's *not* going on these tables."

"Groom's wishes. Bride concurs." Liam tapped his phone screen, and it went dark. "Shall we eat?"

Liam wrestled dueling urges: he wanted to cringe at his undiluted lies. He wanted to laugh at the look on Ella's face. Neither won. Instead, he smothered both urges with brutal efficiency.

Murdering emotions and flights of fancy. A new tagline for my personality type.

His mouth tightened until he felt the corners curl down.

Sitting next to him, Ella made small talk, guiding the conversation with an easy grace through each course, from appetizers through salad and well into the main course. She was a great conversationalist, seeming to truly listen to what Liam had to say and asking intelligent questions in turn. She was an anomaly, a complete about-face compared to the women he typically entertained, who were interested in his money and his social status and focused almost exclusively on what he could do for them. They were piranhas in Prada, jackals in Jimmy Choo. They looked at him and saw unlimited dollar signs and a season's pass into society's elite, whereas Ella— without knowledge of who he really was—saw a relatable man.

It dawned on Liam that, for the first time in his life, he had the chance to get to know a woman without presumptions laid out by society matrons and their husband-hunting daughters. Those women had proven time and again that they'd do anything to become Mrs. Liam Baggett, and he'd shut them down, each and every one. Yet now, having met a woman who genuinely piqued his interest, he was unable to capitalize on the opportunity.

My, how the tables have turned.

"Liam?"

He glanced up. "Beg your pardon?"

Ella paused, fork held out with a seared scallop on the end. "I asked if you were aware scallops had been added to the main course. I thought the groom hated seafood, particularly shellfish." She set her fork down and picked up her wineglass, sipping slowly as she watched Liam with undisguised assessment.

"I know he doesn't care for seafood in general, but I was under the impression scallops were the lone exception to that rule. It's shrimp that will send him into a righteous fit of temper."

"Shrimp? Why?"

"The first time I met the man was at a private dinner with my sister. She was in London for…" He waved off the explanation, not ready to disclose his sister's identity. "Regardless, that's where she chose to introduce me to him."

"I take it things didn't go well."

"He ordered steak. There was a shrimp skewer on his plate as garnish, and the guy absolutely lost it. Berated the server, demanded to speak to the manager, told my sister to mind herself when she attempted to intervene and defuse the situation. Her fiancé humiliated her. Over shrimp." Liam picked up his wineglass and swirled the contents but set the glass down without drinking. "It's safe to say I'm not his biggest fan."

"I'm sorry."

Liam looked up, focusing on the woman across from him as the last wisps of the memory fanned the flames of temper. That had been a disastrous night. "Why are you sorry? You had nothing to do with it."

"It's clear it still bothers you."

Liam shrugged then forked up a scallop and popped it into his mouth, enjoying the buttery flavor. He picked his glass up again but, this time, followed through and drank. The tannins in the wine cut the richness of the butter, the pairing perfect. If only he could say the same of his sister and her choice of groom. Setting his glass down once more, he met

Ella's direct gaze. "It's over and done. She's marrying him despite my suggestion she do otherwise."

Arvin approached the table, stopping at Liam's seat. "How is everything?"

Liam rose from his low seat and offered the other man a brief handshake. "Your staff has outdone themselves. The meal was incredible and the musicians positively brilliant."

Arvin stammered as he tried to articulate his thanks.

Liam interrupted, waving him off. "I understand how much effort went into the planning and execution. You have my thanks and the same from my sister, I'm sure. If you'd have dessert served while the event's primary entertainment performs, that would be lovely."

"Of course, sir." Arvin bowed deeply and then gestured to the musicians, saying something in Polynesian. The music grew softer and softer until it completely faded away. The ocean's susurrus rush and retreat filled the void. Liam found himself able to breathe and, for the first time, truly appreciate the perfection of the locale Ella had selected for Jenna's wedding. His sister was going to be thrilled with every aspect Ella had selected and designed.

And he was going to ruin it all.

He had no choice, though. Jenna's fiancé was a fame-seeking, moneygrubbing, coattail-riding leech. Mike had moved in to her home, assumed use of her staff and drove her cars at his leisure. To the best of

Liam's knowledge, Jenna was footing the entire bill until the baseball player "made it big."

Perhaps Liam would be able to convince her to spend a few days here with him after the wedding plans dissolved. She'd need the downtime. This would be the perfect place for her to recenter herself before she headed back to Hollywood. And, with Jenna here for a while, her publicist would be able to spin the breakup and place his sister in the best possible light. As for the groom? Mike could rot in hell as far as Liam was concerned. Let his dime-store publicist work out his personal spin.

A low, slow drumbeat began, and Liam swiveled to find a group of six women making their way onto the stretch of sand between the table's edge and the surf. Each carried a large, lit tiki torch. They took their places and began to move as the drumbeat increased in tempo. Hips undulating, the women— clad in sarongs and bikini bottoms—swung the tiki torches like they were batons, splitting into two groups of three and holding the lights high before stabbing them into the sand as the drum thundered a final beat. Two performers moved to stand in front of the table. They swayed as the drums began to beat out a hypnotic rhythm, their hips seeming to move independent of the limitations set by the human body. They swiveled and shook while the women's shoulders stayed straight and almost still, their arms so fluid as to seem boneless. Two more women joined, and then two more, and all six moved in a way that embodied the allure of the tropics, the appeal of intimate meals shared on fire-lit beaches and the promise of seduction that lay in the music's every note.

One stepped forward and held out a hand to Ella. "Come."

"Oh, no," she replied, laughing, her eyes bright. "I don't dance."

The moon cast its light on Ella's lush mane, highlighting it with luminous silver streaks. Her face was flushed from wine. The self-deprecating smile that decorated her face was so open, so unapologetic, so real. The last thread of his control began unraveling. When the dancer reached for her and Ella shook her head, Liam found himself moving forward without any awareness he'd set himself in motion. All he knew was he had to touch Ella. Right then. To see if the silver streaks in her hair were as cool as they appeared or, just maybe, as warm as the woman who bore them.

The distance between them disappeared, and Ella turned just as Liam reached out.

Warm. She was so warm.

"Liam?"

He didn't say anything, simply took her glass and blindly held it out with the unspoken command that the dancer take it.

She did.

"Dance, Ella." The murmured command rumbled up from within him, so deep that his chest vibrated with the sound. With the need that fueled it.

"I don't dance," she whispered.

"Tonight you do."

"Liam—"

"If you won't dance there, with them, then dance now." He took her hand and pulled her into his embrace. "Here." He began to sway in time to the lilting notes of the traditional bamboo flute, its sound as light as the drums were heavy. "With me."

She began to move in time to the music. They swayed back and forth, letting their bodies go where the music led them.

His hands slid across the smooth, silky skin of Ella's back. He loved her dress, the way it hugged her body, hinted at its lean form but enhanced her lush curves. He would have a dozen made so she had one to wear for every occasion. Hell, he'd plead with her to never wear anything else.

When he pulled her closer, Ella glanced up through thick lashes, her eyes burning with untempered heat. "Is this how you'd treat a date in Los Angeles?"

"This is how I'd treat you, Ella. Only you." He spun her around, guiding her to the water's edge and into the very edge of the surf, the waves rushing in to slip over their bare feet and wick up the fabric of his trousers and her dress. "Just dance."

She closed her eyes then, and gave herself to the music. Her chin tilted toward the sky. Starlight shone brighter than he ever remembered it, bathing her in a surreal glow. The hand that held his tightened, and the hand on his chest fisted the linen of his shirt. "You're a dangerous man, Liam Baggett."

Something in him snapped. No one could have heard, but it was as clear to him as the starting bell at a horse track. He moved with as much grace as he could muster, leading Ella from the water's edge and back onto the sand.

The surf rushed after them, licking at their heels.

Ella's lips parted on a sigh. Lifting her face to his, her gaze came to rest on Liam's mouth.

His cock swelled in response to the undisguised hunger that swam in those green depths.

Ella didn't look away, didn't try to hide the emotional riot she experienced. Instead, she whispered his name, just his name, in that sultry voice of hers. In it lay a plea he heard and responded to in kind.

"Ella."

She rose on her tiptoes, clutching his shoulders for balance in the shifting sand, and closed the distance between them...then stopped less than an inch from his mouth, waiting.

She would pursue so much as she was pursued. She would give what she was given and take what was offered. Nothing more. Nothing less.

Liam could live with that.

He dipped his head low and brushed his lips over hers. She tasted of crisp white wine and the sun's warmth and just a hint of mint in the dessert she'd sampled. He could get drunk on her. His senses heightened even as his mind grew sluggish, intoxicated by the woman in his arms. Never had it been like this with anyone.

Breaking the kiss, he took her hand and started toward the bungalow.

CHAPTER SIX

TENSION RACED THROUGH Ella's body like her nervous system was a never-ending zip line. Fine tremors in her hands made her clumsy as she gathered the hem of her dress before climbing the stairs that led into the thatch-roofed hut. Liam stood across the room, his shirt unbuttoned and one thumb hooked behind the button of his pants. He drew in a deep breath and let it out slowly. "I haven't been able to think clearly since I saw your toes."

She glanced down. "My...toes?"

"They're pink, Ella." He chuffed out a short, harsh laugh. "You've reduced me—the head of Europe's premier financial firm—to obsessing over the color of your nail polish."

She smiled at him, a wicked gleam in her eyes. "So, you get off on feet, then. Or is it the color pink? Because if it's pink, you're in for it. I'm wearing one other item that's pink."

"If you're telling me your lingerie is pink, don't expect to find them in the morning."

"You'd steal my underwear?"

He met her curious stare, his eyes filled with a predatory hunger that made her want to run *only* to ensure he chased her. Took her down. Commanded her body as the spoils of some as-yet unfought war. Then he sealed her fate as well as his.

"Of course, I'd steal other things from you first."

"Such as?"

"I intend to steal your breath followed by your sense of reason followed by your self-control."

Her heart tumbled through her chest like she had just come off a carnival tilt-a-whirl. "You're telling me you're capable of taking all of those things. And with such confidence."

He leaned against the bathroom door frame and, with one flick of his wrist, undid the top button of his trousers. "Yes, Ella. I am."

"How can you be so sure?" she asked, voice strangled.

He pinched the zipper tab between thumb and forefinger. "I haven't been able to stop staring at you all night. That dress… God, Ella. That dress. I want to peel it off you slowly, but I'm afraid I won't have the patience. I want to see you bare, wearing nothing but candlelight, far too badly. I want to touch you, to find out if your nipples are a similar pink to your toes or if they are, in fact, paler."

Ella traced a hand along the outside of her breast, his eyes following her every move. It was thrilling, knowing she had seduced this man simply by being herself. Erotic in a whole new way.

Liam's gaze slid back to hers. "I'm done chatting, Ella. Lose the dress."

She smiled, the coquettish move morphing to something more carnal as her gaze dropped to the smattering of dark hair revealed just above Liam's zipper. He had an impressive erection going on. Mouth dry, she forced herself to swallow. "We need to set the ground rules."

"Fine, but be quick about it." He pulled his zipper down an inch.

"What happens inside this bungalow has no bearing on what happens outside."

"Spell it out clearly, Ella."

"What we do here, privately, has nothing to do with who we are professionally. The two—personal and professional—are essentially two different people."

"I'm fine with that, but I'm more interested in the rules that apply right here. Right now. Tomorrow will be whatever it is."

Ella licked her lips. Liam's gaze zeroed in on the movement, and her nipples pearled.

"Lose the dress."

"Bossy bastard."

He shrugged, eyes blazing with unchecked desire.

Clutching the bodice of her dress with one hand, she reached up and untied the slender bow at her nape. Strings fell away and the dress sagged around her, held in place but not covering much. "Bedroom rules are simple. If either of us doesn't like something, we say so, and whatever it is stops."

"And if you don't tell me to stop, Ella? What then?"

"Then take it as an official endorsement—hell, take it as a challenge—to pull every other damn word in the English language out of my mouth using only your body. Make me scream, Liam. Make me forget my name. Make me forget every man who has been here before and be the man I'll compare every future lover to."

Liam's lip curled. Before Ella could ask what his issue was, he'd dropped his pants, stepped out of the puddled linen and started toward her, his long strides eating up the distance between them with alarming quickness.

He stopped so close to her she could smell the fragrant musk of his cologne. "Here's hoping you have a huge vocabulary, Ella. Challenge accepted."

Then he kissed her.

Ella's self-control dissolved under Liam's undivided attention. She let her dress fall to the floor, the silky fabric puddling around her feet like spilled ink. Kicking free, she moved closer to the scalding heat of Liam's bare skin. She gave herself free rein to explore his chest's contours with hands and lips, discovering the sculpted hills and salty valleys of muscle defined in stark relief in the moonlight. She shoved his shirt off his shoulders and let it go. It landed somewhere. They'd find it later. For now? There was only her.

Him.

Them.

And the moment demanded her full attention if she was going to keep up with his agenda.

As if he read her mind, he broke away from the kiss and leaned in to nip her earlobe. "Stop trying to make sense of this, Ella. Let it be what it is."

"And what is this?" she whispered, letting her head tip back, exposing her neck.

His answer, whispered in kind, raked over her skin. "Madness."

Madness.

She intended to respond, but Liam chose that moment to dip lower and, lifting the globe of her breast, take the nipple into his mouth, where he attended it with lips and tongue and teeth. An invisible line ran through her breast, down her abdomen and settled in her sex. It was hot, tantamount to a lit fuse, and it promised an explosion when it reached her core. Already the embers were burning.

Ella rubbed her thighs together and moaned, raking her fingers through Liam's thick hair and fisting it. She pulled him closer.

He hummed his approval against her skin.

The fine vibrations did impossible things to her already distended nipple.

"Please," she gasped. Desperation made her awkward, but her hands sought out his erection and she gripped it, sliding the broad girth through her fist. So smooth. Hot. Hard. She followed the length back up with slow calculation and discovered a fine sheen of arousal coating the head. Shifting her grip, she smoothed her thumb through it and across the sensitive tip.

Liam huffed out a wordless sound and then lifted

his head to reclaim her mouth. Their tongues dueled, desperation flavoring every touch, fueling every nip, shaping every sound. Alternately pushing and pulling, he directed her toward the bed as if he were a choreographer. Mosquito netting slithered across her bare shoulder and arm, and Ella shivered. Then the edge of the mattress was there, and she found herself being laid down with extreme care, his kiss never ending, his touch never ceasing.

She wallowed in myriad sensations, her body fluid, molten, under his heat.

Liam broke the kiss, and she mewled in protest. There were no words to ask him to return to her mouth, particularly when he began trailing kisses down her body, tracing his tongue around each nipple, circling her belly button and then—

Ella arched off the bed when Liam's mouth closed over her sex, where she most craved touch, stimulation, manipulation. Anything.

Everything.

She cried out in protest when he let go, falling back on the bed as he tugged her hips to the very edge.

"Patience," he said, mouth barely touching her overheated skin.

"Screw patience," she ground out, lifting her hips to him in a wordless demand.

She felt him smile. "That's the plan."

Liam's control had begun to unravel on the beach when he'd taken Ella's mouth in that first kiss, but this—the taste and sound and feel of her—dismantled him in a rush. His mouth worked her hard, driving her to the brink of orgasm before backing off, until Ella shook with the need.

Her frustrated cry had him sliding a single finger into her tight sheath and using his thumb to caress that sensitive nerve bundle as he used his free hand and teeth to rip open the condom he'd tossed on the bed. Unchecked need had him shaking so badly it took both of his hands to roll the condom down his length, but he managed. Barely.

Looking up, he found Ella's glazed eyes locked on the jutting length of his cock. She whimpered, hips undulating with primal need.

Liam was undone.

He gripped her hips and pulled her toward him. Then, eyes on hers, he surged forward and sheathed himself in her tight, hot sex with a single thrust.

Ella arched her back so hard only her shoulders and feet were on the bed. She took him to the root even as her hands scrabbled and fisted the duvet, seeking purchase.

There was little finesse and even less control as instinct took over, driving his hips in a base thrust-retreat-thrust motion echoed by the sound of skin striking skin with a rhythm that spoke of bodies in motion.

Ella gripped his arms for leverage and gave as well as she received, lifting her hips to meet his every drive. She was wild and uninhibited and everything he'd ever dreamed of in a lover. He wanted more of her, all of her, and would settle for no less as he fucked her with a brutally raw passion he'd thought himself incapable of.

Reaching between them, he found her swollen clitoris and pinched it.

"Liam!" she cried out, eyes going wide.

The first flutters of her orgasm clutched his cock, and his balls drew impossibly tighter. The base of his spine burned with warning a mere second before heat scorched his length and his own orgasm overtook him. No more warning than that.

He was reduced to a frantic pumping of hips and ragged breaths and shattered thoughts as he rode out the sensations that threatened to dismantle him, body and soul. Grinding his hips into hers, he gave a final thrust as she went limp. Straining, a final pulse rocked him and he collapsed forward onto her.

Their hearts thundered one against the other, the frenzied beats adopting a kindred rhythm.

She shifted beneath him, and he managed to move his body onto the bed beside her, rolling to take her into his arms in a move as foreign to him as democracy was to dictatorship. He'd never been one for postcoital cuddling, but just then, the idea of letting Ella go wasn't acceptable.

His chest tightened with an unnamed emotion when she snuggled back into him so that he spooned her. They fit together as if they were a two-piece puzzle. He felt like he should say something, offer some sort of commentary on their situation, but Ella beat him to it.

"You're way behind, Webster."

"Webster?"

"The dictionary. I suggested you pull every word in the English language from my mouth. All you managed was your name."

He smiled into her hair. "That was enough, darling." The pet name fell from his lips with ease and, for once, it wasn't just an empty platitude meant to pave the way for a smooth departure from his lover's bed. The truth rattled him, and he lost his train of thought.

She was quiet, presumably waiting on him to finish his thought.

He rolled onto his back and took her with him, situating her so she straddled his hips before offering her the truth. "Dawn is hours away. We've plenty of time to work on your vocabulary."

CHAPTER SEVEN

ELLA SAT NEXT to the pool, laptop open, and flipped through the list Liam had given her before he slipped out this morning. The warmth of the early-afternoon sun soothed muscles that ached from overuse through the night.

She grinned.

Maybe she'd arrange for a massage later this afternoon. Or she'd talk Liam into doing it. Yeah, that had some real potential.

Her grin widened.

"Work first, play second." She murmured the reminder under her breath.

Getting back on task, she continued to read through Liam's paperwork. There, at the bottom of the first page in bold male handwriting, was a note with the groom's request for a shellfish pairing with the main course. She typed the request into the file she'd started to track Liam's changes. It wasn't that she didn't trust him. She didn't know him enough to either trust or distrust him when it came to her career. But she felt better keeping their individual choices clearly defined in the event the bride or groom wanted to know why a specific change had been made.

She continued through the notes. There were quite a few handwritten amendments on the second and third pages—things like the flowers to be used in the bride's bouquet, the number of guests attending, requested activities, food choices, the orientation of the chairs relative to the sea and more. Each change left Ella a little more concerned than the last. Sure, the revisions were minor, but they altered the feel of the preceremony celebration and the nuptials...enough to make Ella question whether she'd had it right from the beginning. Was she losing her touch? Liam had been so confident in giving her the changes, so sure about what the couple desired for their big day. And he would know, wouldn't he? Had she misread the bride's wishes so significantly?

At the thought, her belly rolled over, the sensation as lazy as it was insolent.

A shadow cut across her computer screen. "Finding everything in order?"

Ella glanced up and discovered the very man she'd just been thinking about standing beside her lounge chair. Liam's broad shoulders blocked the sun. He wore nothing but a pair of pale blue board shorts. Water dripped from the hems and puddled around his bare feet. His dark hair was slicked back, making his deep brown eyes all the more prominent in that sculpted face. He shifted his weight from one foot to the other, and the waist of his trunks slipped a fraction of an inch down his hips. Tanned warmth gave way to a thin white strip of skin.

He moved to tug the shorts up, and she reached out to rest a hand on his knee. "Don't."

A smile teased one side of his mouth. "Don't what?"

"Don't pull your shorts up."

"The lady allows me to command her body in the dark but thinks to command mine in the light of day?"

She tugged on the end of the wet suit, exposing a bit more skin, and took him in, one visual gulp at a time.

"If memory serves, you were quite vocal in your approval."

"I'm all about positive reinforcement."

He chuffed out a small laugh.

"Besides," she continued, "how else was I supposed to let you know you were doing what—*exactly* what—I wanted?" Batting her eyes, she lowered her voice. "And if *my* memory serves, you were all too anxious to have me command your body under yesterday's sun."

He touched two fingers to his forehead in mock salute. "Touché."

A short laugh, breathy and shallow, escaped her, and she fought the urge to cringe. She'd never been *that woman*, the one who flirted with inane comments and superficial behavior. This man wouldn't turn her into that woman, no matter how spectacular a lover he'd been.

Ella cleared her throat, gathered her paperwork and then stood, forcing Liam to take a step back and give her some space. She needed to do something proactive on this account, something to prepare for the arrival of the bride and groom in just four short days.

Four days.

The timeline was so tight. If she screwed this up, there would be no time to fix it. This was a one-shot opportunity to reclaim her career and her self-esteem. She wouldn't, *couldn't*, screw it up.

"I have some questions about the changes you requested."

Liam crossed his arms over his chest, took a deep breath and widened his stance as if preparing for battle. "Do you, now." His tone was measured. "I was under the impression my notes were self-explanatory."

She tilted her head to one side, looking him over. "Does this happen often?"

"Does what happen often?"

"This." She gestured toward him. "Do you have frequent episodes where your superiority complex interferes with common courtesy? If so, you might consider seeing someone about it."

His eyes flared for a moment before his lids slid down and gave him the appearance of bored but focused irritation. "A little respect, Ella."

"Absolutely, Liam," she said, emphasizing the two syllables of his name and meeting his stare head-on. "When it's earned." She squared her shoulders and tipped her head toward a table situated in deep shade. "Let's move over there. We'll be able to spread the paperwork out, and I can share sketches and initial plans on the guest seating, ceremony timing and reception setup. I believe that when you view the ideas your sister first approved, you'll be able to help me incorporate the modified requests."

"Certainly, though I'm deferring to you and your expertise."

"Yes, but you know the couple. I don't." She moved past him, still talking as she went. "Consider it a different type of boardroom negotiation and you'll be fine. But treat me like the expendable lackey, and we're going to butt heads all the way to our departing flights."

"And that wouldn't do, would it."

Ella rounded on Liam and forced herself to hold her ground when she found him much closer than she'd anticipated. Tilting her head back and shielding her eyes from the sun, she fought to keep her tone level. "You're trying to provoke me. I'm not sure why, but stop it. Neither of us gains anything if this wedding is a wreck just because you couldn't separate the personal and professional aspects of our acquaintanceship."

"Acquaintanceship." Liam's brow furrowed and his eyes darkened. "Is that what you're calling this thing between us?"

Ella shrugged. "I don't need to label it to enjoy it, so feel free to call it what you want. But whatever you do? Don't, and I mean *do not*, allow it to interfere with my job. Understand?"

He inclined his head but didn't meet her challenging stare as he waved her toward the table she'd indicated moments before. "After you, then."

And that...that easy capitulation left the skin across her shoulders tight even as he placed a hand so low on her back that a small shift let him slip lower, one finger caressing the skin below her sarong and bikini-clad bottom, sending warmth coursing through her. Both sensations were strong, both messages loud and clear.

The question was, which one should she listen to first?

Five hours later, with the sun beginning to set, Liam had demanded Ella take a break. The woman had grown frazzled, frustrated and kept retracing steps she'd already taken. She'd argued with him, as predicted, so he'd signaled the waiter, signed off on the check and asked her to meet him at the bungalow. Then he left, Ella still stewing in her seat. There was time yet to get her to come around, even if the timeline was tight and growing tighter. The approach had to be gentle, even subtle. If he pushed her too hard, too fast, she'd become suspicious. He didn't want to lose the best chance he had in getting his sister to see the truth about her fiancé. Though he was feeling inexplicably guilty about the consequence to Ella should he successfully dismantle the wedding.

Settling deeper into the porch hammock, he used one foot to push off and start the swing rocking. He could fix whatever went wrong, set Ella's business to rights with just a few well-placed calls, a timely recommendation or two and a couple of high-profile jobs he'd create on his own if he had to. And surely Jenna would use her star power and social influence to help as well. His sister was softhearted. Too much so. That had gotten her into this mess of an engagement in the first place. If she'd been more practical instead of so emotional, she'd have seen what her fiancé was after from the beginning. Thankfully, Liam had no qualms about protecting his sister. He would do what needed to be done to ensure Jenna wasn't taken in by a con man. If love existed, his sister deserved nothing less.

One of the bungalow's French doors opened with a soft *snick* before closing with a sharp *kabam*.

No apology followed.

Yep. Ella was still irritated. Maybe "pissed off" was more accurate. His insistence that Jenna wanted freshly imported tulips from Holland had seemed to send Ella over the edge. She'd typed the amendment into her computer, fingers slamming against the keys in rapid-fire fashion, and then eyed him through narrowed lids. "Anything *else*?"

That's when he'd made his stage-left exit.

He knew he needed to smooth the proverbial waters between them to keep her focused on his revisions. The trick was to do so in a way that wouldn't make his concerns seem overdone or his directives too controlling. He couldn't allow her to get to the point she considered reaching out to Jenna's assistant for confirmation. There had been a moment, maybe two, this afternoon where it had been a near thing.

The woman was sharp as hell. But he'd been able to redirect her by suggesting outrageous alternatives to his "amended" requests in the hopes of making his changes seem less, well, outrageous. Which they were. He was well aware some of what he'd written in was over-the-top. He'd drafted a mental checklist of things he would need to handle himself. Then he had offered to take those tasks off her plate to help her. The blatant lying didn't sit well with him. At all. But he'd do that and more, even worse, to spare Jenna the heartache Mike would, without a doubt, foist on her.

Liam had watched over Jenna since she'd taken her first steps, always there to ensure she wasn't hurt if she fell, helping her get back up and take her next steps with confidence. And she had because she knew he was right there to catch her should she fall again. Liam had tended her wounds, from skinned knees after falling off her bicycle to a broken arm following a horseback-riding incident. He'd talked her through her first broken heart. He'd celebrated her first major nomination for lead actress. He'd always been there for her. Always. She'd even once admitted to him that part of her fearlessness was the knowledge he'd always be there to support her.

And then there was the oath Liam's father had demanded from his deathbed.

First, Liam had to give his word that he would watch over Jenna. Second, his father had demanded that Liam keep Baggett Financial Services in the family and ensure that voting rights and ultimate ownership would remain at 51 percent or greater in the Baggetts' favor. Should Liam fail, the board was ordered to replace him with a second cousin. The boy was only fourteen but had already proven a head for numbers in his boarding school. Liam had been insulted. He'd also been emotionally wrung out. The former his father dismissed; the latter was never acknowledged. Not by either Baggett.

And while he'd resented the hell out of his old man, he fully intended to keep true to his word. He didn't take vows lightly.

Ella stepped closer, scattering his darkening thoughts like light permeating shadow. The wind toyed with loose curls that had slipped free of her sloppy topknot. Her semisheer sarong fluttered around her long, toned legs.

Liam let his eyes drift closed even as his sex awoke with a hard pulse.

He knew exactly how those legs felt when they were wrapped around him.

The wind shifted and carried with it the floral bouquet of her perfume. She was a siren. How could she be anything else? She was smart as hell, beautiful, charming, witty—all traits Liam valued in friends as well as in lovers. He'd never been lucky enough to find all of those things in one person, though. Until now. The realization was a stinging buzz in his chest, a feeling not unlike the vibration of a large gong struck in close proximity. It vibrated through him until he was forced to rub the valley between his pecs in an attempt to assuage the feeling.

"The tulips will be here on Tuesday, in tight bud condition, with a guaranteed arrival of no later than 3:00 p.m. That gives me time to put together the bouquets and boutonnieres without the heat forcing the flowers open prematurely." She sighed. "I have Arvin speaking to the resort's contracted fishermen about harvesting the scallops, but he's not sure what they'll be able to gather this time of year. We may have to add them to the seafood croquettes, but there will be shellfish in some form or another."

Liam hooked his arms behind his head and watched Ella pace the length of the deck. "You need to relax, Ella."

She sucked in a short breath, tension carving deep grooves in the soft skin beside her lush mouth. "I'll relax when this wedding is a success. There'll be time and opportunity then. But right now? I can't. Too much is riding on luck showing up to play for my team, and in my experience she tends to avoid critical situations where I'm involved. She'll show up afterward and be all, 'What? You needed me? My cell never rang.'"

Liam smiled. "You're sexy when you're strung out."

"You think so?"

"I do."

She shook her head and laughed softly. "Then you ought to find me completely irresistible by Monday night."

"It will work out the way it's supposed to, Ella.

Trust me on this. And I find you irresistible right now."

"Sweet talker." Her smile faded. "If all that mattered was an exchange of vows, I'd agree. But there's so much more to making a bride's dream manifest as reality. I was under the impression she wanted butterflies, not birds, released at the close of the ceremony. Now I find out she wants four dozen birds released with the kiss. So while I figure out the best place to release the butterflies that will arrive Monday, I have Arvin trying to source the birds. It's all last-minute, of course, and all he can come up with are pigeons. Not quite the same effect as white doves soaring free."

Sitting up, Liam straddled the hammock and motioned her forward.

She moved toward him like a cautious cat, lithe and smooth but ready to bolt if threatened. "What?"

He wiggled his fingers in an impatient gesture. "You need to take a few minutes and relax."

"I don't *have* a few minutes to relax. I 'relaxed' last night and slept through my alarm this morning."

He stood and moved toward her, silently celebrating when she held her ground and squared her shoulders. This woman was no shrinking violet. It made the battle of wills sharper and conquest that much sweeter…no matter who won. And Liam wasn't averse to being conquered now and again.

Pulling her into his embrace, his hands skated down her back, over the expanse of bare skin and, cupping her butt, pulled her into his semierect cock.

"If you won't take a break for your own well-being, take one for mine."

Ella slid her arms around his waist at the same time she twined her right leg around his left. "You're bribing me to slack off on your sister's wedding."

"No." He lowered his head and nibbled his way along her jaw to her neck, down and then down some more until he reached her collarbone. A quick nip drew a sharp intake of breath from her, and his cock swelled hard and fast. "I've no doubt you'll handle what needs handling." Taking her hand, he rested it on his erection, his nostrils flaring when she closed her hand over his length and stroked him through his shorts.

Ella's breath came faster, scalding the skin of his neck. Backing toward the bedroom, she tightened her hold on him and whispered, "And what about you, Liam? Do you need to be handled?"

"By you?" he asked. "Always."

CHAPTER EIGHT

ELLA'S PHONE BUZZED. Face buried under her pillow, she blindly searched the tabletop until she found it, but the call went to voice mail before she managed to answer.

"Don't you dare leave this bed." The commanding male voice was still laced with sleep. "Whoever it was will call back, and whatever they want will keep until then."

Sunlight slipped through the window, softened by the gauzy mosquito netting that surrounded the bed and created a haven within the tropical paradise. "Says the man who left me without even a note yesterday morning." She stretched until her muscles shook and then went limp, letting her arms flop onto the expansive mattress. One hand made contact with her lover's arm.

He grunted his objection.

The temptation to lie there until noon was too real. "I need sustenance." She weakly clapped her hands. "Breakfast in bed, man. Make it happen."

The bed shifted. Small electronic notes indicated

Liam was placing a call. Still, it surprised her when his sleep-roughened voice greeted the person on the other end with "And good morning to you, Marise. This is Liam Baggett. I'd like to place a room service order, please." A pause. "Crepes with fresh cream and strawberries, fruit, granola, Belgian waffles, sourdough toast, bacon, orange juice and a carafe of regular black coffee." Another pause. "That's it. Just charge it to my room. Oh, and if you would have the meal set up on our patio, that would be lovely."

Ella's stomach rumbled in appreciation. The man certainly had good taste. She rolled onto her back and draped one arm over her eyes as the beep of the phone said Liam had disconnected the call. "How long before I can put caffeine in my system?"

He chuckled. "Twenty minutes."

A warm hand slid across her abdomen, and she sucked in a sharp, short breath. "Too long."

"Just long enough for me to distract you," he countered, reaching for her.

She rolled away before he could get a good grasp on her. "No. Nope. Not happening." Standing, she swayed with a bit of dizzy exhaustion. They'd stayed up too late last night, making love in far too many locations in and around the bungalow—the porch, the hammock, the bed, the tub, the floor. She was satisfied—so satisfied her muscles felt like overcooked noodles. It was a wonder she was able to stand without support. Not that she was complaining. At all. But the time she'd spent in personal indulgence was time that hadn't been spent working on the wedding.

Snatching up her cell, she thumbed to the messages and read the transcription of Arvin's voice mail.

> Birds located. Aviary only had one dozen available. Breeder recommended another aviary on neighboring island. If the expense is acceptable, let me know and I'll have the doves delivered. I need to order them today in order to receive them in time for the ceremony. Arvin.

Ella pinched the bridge of her nose and focused on taking slow, deep breaths. This was another expense she hadn't planned on. Every change Liam made came with a new cost. Like using flowers flown direct from Holland. She had expressed her concerns, but Liam dismissed them with a wave of his hand. He'd insisted that his sister had given him free rein to go over the budget. Ella had asked him to send her an email confirming that the additional costs were acceptable. He'd pulled out his phone and written the email on the spot, going one step further by promising he'd cover any cost to which his sister objected.

But Ella was still anxious. The energy drinks, the doves, the excursions…additions and subtractions to the welcome baskets. If Liam failed to honor his word to cover costs, the bride and groom could come after her and demand she pay out of pocket.

Driven by caution, she figured she'd improvise. Somehow. Maybe hold a less expensive group activity than the private sail and scuba dive currently scheduled for the bride, groom and their guests the day prior to the ceremony. That would be one place Ella could cut a few corners.

Leaving Liam lounging in bed, she went into the living room and opened her computer, pulling up the resort's activities website. She traced a finger along the keypad, scrolling—scuba diving, deep-sea fishing, snorkeling, hiking. She paused. *Parasailing and horseback riding.* Each activity was easily one hundred and fifty dollars less per person, and she'd bet she could negotiate a better rate.

"Liam?"

An inarticulate sound was her only response.

"What do you think about parasailing and horseback riding?"

"I'd never recommend trying the two at the same time."

"I'm sure that's sound advice, smart-ass. I'm asking if you think either of those activities might be a better choice for the guests instead of the sail and dive."

Covers rustled followed by the sound of bare feet padding across the hardwood floor. Liam appeared in the doorway, a sheet wrapped about his waist. Sunlight came down from the skylight, showcasing the hard planes and muscles of his torso, making him look like a chiseled work of art. Natural highlights in his hair softened his features. But his eyes—they were infinitely deep and far more sensual than she'd ever seen them.

Ella wanted to abandon all attempts at work and take this man back to bed. He might frustrate the hell out of her, but he had learned his way around her body in no time at all. He could dissolve stress better than a stiff drink, relieve anxiety better than any prescription. Yeah, she'd take one of him to go, thanks.

Blinking rapidly, she shook her head. "Stop distracting me."

He smiled then, slow and suggestive, and tilted his head toward the bedroom. "We still have ten minutes before breakfast gets here. Enough time for a quickie."

The problem was, she didn't want a quickie. She wanted more time with him, wanted more time than this event would afford them. Already she'd begun dreading the day they'd part ways. This wasn't like her. At all.

But the truth was what it was.

The only practical solution was to keep things between them light. Fun. Relaxed. She needed to keep her head in the game and her heart off the table. Period. And there was no better time to enforce her "no emotional connections" pledge than the present.

Closing her computer, she set it aside and stood, stretching her arms above her naked body.

Liam's eyes grew hooded as he pushed off the door frame he'd been leaning against.

She started toward him. "What can you do with six minutes?"

He reached out and pulled her close, his erection prodding her belly. "More than enough, Ella." His lips brushed hers and he smiled, the look utterly wicked. "More than enough."

Liam spread out the newspaper and read through the financials before opening his computer to do a little catching up with the London office. He answered a handful of critical emails and delegated the rest to his personal assistant. He was in the process of reviewing a high-profile client's returns, making notes on changes and calculating potential returns on amended investments when his cell rang. The ringtone was a snappy show tune, one he'd set for his sister after taking her to see a live performance on the West End for her sixteenth birthday.

He reached for the phone and swiped to answer the call, silently thanking the powers that be for getting Ella out of hearing distance so he could speak freely. "What's going on, squid?"

Jenna laughed. "How long are you going to call me that awful nickname?"

"Until I can forget you clinging to me, afraid to jump off the diving board unless I went with you."

"I was being cautious!" she retorted.

"You nearly drowned the both of us," Liam groused, though even he could hear the undiluted affection in his voice.

"Whatever. How's the wedding stuff going?"

Liam leaned back in his chair and closed his eyes, focused on keeping his breathing even, his tone level. "Right on schedule. You hired a stellar event coordinator."

"My assistant said she was pretty awesome. I hate doing this so cloak-and-dagger, but it's the only way to keep the paparazzi off my ass."

"What are you telling your guests?"

She laughed. "Nothing. We've handwritten notes to invite them to join us on a brief getaway. Doesn't look like a wedding invitation at all. That was the event coordinator's idea. What's her name again?"

"Ella."

"Right. Anyway, we're inviting everyone like it's an individual thing and asking them to keep it tucked under their hats so we have a chance of a paparazzi-free vacay. Most are Hollywood names and faces, so they'll appreciate the opportunity for a private vacation. It wouldn't surprise me if most of them suspect a wedding, but the guest list is small enough I'm not too worried about gossip."

"I'll bet you a hundred pounds one of them sells you out."

"You're such a cynic."

"Yet you didn't take the bet."

"Oh, I'll take it. But when I win, make sure you pay up in British pounds. Don't try to cheat me by giving me American dollars. Not with the exchange rate what it is."

Liam chuckled. "As if you'd best me. I'll take *my*

winnings by way of a single Benjamin, you trusting soul."

"We'll see who's handing out money when this is all over." She sighed, a small hitch sounding across the connection. "Is the wedding really coming together well, Liam? I've been worried. It's not that I don't trust you. You know that. It's just..." Jenna hesitated, seeming to hunt for the right words.

It's not that I don't trust you. Liam felt as if his heart had been steamrolled, backed over and steamrolled again. She had entrusted this—what was supposed to be the happiest day of her life—to him. And for the first time ever, he was going to absolutely disappoint her.

His chest tightened at the realization. Every breath grew shorter and shorter until he struggled to breathe at all.

"Leem?"

She hadn't been able to pronounce his name as a toddler. Instead, she'd called him "Leem," and it had evolved into her nickname for him. Now she only called him that when she was out of sorts and unsure of herself. It didn't happen often anymore.

"Ella is top-notch, Jenna, truly in a class of her own. She has ensured that every idea presented, whether from you or I, becomes a reality." Total truth so far as that went. Perhaps the most truth he'd spoken regarding the wedding since he'd set foot on the island.

"There haven't been any issues with the stuff I asked for? I know some of it will be hard to manage in such a remote location, but she was positive she could make it happen."

"Jenna, there's nothing to fret over." *Except the groom.* "What was it your mother always told you about getting married to our father?"

"That she could've been married in a cornfield under the blazing noon sun wearing nothing but a gunny sack while holding a bouquet of thistle. She married the man she wanted to spend the rest of her life with, and *that* was what mattered."

"So hold on to that."

"I am."

"Are you quite certain about this, squid? You don't have to marry him simply because he asked, you know."

"I know you and Mike haven't exactly hit it off, and it's clear you don't like him much, but he's the one. *My* one, Liam. I love him."

"Then that's the answer, I suppose." But it didn't have to be. She didn't have to marry this guy just because he'd convinced Liam's softhearted sister he was a prince among paupers.

"It is," Jenna answered in kind, her voice soft. "And you'll be there to stand in for Dad, to walk me down the aisle and give me away. I wouldn't have it any other way."

Emotion welled, stealing Liam's ability to speak. He made a noncommittal noise and then choked on the sound, coughing harshly.

"Leem?"

"I'm fine."

"I've got another call. Hold on." She was gone and back in a flash. "That was Mike. The car service is here to pick us up. We're headed to the airport!" she nearly squealed. "This is really happening, Liam!"

She sounded so damnably happy...

Leaning forward, he propped his elbows on his knees and raked his free hand through his hair. "Travel safe, squid. You're all that matters, you know."

"Don't worry so much," she chastised. "I'll be there soon enough and you'll see."

"Jenna," Liam wheezed. "I gave our father my word that I'd look out for you, ensure your happiness before all else..." He couldn't finish that particular train of thought because a new realization was barreling down on him at breakneck speed.

What if I'm wrong—wrong about the groom? Wrong about stopping the wedding? And, God save me, wrong about what would truly ensure Jenna's happiness?

If he was wrong, his sister was about to pay the price for his mistake.

But he'd seen Mike treat Jenna poorly, and more than once. His boorish behavior, lack of manners and general indifference had soured Liam on the man. There was no undoing the damage. He had to protect Jenna.

"Leem?" she prompted.

"I only want you to know you have options. Even if you're pregnant, we can—"

"I'm not pregnant, Liam," Jenna said in as sharp a tone as she ever took with him. "Would you please relax? It's going to be fine. After all, you said so, and who would dare defy you?" She sighed. "We'll be there soon, Liam. Please stop worrying. Mike is my one. I know what I'm doing."

Liam remained silent, unsure what to say in the face of her frustrated plea.

Jenna took the decision out of his hands, disconnecting the call without a goodbye.

Liam was left holding the phone, still wondering what he should've—could've—said that stood even a remote chance of making things better between him and Jenna. Things couldn't be broken now, before the rug was pulled out from under her.

With their father gone and her groom likely to bail when things got tough, Liam would be the only one there to help her pick up the pieces of her dream.

Even though he was the one who would shatter it.

CHAPTER NINE

ELLA SAT AT the beachside bar, the seating chart for the wedding dinner spread out in front of her. Her initial notes had stipulated no bride and groom table—Jenna and Mike had wanted to sit *with* their guests. The revised arrangement had guests clearly segregated, each one labeled "B" for bride or "G" for groom. The two groups had been seated in different locations, each one opposite the new table where the bride and groom sat. Alone. The arrangement made little sense. It felt wrong, far too unlike the original plans.

Shoving her hands through her hair, a low growl escaped her. Should she follow Liam's revised plans and ignore the inner voice that was screaming at her to disregard his changes? Surely Liam wouldn't screw her over. What could he possibly gain from ruining his sister's wedding? More than once he'd said that he wanted his sister's happiness above all else.

But things weren't adding up, and Ella couldn't swing many more changes. Not with the wedding so close. The resort—thanks to her relationship with Arvin—had been willing to extend a significant rate reduction for horseback riding on the beach. Liam had never answered her about substituting horseback riding or parasailing for the dive trip, so she'd chosen horseback riding based on his notes. No one indicated a fear of animals. No one claimed any allergies. So she'd offer two excursions, each with the bride and groom present, and guests could choose which one they wanted to participate in. That would work.

Letting her gaze drift over the seating arrangement, Ella traced her fingers along the far table, the one labeled with the groom's guests, then finger-walked across to the bride's guest table. The groups were small, but… "This can't be right."

"What's wrong with it?"

She looked up sharply into eyes the color of luxurious dark chocolate—sweet but with a bite.

Liam's brows drew together. "Ella?"

Shaking off the ridiculous wanderings of her mind, she focused on the moment at hand. Now was the time to get this mess straightened out. Ella had a short window of time left to make sure everything was in order for the Wednesday morning walk-through and Wednesday afternoon excursions. Then? The wedding.

Two. Days.

The butterflies in her stomach took up dogfight maneuvers, zipping left and then right, flying up only to plummet to the depths of her belly. Rather sickening, all in all.

"Ella?" Liam repeated.

"I have two days to piece together what you say your sister wants versus what her personal assistant said she wants. I have to make sense of this and make it work, Liam, because anything less could potentially doom me to planning children's parties for the rest of my life." Running her hands over her face, she traced the lines marring her forehead and the grooves etched alongside her mouth. She had to look as haggard as she felt. "This is wrecking me. I'm going to need a week at a spa just to undo the damage the stress is doing to my skin. I swear I've aged five years in four days. This is ridiculous, Liam."

He sank into a canvas sling chair and scooted forward, pulling together the plans she'd scattered around her. It took him seconds to organize them, but then he seemed to hesitate. With careful consideration, he folded up the sheet he'd given her and moved the original plan to the top of the pile. "Trash the seating plan I gave you and go with the one my sister's assistant originally laid out."

Ella started and then sank back into her chair. "What? Why?"

"Because this is more in line with what she truly wants." Liam looked at her, smile sardonic and eyes sad. "It's something I shouldn't have messed with."

The knot that had formed in Ella's stomach unraveled, and she drew her first full breath since hearing Liam had a modified wish list. Until now, she hadn't realized exactly how messed up she'd been. Not really. But this...this sudden about-face Liam was pulling? It eased her fears. Surely there was a reason behind it, but she wasn't going to look for it. All that mattered was she'd suddenly found the confidence to move forward. "So what would you say to horseback riding on the beach or parasailing instead of snorkeling and diving?"

He was shaking his head before she had finished asking the question. "Groom has allergies. I'm not sure if horses fall under that umbrella, but I'd avoid it just to be safe."

"Good to know." Reaching across the table, she laid her hand over his, which was resting on the original seating chart. "Thank you, Liam." There was more to those words than courtesy. There were layers of gratitude and an acknowledgment that she knew this was hard for him. She wanted him to know, to realize she understood he was struggling.

He squeezed her hand in return before pulling away. Looking out over the quiet beach, his mind seemed even farther away than his gaze. "Ella, do you know who my sister is?"

No reason to play games or be coy. "I have an idea."

"Who do you think she is?"

"I'm guessing she's Paige Jennings."

He smiled. "Nope. Guess again."

Ella sat farther forward and rested her crossed arms on the table's edge. "I almost asked if you were sure," she said with a small smile. "I was pretty sure myself."

Liam's gaze came back to her. "No idea, then?"

"I suppose she could be any number of starlets in Hollywood."

He grinned. "Don't let her hear you say that."

"Now you're scaring me."

"My sister is Jenna Williams. Her fiancé—"

"Is Mike Feigenbaum." Ella swallowed hard. "Award-winning actress meets the rookie MVP for minor league baseball and starting pitcher for Utah's triple-A team, the Hellcats. An insanely fast, well-publicized romance follows, culminating in a proposal right before Mike opts out of his contract negotiations and very publicly becomes a free agent. He then moves to Hollywood to be with Jenna." Flopping back into her chair, she shook her head. Or maybe it was her whole body shaking. Yeah, that was more likely. "Jenna Williams is your sister?"

"My father married Jenna's mother when I was seven. They had Jenna when I was nine." One corner of his mouth curled up in a tender smile. "I couldn't stand her when she was born. But then, when she was about nine months old, she took her first steps…and they were toward me. She followed me everywhere after that. And when she began to talk? Good God, she chattered at me nonstop. It didn't matter if I understood a single word she said. Like everyone she meets, she won me over by simply being herself."

"Jenna Williams," Ella repeated through numb lips.

"You'll love her." It was half statement, half command.

"I'm sure I will—if she's even half as lovely in person as she has been in every interview I've ever seen. But why tell me now?"

She watched as something haunted passed through his eyes. "You need to know who she is."

Ella heard the two words he'd left unspoken. *To me. You need to know who she is to me.* She scooted her chair closer to the edge of the pavilion and wiggled her toes until they were buried in the sand. There were a hundred things she could say, at least two dozen she probably *should* say, and not a single one seemed absolutely right.

As if he read her mind, Liam said, "I expected something…more."

"More?"

"In your reaction to my sister's fame."

Ella shrugged. "I've dealt with celebrities before. And everything I know about her indicates she's a delightful woman. I don't know much about her fiancé, but I'll meet him soon enough."

At the mention of the groom, Liam's face clouded over.

"So it was an understatement when you said you're not his biggest fan." Ella leaned over and picked up her mimosa, sipping the drink slowly as she considered what to say next. She needn't have bothered, as Liam plowed through the opening she'd provided.

"There aren't civil words strong enough to accurately convey my feelings toward the groom," he snapped.

"Good thing you're not the one marrying him, then." The words hung between them before falling with an inaudible *splat*.

"No, I'm not." He stood, brushing invisible lint

off his shorts before tugging at his linen shirt. "But the most important person to me in the whole world is, and she deserves better."

"Is she happy?" Ella asked quietly, the knots that had unraveled beginning to bind themselves all over again just behind her belly button.

Liam slipped his sunglasses on and looked at her, eyes blocked by the dark lenses. "If he's not good enough for her, if all he's doing is riding her coattails to fame and fortune, does it matter?"

She opened her mouth to answer, but he waved her off, spun and, with a spine that appeared totally unbending, stalked away.

Despite the fact that he couldn't hear her answer, she offered it anyway. "I'd be willing to bet it matters the world to her."

Liam stomped into the bungalow, his insides a bloody riot of opposition. He wanted to throttle himself for thinking he could disrupt a wedding by giving poorly placed and outright gaudy suggestions.

He wanted to strangle Mike Feigenbaum when he got off the plane. Liam would send the body to some remote region to be dumped. He had the funds to pay people who knew people.

He stumbled to a halt. Sweet mother of God, what was he thinking? He'd never order a murder even under the worst of conditions.

Doesn't this qualify—breaking a deathbed vow?

He shook the thought off and then stilled as he realized what he really wanted to do: grab Ella

Montgomery and run. He wanted to stay in bed with her for a week, to talk and make love and order room service and, shockingly, talk some more. Everything about her calmed him. She was the counterbalance to his personal crazy, and he craved her nearness, hungered for her touch, longed for the scent of her perfume on his pillow. All that and more. So much more. Emotions he refused to look at head-on and was unwilling to name thundered around him in a war chant, demanding he take up the fight to win her, claim her and, above all, keep her.

But it would never happen. Liam wasn't programmed for happily-ever-afters. Hell, he was trying to stop that very thing from happening because if life had taught him anything, it was that fairy tales were best suited to paperbacks and afternoon matinees. They didn't hold a place in the real world because *they weren't real*.

He'd seen friends marry and divorce and become bitter shells of their former selves.

He'd seen heartbreak and hurt in abundance, but never had he seen that thing called love, *romantic* love, rise above any given situation and conquer all.

It simply didn't happen.

Loyalty was a far more desirable trait. Tangible. Reliable. Measurable.

Liam rolled shoulders gone tight with that bevy of emotions. What lay ahead of him was a combination of obligation and love of family. That kind of love could be compared to loyalty, and Liam was comfortable with that. It was, after all, the characteristic he valued most.

The latch on the door snicked open, and Liam turned, expecting housekeeping. What he found was a wedding planner, arms overflowing with fresh flowers and a flush of sun on her skin.

"Hey. I wanted to tell you I didn't mean for us to part like that earlier. I really—oomph!"

He crossed the room and pulled her into his arms, crushing delicate blooms between them so that the spicy fragrances swirled around them like nature's perfume. His mouth found hers and swallowed her gasp of surprise even as one hand grabbed her ass to pull her closer and the other hand relieved her of the floral bounty. One word repeated through his mind.

Mine.

There were whispers of other words, words he'd spent the last hour denying.

Liam didn't care.

The only thing that mattered was finding the solace he'd been so sure he could do without. Solace only this woman offered him. He needed it like a diver needed air.

Their tongues dueled in the most intimate dance—thrust, parry, retreat. She met him move for move, never backing down, never giving him permission to take the lead. No, not this woman. She was fierce. A woman who held her own, and he found her strength, her determination, her give-as-good-as-she-got absolutely sexy as hell.

Her hands went to his chest and yanked at his

shirt. Buttons flew, plinking across the hardwood floor. She shoved the destroyed garment off his shoulders, her hands roving over his upper body with a possessiveness he'd never cared for...until now. She nipped his bottom lip before breaking the kiss, her mouth tracing his jaw, down his neck, between his pecs—all with stinging nips followed by soothing kisses.

A wildcat. That's what she was.

And he loved it.

Reaching his pants, she made an inarticulate sound of frustration when the tie at his board shorts knotted. He tried to help, but she pushed his hands away. Warm feminine hands and nimble fingers slipped underneath the waistband of his shorts and the fabric slithered down his legs, setting his cock free.

Ella dropped to her knees and, before Liam could say a word, she took the length of him in her mouth. Deep, so deep. The head of his cock bumped the back of her throat and she hummed around him with pleasure as he shouted out the same. She swallowed his length even deeper, cupping the ridged underside of his cock with her tongue as she worked him slowly, so slowly. Then she eased off and started all over again.

Clever fingers slipped up his legs, higher and higher until she parked one on his thigh for support and the other—

Liam shouted again, louder this time.

Ella gently cupped his balls, rolling them deftly

between her fingers as she squeezed tenderly and pulled on his sac. Never did she cease laving him from root to tip, cheeks hollowing as she sucked him deep, tongue working magic he had never fathomed she possessed.

Winding his hands through her hair, he found himself mesmerized by the sight of her kneeling before him, surrounded by the flotsam of scattered flowers. She'd spread her knees, bracketing his feet. Her hair mounded around his hands. Her breasts were lush. Sun kissed. He knew what they tasted like, knew the way her nipples felt as they pearled on his tongue. Knew the way her breath hitched if he drew a bit stronger, if he let his lips pluck at the hypersensitive skin before letting go to breathe cool air across their tips.

He was torn between wanting to experience Ella's gifted mouth and wanting to lose himself in the pleasures of her body. Watching her for another moment made up his mind.

He reached down and lifted her chin.

She let his cock go with a soft sound of disapproval.

"Up," he ordered.

"Bossy bastard. I'm not done."

"While I appreciate your damn fine skills, we'll get there together or not at all." He let go of her hair to grasp her arms and pull her to her feet. Their mouths fused once more, her lips swollen, and he pulled her close, groaning when she shimmied out of her bikini bottoms without breaking the kiss.

Wrapping a long leg around his waist, she ground

her sex against his. His grip on her tightened as her desire slickened his shaft. Passion fogged his mind.

"Take me to bed, Liam."

"As my lady commands."

Without warning, he swept her up in his arms, grinning at her alarmed squeak. He delivered her to the bed, setting her down with tender care, and left a trail of kisses in his wake as he moved up her body. They fit together like two pieces of a puzzle, his cock nestled against the apex of her thighs, his forearms resting comfortably on either side of her shoulders.

She wrapped one leg around him and, with a swift push-pull, reversed their position so she straddled him.

Resting his hands on her hips, he stared up at her. "My body is yours, Ella."

A shadow crossed her face, so fleeting he half wondered if he'd imagined it, particularly when she took his hands and moved them to cup her breasts. But he knew what he'd seen. "What's wrong, love?"

She shook her head, her hair tumbling around her shoulders. "Not a thing."

Rising, she let him slip the condom on before she took over again, gripping his cock at the base and positioning him between her slick folds. With careful control, she slid down his length, her heavy-lidded gaze locked on his.

Liam took hold of her hips and thrust up, the move driven by sheer instinct.

She squeezed her thighs around his hips. Hard. "Uh-uh. I'm in control here. Patience."

He growled, the sound reverberating deep in his chest. Patience wasn't what he was after. He wanted fast, hard, blank-the-mind sex. He wanted to make love to her with mind-numbing results. Instead, she was the one working him over, demanding his body acquiesce to her demands, attentions, skills. Then she wrecked him.

"Let me take care of you."

She rose on her knees so high that the very tip of him nearly slipped free, then she sank back down. Every inch she took was pleasure paired with pain. The tight grip of her sheath stole his control and he bucked.

Again, she squeezed her thighs around his hips.

The urge to protest tripped over his tongue, but she placed a finger on his lips at the same moment he started to speak. "Hush, Liam. Let me."

So he did. Relaxing the hold he had on her hips, he lay back and gave her something he'd given no woman before: absolute control.

Ella rode him, slow and sure, until a fine sheen of sweat broke out over her skin. It shone in the afternoon sun, casting an ethereal look over every inch of her body. Running her hands up her torso as she rose and fell, she cupped her breasts and then tweaked her nipples.

Liam shuddered beneath her, twisting his hips in an effort to be still as she took him all the way inside her.

"Do that again," she said, voice husky with passion.

He hadn't meant to move that way, but if she

wanted more of that? Yeah, he could give her what she wanted.

Hands on her hips, he let her set the pace, occasionally twisting his hips as directed. Every time he did, her core tightened around him to the point her sex gripped his cock like a damn vise. The urge to give her what she wanted warred with his need to drive into her, to force the orgasm she was dragging out for both of them, to make her scream his name to the heavens.

She must have been on the same page because, without warning, she leaned forward, parked her hands on his shoulders and began to ride him in earnest. Sounds of hard, fast sex—skin on skin, harsh breaths, little moans—saturated the air, filled his head and dominated his awareness. There was only this moment, only this woman, only one possible outcome.

Liam's balls drew up tight. Release roared toward him, and he was a slave to its timing. But he could—*would*—bring her with him. Reaching between them, he found her clitoris and stroked in time with the pace Ella set. She faltered before increasing her speed, pumping harder, digging her fingers into his shoulders until her nails scored his skin. Her eyes widened a fraction, and Liam struck.

Knees bent, he pitched her forward at the same time he pinched that bundle of nerves between two fingers and strummed it with his thumb. He rolled his hips and drove into her, meeting her thrust for thrust.

Ella's head fell back and she called out his name.

Liam increased the tempo even more, thrilling as she lost control and called out his name.

Hair loose and wild, she let go of his shoulders and reached back, gripping Liam's knees as she ground her sex against him, taking him as deep as she could. Her cry was magnificent, seeming to originate from the very heart of her before flinging itself free without a care as to who heard her or what they might think.

Liam's own release ripped through him, boiling out of the tip of his cock as if she'd summoned it.

Nothing had been this good. This right. This whole. Not ever.

Ella was brilliant, wild, so fucking alive he couldn't look away. She was everything.

And he was lost.

CHAPTER TEN

STORM CLOUDS DOMINATED the horizon, obscuring the setting sun as Ella stepped out of the shower. Body lax, muscles loose, she toweled off and wrapped up her hair atop her head. There were a dozen different things she needed to focus on, but her first priority was sorting herself out.

She and Liam had been right on the cusp of falling into each other earlier when Liam had said four words—just four words—that had shredded Ella's heart. *My body is yours.* His body. And only his body. She'd realized then that she wanted more. Not that she had any right to any of him, particularly after they'd agreed this was a fun-while-it-lasted affair. No strings. No regrets. Hell, she'd even given herself a stern talking-to a couple days ago about keeping things light and enjoyable until they left the island.

But somewhere in there, she'd begun to feel… something. What that something was, she couldn't be sure. Not yet. And with the way Liam viewed relationships, not ever. That meant Ella needed to stick to her initial ground rules or remove herself from the equation altogether.

Touching her fingertips to the tops of her breasts, she watched the peaks swell and rise, and she wondered if she could actually give him up. He loved her body like no one ever had. He made her tremble with a single word, yearn for his touch, forget how to breathe, come apart on command. She was the instrument to his virtuoso. Her sex throbbed, a sweet ache of memory.

His form filled the doorway, mouth fluttering at the corners in a half smile. "And I was under the impression I'd done a thorough job so you wouldn't need to supplement my efforts."

She dropped her hands and shrugged, looking away as she unwound the towel from her head. "Condition check. Nothing more."

"Everything okay?"

She smiled at him in the mirror. "You'll be pleased to know you left everything in working order." Grabbing her brush, she began working the tangles from her wet mass of hair. Sometimes she loved having naturally wavy hair; others, not so much. Like now. She pulled a little too hard and winced.

"Here," he said, closing in behind her and taking the brush. "Sit. Let me."

She sat on the vanity stool, body vibrating, heart numb. How could she possibly keep her emotional distance if he was going to do things like brush her hair? That certainly wasn't some random act of kindness. It was blatant intimacy, the one thing he had kept out of their interactions.

Except the dance on the beach.

Except for ordering breakfast served on the porch.

Except carrying you to the bedroom.

Her heart ached like a bad tooth, and she fought the need to rub her chest and soothe the discomfort that bordered on pain. It wasn't like this could be serious anyway. People didn't fall for each other this fast. Not if it was real. Infatuation? Sure. She had that in spades. And, if she were honest, she'd had *that* particular affliction since he'd landed on her lap on the plane.

If her feelings for him were serious, she'd be… what? What would she be feeling that would be any different than what she felt now?

Ella's breath caught.

She was so not falling for Liam Baggett, brother of Hollywood's darling, famous in the world of finance, infamous among socialites as the unattainable, unchainable bachelor. Yeah, she'd looked him up this afternoon. Article after article labeled him a jet-setting playboy, a millionaire so many times over even *Time*'s Top 100 had lost count, a shark in the boardroom and a lover of women worldwide.

I'm one of those women.

It shocked her that it stung to be one of ten, twenty, fifty, one hundred women he'd called "lover." She'd had affairs before, but she'd never become so emotionally involved that she struggled with the inevitable end.

Liam paused behind her. "What's with the long face?"

She forced herself to smile. "My face is oval, thank you. Not long."

"Talk to me, Ella." The quiet command hung there, his eyes on hers in the mirror.

"If you don't get the tangles out before it dries, my hair turns into a giant nest that will haunt me until I shower again."

He began brushing. "Don't hide from me."

"I'm sitting right here. Naked, in fact." She smiled brighter but couldn't maintain eye contact, instead leaning forward to reach her moisturizer. Removing the lid, she scooped out a dollop and slapped it on her face, rubbing in the expensive cream with brisk, sweeping strokes.

"Ella," he said in that warning tone of his.

As if she were a child to be admonished.

She huffed out a sharp sigh. "Leave it alone, Liam. I'm fine."

He paused. "There's this look on your face—"

"That's probably because I keep thinking about the metric shit ton I have yet to accomplish before this wedding." He opened his mouth to say something else, likely to press if she knew him at all. Reaching back, she held his wrist. "Let it go, Liam. I'm stressed. That's all."

"Don't regret the time we've spent together." A command couched as a request.

"I don't," she said, fighting for a normal tone and nearly succeeding. She tried not to focus on the words he hadn't spoken—that their time was limited, that they had best make the most of what was left—over what he'd said.

"Neither do I." He stared at her for what felt like an eon before handing her the brush. "I need to answer a few emails from the London office. Shouldn't take more than an hour. Join me for dinner when I've finished?"

She considered, thinking how nice it would be to have a quiet dinner with him, to get to know him better, to discover who he was beneath the polish and responsibilities. And she realized she'd only be setting herself up to fall harder.

"I shouldn't," she said around the bitter regret lodged in her throat. "I have so much to do before Jenna and Mike get here."

"You…we…have another full day. Dinner, Ella." He rested his hands along her jaw, gently turned her face toward the mirror and waited until she had no choice but to look at him. "Please."

She might not know Liam well, but she knew enough to be sure he didn't use that word often.

"Say yes." Again with that half smile.

She debated with herself, going back and forth as she rapidly created a mental list of pros and cons. But then Liam leaned in and sealed his mouth over hers in a persuasive kiss.

He broke the kiss but his lips still caressed hers when he spoke. "Dinner, Ella. One meal where we're just a couple of people on holiday. No talk of the wedding or my work or anything remotely related."

She looked into eyes fringed with dark lashes—

eyes she'd seen amused, angry, aroused—and she answered the way she'd known she would from the beginning.

"Okay."

A quick buss of the lips and he was walking out of the bathroom, calling over his shoulder, "I'll meet you back here in an hour."

"Make it two," she called after him.

If she was going to do this—go on a date with this man—she was going to make sure he remembered everything about her. From what she wore to what she didn't, she would etch herself into his memory.

It was only fair seeing as he'd already done the same to her.

Liam had sent word via a runner asking Ella to meet him at the head of the beach path nearest the main pavilion. The runner had returned with the message she'd be there. But she was late. Fifteen minutes, to be exact. Every second felt like ten. Every soft footfall against the boardwalk had him searching the evening shadows for her. And then she was there, rounding the bend with the resort lights behind her creating a nimbus around her lithe form.

She wore a short, sleeveless dress in a green silk that was so dark it appeared black in the shadows. Around her throat was a black choker with a single diamond-encrusted emerald in the center. Matching earrings hung from her ears. The sides of her hair had been pulled up to a loose knot at the crown of her head, leaving waves hanging down her back. The style emphasized her natural beauty. Whatever makeup she wore was understated and enhanced her elegant features. Her tan legs were bare. Dark stilettos with heels so high she moved in a hip-swinging strut made him want to forgo dinner and have her for dessert. His cock was ready to place that order.

She stopped a couple feet short of him. The air carried the hint of her perfume, a scent he would always associate with her—earthy with a floral undertone, so bold yet feminine.

He wanted to tell her she looked amazing, but the words were lost, carried away by the flood of testosterone raging through his veins. Every thought in his head involved her, him and a Do Not Disturb sign on a door that would remain locked for the next three days.

She arched a brow. "Either I'm overdressed or I look like hell and you're trying to find a nice way to say it."

"I've been trying… That is, there aren't words…" Liam cleared his throat. Twice. When he finally spoke, the words were gruff, one hand reaching for her. "Come here."

She laughed then and stepped forward, allowing him to pull her into a warm embrace.

On the patio nearby, a quartet struck up soft dinner music. Liam spun Ella away from him and brought her back, turning her in slow circles, watching her carefully.

She looked up at him, then tilted her chin even farther and stared at the night sky. "What?"

"I'm trying to figure out what's different about you tonight."

"Nothing."

"Not true. There's an air about you, something less…intense, maybe? Different, definitely."

"My give-a-damn broke."

"Pardon?"

She laughed, softer this time.

He couldn't help but think that, if he had to name the color of her eyes tonight, it would be Somber Green in Starlight.

When did I become such a bloody maudlin poet? Next thing, I'll need a cigarette and bottle of cheap wine as I tap out bad rhymes on a run-down laptop.

"So what broke your give-a-damn? I didn't even know that was a real thing," he teased.

"Oh, it absolutely is. And you, Mr. Baggett, will be receiving a bill for breaking it. Shattering it, really."

His brows shot up. "Me?"

"You."

"How?"

"You invited me to dinner without work as a buffer."

"I fail to follow your logic."

She stopped following his lead, forcing him to cease the intimate dance he'd begun. Moving out of his arms, she took a few steps down the cultivated path, stopping where the sand began. Ella, one hand on a palm tree, balanced on one foot and then the other as she removed her shoes. Then she headed toward the beach.

"Ella, stop."

A short glance back and she did as he bade.

It took him a second to catch up to her. Toeing his dress shoes off, he retrieved them in one hand and took hers with the other. "I had dinner set up on…" He paused, surprised to find he didn't want to ruin the romance of the moment he'd spent the last hour creating. "Would you do me the honor of allowing me to escort you to our table?" She started to put her shoes back on, but he stopped her. "You won't need those."

One of the event staff approached with a small basket extended. "For your shoes. They'll be returned to your bungalow, Ms. Montgomery, Mr. Baggett."

Curiosity made her tuck her chin in, but she handed her shoes over without comment.

Liam did the same and then reclaimed her hand. "This way."

He led her down the beach and around a bend to a private cove. There, a teak daybed had been set up complete with a champagne bucket staked in the sand, bottle open and chilling. Flowers were scattered across the daybed, and a plate of hors d'oeuvres sat near the foot. A blanket lay artfully over a top corner. At least four dozen large pillar candles were scattered about, their flames whipping in the slight breeze. The flickering candlelight made the night feel more alive and yet more secluded, like they were miles from civilization. On a portable table, four silver domes—two large, two small—covered the meals the chef had prepared.

Ella paused, seeming to take it all in. She didn't say anything, but her hold on Liam's hand tightened.

He would have given anything to know exactly what that squeeze was meant to convey. Irritation? Surprise? Joy? Anxiety? Too many options ran through his head. She'd reduced him to this person he'd never been, someone who sought the approval of another, someone who wanted nothing more than to make his lover understand what she meant to him.

He'd been unable to articulate that and so much more, so he'd tried to show her.

He squeezed her hand back after several more seconds.

Still, she was silent.

And he broke. "For the love of God, woman, would you say something?"

Her eyes sparkled as a wicked grin spread across her face. "Something."

The single whispered word took a moment to register. When it did, Liam let go of her hand and doubled over with laughter. He couldn't catch his breath. No one was that ballsy with him, pushing him when he was so clearly on edge. He loved that about her, that she refused to let him intimidate her. She was perfect the way she was.

The sobering thought stole the last peal of laughter, cutting it short.

...*loved that about her*, he'd thought. *Perfect the way she was.*

Too much was happening at once.

"Liam, I can't believe you did this."

"Neither can I," he said. Liam had discovered the one woman who possessed the ability to convince him love might exist after all.

And after the last-minute wedding changes he'd made late this afternoon, love might not be enough to save them.

CHAPTER ELEVEN

ELLA HADN'T REALIZED that Liam could be quite so charming. While they ate, he was as entertaining as he was attentive, asking about her childhood and telling her stories of his boarding school days and, later, tales that involved a younger American half sister who wanted nothing more than to be one of the boys—right down to her poorly imitated British accent.

"My mates would chuckle at her behind her back, but Jenna knew. She'd get so cross she would stomp her feet and threaten to divest them of their bollocks long before she knew what bollocks were."

He'd been so descriptive that Ella could imagine the pigtailed girl's tantrums. "Where did she get the idea bollocks were important?"

"I'm quite sure, us being strapping young lads with quite exaggerated prowess where young ladies were concerned, that she heard us bragging."

"As boys…and men…are wont to do," she added.

He tipped his wineglass toward her in unspoken agreement. "She's a smart girl—always has been.

She'd have figured out that, whatever bollocks were, we valued ours greatly, so why not threaten to take what we clearly held in highest esteem?" He laughed then, eyes warm with love for the girl his sister had been. "And what of you, Ms. Montgomery? Any siblings?"

"I was an only child."

"Ever wish for siblings?"

"All the time." She sipped her wine, opening her mouth to accept a piece of fruit Liam offered. Exotic flavor burst across her tongue, something similar to cantaloupe but with a slightly softer aftertaste.

Head canted to the side, he considered her. "Would you have had a brother or a sister?"

"One of each, if I'd been able to choose, and I'd have been the baby."

"And if you could only have one?"

"A sister, hands down."

Liam clutched his heart with his free hand and furrowed his brow. "A shot to the heart of all mankind. A brother would have looked out for you. What would a sister have done but steal your dolls and borrow your clothes?"

"Since it's my perfect world, my sister would have been my best friend. Older than me, she would have had all kinds of worldly advice about men, clothes and—" she cringed "—makeup that would have spared me the humiliation of my seventh-grade yearbook photo."

"That bad?"

"Baby blue eye shadow and white lipstick immortalized together, forever." She raised her glass in a mock toast. "Top that."

"I share this with no one, so repeat it and I'll disavow any knowledge of this conversation before I hunt you down and—"

"Not a word." With two fingers, she made a zipping motion across her lips.

"I had my hair permed so I could style it like Donnie Wahlberg from New Kids on the Block."

Her laughter bubbled up and escaped, peal after peal. Nothing tempered her reaction as she considered this man first in perm rods, then with perm solution dripping around his hairline and, finally, using a plastic hair pick to gently tease out the curls of his new hairdo. "A...perm..."

"Oh, it gets worse."

"Worse?"

He grimaced. "The band was an American sensation, not so well known in the UK, and my stepmother's stylist didn't know who he was. First time around, I ended up looking quite like Weird Al. I believe it's called a bouffant?"

That did it. Ella handed him her wineglass before rolling onto her side and, clutching her aching stomach, laughing until she cried.

Liam set the glasses down on the side table, retrieved a cloth napkin and handed it over. "You mock me?"

"I don't need to," she gasped. "I'm sure your friends did quite well on their own."

He grinned and chuckled. "They took the mick out of me, that's for sure."

"Why in the world did you use your mother's hairdresser?"

"I could hardly go to a salon, now could I? All of thirteen and wanting to be cool. What if a girl from the area had seen me or, God forbid, been in having her hair done as well? Mum's hairdresser came to the house, so I had the privilege of being attended privately."

"And after? When she'd finished with your hair?"

"I may have been single-handedly responsible for the introduction of the ball cap into British society."

Ella flopped onto her back and dropped one arm over her face. She'd laughed so hard her belly hurt, grinned so wide her cheeks ached. "I can't imagine you like that. You're so polished now. So *GQ* in all the right ways."

"I'll take that as a compliment and respond simply by saying a good stylist goes a long way in making the man fit the mold."

Dropping her arm, she rolled her head to the side. "What mold?"

This time he didn't look at her when he answered. "The one my father expected I shoehorn myself into."

She rolled onto her side again, curling her knees so her feet tucked up behind her, her head resting on one arm. "He had expectations, I guess. Given that you came from society."

"Not just society, but high society. My lineage has been charted since the 1400s. My family tree has been propagated by arranged marriages and pruned by a pragmatic hand when things weren't just so. I was the only son, so my father was determined from my first breath that I'd carry on the Baggett legacy, and he raised me, groomed me, with that singular goal in mind."

"And if you didn't want to be a financial investment guru?" She waggled her hand at his quizzical look. "Or whatever it is you do."

The bed shifted slightly as Liam rolled onto his back and stared at the star-saturated night sky. "I was never given the option, Ella. Had I gone to him and said I wanted to be a teacher, he would have simply told me, 'Baggetts do not engage in common occupations.'"

"Teaching is far from common," she said a bit tartly. "My mom's a teacher."

"I'm not demeaning the occupation by any means." The short laugh that followed was decidedly bitter. "I had him to do that."

"So what did, or does, being a Baggett mean?"

"I was raised to understand that it meant loyalty at all costs. Behaving honorably, but 'honor' was measured by the outcome of one's choices, not by any bourgeois definition. Carrying on tradition no matter the cost. Carving out the most direct path to your success no matter whom you had to cross, run over or destroy to get to that end goal." He sighed.

"It meant doing your duty even at the cost of extinguishing your desire."

To hear him speak so calmly of a household with such dogmatic, patriarchal values simply crushed her. She wanted to comfort the child he'd been before the worst of the rules were instilled in—or inflicted on—him. He never had a chance to just be a boy, to get his Sunday clothes dirty, put frogs in his pockets or build forts out of cardboard boxes. Ella might not have had siblings, but she'd had friends. She had been encouraged to run and play and discover and dream, to figure out who she was and where she fit in the world. Happiness had been her parents' end goal for her. Nothing else had mattered. Certainly not to the extent that they would've robbed her of free will, enforced antiquated expectations on her contemporary lifestyle or forced her to follow in the footsteps of ancestors who were long since dead.

But nothing she said would change his past, and she had the distinct feeling that showing pity would force him, by conditioning, to defend his heritage. More specifically, his father.

Instead, she asked the only question she could think of. "Are you happy?"

He looked at her, really looked at her, and a slow smile carved its way across a face that had been bordering on solemn. "Right now? Very."

Her heart tumbled, and not because she rolled onto him and straddled his lap.

Not because his hands slipped up her bare thighs,

his thumbs discovering that she, too, could pull off the commando routine with aplomb.

Not because he said, "Gladly," when she whispered, "Take me to bed, Liam."

No, her heart tumbled because he'd given her more than a glimpse of who he was, where he came from and what had shaped him into the man he had become. Her heart longed for him in a way that was personal.

Intimate.

Profound.

And what she wanted from him was more than a love affair. She craved the thing she'd never wanted from another man. Not an affair of bodies but of hearts. The free-fall sensation she'd heard about, read about and listened to in songs her whole life. She wanted to feel her stomach wobble, her heart quake and her sense of reason dissolve. She wanted to fall in love.

As she took her own measure, checking off symptom after symptom, feeling after feeling, she realized she was already out of control—well and truly falling.

She could only hope Liam would catch her.

Linen sheets slid over Liam's body as he stretched, slowly coming awake. A glance at the clock surprised him with the late hour. Breakfast would be over. He'd have to make arrangements to have lunch brought in for Ella.

Ella.

He glanced over at the woman sprawled out beside him, the sun pulling rich highlights from her hair where it fanned out over her pillow. Last night seemed like a dream now, and if it weren't for the fact she was here he might wonder if he'd imagined the whole thing.

Conversation had flowed so easily. Hell, he'd even talked about his childhood—something he didn't do with anyone, even Jenna.

After hearing about how Ella had been raised—in a loving, happy home—Liam couldn't help but think she'd make an excellent mother. The kind who made a house into a home. Someone who'd bake cookies and have pillow fights but wasn't a pushover. A woman who would be able to act as parent and friend to her children.

He respected her even more than he had before, and that respect drove him out of bed, albeit silently, and had him pulling on his shorts before, shirt and shoes in hand, he tiptoed to the front door.

The pile of paperwork she'd left next to her computer caught his eye. Given what he was about to do, he thought it wise to lift the list he'd given her. Maybe he could amend a couple of items before giving it back to her. Nothing major, just…

Without trying to rationalize his actions, he slipped the stapled list free and stepped out the front door, closing it as quietly as possible. He shoved the papers in his back pocket and then finished dressing on the porch before heading toward the resort's main building. The one benefit to having slept in was that Arvin and his staff should be at work. Arvin would be Liam's best—only—chance of undoing what he'd done yesterday. And the lead guilt weighing on his shoulders meant he had to try.

Scanning the massive lobby, he didn't see Arvin anywhere. The event planner's area, right beside the concierge, was vacant. So he opted for the concierge instead.

"Good morning." The chipper young woman behind the desk smiled at him. "How has your stay been so far?"

"Excellent, thank you," Liam answered absently, scrubbing his hands through his hair. "Do you know where I might find Arvin?"

The woman affected a concerned look. "I'm sorry. Arvin is off island this morning retrieving some materials for a private event. He should be back by midafternoon, late afternoon at worst. May I leave a message for him?"

"Right. The event he's out for is actually mine."

"Congratulations," she said, beaming up at him.

"It's not…" He shook his head. "Never mind. Does he have any other staff on hand, anyone who might help me resolve an issue with a change I made to the event?"

"His staff is out this morning, running errands related to your event. However, I'll certainly have someone call you as soon as they're back."

"I really do need to—"

"Liam!"

He whipped around in time to catch the petite blonde who threw herself at him. His mouth opened and closed several times before he set the woman back. "What are you doing here?"

"Um… I'm the bride?" Jenna answered, laughter making her eyes sparkle.

"You're earlier than I expected."

"Liam."

The deep voice drew his attention to the man standing several paces away, arms crossed over his chest.

"Mike," he returned.

"Nice place," the groom said, looking around.

"It's perfect!" Jenna chirped. "I love it. It's exactly what I wanted. And everyone is so friendly." She stepped out of Liam's embrace only to slide an arm around his waist and snuggle into his side.

He instinctively settled an arm around her shoulders as he looked down. "I'm confused, Jenna. Your flight left New York yesterday with a long layover in Paris. I wasn't expecting you until tomorrow."

"Nope. We got to Paris so early that we were able to get seats on an earlier flight."

"The guy at the airline desk was a huge fan," Mike said, smiling down at his bride-to-be.

Liam tried to think, tried to put things in order, but his mind had blitzed out. Jenna was early, and Ella was going to flip out.

Ella.

Again, her name whispered through his mind like an invocation, his heart beating faster and breath coming a bit short.

"Liam?" Jenna asked as she wiggled in his embrace. "I mean, I know you're glad to see me and all, but you're going to bruise me if you clutch me any tighter."

"Apologies." He forced himself to relax and take a deep breath. Ella was going to flip her shit when she found out Jenna and Mike had arrived a day early.

"Mr. Baggett?"

The young lady from the concierge's desk held out a cordless phone. "I have Arvin on the line for you, sir."

"Thank you—" he glanced at her name tag "—Becky." Taking the phone, he stepped away from Jenna and Mike. "Arvin."

"What may I do for you, Mr. Baggett?"

Liam lowered his voice. "Arvin, my sister and her groom have arrived a day early. I need to know where you're at on the task I gave you yesterday."

Arvin swallowed so loud Liam heard it. "It's done, sir. It wasn't easy, but I do think you'll be pleased with the…results."

Stomach clenching hard, Liam lowered his voice further still. "I'm not certain it will be in the bride's best interest to have it done as I requested."

"I—I'm sorry, sir? Are you asking me to undo it?"

"Yes. That's exactly what I'm asking."

"It's temporary color, sir, but it won't wear off for several days."

Damn it.

"I'll figure something out, Arvin. Thank you."

"Yes, sir. I'll be back this afternoon and—"

"I'll see you then." Liam hastily disconnected as Jenna bounced over to him.

She poked him in the ribs. "I hope you weren't working."

"Uh, no. It was nothing." Handing the phone back to Becky, he smiled. "Thank you. It's all in order."

He turned back to Jenna. "So what would you like to do since you're here early?"

"I want to walk through everything for the wedding, see what it's going to look like." She grinned back at her fiancé beatifically. "It's going to be incredible, getting married in paradise. Perfect way to start our lives together."

"If it makes you happy." Mike moved closer and held his arms open.

Jenna slipped out from under Liam's arm and into Mike's embrace. She whispered something in his ear, and the man leaned down and kissed the top of her head. "You're footing the bill, so I'll shut up. Most important thing is that we end up husband and wife."

Liam bit back the caustic words that burned his throat. Mike had just confirmed what Liam most feared—that the minor league baseball player was, indeed, riding along on his sister's dime. And now the guy was officially a free agent, which was sportsspeak for "unemployed."

Jenna deserved better than a tag-along kind of guy. She deserved someone who was her equal. Sure, Mike might be considered a handsome man, but there were issues beyond looks. Serious issues. Things like the guy's temper and his tendency to take his frustrations—*any* frustrations—out on Jenna. Add his just-confirmed financial leeching and it came together to equal one fundamental truth: the man wasn't remotely fit to be Jenna's husband.

If Liam were to compare Mike to, say, Ella, she would take the win in every category. She was far more loyal, driven and accomplished than the baseball player ever would be.

As if she'd heard his innermost thoughts, Jenna glanced up at Mike and said in a rebellious stage whisper, "I'm telling him."

Her groom rolled his shoulders, looking back and forth between his soon-to-be wife and future brother-in-law. "It hasn't hit the news, sweetheart."

"So? It's happening, Mike." She twisted inside his embrace and faced Liam. "Mike's been called up."

Liam's brows rose. "To what?"

"You're so British," she said, laughing. "The major leagues, Liam. He's been called up as their relief pitcher. He'll be going to spring training with the team."

"I assume that comes with a paycheck." He stared at the other man, who simply stared back.

"A good one."

"And what, exactly, is 'good' in your ledger? Does 'good' provide for my sister under any and every circumstance?"

"Liam!"

Mike moved in front of Jenna, all but physically shoving her aside. "What the hell is your problem, Baggett?"

"Problem?" Liam laughed out loud. "It begins, and ends, with you."

"Stop it." Jenna's hissed command was ignored until she wedged herself between the two men. "Just stop it. This is my wedding."

"Our wedding," Mike corrected, his sharp tone cutting through the air.

She shot him a look. "Our wedding." Rounding on Liam, she drove a finger into his chest. "You need to stop provoking Mike. Now. And I don't want either of you ruining the wedding with this bullshit posturing and chest thumping. Do you hear me?"

"I wouldn't dream of it," Mike said softly before kissing the top of her head.

Liam said nothing.

Jenna glared at him.

Silence.

Mike broke into what was fast becoming a battle of wills. "The concierge was able to get us into rooms early. Some family ended up having to go home early, so we're taking their rooms until the ceremony, when we'll be moved to the honeymoon suite."

Liam almost choked.

Mike continued, unaware. "Let's go check out our rooms, unpack and get settled in. Then you can call Liam, maybe have him introduce us to the event coordinator you hired. She can show us around."

"Sounds good." Jenna's words were tight. She grabbed the handle of her carry-on bag and walked away. She stopped after several feet, seemed to think something over, then turned back to Liam. "Don't be a dick, brother mine." Then she gave him her back and stalked across the expanse of tile floor to the elevator bank, where she jabbed the Up button several times.

"Wouldn't dream of it," Liam muttered.

"Good," Mike said. "Do *not* ruin this for her…or you'll answer to me."

The warning couldn't have been any clearer.

Liam wanted to respond with his own warning, to tell this clown that he knew why the guy was marrying Jenna, but all Liam could do was stare and say nothing at all.

They wanted to see what was in store for their wedding. But what they were going to encounter over the next twenty-four hours would show Jenna exactly what type of man Mike was. Because watching Mike physically move Jenna aside, speak over her, tell her how they'd handle check-in followed by the suggestion that Ella could show them around, thus bypassing Liam?

No. To all of it, no.

Liam could only hope for two things. First? He hoped Jenna would understand what he'd done to make her see the truth about Mike's character…or lack of.

And second, he had to hope Ella would forgive him and accept his efforts to make amends when the wedding went straight to hell in handbaskets she'd decorated.

CHAPTER TWELVE

ELLA WAS UP to her elbows in fresh flowers. She loved floral arranging and had taken on some of those duties as a sort of indulgence. Designing was cathartic, forcing her to focus on the flowers and their shape and size and smell, the orientation of each bloom and the way they were placed for maximum impact.

Working beside her was a master baker who was applying fondant to the cake for tomorrow night's rehearsal dinner. Both this cake and the wedding cake would be adorned with floral toppers made by Ella herself.

She'd just placed a water pick on a bird of paradise stem when her cell buzzed. Gently setting the flower down, she dug her phone out of her back pocket. The display showed a number she didn't recognize. "Ella Montgomery."

"Don't panic."

"Any time you tell someone not to panic, Liam, it's the first thing they do. Hold on a second. I need to step outside." She waved at the baker and mouthed, "Be right back." Maneuvering around the work space, she made it to the side door and stepped into the sunshine. The air felt warm, especially after working in what was essentially a cooler. A bloom of sweat decorated her hairline, and she rubbed it off with the back of her forearm. "Go ahead. Tell me what I'm not supposed to panic over."

When Liam spoke, the urge to scream welled up in her throat, choking off her air and, with it, any ability to respond.

"Did you hear me, Ella? Jenna and Mike are here."

She nodded as she tried to force her lungs to work, her mouth to open, her lips to form words. "When you say 'here,' what exactly do you mean?"

"I'm not sure there's another way to interpret 'here.' They've checked in to their rooms, are currently getting settled in and would like to do a walkthrough of the event this afternoon," Liam bit out.

"You know, if I'm not allowed to panic, you don't get to be an ass," she retorted.

"I'm not being... Never mind. The point is, they want you to take them through the rehearsal plans and ceremony setup. They're calling me after they've unpacked their bags and want me to perform introductions."

"I'm not ready! I was supposed to have another day! There are some key things I need to finish before I can do a proper walk-through with them!" She fought the suffocating panic that ballooned in her chest.

"What would you have me do, Ella?"

There was no good answer. "Buy me some time and I'll find a stopping place here. Can you do that— entertain them, walk the resort, something? Just let me finish this bouquet and I'll meet you in the lobby in—" she looked at her watch "—an hour. What have they asked to see today?"

"They want to see what you've put together. All of it. Jenna's excited."

The tone of his voice told her he was anything but.

Yanking at the tie that held her hair up in a loose topknot, Ella dropped her phone. A wide crack split the screen corner to corner. "Shit," she snapped. Retrieving her phone, she looked it over. Hopefully, it would keep working until she could get home and replace it.

"What's wrong?"

Hysterical laughter rose up the back of her throat and emerged as a croak. "Everything is wrong, Liam. If you're asking what just happened? I broke my phone. It's one more expense I don't need, one more thing I'll have to pay for because I can't do without it. And you're calling, asking me to do the walk-through when only half of what needs to be done is actually *done*."

"Ella, I can't do this for you."

"I'm not asking you to. I'm asking you to stall them, Liam. Make small talk over drinks until I can pull together a walk-through that won't leave them regretting the choice to hire me."

Swallowing past the almost debilitating fear, she closed her eyes and focused on her breathing.

"Ella?"

"Just…give me a second."

She ran through the list of things that had been fully prepped, things she could share with the bride and groom. There were excursions to walk through, the menu, entertainment, the ceremony site. She could call Arvin and get him to set up a taste test of the wedding dinner. All that would take up the rest of the day. There would be plenty of time to finish the flowers tonight. Then tomorrow she could actively manage the guest excursions and the rehearsal, see the couple and their guests through the rehearsal dinner, and, finally, put the finishing touches on the wedding ceremony and the reception. The end was in sight. She just had to push through and get there in one piece.

The initial shock having passed, she took a deep breath and relayed her plan to Liam.

"That's fine. Jen and Mike will meet you in the lobby. What time?"

"I said an hour. I'll stick to that. After I've finished here, I'll grab my portfolio so I'll be able to show them the sketches. That'll help them visualize what the actual ceremony will look like. Otherwise? They'll be wholly dependent on my descriptions to fill in the blanks."

"I'll be there."

"You're coming, too?"

"I want to support my sister no matter the outcome."

"'No matter the outcome?'" she parroted. "What does that mean?"

"Poor choice of words. I'll see you shortly."

An odd feeling settled low in her gut. "Don't screw this up, Liam."

"Pardon?"

"Just...forget it. I'll see you in a little while."

A single tap on her cracked screen and the call disconnected. She finished the bouquet and headed back to the bungalow, thankful that her phone at least worked. She'd struggled with this event so much she'd begun to think the universe hated her, but maybe—just maybe—she was wrong. Maybe the universe didn't hate every cell in her being.

Just most of them.

Liam stood on the balcony just off the lobby. Jenna and Mike were several steps away, their heads together as they whispered, laughed and sneaked kisses. They were trying to stay away from the main foot traffic at the resort, but they'd insisted they wanted to get a feel for the ambience and see some of the decor.

Mike said something to Jenna and she laughed, a low, throaty sound that moviegoers worldwide would recognize. Liam looked over to find them slow dancing on the balcony.

"Get a room."

"We got two," Mike said, sotto voce.

"I'm sure Jenna did."

Mike stilled.

Jenna turned and looked from one man to the other. "What? What did I miss?"

Tension built until it crackled on the air like a summer storm. Mike didn't look away from Liam when he answered. "Your brother's suggesting I'm a gold digger."

Jenna's eyes flashed with anger. "Liam? What is wrong with you?"

"Just protecting your assets, sister."

"My assets are mine, Liam. I'll do as I please with them. That means if I want to invest in an alpaca farm in Nepal, you'll smile and wish me good returns. Likewise, if I want to pay for my own wedding, you don't have a say in that choice."

Liam clenched his jaw tight, but it wasn't enough to stop his damning judgment from spilling out. "No? Fine. But your choice doesn't change my opinion. I'd rather you had someone willing to carry his own weight in the relationship."

Mike took a step forward. "And how do you know I don't?"

Liam's laugh was so bitter it left an aftertaste. "How do I know? You certainly didn't buy that designer three-carat bauble on her finger on a farm league salary. You moved in to her place instead of her moving in to yours. You're driving her cars everywhere you two go. You were unemployed and now claim to be moving up to the big leagues, but it hasn't hit the trade papers. Need more examples?"

"You have no idea what I make or what I'm worth."

Liam arched a brow, his sole intent to piss the other man off. "It so happens that I do. Your farm salary was reported in the trade papers. The right word in the right ear and I found out what your endorsements paid. Added together? Your value isn't even half of what Jenna makes for a single film. I can't imagine it has improved since you quit."

"You son of a bitch," Mike spat, starting for him.

Ella cleared the large French doors just then, taking in the situation. In one fluid move, she stepped between Liam and Mike, extending her hand to the groom. "Hello. You must be Mike Feigenbaum, the lucky groom. I'm Ella Montgomery, your event coordinator."

Mike drew up, social custom and common courtesy partnering to halt what would likely have been a bloody good fight. Liam watched as the other man shook Ella's hand and forced a tight smile. "Nice to meet you, Ms. Montgomery."

"Please call me Ella." Then she turned to Jenna. "And you, Ms. Williams, are even more beautiful in person than on screen, which I wouldn't have believed possible. It's lovely to finally meet you. Your brother has spoken so highly of you."

"It's lovely to meet you as well, Ms. Montgomery... Ella." Jenna smiled the smile she used for publicity shots, paparazzi and interviews. "And while it's good to know Liam has spoken so highly of me, I'd be more interested in hearing what he's had to say about my groom."

Liam didn't miss Jenna's word choice—*my groom*.

Ella didn't miss a beat. "He's been nothing but complimentary of the choices you and Mike have made for your wedding. Beyond that, he's said that your happiness is the most important thing in the world to him."

The tension around them fractured into a thousand pieces that the trade winds carried away.

Liam was dumbfounded, watching Mike and Jenna relax into each other as Jenna's smile morphed into the one reserved for friends and family—the *real* smile. Mike became engaging and, damn it all to hell, charming as well. Liam couldn't say what it was Ella had done, but her presence, her word choices, her approach—all of it had defused a situation that was fast devolving into something that would have made the papers.

The papers.

Jenna had been most clear about that—she didn't want news outlets carrying the story of her wedding or gossip rags featuring it on their covers. She'd been so worried about that one specific thing, and he'd nearly brought it down on her head.

He owed Jenna, at the very least, an apology. He stepped forward a fraction of a second after Mike took her hands and claimed her attention, face solemn.

"I owe you an apology, sweetheart. I let Liam bait me even after you asked me to keep my cool. I nearly caused a scene when I know you don't want anything to draw attention to us being here. I'm so damn sorry, baby. It won't happen again." He kissed her then, gently but thoroughly, before stepping away.

Flushed, Jenna smiled up at Mike. "Thanks, baby. I know he can be a lot to handle at times. He'll get better." The "or else" was implied. Heavily.

"I'm sure Mr. Baggett didn't intend to start a fight," Ella started, but Liam waved her off.

"No, Ella. Mike is right. I baited him. I'll not do it again."

Mike and Jenna nodded, but neither spoke.

Ella gestured toward the stairs that led to the resort's largest lawn and a raised garden that was framed in hedges and looked out over the ocean. "Let's head down to the garden, and we can discuss the rehearsal and ceremony."

Jenna and Mike started out ahead, Liam falling in step with Ella just behind them. "That was well done of you. Thanks."

She barely spared him a glance. "It was clear there was about to be bloodshed."

"Without a doubt."

"Why didn't you just apologize?" she asked. "It's the least you could do given that this is their big day."

"I beg your pardon," he snapped. "I bloody well did apologize."

"No, Liam. You didn't. You said you shouldn't have baited Mike."

"And?"

She sighed and shook her head, crossing her arms

under her breasts. "The words *I'm sorry* never passed your lips."

"She knows I meant it," he said, rationalizing his choice despite the voice in his ear that whispered Ella was right.

"It would have gone a long way with her, and him, to have heard those two words from you."

"I don't give a rat's ass what he thinks of me."

This time Ella laid a hand on his arm, forcing him to stop with her. "The thing is, Liam, this isn't about you or your decisions or your wants. This is about her—her future husband and the life they're about to build together."

The skin across Liam's shoulders grew tight. "He's not good enough for her."

"That's not your decision to make."

Her words, so softly delivered, set him back a step. "I want what's best for her."

"And you don't trust her to know what that is?" Ella countered.

"I've seen that man's true character, Ella. He has repeatedly talked over and around my sister. He has disrespected her in front of me, and I won't have it."

"How is what he's done so different from what you just did?"

"I love her!" he bit out.

Ella reached out and took one of Liam's hands, squeezing gently. "It would seem Mike does, too." She dropped his hand and then strode forward to catch up to the couple.

Liam stood there for several seconds, his mouth

hanging open like a fool's. Ella was absolutely right. He was no better than Mike. Liam had been presumptive, domineering, controlling and brash—all traits he'd criticized in the other man.

Could Ella be right? Could Jenna have found her miracle in this man who professed to love her? Could it be possible that he'd so severely underestimated Jenna's choices?

It seemed that he had.

Shaking off the stupor the truth had wrought in him, he strode toward the couple and their event co-ordinator. His lover. The woman who wasn't afraid to tell him the truth no matter the cost, and he vowed he'd make this right.

It dawned on him as he reached the steps to the garden that what they were about to encounter was as wrong as wrong could get. And he had no way to stop it.

CHAPTER THIRTEEN

ELLA WAS HALFWAY up the stairs when the scream hit her. She tripped up the last step and stumbled to a halt at the garden's back wall. Something pink darted left. Something darker pink darted right. And there, fifteen feet away, stood Hollywood's it girl, Jenna Williams, screaming as if an ax murderer was closing in. But it wasn't an ax murderer. It was…a peacock? No. It was a *pink* peacock.

Two.

Three.

Four pink peacocks ran amok, long tails flowing behind them.

And one, presumably the appropriately named cock, strutted toward Jenna, his red eyes sinister, his cotton candy–colored tail on full display, his head bobbing to and fro as if to mesmerize Jenna before slaying her.

Mike wrapped Jenna in his arms and looked about wildly.

Ella lurched forward as Liam crested the stairs and ran smack into her.

"What's going on?" she demanded.

"Where the hell did the peacocks come from?" Mike shouted, partly from obvious fury and partly to be heard above the bride's screaming and the birds' squawking.

Liam rushed past her and reached for Jenna, but Mike swung her up into his arms and carried her toward the nearest exit at a swift jog.

"Mike?" Ella called, following after them.

"She's terrified of birds, Ms. Montgomery," Mike bit out. "Actually diagnosed as ornithophobic. That's why the paperwork said 'Absolutely No Birds.' And why the hell did you dye them pink? Jenna is an animal activist, very vocal on animal rights and environmental preservation."

"I know. I didn't order the birds," Ella said, forcing herself to stand up straight and meet Mike's accusing stare.

Jenna peered up at her, tears having turned well-applied mascara into raccoon eyes. "Someone did, Ms. Montgomery, and there are only two people who would have. Liam, who knows I'm scared of birds, and you. I can't imagine Liam doing something like this when he knows I'm petrified of the things." She shuddered. "So who else would've done it if not you?"

"I don't know," Ella answered.

Looking around, she found Liam herding the last bird through the far exit and shutting the garden gate behind it. He turned and found them all staring. "They're contained, Jenna. The gate is locked.

They won't get out again. Mike, if you'd kindly remove my sister from the garden."

"I'm not leaving until I know who did this," Jenna said. "Liam wouldn't have."

"I have the paperwork here," Ella said. "Let me look at what your assistant filled out."

Mike consoled Jenna as Ella dug through her messenger bag. She'd left the paperwork in her bag last night, both copies, in fact—the original and the one with Liam's changes. But now the only one she could find was the one Jenna's assistant had originally sent over.

The groom said something soft in his future wife's ear, and she sagged against him, her sobs reduced to hiccuping little gasps. "Shh," he said gently. "I've got you. Deep breaths."

"I feel like such a fool," she said, voice muffled by his shirt. "Did anyone see me?"

Ella wanted to crawl into a hole and die. She hadn't ordered the peacocks, and certainly not *pink* peacocks, but she *had* ordered the flock of doves that were to be delivered tomorrow. Liam had made sure the order had been placed. She'd questioned him, referring to the "no birds" stipulation in the original paperwork, but he'd insisted his sister wanted the doves released. According to him, "no birds" meant she had wanted the area cleared of any indigenous animals—domesticated parrots, flocks of pelicans or whatever else might have been curated by the resort.

She'd done as he asked, but she'd kept the paperwork for reference.

Page after page, she flipped through the original paperwork. She finally came to the "Ceremonial Release Option," and there, in bold Sharpie next to the checkbox labeled "Birds," was the word *NO* in capital letters, underlined twice.

She wanted to vomit.

Instead, she grabbed her bag and dug through, determined—desperate—to find the copy Liam had provided, to redeem herself. But the copy he'd provided her wasn't there.

Mike must have been watching her, because he asked, "What's on the paperwork?"

Ella couldn't lie. God, she wanted to, but it went against everything she was.

"No birds," she answered, throat so dry she could've been labeled a fire hazard. She glanced over to where Liam stood. "I know there was something about a request for birds on the subsequent paperwork."

"Subsequent paperwork?" Mike asked.

Ella clarified. "The paperwork Liam, Mr. Baggett, provided."

"Liam didn't do it, Mike." Jenna looked up at him with doe eyes. "He wouldn't."

"Ms. Montgomery," Mike started, but Liam chose that moment to close the distance between them.

Liam reached out and gently touched Ella's arm, trying to gain her attention.

"Not now, Liam," she bit out.

"I'd like to see the paperwork."

"You've seen it plenty of times."

"Ella—"

"This is mine to fix, Liam. Somewhere, somehow, someone made a mistake. It appears that someone was me." She shrugged off Liam's hand and stepped toward Jenna. "I can only apologize profusely, Ms. Williams. I'll make this right and ensure there are no birds anywhere near the ceremony. You have my word."

"Why were they pink?" she asked, slipping into a hazy awareness. "I hate pink."

"I have no idea," Ella answered.

Jenna just looked at her, the accusation in her eyes unquestionable.

Ella's stomach was threatening a full-scale revolt. She swallowed several times before she was able to get her mouth to stop watering excessively and her eyes to stop tearing up. "I'm so sorry. We'll find out where the mistake was made. Perhaps it was for another wedding."

"Whatever the reason, I expect you to ensure nothing like this happens at the ceremony. I will not have our day destroyed by someone's mistake, no matter how innocent it allegedly was." Mike shifted his hold on Jenna. "I'm going to take her back to the room to clean up. We'll forgo the rest of the walk-through to give you time to make sure everything is in order. Guests begin arriving in the morning. Don't screw this up for us, Ms. Montgomery. If this goes well, it could make your career. If it goes poorly, it *will* ruin it. Don't make me regret hiring a relative unknown event coordinator."

And with that parting shot, Mike gently steered Jenna back toward the resort.

Liam laid a hand on Ella's arm. "I know—"

"No, Liam. *I* know. I know!" she shouted. She knew exactly who had ordered the peacocks. The same person who had encouraged her to include the dove release at the end of the ceremony. The only man who had the ability to authorize changes to the prewedding events. The man with the power to destroy her career without doing more than initialing changes he'd initiated on behalf of his sister. The only man she'd ever cared for so much that she'd overlooked changes she should have known better than to blindly accept.

Liam Baggett.

Liam had let Ella be, taking a walk along the beach to sort out the riot of emotions burning through him. He should have stepped up and taken responsibility for the bird debacle, but he hadn't. Planning on ruining the wedding had been one thing; seeing his plan come to fruition had been another.

When Jenna had experienced a full-blown panic attack this afternoon, Liam hadn't been able to make himself say the words. Accept blame. Look into his sister's eyes and tell her that he was the one who had scared her in the hopes her precious Mike would show his true colors.

Had he an ounce of chivalry, he'd have spoken up. But he hadn't. And he was disgusted with himself.

It had been seeing Ella step in and bear the brunt

of Mike's anger that gave his guilt a voice. Jenna might put up with that shit, but Liam wasn't going to allow Mike to treat Ella that way.

He'd stepped in, intent on clearing the issue up. But Ella had stopped him dead in his tracks. She shut him down, telling him, all of them, that she'd make it right. She'd fix the mistake, see the wedding through as promised and ensure there were no birds at the ceremony.

The least he could do was respect her wishes and let her save face by handling it as she saw fit.

He owed her that. That, and so much more.

He had to find a way to make it right for his sister and to salvage what lay between Ella and him. Part of his plan had failed in ways he hadn't been fully prepared for, but that didn't mean all was lost. There was still time to ensure Mike showed his true character before vows were exchanged. Liam would just have to be careful. He'd have to find a way to shield Ella as much as possible while still getting Mike to show Jenna he was the worst possible choice she could make. There was still the rehearsal and dinner. Time enough.

Standing on the bungalow's porch, his hand on the doorknob, Liam hesitated. Making the decision to go through the door and face Ella's anger was simple enough. It was her presumable disappointment in him that he didn't want to confront. So there he stood, the deep shade of early night settling around him, the winds stalling and the waves shushing. On the other side of the door, he heard Ella throwing things around with fervor, cursing his name with such creativity and thoroughness that it was clear she thought he and the devil himself were on a first-name basis.

With a deep breath, he turned the doorknob and stepped inside.

The one-bedroom suite was clean. As in, sparkling. No papers lay strewn about. No seating chart was tacked to the bulletin board. No computer with its portable printer sat on the desk. Nothing.

A shadow moved past the sliver of light that escaped through the bedroom door and door frame.

Ella.

Heart in his throat and pulse pounding out a heavy-metal drumbeat in his ears, he forced himself to knock.

She didn't answer, but he opened the door anyway.

Ella was packing. Or, in actuality, had already packed.

She let out a shout when she saw him. "You scared the shit out of me, Liam," she snapped, hand fluttering back and forth between her chest and throat like a hummingbird that wasn't sure where to land.

"I…" The word *sorry* hung up in his throat yet again. "You've packed."

"Brilliant observation." She shot him a bland look. "Next you'll tell me your London offices are at 221b Baker Street."

"Where are you going, Ella?" The question was

delivered with a quiet severity he managed only by keeping a fierce grip on his emotions—emotions that threatened to erupt in a bout of rage and desperation. She couldn't leave. If she left, he'd be forced to chase her down. His father's voice resonated through his head.

You're a Baggett, by God. You do not *lower yourself to such plebian behavior.*

"Ella?" he pressed when her silence broke through his father's posthumous rant.

"Away, Liam. I'm going away."

"Where? There aren't any rooms on the island."

"I've found a place."

"Where?"

She rounded on him then, all fury and fire. "Who the hell do you think you are, sabotaging my job and then demanding answers from me like I'm some bought-and-paid-for dinner date? Not to mention the fact that you stole my notes!"

"I didn't steal them," he ground out.

"What, you 'borrowed' them?" she asked, her air quotes exaggerated. "Couldn't keep up with all the shit you'd changed so you needed my paperwork to be in the right place at the right time to see this house of cards fall?"

"It wasn't like that." But nothing he could say would change her mind, and he knew it. Besides, part of her accusation stung with truth. Perhaps he'd wanted this more than he'd thought. "I don't want…" He tugged at the neck of his suddenly tight shirt.

"What, Liam? What is it you don't want so badly

that you'd destroy my career?" When he didn't answer right away, she shouted, "Tell me."

Something in Liam snapped, and the truth poured
out of him in a tsunami. Devastating. Unstoppable.
Catastrophic in force. "I don't want Jenna marrying
that son of a bitch, okay? She deserves better than
him. All he wants is her money, her fame—a key
to her house and her car and her heart. But what's
he giving her in return? What is it he brings to the
table, Ella? The answer is nothing. The man brings
nothing."

She stared at him, mouth slack with shock. "You're
standing in front of me telling me you truly believe
you're a better judge of what's best for your sister
than she is?"

"She's blinded by love, or what she thinks is love."

"Did you stop even once to think that maybe love
is *exactly* what she's found?"

"It's not possible."

"Why, Liam? Why couldn't she have fallen into
something beautiful and grand and promising? Tell
me. Convince me it's not possible."

"Because love isn't real, Ella!" The shouted words
echoed in the heart of who he was. "It's a figment
of imagination, something propagated by industries
like yours. You lie to people every day to get them
to buy in to the idea that there's this utopian life on
the other side of commitment where it's sunshine
and champagne every damn day, where people love
each other forever and no one ever leaves."

Ella looked so sad just then, standing there staring at him like she'd never seen him before. "You're wrong, Liam. So wrong. Love is a very real thing. And what I do isn't propagating a lie. It's celebrating a new beginning. It's rejoicing that you've finally found that one person who truly gets you. The person who always has your back. The one who will be there on Sunday morning so you don't have to do the crossword puzzle alone and when you need someone to hold back your hair because you're sick."

"So, if love is real, why is the divorce rate so high? Why are there a million country songs and rock ballads about heartache and loss? Why are there weekends with dads and visitations with moms for kids from divided households? Where's the power of love in these people's lives, Ella? Tell me, because I don't see it."

"It's right in front of you," she whispered. "People make bad choices sometimes, but—"

"Which is what I'm trying to prevent Jenna from doing," he said.

"Don't you get it? It's not your decision to make, Liam. Her life is not yours to micromanage."

"I promised our father I would make sure she was happy." Raking his hands through his hair, he spun away from her and stalked to the open patio doors. Beyond the railing lay the infinite sea, as dark at night as it was brilliant during the day. "I swore I would make sure Jenna was happy."

"Then trust her to make sure that happens and be there to help if she asks for it. But don't you dare take over her life and try to make it into your version of happy."

He didn't respond right away, just stood there staring out over the water.

"You don't get to choose for people, Liam. You don't get to live others' lives by proxy, to decide what's best for them under any given circumstance." The soles of her shoes tapped across the hardwood floor, the sound telling him she'd stopped somewhere nearby. "What did you see happening here, between us?"

There were a hundred things he wanted to say, each of them the truth, but like the apology that wouldn't come, neither would a single answer to her question.

"Did you seduce me so you could have free rein where this wedding was concerned, or did you seduce me because you wanted me?"

There was heartache in that question, and fury as well. What struck him the hardest was the sour note of regret she couldn't, or didn't bother to, hide.

So no more lies. No more deception. "Both."

She laughed, the sound brittle on the soft night air. "I can't believe I fell for you, let you use me like you did."

He rounded on her. "I didn't use you."

She looked up slowly as if she'd been stunned. "You did, and by your own admission. You seduced me. And I fell for it." She shook her head. "You must really think I'm a fool. I sure as hell do." She stepped away from him, and he moved to catch her when she swayed. She stumbled out of his reach and then froze, not looking at him when she spoke. "Touch me again, Liam Baggett, and I swear I will cause you a world of hurt."

Liam stepped back, and she shot him a look that would haunt him for the rest of his life. "I wouldn't hurt you, Ella."

She grabbed the handle of her bag and started for the door. Drawing parallel to him, she stopped and leaned in. "You already did."

And then she was gone.

CHAPTER FOURTEEN

ELLA REFUSED TO CRY. That man didn't deserve her tears any more than he deserved her forgiveness. He'd thrown her under the bus with so much force she'd nearly come out the other side. Had he apologized with an ounce of sincerity, she might have been able to forgive him. But hearing him admit that he'd seduced her not only for pleasure had wounded her pride. Not as much as it wounded her heart, though. Because as stupid as it was, she'd fallen for him.

She wandered the grounds for a while before collapsing onto an empty beach chaise. They were plentiful this late at night, but she craved one away from wandering beachgoers. Midnight strollers. Lovers. She'd lied to Liam when she told him she'd found a place to stay. There still wasn't a room available, but she'd be damned if she'd be dependent on his good will. Never again.

When dawn finally came, she made her way to the concierge's desk, asked them to stow her two bags and went to the dining room for breakfast. It was a quick trip through the buffet before Arvin called to inform her the first shuttle of guests had arrived and checked in to the block of rooms Liam had reserved under a fictitious party name. The whole thing had been set up under the guise of a family reunion. So far, it had worked.

Ella went to the event coordination desk and made sure the welcome bags for each guest were ready and labeled; she double-checked the contents and then went out to the docks to check on the boats reserved for parasailing.

At one o'clock, Ella confirmed all the guests had arrived and then had a member of Arvin's staff call each room and ask guests who had signed up for the excursion to meet her on the lawn behind the main dining room.

The guests trickled into the tent in twos and threes. Liam came somewhere in the middle, trying to speak to Ella. She avoided any conversation by saying, "I believe the bride is in that corner, Mr. Baggett. You'll want to see her, I'm sure." Then she focused on the guests behind him. Ella greeted each one, provided them with the courtesy towel, bottled water and sunscreen, and she explained that, after their excursion, there would be a champagne bar set up and in-room spa treatments available before the rehearsal dinner. Despite the fact she'd done it before, it was a bit intimidating to be mixing with Hollywood's elite. There was so much riding on this job. She had to get it right. From the positive responses coming from the group, it seemed she had. It was just too soon to cash that particular check, though.

They all went down to the docks, Mike and Jenna walking with her. When they reached the power-boats, Mike stopped short.

Jenna looked between the boat, her fiancé and Ella. "What are we doing?"

"Parasailing?" Ella's response came out a timid question.

Mike shot her a sharp look. "I thought we'd agreed on diving."

Ella took a deep breath. "It was suggested that more people would take part in parasailing, so the event was changed."

Jenna stepped in close to Mike and took his free hand in hers. "It will be okay. You don't have to do this."

"Is there a problem?" Ella asked under her breath.

"Mike is, um…" Jenna glanced at her feet.

"I hate heights," he said between gritted teeth.

Oh. Shit.

Ella wanted to curl in on herself as much as she wanted to explode with rage all over Liam. *He'd* picked parasailing over horseback riding, and she'd agreed. He'd done it again—thrown her to the wolves and left her to be eaten alive.

She went into disaster intervention mode. Stepping back, she turned to the guests who were milling about, shooting curious glances their way. With a broad grin, she said, "Jenna was torn between going up with Mike on the first run, or going up with her brother. Mike, being his typical gracious self, offered to let brother and sister go up first. And since we're an odd-numbered group, Mike has offered to man the ladder for everyone. After you land in the water at the end of your ride, an instructor will get you unhooked from the sail. You'll swim to the side of the boat and Mike will help you up the ladder if you need assistance." She beamed at Mike, maybe a little too overdone, but she beamed all the same. "Thank you, Mike, for being ever the gentleman."

A smattering of applause sounded.

Mike took a small bow.

Jenna nudged him aside and reached for Liam. "We're first!" She hauled her brother away as if the dock was on fire, shoving him into the first boat so hard he tripped and nearly fell in the water.

"Everyone else, pick your ride partner." Numb with anxiety, Ella moved like an automaton, helping people pair up and sorting them onto boats. Then she followed Mike onboard, fully expecting to get reamed out.

"Thank you," he said from the side of his mouth.

Ella shot him a speculative glance. "You're… welcome?"

"For not making a big deal about it *and* getting my ass out of that obligatory ride." He wiped actual sweat from his forehead. "You have no idea what that would have cost me."

"I didn't know."

His face darkened. "I'm sure you didn't." He waved her off when she started to apologize again. "Let's get through this and the rehearsal dinner, and we'll be golden. How bad can it actually be? As long as I come out of this married to that woman, it's all good."

Six hours later, as Mike was loaded into an ambulance, Ella realized exactly how bad it could be.

Liam had shown up at the rehearsal dinner late and taken his seat with a table of guests. When the appetizer came out and his plate was set before him, he'd shoved out of his chair and scanned the room. Eyes lighting on hers, he started toward Ella with long strides. She'd directed him back to his seat with a sharp point of her finger and a glare.

He'd kept coming.

So she'd jabbed her finger in the direction of his seat and mouthed the word *Now.*

Still, he kept coming.

Her stomach had twisted itself into a complex series of knots that tightened with every step Liam took toward her. Then he slipped his arm through Ella's and directed her to the back of the room, smiling as they went.

He leaned in, his lips brushing her ear, the move as sensual as his words were chilling. "Where are the scallops?"

"Don't worry, they're here. I had them added to the salmon croquette sauce because there weren't enough harvested to make them part of the main course."

"Ella, Mike hates shellfish. Absolutely abhors the things. Gags on them."

Everything after that happened in slow motion.

She turned toward Mike to find him choking and Jenna panicking. Someone shouted for a doctor. Another person rose and started toward him. Liam lifted his phone, dialed the front desk and requested emergency medical services in the dining room.

And Mike began to turn a weird puce color.

"Oh, God." She stumbled, and Liam caught her. "Liam, he doesn't hate shellfish. He's allergic."

"Oh, sweet hell."

She looked up at him, then, not sure what she'd find. He was so pale he appeared almost corpse-like.

The resort doctor rushed into the room moments later and, hauling a monster-size syringe out of his bag, stabbed Mike in the thigh. Seconds passed like minutes, hours, and then Mike took a ragged breath.

Sirens wailed, coming closer with every subsequent breath he took.

"Did you know?" she croaked out.

"I swear to you, I didn't. I intended to annoy him to pieces, but I didn't have a clue he was allergic. Only that he was a royal prick about not having them touch his food the first night I met him at dinner with Jenna."

Paramedics had Mike on a gurney and were wheeling him out before Ella was able to move. She rushed to the bride's table, where Liam was talking to Jenna in a low, calm voice.

Jenna caught sight of Ella and, with a tear-streaked face, said, "You served shellfish. Why? *Why?*" The last word was screamed, a demand for an unanswerable question.

Behind Ella, the crowd began to murmur.

"The why isn't important right now," Liam said. "We need to get you to Mike so you can be with him." Taking her by the arm, he steered her toward the exit at a brisk pace, not once looking back to where he'd left Ella…standing at the front of the room, under the weight of glares from people who believed she'd just poisoned the groom. What was worse, she couldn't remember if she'd made the change or if Liam had.

Regardless, Mike had suffered for the choice. Badly. And she'd never forgive herself.

Her career had been on life support, and Liam had just pulled the plug.

Liam stood in the corner of the hospital room and watched Jenna and Mike. Heads together and hands clasped, they whispered to each other and shared small, intimate kisses despite Mike's swollen face and lips. Hell, his swollen upper body. Even his fingers looked like sausages. His eyes were slits in his head. At least he was breathing.

And it was all because of the shellfish.

Liam stood quietly, hands in his pockets and chin to his chest. Damn, but that had been close. Mike had all but stopped breathing when the resort physician had arrived with an EpiPen. Mike had left his own in the hotel room.

God alone knew how guilty Liam felt. He'd known Mike didn't *like* scallops. When Liam had treated Mike and Jenna to a rather fancy dinner in London, the man had turned down the scallop appetizer. Liam had prodded him about being a burger-and-beer guy. Common. Mike had blown Liam off without mentioning that it was an allergy versus a preference. If he'd left Ella to do her job, it would have been fine. If he'd not insisted on poking at Mike until his temper exploded, this wouldn't have happened. If he'd only—

"Liam?"

He looked up and found Jenna focused on him. Mike had drifted off to sleep.

His little sister took a deep breath, stood and squared her shoulders. "I want you to fire the event coordinator."

"I'm not sure that's the best course of action."

Her brows winged up so far they nearly met her hairline. "Not the best course of action? How can you say that when she nearly killed my fiancé? Look at him, Liam." She tipped her head toward the sleeping man. "His oxygen saturation only just topped ninety. According to the doctor, it should be ninety-nine given the excellent shape he's in. I know you were involved in the peacock thing—" she held out her hand when he tried to interrupt "—don't bother denying it. But she knew I was scared of birds. It was on the original paperwork. The excursion was supposed to have been diving. It's what we picked. She changed that to parasailing. And we had specifically requested a native meal for the rehearsal and wedding dinners, listing things we wanted included. Shellfish wasn't on the list for a reason. And you don't serve something like that, let alone hide it in a sauce, without knowing if someone is allergic." Her voice had risen as she listed her complaints, and Mike stirred beside her. "Shh, baby. Rest."

"Want to get married."

"And we will," she said softly, smoothing a hand over his hair. "We will."

Liam had a difficult choice to make. He could respect Jenna's wishes and use Ella's termination as a means of cutting ties with the woman. He could still fire her but keep to his original plan and hire her to coordinate several high-end functions, thus helping her get things back on track. He could even leave everything to his sister and let her terminate Ella, keeping his hands out of it completely.

But he was the direct cause of everything that had gone wrong. Ella had changed the dive excursion to parasailing because the changes Liam had insisted upon were eating into her profit margin. He'd been directly responsible for the peacocks—*pink* peacocks, at that. And the doves. And the changed flowers, from the bride's bouquet to the groom's boutonniere to the table toppers. And the revised seating chart. And, worst of all, the addition of scallops to the menu. While he wanted to deny it all, to affect having no conscience, he couldn't. Not this time. Ella had paid, and dearly, for his mistakes. He wouldn't let her take the fall, again, for his screwups.

Regret bound his chest like a vise. And he knew that whatever he was suffering, Ella had to be suffering a hundredfold. Her career's recovery had hinged on the success of this job. People had seen what had happened. Influential people. And they would talk. He might not be able to stop them, but he would do what he could to help her find her path forward.

If he could manage to salvage this, maybe he had a chance at getting her to forgive him.

Better luck betting the contents of my wallet on the afternoon races.

But he had to hope. It was all he had.

Then there was Jenna. And, more consequently, Mike, he acknowledged grudgingly. Watching them together in this intimate setting, he saw something between them he'd somehow missed before. They'd gotten together so quickly, had already been engaged when Jenna introduced him to Mike. Liam hadn't had the chance to observe them like this, to watch how the man tended to Jenna's every want, met her every need and cared for her without apology. Liam had been wrong about the man and his motives, and he'd have to admit it. Not just to Jenna, but to the man himself. So many apologies in front of him, the first of which would be hard, the last of which would be the hardest but also the most important.

Looking at Jenna, he struggled to find the right words. Liam blew out a hard breath, gave up what little semblance of control he had left and did what he'd never done before. He spoke from the heart. "Jenna, I've made a right mess of things."

"It's not your fault Ella nearly killed Mike."

Ever faithful, his little sister.

"Actually, it is." If he could just keep his voice

steady. "Your assistant provided her with your wish list. I have a copy of it on my computer."

Jenna just looked at him.

"I also have the digital copy as well as Ella's hard copy of that list with... Damn it." He raked his hands through his hair and grabbed fistfuls in frustration. This was proving even harder than he'd expected it would be.

"Leem, what's going on?" Jenna's skepticism was beginning to trump her faith in him, and witnessing the change devastated him.

Treat it like a bandage. Grab the edge and rip. "I'm responsible for every change that was made to the original wedding plans." And he waited.

She stared at him, eyes wide. "You."

"Yes. Me." He blew out a breath. "I didn't believe Mike was the best choice for your husband, squid. You ran off and fell in love between Christmas and New Year, accepted a proposal without consideration and began planning a wedding by Easter. It was too fast. And my first impression of Mike was poor, to say the least."

"Your first impression trumps mine?" she wheezed. "What, he wasn't high enough on society's scale of 'Rich and Richer' for you? What about me, Liam? What about what I want? I told Ella precisely what my dream wedding would look like. It was her job to make that happen. Your only job was to be happy for me."

"Ella only did what I told her to do. She was operating in good faith and believed I was acting in your best interest as your proxy. I wasn't, and I own that."

"You *own* that?" she asked, voice deceptively calm. Her eyes? Not so calm. In them, a tempest raged, coming closer to the surface with every heartbeat. "How dare you, Liam. How dare you come in here to Mike's room, a room he wouldn't be in if it weren't for your callousness, your narcissistic belief you know what's right for everyone. How. Dare. You." She turned away from him and picked up Mike's hand. "Damn you, Liam. Your arrogance could have killed this man. Killed my heart. In turn, you would have killed me. You were okay with that?" Blond curls slid forward, curtaining her face, shielding her from him. "You aren't the man I thought you were. Please leave."

"Jenna—"

"Leave," Mike whispered, voice raspy. "We'll work out what's best for us and let you know where we go from here."

Liam swallowed the argument he'd been mounting, the words scraping his throat raw before plummeting into the depths of his belly.

He left.

CHAPTER FIFTEEN

ELLA DIDN'T BOTHER trying to sleep. There were no available flights off the island until the following afternoon, so she had time to kill and nowhere private to do so. She spent the first part of the night on a beach chaise again, but the resort's security patrol asked her to return to her room for her safety given that the height of the carnival was nearing. She couldn't argue with that, so she went to the hotel lobby, powered up her computer and opened her accounting file. No need to put off the truth of her financial situation. With a new spreadsheet, she began compiling a list of bills, a second sheet with a list of physical assets she could liquidate and a third sheet with a list of liquid assets. The last was the shortest list. She was broke, and it was only going to get worse before it got better.

Her eyes were heavy and she found herself bobbleheading as the hour hand slipped past two in the morning. No doubt she'd lost the job, and that meant she had nothing better to do. She was about to give in and lay her head on the table when someone slid a cup of coffee toward her.

"Brain juice," she whispered. Slurred? Whatever. She needed the caffeine like a newborn babe needed its mother's milk. Her hands shook as she lifted the cup to her mouth. Had she ever been this tired? She took a big sip.

"It's hot, Ella."

She spat the contents out. Yes, it was hot. But the warning was delivered with a British accent.

A *male* British accent.

Adrenaline crashed through her, and she started to shake even as her bleary vision cleared. Liam sat across from her, wiping coffee from his face. All the things she wanted to say rushed to the tip of her tongue and fought for their right to be the first words chosen, the first threat delivered, the first curse uttered. But instead of saying anything intelligible, she sputtered and tripped over her thoughts, managing single syllables.

"Not the greeting I expected, though not as bad as it could have been." Liam's words were muffled as he dragged his arm across his face and blinked a few times to clear the last of the coffee from his eyes.

"That you expected anything from me after all you've done tells me what a fool you really are." Ella gathered her personal flotsam, closed her computer and began shoving things into her bag.

"Ella, please." He settled a hand over hers.

Shock raced through that point of contact and up her arm. Heat followed, so intense it was nearly unbearable. She jerked away from him and knocked over the coffee cup and the saucer it sat in. Porcelain splintered on the tile floor and bled black as the still-hot brew seeped out of the mess in every direction. Shoving her chair back, she stepped around the mess and hoisted her messenger bag over her shoulder.

No matter what he'd done, seeing Liam hurt on a deep, personal level. But there were a couple of things she had to say or she'd never forgive herself. Steeling herself, she lifted her chin and met his dark gaze head-on. "It breaks my heart on a variety of levels that you lied to me, Liam, that you used me and proved yourself to be someone other than the man I thought I'd come to know."

"Ella," Liam interrupted.

But she was having none of it. "I'm. Not. Done." Her jaw was so tight she didn't know how she'd get the next words out, but they were burning a hole in her self-worth, and pride demanded she fling them out so she alone didn't have to bear the burden of their being. "You destroyed my career, Liam. You have made it impossible for me to go back to Los Angeles and get any type of respectable work in event planning. You screwed me—physically, mentally, emotionally and, above all, professionally. My only solace is that karma's a bitch, and her memory's infallible."

With that, she hoisted her bag higher and strode across the lobby, out the main doors and across the grass. She shook, an emotional tempest whipping her thoughts into a frenzy, the vortex dropping into her chest and battering her heart. She should've let him have it—*really* let him have it. She could've ripped him to shreds, could have left a tattered mess in her wake.

"Pretty to think so," she said to herself, kicking at a small coconut that had fallen on the path to the beach.

All night she'd been skirting the truth, coming close and then racing away. But when she'd stormed off, her heart aching with every beat and her eyes stinging with caustic tears, she'd realized that avoidance might work for others, but she wasn't programmed that way.

The truth? She wanted to hurt Liam, deliver a little tit for tat, but she couldn't. Because she'd fallen for him.

Sincerely.

Thoroughly.

Completely.

She stepped off the end of the path and onto the beach, feet sinking ankle deep into the soft white sand. The moon cast a silvery beam across the water. Waves rolled in and crashed against the shore.

Ella sighed. At least she had this last memory, the beauty of this place emblazoned on her mind.

"Ella."

Ella whipped around, fists clenched.

Keeping out of arm's reach, he pushed his hair off his forehead before shoving his hands in his pockets. "I want… I need to make this up to you."

"How? You think you can, what, demand others respect me after this? Maybe hire me despite the sheer fuckery this event turned into?" Her harsh laugh scraped her throat raw.

And wasn't it telling he wanted to fix the business

side of things while the personal side was far more devastating? How could he not know?

"I have connections, Ella. I can make people hire you."

"Make...people..." Against her will and despite her pride, her chin began to wobble. "Make them hire me. Buy my way into good graces with your financial backing."

"I didn't mean it that way."

"Then how did you mean it, Liam? Be very clear so I don't hear the wrong thing. Again."

"You're wildly talented. Look at all you did for my sister's wedding."

"I nearly killed the groom. That's a real résumé builder. How much money would it take to hide that little 'oops'?"

He looked out over the beach, his gaze fixed somewhere near the horizon. "I can't undo that, but I want you to know I can help you regain what was lost. I can arrange high-profile events, hire you to coordinate them, make sure there's media coverage and promote the rebuilding of your brand."

"And what about me, Liam? As an entrepreneur or, better, as a woman? What about my self-respect? My pride at having recovered from being screwed over the first time by my former business partner? My sense of self-worth that people desired my skills, my name on their registry, my vision for their perfect day? How do you propose to buy those back?" she demanded.

"I have resources you can't imagine. I have contacts with more power and influence than the combined social power of the entire guest list at that rehearsal dinner. I can pave the way for you to reclaim your social status and reassert your position as the elite event planner in more than just LA." He shifted his gaze to her and threw his hands in the air. "Why is this so hard for you to see?"

"Because what I see is you throwing your name and your influence and your money at a problem thinking you know the best way to fix it. Here's the thing, Liam. You might be able to buy my way back into society's good graces. You might even be able to save my business. But you can't *buy* my reputation. And if you can't buy that, you sure as hell can't buy my pride or my self-worth or my ethics. They were never for sale. Everything I did, I did because I thought it was the right thing to do. You broke that..." She paused and then thought, *What the hell*, and threw down the truth. He could do with it what he would. "You broke that, Liam, and you broke my heart."

With that, she turned and walked away from him. This time, he didn't follow.

Liam had always known where he belonged in the grand scheme of things, always knew just what he was supposed to do, who he was supposed to be, how he was supposed to act. From which fork to use at a formal dinner to the right putter on the golf course to the best wine to pair with steak, *he knew*. But just then, sitting on the beach in his suit pants and his tailored shirt with French cuffs and his polished wing tips, he had no clue what to do. He wouldn't have been surprised to look in the mirror and find a stranger staring back.

There were so many things he'd planned to say and do, so many ways he was going to make things right, and not a single one would come to pass. Not with Jenna and certainly not with Ella. Both women had made it clear that they were done with the whole debacle. They hadn't been talking entirely about the wedding, either. They'd been talking about Liam. They were done with *him*.

The image of Jenna's hurt but furious face flashed through his mind and was followed immediately by Ella. He remembered everything he'd said and done, from their initial meeting where he'd landed in her lap to the first time he'd kissed her to the first lie he'd told and his moment of conscience when he'd told her not to change the seating charts. Memory after memory flashed through his mind, the more personal ones—the scent of her perfume, the sound of his name sighed across her lips, the feel of her arching beneath his hand, her laugh, the way she looked when she slept—becoming rapid-fire kill shots that left him struggling to breathe. A single truth threaded its way through every interaction, every conversation and every moment he'd spent with her: the way she made him *feel*.

She'd made him doubt his cynicism and believe that, just maybe, finding his own happily-ever-after was possible.

He'd been such an ass.

"Oh, Leem," said a soft voice behind him. "What have you done?"

He whirled around and found Jenna standing there, the sun beginning to stain the darkness with dawn's light. Jenna, the sister he loved to the ends of the earth.

"Jenna. I'm so sorry." His voice broke on the last word, a word he couldn't remember offering to anyone before.

She crossed the sand and, in seconds, held him in her embrace. So huge, so all-encompassing for such a pixie of a woman. Arms tight around his waist and cheek against his chest, she spoke low but with undeniable fervor. "You really screwed up."

"You don't know the half of it."

"Ella?"

His entire body twitched in her embrace, but she didn't let go.

"I thought so." A smile lurked in her voice and he wanted to chastise her for relishing his defeat, but he'd earned her scorn. Then she surprised him by hugging him impossibly tighter. "You know, I still love the pudding out of you, but you *really* screwed up."

"I did," he admitted, breathing easier at her reassurance. "And with a self-righteous vigor reserved for few of my ilk."

She tilted her head back and considered him. "Your ilk?"

"I'm a capital ass, Jenna."

She smiled beatifically. "You so are."

Something in him—the fear he'd lost her—suddenly eased. She would forgive him. And somehow, some way, he would earn her trust as well as her respect again.

Jenna let him go and stepped back. "What happened?"

He'd always been there for his sister, always been her sounding board and confidant, but he'd never confided in her, thinking it was a show of weakness. Not anymore. So Liam did something he'd never done before: he told her everything. Too much, probably, if some of her reactions and the repeated "TMI" were any indication.

Jenna sat on the sand halfway through his story, listening and watching him pace. When he stopped speaking and went still, she popped back to her feet. "So, do you love her?"

He started to deny the emotion out of habit, but her stern look stopped him and he answered the only way he could. "I… How do I know? For sure, I mean."

"Nothing's guaranteed, Liam. Not even love. You have to take a chance."

"I deal in statistical probabilities and historical trends, not chance."

She punched him lightly on the shoulder. "You and that ilk thing. Cut your crap." She took both of his hands and stared up at him. "There are a hundred, a *thousand* questions I could ask you—does she make your breath come short? Do you relax, really relax, around her? Do you feel like you could tell her anything? Do you trust her? Do you love waking up to her face? Do you miss her the minute she begins to walk away? They're all valid, Liam, but there's only one question that really matters."

He waited.

"If she walks out of your life, walks out and never comes back, will you be a better man or a broken man?"

"Broken," he whispered.

"There's your answer." Jenna smiled, her true smile. "No matter what you think of Mike, I am crazy in love with that man. Your opinion—the world's opinion—will never change that for me. He's my One, capital *O*. I would give up everything for him, Liam, and he'd do the same for me. The beautiful thing, though? Love doesn't mean losing one thing to gain another. It's gaining something that enhances everything else in your life. There are compromises, yes," she said, one hand waving those invisible compromises off like they were a swarm of gnats. "But compromise isn't loss, either. It's just bending what you want to make it suit two lives instead of one. Only a fool would miss his shot at his one, Leem, and you're no fool."

He pulled her back in for a tight hug. "I've been exactly that."

"You've certainly been fool*ish*," she admonished, her words a bit warped as he had her face mashed into his chest. "But a fool? You're a Baggett, dear brother. Dad neither raised nor tolerated fools within his clan."

Only Jenna would call the elder Baggett "Dad." The thought made Liam smile, an action not at all common when remembering the old man. "Just so."

"Mike and I got married."

He stiffened. "Beg your pardon?"

"In the hospital. Ella showed up with a beautiful bridal bouquet, my dress, his tux jacket and the rings. I guess she got some guy named Arvin out of bed in the middle of the night and got our stuff together. She made my bouquet." Jenna pulled her phone out of her little handbag and showed Liam pictures. "She asked us if what we had was worth fighting for—no matter who fought against us." She looked up. "Ella so meant you, Liam."

"I got that." His tone was dry as dust.

"Just making sure you're keeping up. Anyway," she continued, "she asked us and we both said yes. She'd asked the doctor about Mike's possible release and they're keeping him for at least twenty-four hours of observation, so he wouldn't have been out in time for the wedding. So she said we should get married by the hospital chaplain and then show up, after they let Mike go, for the wedding dinner and share the good news that way." She grinned. "She repeated something Mike had said about how it couldn't be all that bad if he left here married to me, so she made it happen." Jenna sighed. "She's a total romantic, and the ceremony was beautiful and we had Mike's doctor give me away and the charge nurse was my maid of honor. It was lovely."

"You got married…in a hospital?" he choked out.

"Like you gave me any other option," she retorted. And he shut up.

"Don't let her go, Liam. Please. I'm going to tell everyone what happened and encourage my agency and my studio to use her for events. I'm going to ask my friends to use her. Whatever it takes, I want to help her get back on track. But most of all? I don't want you two to lose each other. Please."

Liam nodded, his vision watery with what he deemed gratitude. "Where is she?"

The sun had long since cleared the horizon and begun to warm the day. "I think she was going to catch the first available flight to the main island and head home from there." She glanced at her watch. "If you hurry—"

"I'll catch her," he said. He kissed Jenna's cheek. "I love you, Jen."

"And I you, Leem." She beamed up at him. "Go get your one."

CHAPTER SIXTEEN

ELLA STOOD IN line waiting to board the tiny puddle jumper for the first of four flights she'd take to get home. Professionally, she'd done what she could to pull a rabbit out of the hat and save the wedding. At first, Jenna had been unsure of Ella's plan to have them married at the hospital. Sure, it had been a long shot. *But no shot will make it if you don't take it.* Her dad's words had marched around inside Ella's head as she pulled things together and took the shuttle to the hospital. They hadn't even faltered at Jenna's reserved greeting. But when Mike had looked at Jenna, motioned her over and said, "Be my wife. Now and always," Ella had wanted to melt *and* pump a fist in the air.

The ceremony had been short but sweet, and it had been evident how in love the bride and groom were. Whatever came their way, they'd handle it. And provided Mike continued to improve, there would be one hell of a reception on the beach tonight. Thanks to Arvin, there would be no shellfish anywhere near the food, and he and his team would be following the original plans, save one thing. The bride and groom had thought it was kind of cool to have the sports drinks incorporated—despite their garish color. So those would stay, just not on the table. They'd be going home in everyone's swag bags.

The door to the plane opened, and the pilot stepped out onto the boarding ladder clipped to the side of the plane. "Good morning! This is flight one-nine-one-Alpha-Tango-Delta that will take you to the main island. It's a forty-minute trip from takeoff to touchdown. Welcome aboard."

Ella climbed the steps and shoved her suitcase in the small overhead bin. It barely fit, and she had to wrestle it into place. She'd probably never get the damn thing out. Figured. If she could just get home… She'd deal with the fallout there.

Her phone chimed, and she checked it, froze and blinked rapidly, trying to comprehend what she was seeing. It was a request from Jenna to coordinate her and Mike's reception in Hollywood. They'd decided to throw a big party once they were back from their honeymoon and sell the photos, with the proceeds going to their favorite environmental charity. A second email followed, this one from Jenna's studio, asking Ella to coordinate a small, intimate event where well-wishers from the studio could congratulate the bride and groom. The initial guest list of seventy-five people made Ella light-headed. The budget forced her to drop into her seat like her ass was made of granite.

Whatever was happening, it was like karma had

finally decided Ella deserved a little recognition and had upped the wattage to "spotlight." Jenna had sent the kindest thank-you note for their ceremony and said she hoped Ella would meet her for lunch to discuss the reception as soon as Jenna was back in town.

Ella tried to type a response, but her fingers shook so badly that what came out was something not even autocorrect could untangle. She tucked her phone away, determined to answer when the plane set down at the international concourse on the main island. She had a three-hour layover anyway. Plenty of time to get her nerves under control.

The door to the plane closed, the engines started and the noise echoed around inside the hollow pit in Ella's stomach. No matter how far Jenna's request went toward soothing Ella's fear she'd never work again, there was still the matter of Liam. The pain of losing him was far worse than she'd ever imagined it could be. It made little sense that she'd fallen for him so hard and fast. But it simply was what it was. She was sure she'd recover, but she'd have felt much better if she had a timeline. Right now it felt like it would be years before she could even stomach the idea of drinks with a stranger. She would simply have to fight her way back to her old self. Period.

"Even if it kills me a little bit each day," she murmured.

The plane taxied away from the tiny terminal, bouncing around as it crossed the cracked and broken asphalt that led to the slightly more even runway.

Ella closed her eyes and let her head rest against the seat back, the dull roar of the engines fueling a burgeoning headache. She was so tired. Maybe she'd be able to get some sleep, if not now then certainly on the next flight to Honolulu.

The engines powered down at the same time the pilot's voice came over the speaker system. "Ladies and gentlemen, there has been a slight delay in our departure. We'll be returning to the gate for a moment to resolve an outstanding issue and then we'll be on our way."

Grumbles and protests were soft, subtle.

Ella sat up, rubbing her temple. The plane came to a stop and the pilot emerged, opened the door and said something to someone outside.

"I'd come back for a piece of that pie," a woman murmured.

Something stirred in Ella's belly, something suspiciously similar to hope.

The pilot stepped back into the cockpit, leaving plenty of room for Liam to enter the cabin.

Ella stared at him, dumbfounded. "What do you think you're doing?"

He came toward her, movements lithe despite the cabin's tiny confines. "We're not done here, Ella."

"I am."

He stopped beside her seat, deep brown eyes meeting hers with an unfamiliar somberness. "If you really mean that, I'll get off this plane. I'd ask that you hear me out first."

Ella looked around. "Here?"

"Here," someone called out from farther back.

"Then here it is," Liam replied. "I'm an ass."

"News flash," Ella muttered. "You forgot a few adjectives, mostly *controlling, superior, vain, boorish, arrogant, egotistical, conceited, self-important.* Should I go on?"

"No need, seeing as I agree with everything you've said." Liam closed his eyes and took one deep breath, two, three, as he seemed to search for words. Finally, he opened his eyes and focused on her with an intensity that kept her silent. "It's become clear to me that I'm a rather self-righteous jackass who, until recently, operated on the assumption that I knew what was best for everyone." He held up a hand when she opened her mouth to respond. "Please. I'd like to get this out before I lose my nerve."

"You never lose your nerve," she whispered.

He traced a finger along her jaw. "I've never had something I was so scared to lose."

She couldn't speak, could only nod and pray that he didn't expect more from her.

"I have made mistakes in life, the most egregious ones this week. But if I let you leave this island without hearing how I feel about you—about *us*—it will be the biggest mistake I'll ever make. You see, I've always chosen duty over desire. It was the Baggett way. Emotions weren't a factor when one had to make a choice. Baggett men did what they were conditioned to do."

"Achieve the desired outcome at any cost." Ella

swallowed hard. "I remember this part of the program."

A smile teased one corner of his mouth. "I'm the boss, so I'm exercising my right to change the program."

Her head was spinning. This wasn't happening, wasn't real. It couldn't be. "You don't make yourself vulnerable, Liam. It's not who you are. You've said as much yourself."

"Words I'd take back if I could, but I can't. So, that leaves me with two choices."

"Which are?" she whispered, scared to death to hope.

"I can stay the course, or I can change. I can remain a closed-off, narcissistic, self-serving asshole, or I can open myself up to be the man I want to be—a man not quite so Baggett-like as my father would have preferred."

Change the course. A spark of hope flared in her heart and burned hot. "Why?"

"Because I'm still Baggett enough to do whatever is necessary to achieve the desired outcome. But a smart woman showed me that vulnerability is actually strength manifest. It takes a brutally strong person to put themselves out there, knowing they could be hurt, and yet still take the risk in pursuit of the reward."

"Sounds like a smart woman."

"She is. Smart, funny, loyal, brilliant, creative, sexy as hell. I could go on if you'd like."

She shook her head, the movement minute. "No. What I mean is, why now, Liam? Why me?"

"Jenna asked me the most profound question. 'If she walks out of your life, will you be a better man, Liam, or will you be a broken man?'"

Ella waited, not sure where Liam was going with the question. She knew—God help her, she *knew*— what she wanted, needed, to hear from Liam. But she wasn't going to put herself out there, refused to offer even a single word of encouragement that might change his authentic answer, the answer he had to come up with on his own if it was going to matter.

"I will be a broken man if you leave this island without me, Ella. I don't know how we'll make it work. But I know with absolute certainty that there is no obstacle so insurmountable that I can't conquer it with you."

With her. Not *for* her. "Sounds like a pretty intense partnership," she said quietly.

"I can only hope." He held out a hand. "I'm far from perfect. I'll make missteps. I'll stumble. I'll be an asshole of ridiculous proportions more often than not…but only until you've polished my roughest edges and helped me shape my vulnerability into strength."

She took his hand, and he pulled her to her feet.

"You are the only woman who has ever made me believe in love, Ella Montgomery."

"May it always be so." She smiled. "Unless we have daughters."

His eyes went comically wide. "God save us all. I

botched up having a little sister. Any daughter would be doomed...save for the fact she'd have you as her mother."

"Is she staying or going?" someone asked in a stage whisper. "I'm going to miss my connecting flight if she doesn't choose quickly."

Liam looked down at her. "What will it be, Ms. Montgomery? Will you stay?"

Ella took his face in her hands, rose to tiptoe and kissed the man who had won her heart.

Liam pulled her into a fierce hug. "Captain," he called out, "file your flight plan with one change. Your passenger count is minus one."

* * * * *

THE WEDDING PLANNER'S BIG DAY

CARA COLTER

To all those readers who have made the last 30 years
such an incredible journey.

CHAPTER ONE

"No."

A paper fluttered down on her temporary desk, slowly floating past Becky English's sunburned nose. She looked up, and tried not to let her reaction to what she saw—or rather, whom she saw—show on her face.

The rich and utterly sexy timbre of the voice should have prepared her, but it hadn't. The man was gorgeous. Bristling with bad humor, but gorgeous, nonetheless.

He stood at least six feet tall, and his casual dress, a dark green sports shirt and pressed sand-colored shorts, showed off a beautifully made male body. He had the rugged look of a man who spent a great deal of time out of doors. There was no sunburn on his perfectly shaped nose!

He had a deep chest, a flat stomach and the narrow hips of a gunslinger. His limbs, relaxed, were sleekly muscled and hinted at easy strength.

The stranger's face was mesmerizing. His hair, dark brown and curling, touched the collar of his shirt. His eyes were as blue as the Caribbean Sea that Becky could just glimpse out the open patio door over the incredible broadness of his shoulder.

Unlike that sea, his eyes did not look warm and inviting. In fact, there was that hint of a gunslinger, again, something cool and formidable in his uncompromising gaze. The look in his eyes did not detract, not in the least, from the fact that his features were astoundingly perfect.

"And no," he said.

Another piece of paper drifted down onto her desk, this one landing on the keyboard of her laptop.

"And to this one?" he said. "Especially no."

And then a final sheet glided down, hit the lip of the desk, forcing her to grab it before it slid to the floor.

Becky stared at him, rather than the paper in her hand. A bead of sweat trickled down from his temple and followed the line of his face, slowly, slowly, slowly down to the slope of a perfect jaw, where he swiped at it impatiently.

It was hot here on the small, privately owned Caribbean island of Sainte Simone. Becky resisted a temptation to swipe at her own sweaty brow with the back of her arm.

She found her voice. "Excuse me? And you are?"

He raised an arrogant eyebrow at her, which made her rush to answer for him.

"You must be one of Allie's Hollywood friends," Becky decided.

It seemed to her that only people in Allie's field of work, acting on the big screen, achieved the physical beauty and perfection of the man in front of her. Only they seemed to be able to carry off that rather unsettling I-own-the-earth confidence that mere mortals had no hope of achieving. Besides, it was more than evident how the camera would love the gorgeous planes of his face, the line of his nose, the fullness of his lips…

"Are you?" she asked.

This was exactly why she had needed a guest list, but no, Allie had been adamant about that. She was looking after the guest list herself, and she did not want a single soul—up to and including her event planner, apparently—knowing the names of all the famous people who would be attending her wedding.

The man before Becky actually snorted in disgust, which was no kind of answer. Snorted. How could that possibly sound sexy?

"Of course, you are very early," Becky told him, trying for a stern note. Why was her heart beating like that, as if she had just run a sprint? "The wedding isn't for two weeks."

It was probably exactly what she should be expecting. People with too much money and too much time on their hands were just going to start showing up on Sainte Simone whenever they pleased.

"I'm Drew Jordan."

She must have looked as blank as she felt.

"The head carpenter for this circus."

Drew. Jordan. Of course! How could she not have registered that? She was actually expecting him. He was the brother of Joe, the groom.

Well, he might be the head carpenter, but she was the ringmaster, and she was going to have to establish that fact, and fast.

"Please do not refer to Allie Ambrosia's wedding as a circus," the ringmaster said sternly. Becky was under strict orders word of the wedding was not to get out. She was not even sure that was possible, with two hundred guests, but if it did get out, she did not want it being referred to as a circus by the hired help. The paparazzi would pounce on that little morsel of insider information just a little too gleefully.

There was that utterly sexy snort again.

"It is," she continued, just as sternly, "going to be the event of the century."

She was quoting the bride-to-be, Hollywood's latest "it" girl, Allie Ambrosia. She tried not to show that she, Becky English, small-town nobody, was just a little intimidated that she had been chosen to pull off that event of the century.

She now remembered Allie warning her about this very man who stood in front of her.

Allie had said, *My future brother-in-law is going to head up construction. He's a bit of a stick-in-the-mud. He's a few years older than Joe, but he acts, like, seventy-five. I find him quite cranky. He's the bear-with-the-sore-bottom type. Which explains why* he *isn't married.*

So, this was the future brother-in-law, standing in front of Becky, looking nothing at all like a stick-in-the-mud, or like a seventy-five-year-old. The bear-with-the-sore-bottom part was debatable.

With all those facts in hand, why was the one that stood out the fact that Drew Jordan was not married? And why would Becky care about that, at all?

Becky had learned there was an unexpected perk of being a wedding planner. She had named her company, with a touch of whimsy and a whole lot of wistfulness, Happily-Ever-After. However, her career choice had quickly killed what shreds of her romantic illusions had remained after the bitter end to her long engagement. She would be the first to admit she'd had far too many fairy-tale fantasies way back when she had been very young and hopelessly naive.

Flustered—here was a man who made a woman want to believe, all over again, in happy endings—but certainly not wanting to show it, Becky picked up the last paper Drew Jordan had cast down in front of her, the *especially no* one.

It was her own handiwork that had been cast so dismissively in front of her. Her careful, if somewhat rudimentary, drawing had a big black X right through the whole thing.

"But this is the pavilion!" she said. "Where are we supposed to seat two hundred guests for dinner?"

"The location is fine."

Was she supposed to thank him for that? Somehow words, even sarcastic ones, were lost to her. She sputtered ineffectually.

"You can still have dinner at the same place, on the front lawn in front of this monstrosity. Just no pavilion."

"This monstrosity is a castle," Becky said firmly. Okay, she, too, had thought when she had first stepped off the private plane that had whisked her here that the medieval stone structure looked strangely out of place amidst the palms and tropical flowers. But over the past few days, it had been growing on her. The thick walls kept it deliciously cool inside and every room she had peeked in had the luxurious feel of a five-star hotel.

Besides, the monstrosity was big enough to host two hundred guests for the weeklong extravaganza that Allie wanted for her wedding, and monstrosities like that were very hard, indeed, to find.

With the exception of an on-site carpenter, the island getaway came completely staffed with people who were accustomed to hosting remarkable events. The owner was record mogul Bart Lung, and many a musical ex-

travaganza had been held here. The very famous fund-
raising documentary *We Are the Globe*, with its huge
cast of musical royalty, had been completely filmed
and recorded here.

But apparently all those people had eaten in the very
expansive castle dining room, which Allie had said with
a sniff would not do. She had her heart set on alfresco
for her wedding feast.

"Are you saying you can't build me a pavilion?"
Becky tried for an intimidating, you-can-be-replaced
tone of voice.

"Not can't. Won't. You have two weeks to get ready
for the circus, not two years."

He was not the least intimidated by her, and she
suspected it was not just because he was the groom's
brother. She suspected it would take a great deal to intimidate Drew Jordan. He had that don't-mess-with-me
look about his eyes, a set to his admittedly sexy mouth
that said he was far more accustomed to giving orders
than to taking them.

She debated asking him, again, not to call it a circus,
but that went right along with not being able to intimidate him. Becky could tell by the stubborn set of his
jaw that she might as well save her breath. She decided
levelheaded reason would win the day.

"It's a temporary structure," she explained, the epitome of calm, "and it's imperative. What if we get inclement weather that day?"

Drew tilted his head at her and studied her for long
enough that it was disconcerting.

"What?" she demanded.

"I'm trying to figure out if you're part of her Cinderella group or not."

Becky lifted her chin. Okay, so she wasn't Hollywood gorgeous like Allie was, and today—sweaty, casual and sporting a sunburned nose—might not be her best day ever, but why would it be debatable whether she was part of Allie's Cinderella group or not?

She didn't even know what that was. Why did she want to belong to it, or at least seem as if she could?

"What's a Cinderella group?" she asked.

"Total disconnect from reality," he said, nodding at the plan in her hand. "You can't build a pavilion that seats two hundred on an island where supplies have to be barged in. Not in two weeks, probably not even in two years."

"It's temporary," she protested. "It's creating an illusion, like a movie set."

"You're not one of her group," he decided firmly, even though Becky had just clearly demonstrated her expertise about movie sets.

"How do you know?"

"Imperative," he said. *"Inclement."* His lips twitched, and she was aware it was her use of the language that both amused him and told him she was not part of Allie's regular set. Really? She should not be relieved that it was vocabulary and not her looks that had set her apart from Allie's gang.

"Anyway, *inclement* weather—"

Was he making fun of her?

"—is highly unlikely. I Googled it."

She glanced at her laptop screen, which was already open on Google.

"This side of this island gets three days of rain per year," he told her. "In the last forty-two years of record-keeping, would you care to guess how often it has rained on the Big Day, June the third?"

The way he said *Big Day* was in no way preferable to *circus*.

Becky glared at him to make it look as if she was annoyed that he had beat her to the facts. She drew her computer to her, as if she had no intention of taking his word for it, as if she needed to check the details of the June third weather report herself.

Her fingers, acting entirely on their own volition, without any kind of approval from her mind, typed in D-r-e-w J-o-r-d-a-n.

CHAPTER TWO

DREW REGARDED BECKY ENGLISH thoughtfully. He had expected a high-powered and sophisticated West Coast event specialist. Instead, the woman before him, with her sunburned nose and pulled-back hair, barely looked as if she was legal age.

In fact, she looked like an athletic teenager getting ready to go to practice with the high school cheer squad. Since she so obviously was not the image of the professional woman he'd expected, his first impression had been that she must be a young Hollywood hanger-on, being rewarded for loyalty to Allie Ambrosia with a job she was probably not qualified to do.

But no, the woman in front of him had nothing of slick Hollywood about her. The vocabulary threw his initial assessment. The way she talked—with the earnestness of a student preparing for the Scripps National Spelling Bee—made him think that the bookworm geeky girl had been crossed with the high school cheerleader. Who would have expected that to be such an intriguing combination?

Becky's hair was a sandy shade of brown that looked virgin, as if it had never been touched by dye or blond highlights. It looked as if she had spent about thirty seconds on it this morning, scraping it back from her face and capturing it in an elastic band. It was a rather nondescript shade of brown, yet so glossy with good health, Drew felt a startling desire to touch it.

Her eyes were plain old brown, without a drop of makeup around them to make them appear larger, or wider, or darker, or greener. Her skin was pale, which would have been considered unfashionable in the land of endless summer that he came from. Even after only a few days in the tropics, most of which he suspected had been spent inside, the tip of her nose and her cheeks were glowing pink, and she was showing signs of freckling. There was a bit of a sunburn on her slender shoulders.

Her teeth were a touch crooked, one of the front ones ever so slightly overlapping the other one. It was oddly endearing. He couldn't help but notice, as men do, that she was as flat as a board.

Drew Jordan's developments were mostly in Los Angeles. People there—especially people who could afford to buy in his subdivisions—were about the furthest thing from *real* that he could think of.

The women he dealt with had the tiny noses and fat lips, the fake tans and the unwrinkled foreheads. They had every shade of blond hair and the astonishingly inflated breast lines. Their eyes were widened into a look of surgically induced perpetual surprise and their teeth were so white you needed sunglasses on to protect you from smiles.

Drew was not sure when he had become used to it all, but suddenly it seemed very evident to him why he had. There was something about all that fakeness that was *safe* to a dyed-in-the-wool bachelor such as himself.

The cheerleader bookworm girl behind the desk radiated something that was oddly threatening. In a world that seemed to celebrate phony everything, she seemed as if she was 100 percent real.

She was wearing a plain white tank top, and if he leaned forward just a little bit he could see cutoff shorts. Peeking out from under the desk was a pair of sneakers with startling pink laces in them.

"How did you get mixed up with Allie?" he asked. "You do not look the way I would expect a high-profile Hollywood event planner to look."

"How would you expect one to look?" she countered, insulted.

"Not, um, wholesome."

She frowned.

"Take it as a compliment," he suggested.

She looked uncertain about that, but marshaled herself.

"I've run a very successful event planning company for several years," she said with a proud toss of her head.

"In Los Angeles," he said with flat disbelief.

"Well, no, not exactly."

He waited.

She looked flustered, which he enjoyed way more than he should have. She glared at him. "My company serves Moose Run and the surrounding areas."

Was she kidding? It sounded like a name Hollywood would invent to conjure visions of a quaintly rural and charming America that hardly existed anymore. But, no, she had that cute and geeky earnestness about her.

Still, he had to ask. "Moose Run? Seriously?"

"Look it up on Google," she snapped.

"Where is it? The mountains of Appalachia?"

"I said look it up on Google."

But when he crossed his arms over his chest and raised an eyebrow at her, she caved.

"Michigan," she said tersely. "It's a farm community in Michigan. It has a population of about fourteen thousand. Of course, my company serves the surrounding areas, as well."

"Ah. Of course."

"Don't say *ah* like that!"

"Like what?" he said, genuinely baffled.

"Like *that explains everything.*"

"It does. It explains everything about you."

"It does not explain everything about me!" she said. "In fact, it says very little about me."

There were little pink spots appearing on her cheeks, above the sunburned spots.

"Okay," he said, and put up his hands in mock surrender. Really, he should have left it there. He should keep it all business, let her know what she could and couldn't do construction wise with severe time restraints, and that was it. His job done.

But Drew was enjoying flustering her, and the little pink spots on her cheeks.

"How old are you?" he asked.

She folded her arms over her own chest—battle stations—and squinted at him. "That is an inappropriate question. How old are you?" she snapped back.

"I'm thirty-one," he said easily. "I only asked because you look sixteen, but not even Allie would be ridiculous enough to hire a sixteen-year-old to put together this cir—event—would she?"

"I'm twenty-three and Allie is not ridiculous!"

"She isn't?"

His brother's future wife had managed to arrange her very busy schedule—she was shooting a movie in Spain—to grant Drew an audience, once, on a brief return to LA, shortly after Joe had phoned and told him with shy and breathless excitement he was getting married.

Drew had not been happy about the announcement. His brother was twenty-one. To date, Joe hadn't made many major decisions without consulting Drew, though Drew had been opposed to the movie-set building and Joe had gone ahead anyway.

And look where that had led. Because, in a hushed tone of complete reverence, Joe had told Drew *who* he was marrying.

Drew's unhappiness had deepened. He had shared it with Joe. His normally easygoing, amenable brother had yelled at him.

Quit trying to control me. Can't you just be happy for me?

And then Joe, who was usually happy-go-lucky and sunny in nature, had hung up on him. Their conversations since then had been brief and clipped.

Drew had agreed to meet Joe here and help with a few construction projects for the wedding, but he had a secret agenda. He needed to spend time with his brother. Face-to-face time. If he managed to talk some sense into him, all the better.

"I don't suppose Joe is here yet?" he asked Becky with elaborate casualness.

"No." She consulted a thick agenda book. "I have him arriving tomorrow morning, first thing. And Allie arriving the day of the wedding."

Perfect. If he could get Joe away from Allie's influence, his mission—to stop the wedding, or at least reschedule it until cooler heads prevailed—seemed to have a better chance of succeeding.

Drew liked to think he could read people—the woman in front of him being a case in point. But he had come away from his meeting with Allie Ambrosia feeling a disconcerting sense of not being able to read her at all.

Where's my brother? Drew had demanded.

Allie Ambrosia had blinked at him. *No need to make it sound like a kidnapping.*

Which, of course, was exactly what Drew had been feeling it was, and that Allie Ambrosia was solely responsible for the new Joe, who could hang up on his brother and then ignore all his attempts to get in touch with him.

"Allie Ambrosia is sensitive and brilliant and sweet."

Drew watched Becky with interest as the blaze of color deepened over her sunburn. She was going to rise to defend someone she perceived as the underdog, and that told him almost as much about her as the fact that she hailed from Moose Run, Michigan.

Drew was just not sure who would think of Allie Ambrosia as the underdog. He may have been frustrated about his inability to read his future sister-in-law, but neither *sensitive* nor *sweet* would have made his short list of descriptive adjectives. Though they probably would have for Becky, even after such a short acquaintance.

Allie? Brilliant, maybe. Though if she was it had not shown in her vocabulary. Still, he'd been aware of the possibility of great cunning. She had seemed to Drew to be able to play whatever role she wanted, the real person, whoever and whatever that was, hidden behind eyes so astonishingly emerald he'd wondered if she enhanced the color with contact lenses.

He'd come away from Allie frustrated. He had agreed to build some things for the damn wedding, hoping, he supposed, that this seeming capitulation to his brother's plans would open the door to communication between them and he could talk some sense into Joe.

He'd have his chance tomorrow. Today, he could unabashedly probe the secrets of the woman his brother had decided to marry.

"And you would know Allie is sensitive and brilliant and sweet, why?" he asked Becky, trying not to let on just how pleased he was to have found someone who actually seemed to know Allie.

"We went to school together."

Better still. Someone who knew Allie *before* she'd caught her big break playing Peggy in a sleeper of a movie called *Apple Mountain*.

"Allie Ambrosia grew up in Moose Run, Michigan?" He prodded her along. "That is not in the official biography."

He thought Becky was going to clam up, careful about saying anything about her boss and old school chum, but her need to defend won out.

"Her Moose Run memories may not be her fondest ones," Becky offered, a bit reluctantly.

"I must say Allie has come a long way from Moose Run," he said.

"How do you know? How well do you know Allie?"

"I admit I'm assuming, since I hardly know her at all," Drew said. "This is what I know. She's had a whirlwind relationship with my little brother, who is building a set on one of her movies. They've known each other weeks, not months. And suddenly they are getting married. It can't last, and this is an awful lot of money and time and trouble to go to for something that can't last."

"You're cynical," she said, as if that was a bad thing.

"We can't all come from Moose Run, Michigan."

She squinted at him, not rising to defend herself, but staying focused on him, which made him very uncomfortable. "You are really upset that they are getting married."

He wasn't sure he liked that amount of perception. He didn't say anything.

"Actually, I think you don't like weddings, period."

"What is this, a party trick? You can read my mind?" He intended it to sound funny, but he could hear a certain amount of defensiveness in his tone.

"So, it's true then."

"Big deal. Lots of men don't like weddings."

"Why is that?"

He frowned at her. He wanted to ferret out some facts about Allie, or talk about construction. He was comfortable talking about construction, even on an ill-conceived project like this. He was a problem solver. He was not comfortable discussing feelings, which an aversion to weddings came dangerously close to.

"They just don't like them," he said stubbornly. "Okay, I don't like them."

"I'm curious about who made you your brother's keeper," she said. "Shouldn't your parents be talking to him about this?"

"Our parents are dead."

When something softened in her face, he deliberately hardened himself against it.

"Oh," Becky said quietly, "I'm so sorry. So you, as older brother, are concerned, and at the same time have volunteered to help out. That's very sweet."

"Let's get something straight right now. There is nothing sweet about me."

"So why did you agree to help at all?"

He shrugged. "Brothers help each other."

Joe's really upset by your reaction to our wedding, Allie had told him. *If you agreed to head up the construction, he would see it was just an initial reaction of surprise and that of course you want what is best for your own brother.*

Oh, he wanted what was best for Joe, all right. Something must have flashed across Drew's face, because Becky's brow lowered.

"Are you going to try to stop the wedding?" she asked suspiciously.

Had he telegraphed his intention to Allie, as well? "Joe's all grown up, and capable of making up his own mind. But so am I. And it seems like a crazy, impulsive decision he's made."

"You didn't answer the question."

"You'd think he would have asked me what I thought," Drew offered grimly.

A certain measure of pain escaped in that statement, and so he frowned at Becky, daring her to give him sympathy.

Thankfully, she did not even try. "Is this why I can't have the pavilion? Are you trying to sabotage the whole thing?"

"No," he said curtly. "I'll do what I can to give my brother and his beloved a perfect day. If he comes to his senses before then—" He lifted a shoulder.

"If he changes his mind, that would be a great deal of time and money down the tubes," Becky said.

Drew lifted his shoulder again. "I'm sure you would still get paid."

"That's hardly the point!"

"It's the whole point of running a business." He glanced at her and sighed. "Please don't tell me you do it for love."

Love.

Except for what he felt for his brother, his world was comfortably devoid of that pesky emotion. He was sorry he'd even mentioned the word in front of Becky English.

CHAPTER THREE

"SINCE YOU BROUGHT it up," Becky said solemnly, "I got the impression from Allie that she and your brother are head over heels in love with one another."

"Humph." There was no question his brother was over the moon, way past the point where he could be counted on to make a rational decision. Allie was more difficult to interpret. Allie was an actress. She pretended for a living. It seemed to Drew his brother's odds of getting hurt were pretty good.

"Joe could have done worse," Becky said, quietly. "She's a beautiful, successful woman."

"Yeah, there's that."

"There's that cynicism again."

Cynical. Yes, that described Drew Jordan to an absolute T. And he liked being around people who were as hard-edged as him. Didn't he?

"Look, my brother is twenty-one years old. That's a little young to be making this kind of decision."

"You know, despite your barely contained scorn for Moose Run, Michigan, it's a traditional place where they love nothing more than a wedding. I've planned dozens of them."

Drew had to bite his tongue to keep from crushing her with a sarcastic *Dozens?*

"I've been around this for a while," she continued. "Take it from me. Age is no guarantee of whether a marriage is going to work out."

"He's known her about eight weeks, as far as I can tell!" He was confiding his doubts to a complete stranger, which was not like him. It was even more unlike him to be hoping this wet-behind-the-ears country girl from Moose Run, Michigan, might be able to shed some light on his brother's mysterious, flawed decision-making process. This was why he liked being around people as *not* sweet as himself. There was no probing of the secrets of life.

"That doesn't seem to reflect on how the marriage is going to work out, either."

"Well, what does then?"

"When I figure it out, I'm going to bottle it and sell it," she said. There was that earnestness again. "But I've planned the weddings of lots of young people who are still together. Young people have big dreams and lots of energy. You need that to buy your first house and have your first baby, and juggle three jobs and—"

"Baby?" Drew said, horrified. "Is she pregnant?" That would explain his brother's rush to the altar of love.

"I don't think so," Becky said.

"But you don't know for certain."

"It's none of my business. Or yours. But even if she is, lots of those kinds of marriages make it, too. I've planned weddings for people who have known each other for weeks, and weddings for people who have known each other for years. I planned one wedding for a couple who had lived together for sixteen years. They were getting a divorce six months later. But I've seen lots of marriages that work."

"And how long has your business been running?"

"Two years," she said.

For some reason, Drew was careful not to be quite as sarcastic as he wanted to be. "So, you've seen lots that work for two years. Two years is hardly a testament to a solid relationship."

"You can tell," she said stubbornly. "Some people are going to be in love forever."

Her tone sounded faintly wistful. Something uncomfortable shivered along his spine. He had a feeling he was looking at one of those forever kinds of girls. The kind who were not safe to be around at all.

Though it would take more than a sweet girl from Moose Run to penetrate the armor around his hard heart. He felt impatient with himself for the direction of his thoughts. Wasn't it proof that she was already penetrating something since they were having this discussion that had nothing to do with her unrealistic building plans?

Drew shook off the feeling and fixed Becky with a particularly hard look.

"Sheesh, maybe you are a member of the Cinderella club, after all."

"Despite the fact I run a company called Happily-Ever-After—"

He closed his eyes. "That's as bad as Moose Run."

"It is a great name for an event planning company."

"I think I'm getting a headache."

"But despite my company name, I have long since given up on fairy tales."

He opened his eyes and looked at her. "Uh-huh," he said, loading those two syllables with doubt.

"I have!"

"Lady, even before I heard the name of your company, I could tell that you have 'I'm waiting for my prince to come' written all over you."

"I do not."

"You've had a heartbreak."

"I haven't," she said. She was a terrible liar.

"Maybe it wasn't quite a heartbreak. A romantic disappointment."

"Now who is playing the mind reader?"

"Aha! I was right, then."

She glared at him.

"You'll get over it. And then you'll be in the prince market all over again."

"I won't."

"I'm not him, by the way."

"Not who?"

"Your prince."

"Of all the audacious, egotistical, ridiculous—"

"Just saying. I'm not anybody's prince."

"You know what? It is more than evident you could not be mistaken for Prince Charming even if you had a crown on your head and tights and golden slippers!"

Now that he'd established some boundaries, he felt he could tease her just a little. "Please tell me you don't like men who wear tights."

"What kind of man I like is none of your business!"

"Correct. It's just that we will be working in close proximity. My shirt has been known to come off. It has been known to make women swoon." He smiled.

He was enjoying this way more than he had a right

to, but it was having the desired effect, putting up a nice big wall between them, and he hadn't even had to barge in the construction material to do it.

"I'm not just *getting* a headache," she said. "I've had one since you marched through my door."

"Oh, great," he said. "There's nothing I like as much as a little competition. Let's see who can give who a bigger headache."

"The only way I could give you a bigger headache than the one you are giving me is if I smashed this lamp over your head."

Her hand actually came to rest on a rather heavy-looking brass lamp on the corner of her desk. It was evident to him that she would have loved to do just that if she wasn't such a prim-and-proper type.

"I'm bringing out the worst in you," he said with satisfaction. She looked at her hand, resting on the lamp, and looked so appalled with herself that Drew did the thing he least wanted to do. He laughed.

Becky snatched her hand back from the brass lamp, annoyed with herself, miffed that she was providing amusement for the very cocky Mr. Drew Jordan. She was not the type who smashed people over the head with lamps. Previously, she had not even been the type who would have ever thought about such a thing. She had dealt with some of the world's—or at least Michigan's—worst Bridezillas, and never once had she laid hand to lamp. It was one of the things she prided herself in. She kept her cool.

But Drew Jordan had that look of a man who could turn a girl inside out before she even knew what had hit her. He could make a woman who trusted her cool suddenly aware that fingers of heat were licking away inside her, begging for release. And it was disturbing that he knew it!

He was laughing at her. It was super annoying that instead of being properly indignant, steeling herself against attractions that he was as aware of as she was, she could not help but notice how cute he was when he laughed—that sternness stripped from his face, an almost boyish mischievousness lurking underneath.

She frowned at her computer screen, pretending she was getting down to business and that she had called up the weather to double-check his facts. Instead, she learned her head of construction was also the head of a multimillion-dollar Los Angeles development company.

The bride's future brother-in-law was not an out-of-work tradesman that Becky could threaten to fire. He ran a huge development company in California. No wonder he seemed to be impatient at being pressed into the service of his very famous soon-to-be sister-in-law.

No wonder he'd been professional enough to Google the weather. Becky wondered why she hadn't thought of doing that. It was nearly the first thing she did for every event.

It was probably because she was being snowed under by Allie's never-ending requests. Just now she was trying to find a way to honor Allie's casually thrown-out email, received that morning, which requested freshly planted lavender tulips—picture attached—to line the outdoor aisle she would walk down toward her husband-to-be.

Google, that knowledge reservoir of all things, told

Becky she could not have lavender tulips—or any kind of tulip for that matter—in the tropics in June.

What Google confirmed for her now was not the upcoming weather forecast or the impossibility of lavender tulips, but that Drew Jordan was used to million-dollar budgets.

Becky, on the other hand, had started shaking when she had opened the promised deposit check from Allie. Up until then, it had seemed to her that maybe she was being made the butt of a joke. But that check—made out to Happily-Ever-After—had been for more money than she had ever seen in her life.

With trembling fingers she had dialed the private cell number Allie had provided.

"Is this the budget?"

"No, silly, just the deposit."

"What exactly is your budget?" Becky had asked. Her voice had been shaking as badly as her fingers.

"Limitless," Allie had said casually. "And I fully intend to exceed it. You don't think I'm going to be out-done by Roland Strump's daughter, do you?"

"Allie, maybe you should hire whoever did the Strump wedding, I—"

"Nonsense. Have fun with it, for Pete's sake. Haven't you ever had fun? I hope you and Drew don't manage to bring down the mood of the whole wedding. Sour-pusses."

Sourpuss? She was studious to be sure, but sour? Becky had put down the phone contemplating that. Had she ever had fun? Even at Happily-Ever-After, planning fun events for other people was very serious business, indeed.

Well, now she knew who Drew was. And Allie had

been right when it came to him. He could definitely be a sourpuss! It was more worrying that he planned to take off his shirt. She had to get back to business.

"Mr. Jordan—"

"Drew is fine. And what should I call you?"

Barnum. "Becky is fine. We can't just throw a bunch of tables out on the front lawn as if this were the church picnic."

"We're back to that headache." His lips twitched. "I'm afraid my experience with church picnics has been limited."

Yes, it was evident he was all devilish charm and dark seduction, while it was written all over her that that was what she came from: church picnics and 4-H clubs, a place where the Fourth of July fireworks were *the* event of the year.

She shifted her attention to the second *no*. "And we absolutely need some sort of dance floor. Have you ever tried to dance on grass? Or sand?"

"I'm afraid," Drew said, "that falls outside of the realm of my experience, too. And you?"

"Oh, you know," she said. "We like to dust up our heels after the church picnic."

He nodded, as if that was more than evident to him and he had missed her sarcasm completely.

She focused on his third veto. She looked at her clumsy drawing of a small gazebo on the beach. She had envisioned Allie and Joe saying their vows under it, while their guests sat in beautiful lightweight chairs looking at them and the sea beyond them.

"And what's your complaint with this one?"

"I'll forgive you this oversight because of where you are from."

"Oversight?"

"I wouldn't really expect a girl from Michigan to have foreseen this. The *wedding*—" he managed to fill that single word with a great deal of contempt "—according to my notes, is supposed to take place at 4:00 p.m. on June third."

"Correct."

"If you Google the tide chart for that day, you'll see that your gazebo would have water lapping up to the third stair. I'm not really given to omens, but I would probably see that as one."

She was feeling very tired of Google, except in the context of learning about him. It seemed to her he was the kind of man who brought out the weakness in a woman, even one who had been made as cynical as she had been. Because she felt she could ogle him all day long. And he knew it, she reminded herself.

"So," she said, a little more sharply than intended, "what do you suggest?"

"If we scratch the pavilion for two hundred—"

"I can get more people to help you."

He went on as if she hadn't spoken. "I can probably build you a rudimentary gazebo at a different location."

"What about the dance floor?"

"I'll think about it."

He said that as if he were the boss, not her. From what she had glimpsed about him on the internet he was very used to being in charge. And he obviously knew his stuff, and was good with details. He had spotted the weather and the tides, after all. Really, she should be grateful. What if her bride had marched down her tulip-lined aisle—or whatever the aisle ended up being lined with—to a wedding gazebo that was slowly being swallowed by water?

It bothered her to even think it, but Drew Jordan was right. That would have been a terrible omen.

Still, gratitude was not what Becky felt. Not at all.

"You are winning the headache contest by a country mile," she told him.

"I'm no kind of expert on the country," he said, without regret, "but I am competitive."

"What did Allie tell you? Are you in charge of construction?"

"Absolutely."

He said it too quickly and with that self-assured smile of a man way too used to having his own way, particularly with the opposite sex.

"I'm going to have to call Allie and see what that means," Becky said, steeling herself against that smile. "I'm happy to leave construction to you, but I think I should have the final word on what we are putting up and where."

"I'm okay with that. As long as it's reasonable."

"I'm sure we define that differently."

He flashed his teeth at her again. "I'm sure we do."

"Would it help you do your job if I brought more people on-site? Carpenters and such?"

"That's a great idea, but I don't work with strangers. Joe and I have worked together a lot. He'll be here tomorrow."

"That wouldn't be very romantic, him building the stuff for his own wedding."

"Or you could see it as him putting an investment and some effort into his own wedding."

She sighed. "You want him here so you can try to bully him out of getting married."

"I resent the implication I would bully him."

But Becky was stunned to see doubt flash across those self-confident features. "He isn't talking to you, is he?" Becky guessed softly.

She could tell Drew was not accustomed to this level of perception. He didn't like it one little bit.

"I have one of my teams arriving soon. And Joe. I'm here a day early to do some initial assessments. What I need is for you to pick the site for the exchange of vows so that I can put together a plan. We don't have as much time as you think."

Which was truly frightening, because she did not think they had any time at all. Becky looked at her desk: flowers to be ordered, ceremony details to be finalized, accommodations to be organized, boat schedules, food, not just for the wedding feast, but for the week to follow, and enough staff to pull off pampering two hundred people.

"And don't forget fireworks," she added.

"Excuse me?"

"Nothing," she muttered. She did not want to be thinking of fireworks around a man like Drew Jordan. Her eyes drifted to his lips. If she were ever to kiss someone like that, it would be the proverbial fireworks. And he knew it, too. That was why he was smiling evilly at her!

Suddenly, it felt like nothing in the world would be better than to get outside away from this desk—and from him—and see this beautiful island. So far, she had mostly experienced it by looking out her office window.

The sun would be going down soon. She could find a place to hold the wedding and watch the sun go down.

"Okay," she said. "I'll find a new site. I'll let you know as soon as I've got it."

"Let's do it together. That might save us some grief."

She was not sure that doing anything with him was going to save her some grief. She needed to get away from him…and the thoughts of fireworks he had caused.

CHAPTER FOUR

"I'D PREFER TO do it on my own," Becky said, even though it seemed ungracious to say so. She felt a need to establish who was running the cir—show.

"But here's the problem," Drew said with annoying and elaborate patience.

"Yes?"

"You'll pick a site on your own, and then I'll go look at it and say no, and so then you'll pick another site on your own, and I'll go look at it and say no."

She scowled at him. "You're being unnecessarily negative."

He shrugged. "I'm just making the point that we could, potentially, go on like that endlessly, and there is a bit of a time crunch here."

"I think you just like using the word *no*," she said grumpily.

"Yes," he said, deadpan, as if he was not being deliberately argumentative now.

She should argue that she was quite capable of picking the site by herself and that she had no doubt her next selection would be fine, but her first choice was not exactly proof of that. And besides, then who would be the argumentative one?

"It's too late today," Drew decided. "Joe's coming in on the first flight. Why don't we pick him up and the three of us will pick a site that works for the gazebo?"

"Yes, that would be fine," she said, aware her voice was snapping with ill grace. Really, it was an opportunity. Tomorrow morning she would not scrape her hair back into a careless ponytail. She would apply makeup to hide how her fair skin, fresh out of a Michigan winter, was already blotchy from the sun.

Should she wear her meet-the-potential-client suit, a cream-colored linen by a famous designer? That would certainly make a better impression than shorty-shorts and a sleeveless tank that could be mistaken for underwear!

But the following morning it was already hot, and there was no dry cleaner on the island to take a sweat-drenched dress to.

Aware she was putting way too much effort into her appearance, Becky donned white shorts and a sleeveless sun-yellow shirt. She put on makeup and left her hair down. And then she headed out of her room.

She met Drew on the staircase.

He looked unreasonably gorgeous!

"Good morning," she said. She was stupidly pleased by how his eyes trailed to her hair and her faintly glossed lips.

He returned her greeting gruffly and then went down the stairs in front of her, taking them two at a time. But he stopped and held open the main door for her. They were hit by a wall of heat.

"It's going to be even hotter in two weeks," Drew

told her, when he watched her pause and draw in her breath on the top stair of the castle.

"Must you be so negative?"

"Pragmatic," he insisted. "Plus…"

"Don't tell me. I already know. You looked it up. That's how you know it will be even hotter in two weeks."

He nodded, pleased with himself.

"Keep it up," she warned him, "and you'll have to present me with the prize. A king-size bottle of headache relief."

They stood at the main door to the castle, huge half circles of granite forming a staircase down to a sparkling expanse of emerald lawn. The lawn was edged with a row of beautifully swaying palm trees, and beyond that was a crescent of powdery white sand beach.

"That beach looks so much less magical now that I know it's going to be underwater at four o'clock on June the third."

Drew glanced at Becky. She looked older and more sophisticated with her hair down and makeup on. She had gone from cute to attractive.

It occurred to Drew that Becky was the kind of woman who brought out things in a man that he would prefer to think he didn't have. Around a woman like this a man could find himself wanting to protect himself— and her—from disappointments. That's all he wanted for Joe, too, not to bully him but to protect him.

He'd hated that question, the one he hadn't answered. Had he bullied his brother? He hoped not. But the sad truth was Joe had been seven when Drew, seventeen, was appointed his guardian. Drew had floundered, in

way over his head, and he'd resorted to doing whatever needed to be done to get his little brother through
childhood.

No wonder his brother was so hungry for love that
he'd marry the first beautiful woman who blinked sideways at him.

Unless he could talk some sense into him. He cocked
his head. He was pretty sure he could hear the plane
coming.

"How hot is it supposed to be on June third?" she
asked. He could hear the reluctance to even ask in her
voice.

"You know that expression? Hotter than Hades—"

"Never mind. I get it. All the more reason that we
really need the pavilion," she said. "We'll need protection from the sun. I planned to have the tables running
this way, so everyone could just turn their heads and
see the ocean as the sun is going down. The head table
could be there, at the bottom of the stairs. Imagine the
bride and groom coming down that staircase to join
their guests."

Her voice had become quite dreamy. Had she really
tried to tell him she was not a romantic? He knew he'd
pegged it. She'd had some kind of setback in the romance department, but inside her was still a giddy girl
with unrealistic dreams about her prince coming. He
had to make sure she knew that was not him.

"Well, I already told you, you can't have that," he
said gruffly. He did not enjoy puncturing her dream as
much as he wanted to. He did not enjoy being mean as
much as he would have liked. He told himself it was
for her own good.

He was good at doing things for other people's own

good. You could ask Joe, though his clumsy attempts at parenting were no doubt part of why his brother was running off half-cocked to get married.

"I'm sure we can figure out something," Becky said of her pavilion dream.

"We? No, *we* can't."

This was better. They were going to talk about practicalities, as dream-puncturing as those could be!

The plane was circling now, and they moved toward the airstrip.

He continued, "What you're talking about is an open, expansive structure with huge unsupported spans. You'd need an architect and an engineer."

"I have a tent company I use at home," Becky said sadly, "but they are booked nearly a year in advance. I've tried a few others. Same story. Plus, the planes that can land here aren't big enough to carry that much canvas, and you have to book the supply barge. There's only one with a flat enough bottom to dock here. An unlimited budget can't get you what you might think."

"Unlimited?" He heard the horror in his voice.

She ignored him. "Are you sure I'd need an architect and an engineer, even for something so temporary?"

He slid her a look. She looked quite deflated by all this.

"Especially for something so temporary," he told her. "I'm sure the last thing Allie wants is to be making the news for the collapse of her wedding pavilion. I can almost see the headlines now. 'Three dead, one hundred and eighty-seven injured, event planner and building contractor missing.'"

He heard her little gasp and glanced at her. She was blushing profusely.

"Not missing like *that*," he said.

"Like what?" she choked.

"Like whatever thought is making you blush like that."

"I'm not blushing. The sun has this effect on me."

"Sheesh," he said, as if she had not denied the blush at all. "It's not as if I said that while catastrophe unfolded all around them, the event planner and the contractor went missing *together*."

"I said I wasn't blushing! I never would have thought about us together in any way." Her blush deepened.

He watched her. "You aren't quite the actress that your employer is."

"I am not thinking of us together," she insisted. Her voice was just a little shrill. He realized he quite enjoyed teasing her.

"No?" he said, silkily. "You and I seeking shelter under a palm frond while disaster unfolds all around us?"

Her eyes moved skittishly to his lips and then away. He took advantage of her looking away to study her lips in profile. They were plump little plums, ripe for picking. He was almost sorry he had started this. Almost.

"You're right. You are not a prince. You are evil," she decided, looking back at him. There was a bit of reluctant laughter lurking in her eyes.

He twirled an imaginary moustache. "Yes, I am. Just waiting for an innocent from Moose Run, Michigan, to cross my path so that in the event of a tropical storm, and a building collapse, I will still be entertained."

A little smile tugged at the lips he had just noticed were quite luscious. He was playing a dangerous game.

"Seriously," she said, and he had a feeling she was

the type who did not indulge in lighthearted banter for long, "Allie doesn't want any of this making the news. I'm sure she told you the whole wedding is top secret. She does not want helicopters buzzing her special day."

Drew felt a bit cynical about that. Anyone who wanted a top secret wedding did not invite two hundred people to it. Still, he decided, now might not be the best time to tell Becky a helicopter buzzing might be the least of her worries. When he'd left the States yesterday, all the entertainment shows had been buzzing with the rumors of Allie's engagement.

Was the famous actress using his brother—and everyone else, including small-town Becky English—to ensure Allie Ambrosia was front and center in the news just as her new movie was coming out?

Even though it went somewhat against his blunt nature, the thought that Becky might be being played made Drew soften his bad news a bit. "This close to the equator it's fully dark by six o'clock. The chance of heatstroke for your two hundred guests should be minimized by that."

They took a path through some dense vegetation. On the other side was the airstrip.

"Great," she said testily, though she was obviously relieved they were going to discuss benign things like the weather. "Maybe I can create a kind of 'room' feeling if I circle the area with torches and dress up the tables with linens and candles and flowers and hope for the best."

"Um, about the torches? And candles?" He squinted at the plane touching down on the runway.

"What?"

"According to Google, the trade winds seem to pick

up in the late afternoon. And early evening. Without any kind of structure to protect from the wind, I think they'll just blow out. Or worse."

"So, first you tell me I can't have a structure, and then you tell me all the problems I can expect because I don't have a structure?"

He shrugged. "One thing does tend to lead to another."

"If the wind is strong enough to blow out the candles, we could have other problems with it, too."

"Oh, yeah, absolutely. Tablecloths flying off tables. Women's dresses blowing up over their heads. Napkins catching fire. Flower arrangements being smashed. There's really a whole lot of things people should think about before planning their wedding on a remote island in the tropics."

Becky glared at him. "You know what? I barely know you and I hate you already."

He nodded. "I have that effect on a lot of people."

He watched the plane taxi toward them and grind to a halt in front of them.

"I'm sure you do," she said snippily.

"Does this mean our date under the palm frond is off?"

"It was never on!"

"You should think about it—the building collapsed, the tablecloths on fire, women's dresses blowing over their heads as they run shrieking…"

"Please stop."

But he couldn't. He could tell he very nearly had her where he wanted her. Why did he feel so driven to make little Miss Becky English angry? But also to make her laugh?

"And you and me under a palm frond, licking wedding cake off each other's fingers."

At first she looked appalled. But then a smile tickled her lips. And then she giggled. And then she was laughing. In a split second, every single thing about her seemed transformed. She went from plain to pretty.

Very pretty.

This was exactly what he had wanted: to glimpse what the cool Miss English would look like if she let go of control.

It was more dangerous than Drew had anticipated. It made him want to take it a step further, to make her laugh harder or to take those little lips underneath his and...

He reminded himself she was not the type of girl he usually invited out to play. Despite the fact she was being relied on to put on a very sophisticated event, there didn't seem to be any sophistication about her.

He had already figured out there was a heartbreak in her past. That was the only reason a girl as apple pie as her claimed to be jaundiced about romance. He could tell it wasn't just dealing with people's wedding insanity that had made her want to be cynical, even as it was all too evident she was not. He had seen the truth in the dreamy look when she had started talking about how she wanted it all to go.

He could tell by looking at her exactly what she needed, and it wasn't a job putting together other people's fantasies.

It was a husband who adored her. And three children. And a little house where she could sew curtains for the windows and tuck bright annuals into the flower beds every year.

It was whatever the perfect life in Moose Run, Michigan, looked like.

Drew knew he could never give her those things. Never. He'd experienced too much loss and too much responsibility in his life.

Still, there was one thing a guy as jaundiced as him did not want or need. To be stuck on a deserted island with a female whose laughter could turn her from a plain old garden-variety girl next door into a goddess in the blink of an eye.

He turned from her quickly and watched as the door of the plane opened. The crew got off, opened the cargo hold and began unloading stuff beside the runway.

He frowned. No Joe.

He took his phone out of his pocket and stabbed in a text message. He pushed Send, but the island did not have great service in all places. The message to his brother did not go through.

Becky was searching his face, which he carefully schooled not to show his disappointment.

"I guess we'll have to find that spot ourselves. Joe will probably come on the afternoon flight. Let's see what we can find this way."

Instead of following the lawn to where it dropped down to the beach, he followed it north to a line of palm trees. A nice wide trail dipped into them, and he took it.

"It's like jungle in here," she said.

"Think of the possibilities. Joe could swing down from a vine. In a loincloth. Allie could be waiting for him in a tree house, right here."

"No, no and especially no," she said.

He glanced behind him. She had stopped to look at

a bright red hibiscus. She plucked it off and tucked it behind her ear.

"In the tropics," he told her, "when you wear a flower behind your ear like that, it means you are available. You wouldn't want the cook getting the wrong idea."

She glared at him, plucked the flower out and put it behind her other ear.

"Now it means you're married."

"There's no winning, is there?" she asked lightly.

No, there wasn't. The flower looked very exotic in her hair. It made him very aware, again, of the enchantment of tropical islands. He turned quickly from her and made his way down the path.

After about five minutes in the deep shade of the jungle, they came out to another beach. It was exposed to the wind, which played in the petals of the flower above her ear, lifted her bangs from her face and pressed her shirt to her.

"Oh," she called, "it's beautiful."

She had to shout because unlike the beach the castle overlooked, this one was not in a protected cove.

It was a beautiful beach. A surfer would probably love it, but it would have to be a good surfer. There were rocky outcrops stretching into the water that looked like they would be painful to hit and hard to avoid.

"It's too loud," he said over the crashing of the waves. "They'd be shouting their vows."

He turned and went back into the shaded jungle. For some reason, he thought she would just follow him, and it took him a few minutes to realize he was alone.

He turned and looked. The delectable Miss Becky English was nowhere to be seen. He went back along the path, annoyed. Hadn't he made it perfectly clear they had time constraints?

When he got back out to the beach, his heart went into his throat. She had climbed up onto one of the rocky outcrops. She was standing there, bright as the sun in that yellow shirt, as a wave smashed on the rock just beneath her. Her hands were held out and her face lifted to the spray of white foam it created. With the flower in her hair, she looked more like a goddess than ever, performing some ritual to the sea.

Did she know nothing of the ocean? Of course she didn't. They had already established that. That, coming from Moose Run, there were things she could not know about.

"Get down from there," he shouted. "Becky, get down right now."

He could see the second wave building, bigger than the first that had hit the rock. The waves would come in sets. And the last wave in the set would be the biggest.

The wind swallowed his voice, though she turned and looked at him. She smiled and waved. He could see the surf rising behind her alarmingly. The second wave hit the rock. She turned away from him, and hugged herself in delight as the spray fell like thick mist all around her.

"Get away from there," he shouted. She turned and gave him a puzzled look. He started to run.

Becky had her back to the third wave when it hit. It hit the backs of her legs. Drew saw her mouth form a surprised O, and then her arms were flailing as she tried to regain her balance. The wave began pulling back, with at least as much force as it had come in with. It yanked her off the rock as if she were a rag doll.

CHAPTER FIVE

BECKY FELT THE shocked helplessness as her feet were jerked out from under her and she was swept off the rock. The water closed over her head and filled her mouth and nose. She popped back up like a cork, but her swimming skills were rudimentary, and she was not sure they would have helped her against the fury of the sea. She was being pulled out into what seemed to be an endless abyss. She tried frantically to swim back in toward shore. In seconds she was as exhausted as she had ever been.

I'm going to drown, she thought, stunned, choking on water and fear. How had this happened? One moment life had seemed so pleasant and beautiful and then…it was over.

Her life was going to be over. She waited, helplessly, for it to flash before her eyes. Instead, she found herself thinking that Drew had been right. It hadn't been a heartbreak. It had been a romantic disappointment. Ridiculous to think that right now, but on the other hand, right now seemed as good a time as any to be acutely and sadly aware of things she had missed.

"Hey!" His voice carried over the crashing of the sea. "Hang on."

Becky caught a glimpse of the rock she had fallen off. Drew was up there. And then she went under the water again.

When she surfaced, Drew was in the water, slashing through the roll of the waves toward her. "Don't panic," he called over the roar of the water pounding the rock outcropping.

She wanted to tell him it was too late for that. She was already panicked.

"Tread," he yelled. "Don't try to swim. Not yet. Look at my face. Nowhere else. Look at me."

Her eyes fastened on his face. There was strength and calm in his features, as if he did this every day. He was close to her now.

"I'm going to come to you," he shouted, "but you have to be calm first. If you panic, you will kill us both."

It seemed his words, and the utter strength and determination in his face, poured a honey of calm over her, despite the fact she was still bobbing like a cork in a ravaged sea. He seemed to see or sense the moment she stopped panicking, and he moved in close.

She nearly sobbed with relief when Drew reached out and touched her, then folded his arms around her and pulled her in tight to him. He was strong in the water—she suspected, abstractly, he was strong everywhere in his life—and she rested into his embrace, surrendering to his warmth. She could feel the power of him in his arms and where she was pressed into the wet slickness of his chest.

"Just let it carry you," he said. "Don't fight it anymore"

It seemed as if he could be talking about way more than water. It could be a message about life.

It seemed the water carried them out forever, but eventually it dumped them in a calmer place, just beyond where the waves began to crest. Becky could feel the water lose its grip on her, even as he refused to.

She never took her eyes off his face. Her mind seemed to grow calmer and calmer, even amused. If this was the last thing she would see, it told her, that wasn't so bad.

"Okay," he said, "can you swim?"

"Dog paddle." The water was not cold, but her voice was shaking.

"That will do. Swim that way. Do your best. I've got you if you get tired." He released her.

That way was not directly to the shore. He was asking her to swim parallel to the shore instead of in. But she tried to do as he asked. She was soon floundering, so tired she could not lift her arms.

"Roll over on your back," he said, and she did so willingly. His hand cupped her chin and she was being pulled through the water. He was an enormously strong swimmer.

"Okay, this is a good spot." He released her again and she came upright and treaded water. "Go toward shore. I've got you, I'm right with you."

She was scared to go back into the waves. It was too much. She was exhausted. But she glanced at his face once more and found her own courage there.

"Get on your tummy, flat as a board, watch for the next wave and ride it in. Watch for those rocks on the side."

She did as she was told. She knew she had no choice. She had to trust him completely. She felt the wave lift her up and drive her toward the shore at a stunning speed. And then it spit her out. She was lying in shallow water, but she could already feel the wave pulling at her, trying to drag her back in. She used what little strength she had left to scramble to her knees and crawl through the sugar pebbles of the sand.

Drew came and scooped her out of the water, lifted her to his chest and struggled out of the surf.

On the beach, above the foaming line of the ocean, he set her down on her back in the sun-warmed sand. For a moment she looked at the clear and endless blue of the sky. It was the very same sky it had been twenty minutes ago, but everything felt changed, some awareness sharp as glass within her. She rolled over onto her stomach and rested her head on her forearms. He flung himself onto the sand beside her, breathing hard.

"Did you just save my life?" she whispered. Her voice was hoarse. Her throat hurt from swallowing salt water. She felt drowsy and extraordinarily peaceful.

"You'll want to make sure this beach is posted before guests start arriving," he finally said, when he spoke.

"You didn't answer the question," she said, taking a peek at him over her folded arm. "Is that a habit with you?"

Drew didn't answer. She looked at him, feeling as if she was drinking him in, as if she could never get enough of looking at him. It was probably natural to feel that way after someone had just saved your life, and she did not try to make herself stop.

She was in a state of altered awareness. She could see the water beading on his eyelashes, and the sun streaming through his wet hair. She could see through his soaked shirt where it was plastered to his body.

"Did you just save my life?" she asked again.

"I think you Michigan girls should stay away from the ocean."

"Do you ever just answer a question, Drew Jordan? Did you save my life?"

He was silent again.

"You did," she finally answered for him.

She could not believe the gratitude she felt. To be alive. It was as if the life force was zinging inside her, making her every cell quiver.

"You risked yourself for me. I'm nearly a complete stranger."

"No, you're not. Winning the headache competition, by the way."

"By a country mile?"

"Oh, yeah."

"That was incredibly heroic." She was not going let him brush it off, though he was determined to.

"Don't make it something it wasn't. I'm nobody's hero."

Just like he had insisted earlier he was nobody's prince.

"Well," she insisted, "you're mine."

He snorted, that sexy, cynical sound he made that was all his own and she found, right now, lying here in the sand, alive, so aware of herself and him, that she liked that sound very much, despite herself.

"I've been around the ocean my whole life," he told her grimly. "I grew up surfing some pretty rough water. I knew what I was doing. Unlike you. That was incredibly stupid."

In her altered state, she was aware that he thought he could break the bond that had been cementing itself into place between them since the moment he had entered the water to rescue her.

"Life can change in a blink," he said sternly. "It can be over in a blink."

He was lecturing her. She suddenly *needed* him to know she could not let him brush it off like that. She needed him to know that the life force was flowing through her. She had an incredible sense of being alive.

"You were right," she said, softly.

There was that snort again. "Of course I'm right. You don't go climbing up on rocks when the surf is that high."

"Not about that. I mean, okay, about that, too, but I wasn't talking about that."

"What were you talking about?"

"It wasn't a heartbreak," Becky said. "It was a romantic disappointment."

"Huh?"

"That's what I thought of when I went into the water. I thought my whole life would flash before my eyes, but instead I thought of Jerry."

"Look, you're obviously in shock and we need to—"

"He was my high school sweetheart. We'd been together since I was seventeen. I'd always assumed we were going to get married. Everybody in the whole town thought we would get married. They called us Salt and Pepper."

"You know what? This will keep. I have to—"

"It won't keep. It's important. I have to say it before I forget it. Before this moment passes."

"Oh, sheesh," he said, his tone indicating he wanted nothing more than for this moment to pass.

"I wanted that. I wanted to be Salt and Pepper, *for-*

ever. My parents had split up the year before. It was awful. My dad owned a hardware store. One of his clerks. And him."

"Look, Becky, you are obviously rattled. You don't have to tell me this."

She could no more have stopped herself from telling him than she could have stopped those waves from pounding on the shore.

"They had a baby together. Suddenly, they were the family we had always been. That we were supposed to be. It was horrible, seeing them all over town, looking at each other. Pushing a baby carriage. I wanted it back. I wanted that feeling of being part of something back. Of belonging."

"Aw, Becky," he said softly. "That sucks. Really it does, but—"

But she had to tell all of it, was compelled to. "Jerry went away to school. My mom didn't have the money for college, and it seemed my dad had new priorities.

"I could see what the community needed, so I started my event company."

"Happily-Ever-After," he said. "Even though you had plenty of evidence of the exact opposite."

"It was way more successful than I had thought it could be. It was way more successful than Jerry thought it could be, too. The more successful I became, the less he liked me."

"Okay. Well. Some guys are like that."

"He broke up with me."

"Yeah, sorry, but now is not the time—"

"This is the reason it's important for me to say it right now. I understand something I didn't understand before. I thought my heart was broken. It is a terrible thing to suffer the humiliation of being ditched in a small town. It was a double humiliation for me. First my dad, and then this. But out there in the water, I felt glad. I felt if I had married him, I would have missed something. Something essential."

"Okay, um——"

"A grand passion."

He said a word under his breath that they disapproved of in Moose Run, Michigan.

"Salt and pepper?" She did a pretty good imitation of his snort. "Why settle for boring old salt and pepper when the world is full of so many glorious flavors?"

"Look, I think you've had a pretty bad shake-up. I don't have a clue what you are talking about, so——"

She knew she was making Drew Jordan wildly uncomfortable, but she didn't care. She planned to make him more uncomfortable yet. She leaned toward him. He stopped talking and watched her warily.

She needed to know if the life force was as intense in him right now as it was in her. She needed to take advantage of this second chance to be alive, to really live.

She touched Drew's back through the wetness of his shirt, and felt the sinewy strength there. The strength that had saved her.

She leaned closer yet. She touched her forehead to his, as if she could make him *feel* what was going on inside her, since words could not express it. He had a chance to move away from her. He did not. He was as caught in what was unfolding as she had been in the wave.

And then, she touched her lips to his, delicately, *needing* the connection to intensify.

His lips tasted of salt and strength and something

more powerful and more timeless than the ocean. That desire that people had within them, not just to live, but to go on.

For a moment, Drew was clearly stunned to find her lips on his. But then, he seemed to get whatever she was trying to tell him, in this primal language that seemed the only thing that could express the celebration of all that lived within her.

His lips answered hers. His tongue chased the ridges of her teeth, and then probed, gently, ever so gently...

It was Becky's turn to be stunned. It was everything she had hoped for. It was everything she had missed.

No, it was *more* than what she had hoped for, and more than what she could have ever imagined. A kiss was not simply a brushing of lips. No! It was a journey, it was a ride on pure energy, it was a connection, it was a discovery, it was an intertwining of the deepest parts of two people, of their souls.

Drew stopped kissing her with such abruptness that she felt forlorn, like a blanket had been jerked from her on a freezing night. He said Moose Run's most disapproved-of word again.

She *liked* the way he said that word, all naughty and nasty.

He found his feet and leaped up, staring down at her. He raked a hand through his hair, and water droplets scattered off his crumpled hair, sparkling like diamonds in the tropical heat. His shirt, crusted in golden sand, was clinging to his chest.

"Geez," he said. "What was that about?"

"I don't know," she said honestly. *But I liked it.*

"A girl like you does not kiss a guy like me!"

She could ask what he meant by a girl like her, but

she already knew that he thought she was small town and naive and hopelessly out of her depth, and not just in the ocean, either. What she wanted to know was what the last half of that sentence meant.

"What do you mean a guy like you?" she asked. Her voice was husky from the salt and from something else. Desire. Desire was burning like a white-hot coal in her belly. It was brand-new, it was embarrassing and it was wonderful.

"Look, Becky, I'm the kind of guy your mother used to warn you about."

Woo-hoo, she thought, but she didn't dare say it. Instead, she said, "The kind who would jump in the water without a thought for his own safety to save someone else?"

"Not that kind!"

She could point out to him that he obviously *was* that kind, and that the facts spoke for themselves, but she probed the deeper part of what was going on.

"What kind of guy then?" she asked, gently curious.

"Self-centered. Commitment-phobic. Good-time Charlie. Confirmed bachelor. They write whole articles about guys like me in your bridal magazines. And not about how to catch me, either. How to give a guy like me a wide berth."

"Just in case you didn't listen to your mother's warnings," she clarified.

He glanced at her. She bit her lip and his gaze rested there, hot with memory, until he seemed to make himself look away.

"I wouldn't have pictured you as any kind of expert about the content of bridal magazines," she said.

"That is not the point!"

"It was just a kiss," she pointed out mildly, "not a posting of the banns."

"You're in shock," he said.

If she was, she hoped she could experience it again, and soon!

CHAPTER SIX

DREW LOOKED AT Becky English. Sprawled out, belly down in the sand, she looked like a drowned rat, her hair plastered to her head, her yellow shirt plastered to her lithe body, both her shirt and her white shorts transparent in their wetness. For a drowned rat, and for a girl from Moose Run, Michigan, she had on surprisingly sexy underwear.

She looked like a drowned rat, and she was a small-town girl, but she sure as hell did not kiss like either one of those things. There had been nothing sweet or shy about that kiss!

It had been hungry enough to devour him.

But, Drew told himself sternly, she was exceedingly vulnerable. She was obviously stunned from what had just happened to her out there at the mercy of the ocean. It was possible she had banged her head riding that final wave in. The blow might have removed the filter from her brain that let her know what was, and what wasn't, appropriate.

But good grief, that kiss. He had to make sure nothing like that ever happened again! How was he going to be able to look at her without recalling the sweet, salty taste of her mouth? Without recalling the sweet welcome? Without recalling the flash of passion, the pull of which was at least as powerful as those waves?

"Becky," he said sternly, "don't make me your hero. I've been cast in that role before, and I stunk at it."

Drew had been seventeen when he became a parent to his brother. He had a sense of having grown up too fast and with too heavy a load. He was not interested in getting himself back into a situation where he was responsible for someone else's happiness and well-being. He didn't feel the evidence showed he had been that good at it.

"It was just a kiss," she said again, a bit too dreamily.

It wasn't just a kiss. If it had been just a kiss he would feel nothing, the same as he always did when he had just a kiss. He wouldn't be feeling this need to set her straight.

"When were you cast in that role before? How come you stank at it?" she asked softly. He noticed that, impossibly, the flower had survived in her hair. Its bright red petals were drooping sadly, kissing the tender flesh of her temple.

"This is not the time or the place," he said curtly before, in this weakened moment, in this contrived atmosphere of closeness, he threw himself down beside her, and let her save him, the way he had just saved her.

"Are you hurt?" he asked, cold and clinical. "Any bumps or bruises? Did you hit your head?"

Thankfully, she was distracted, and considered his question with an almost comical furrowing of her brow.

"I don't think I hit my head, but my leg hurts," she decided. "I think I scraped it on a rock coming in."

She rolled onto her back and then struggled to sit up. He peered over her shoulder. There was six inches of scrapes on the inside of her thigh, one of the marks looked quite deep and there was blood clumping in the sand that clung to it.

What was wrong with him? The first thing he should have done was check for injuries.

He stripped off his wet shirt and got down beside her. This was what was wrong with him. He was way too aware of her. The scent of the sea was clinging to her body, a body he was way too familiar with after having dragged her from the ocean and then accepted the invitation of her lips.

Becky was right. There was something exhilarating about snatching life back out of the jaws of death. That's why he was so aware of her on every level, not thinking with his customary pragmatism.

He brushed the sand away from her wound. He should have known touching the inner thigh of a girl like Becky English was going to be nothing like a man might have expected.

"Ow," she said, and her fingers dug into his shoulder and then lingered there. "Oh, my," she breathed. "You did warn me what would happen if you took your shirt off."

"I was kidding," he said tersely.

"No, you weren't. You were warning me off."

"How's that working for you, Drew?" he muttered to himself. He cleaned the sand away from her wound as best he could, then wrapped it in his soaked shirt.

She sighed with satisfaction like the geeky girl who had just gotten all the words right at the spelling bee. "Women adore you."

"Not ones as smart as you," he said. "Can you stand? We have to find a first aid kit. I think that's just a superficial scrape, but it's bleeding quite a lot and we need to get it looked after."

He helped her to her feet, still way too aware, steeling himself against the silky resilience of her skin. She swayed against him. Her wet curves were pressed into him, and her chin was pressed sharply into his chest as she looked up at him with huge, unblinking eyes.

Had he thought, just an hour ago, her eyes were ordinary brown? They weren't. They were like melted milk chocolate, deep and rich and inviting.

"You were right." She giggled. "I'm swooning."

"Let's hope it's not from blood loss. Can you walk?"

"Of course."

She didn't move.

He sighed and scooped her up, cradling her to his chest, one arm under her knees, the other across her back. She was lighter than he could have believed, and her softness pressed into him was making him way more vulnerable than the embraces of women he'd known who had far more in the curvy department.

"You're very masterful," she said, snuggling into him.

"In this day and age how can that be a good thing?"

"It's a secret longing."

He did not want to hear about her secret longings!

"If you don't believe me, read—"

"Stop it," he said grimly.

"I owe you my life."

"I said stop it."

"You are not the boss over me."

"That's what I was afraid of."

He carried her back along the path. She was small and light and it took no effort at all. At the castle, he found the kitchen, an enormous room that looked like the kind of well-appointed facility one would expect to find in a five-star hotel.

"Have you got a first aid attendant here?" Drew asked one of the kitchen staff, who went and fetched the chef.

The chef showed him through to an office adjoining the kitchen, and Drew settled Becky in a chair. The chef sent in a young man with a first aid kit. He was slender and golden-skinned with dark, dark hair and almond-shaped eyes that matched.

"I am Tandu," he said. "I am the medical man." His accent made it sound as if he had said *medicine man.*

Relived that he could back off from more physical contact with the delectable Miss Becky, Drew motioned to where she sat.

Tandu set down his first aid kit and crouched down in front of her. He carefully unwrapped Drew's wet shirt from her leg. He stared at Becky's injury for a moment, scrambled to his feet, picked up the first aid kit and thrust it at Drew.

"I do not do blood."

"What kind of first aid attendant doesn't—?"

But Tandu had already fled.

Drew, even more aware of her now that he had nearly escaped, went and found a pan of warm water, and then cleaned and dressed her wound, steeling himself to be as professional as possible.

Becky stared down at the dark head of the man kneeling at her feet. He pressed a warm, wet cloth against the tender skin of her inner thigh, and she gasped at the sensation that jolted through her like an electric shock.

He glanced up at her, then looked back to his task quickly. "Sorry," he muttered. "I will try to make this as painless as possible."

Despite the fact his touch was incredibly tender—or maybe because of it—it was one of the most deliciously painful experiences of Becky's life. He carefully cleaned the scrapes, dabbed an ointment on them and then wound clean gauze around her leg.

She could feel a quiver within her building. There was going to be an earthquake if he didn't finish soon! She longed to reach out and touch his hair, to brush the salt and sand from it. She reached out.

A pan dropped in the kitchen, and she felt reality crashing back in around her. She snatched her hand back, just as Drew glanced up.

"Are you okay?"

"Sure," she said shakily, but she really wasn't. What she felt like was a girl who had been very drunk, and who had done all kinds of uninhibited and crazy things, and was now coming to her senses.

She had kissed Drew Jordan shamelessly. She had shared all her secrets with him. She had blabbered that he was masterful, as if she enjoyed such a thing! Now she had nearly touched his hair, as if they were lovers instead of near strangers!

Okay, his hand upon her thigh was obviously creating confusion in the more primal cortexes of her brain, but she had to pull herself together.

"There," he said, rocking back on his heels and studying the bandage around her thigh, "I think—"

She didn't let him finish. She shot to her feet, gazed down at her bandaged thigh instead of at him. "Yes, yes, perfect," she said. She sounded like a German en-

gineer approving a mechanical drawing. Her thigh was
tingling unmercifully, and she was pretty sure it was
from his touch and not from the injury.

"I have to get to work," she said in a strangled voice.

He stood up. "You aren't going to work. You're going
to rest for the afternoon."

"But I can't. I—"

"I'm telling you, you need to rest."

She thought, again, of telling him he was masterful. Good grief, she could feel the blush rising up her
cheeks. She had probably created a monster.

In him and in herself.

"Go to bed," he said. Drew's voice was as caressing
as his hand had been, and just as seductive. "Just for
what is left of the afternoon. You'll be glad you did."

You did not discuss bed with a man like this! And
especially not after he had just performed intimate rit-
uals on your thigh! Particularly not after you had noticed his voice was seduction itself, all deep and warm
and caressing.

You did not discuss bed with a man like this once
you had come to your senses. She opened her mouth
to tell him she would decide for herself what needed to
be done. It would not involve the word *bed*. But before
she could speak, he did.

"I'll go scout a spot for the wedding. Joe will be here
in a while. By the time you wake up, we'll have it all
taken care of."

All her resolve to take back the reins of her own life
dissolved, instantly, like sugar into hot tea.

It felt as if she was going to start crying. When was
the last time anything had been taken care of for her?
After her father had left, her poor shattered mother had

absconded on parenting. It felt as if Becky had been the one who looked after everything. Jerry had seemed to like her devoting herself to organizing his life. Even her career took advantage of the fact that Becky English was the one who looked after things, who tried valiantly to fix all and to achieve perfection. She took it all on… until the weight of it nearly crushed her.

Where had that thought come from? She *loved* her job. Putting together joyous and memorable occasions for others had soothed the pain of her father's abandonment, and had, thankfully, been enough to fill her world ever since the defection of Jerry from her personal landscape.

Or had been enough until less than twenty-four hours ago, when Drew Jordan had showed up in her life and showed her there was still such a thing as a hero.

She turned and fled before she did something really foolish. Like kissing him again.

Becky found that as much as she would have liked to rebel against his advice, she had no choice but to take it. Clear of the kitchen, her limbs felt like jelly, heavy and nearly shaking with exhaustion and delayed reaction to all the unexpected adventures of the day. It took every bit of remaining energy she had to climb the stone staircase that led to the wing of the castle with her room in it.

She went into its cool sanctuary and peeled off her wet clothes. It felt like too much effort to even find something else to put on. She left the clothes in a heap and crept under the cool sheets of the welcoming bed. Within seconds she was fast asleep.

She dreamed that someone was knocking on her door, and when she went to answer it, Drew Jordan was on the other side of it, a smile of pure welcome on his face. He reached for her, he pulled her close, his mouth dropped over hers...

Becky started awake. She was not sure what time it was, though the light suggested early evening, which meant she had frittered away a whole precious afternoon sleeping.

She wanted to leap from bed, but her body would not let her. She felt, again, like the girl who had had too much to drink. She tested each of her limbs. It was official. Her whole body hurt. Her head hurt. Her mouth and throat felt raw and dry. But mostly, she felt deeply ashamed. She had lost control, and she hated that.

Her door squeaked open.

"How you doing?"

She shot up in bed, pulled the sheet more tightly around herself. "What are you doing here?"

"I knocked. When there was no answer, I thought I'd better check on you. You slept a long time."

Drew Jordan looked just as he had in the dream—gorgeous. Though in real life there was no expression of tender welcome on his face. It did not look like he was thinking about sweeping her into his big strong arms.

In fact, he slipped into the room, but rested himself against the far wall—as far away from her as possible—those big, strong arms folded firmly across his chest. He was wearing a snowy-white T-shirt that showed off the sun-bronzed color of his arms, and khaki shorts that showed off the long, hard muscle of equally sun-bronzed legs.

"A long time?" She found her cell phone on the bedside table. "It's only five. That's not so bad."

"Um, maybe you should have a look at the date on there."

She frowned down at her phone. Her mouth fell open. "What? I slept an entire day? But I couldn't have! That's impossible."

She started to throw back the covers, then remembered she had slipped in between the sheets naked. She yanked them up around her chin.

"It was probably the best thing you could do. Your body knows what it needs."

She looked up at him. Her body, treacherous thing, did indeed know what it needed! And all of it involved him.

"If you would excuse me," she said, "I really need—"

Now her brain, treacherous thing, silently screamed *you*.

"Are you okay?"

No! It simply was not okay to be this aware of him, to yearn for his touch and his taste.

"I'm fine. Did your brother come?" she asked, desperate to distract him from her discomfort, and from the possibility of him discerning what was causing it.

"Nope. I can't seem to reach him on my phone, either."

"Oh, Drew," she said softly.

Her tone seemed to annoy him. "You don't really look fine," he decided.

"Okay, I'm not fine. I don't have time to sleep away a whole day. Despite all that rest, I feel as if I've been through the spin cycle of a giant washing machine. I hurt everywhere, worse than the worst hangover ever."

"You've had a hangover?" He said this with insulting incredulousness.

"Of course I have. Living in Moose Run isn't like taking vows to become a nun, you know."

"You would be wasted as a nun," he said, and his gaze went to her lips before he looked sharply away.

"Let's talk about that," she said.

"About you being wasted as a nun?" he asked, looking back at her, surprised.

"About the fact you think you would know such a thing about me. I don't normally act like that. I would never, under ordinary circumstances, kiss a person the way I kissed you. Naturally, I'm mortified."

He lifted an eyebrow.

"There was no need to throw myself at you, no matter how grateful and discombobulated I was."

His lips twitched.

"It's not funny," she told him sternly. "It's embarrassing."

"It's not your wanton and very un-nun-like behavior I was smiling about."

"Wanton?" she squeaked.

"It was the fact you used *discombobulated* in a sentence. I can't say as I've ever heard that before."

"Wanton?" she squeaked again.

"Sorry. Wanton is probably overstating it."

"Probably?"

"We don't all have your gift for picking exactly the right word," he said. He lifted a shoulder. "People do weird things when they are in shock. Let's move past it, okay?"

Actually, she would have preferred to find out exactly what he meant by wanton—it had been a little kiss really, it didn't even merit the humiliation she was feeling about it—but she didn't want to look like she was unwilling to move past it.

"Okay," she said grudgingly. "Though just for the

record, I want you to know I don't like masterful men. At all."

"No secret longing?"

He was teasing her! There was a residue of weakness in her, because she liked it, but it would be a mistake to let him know her weaknesses.

"As you have pointed out," Becky said coolly, "I was in shock. I said and did things that were completely alien to my nature. Now, let's move past it."

Something smoky happened to his eyes. His gaze stopped on her lips. She had the feeling he would dearly like to prove to her that some things were not as alien to her nature as she wanted them both to believe.

But he fended off the temptation, with apparent ease, pushing himself away from the wall and heading back for the door. "You have one less thing to worry about. I think I have the pavilion figured out."

"Really?" She would have leaped up and gave him a hug, except she was naked underneath the sheet, he already thought she was wanton enough, and she was not exposing anything to him, least of all not her longing to let other people look after things for a change. And to feel his embrace once more, his hard, hot muscles against her naked flesh.

"You do?" she squeaked, trying to find a place to put her gaze, anywhere but his hard, hot muscles.

"I thought about what you said, about creating an illusion. I started thinking about driving some posts, and suspending fabric from them. Something like a canopy bed."

She squinted at him. That urge to hold him, to feel him, to touch him, was there again, stronger. It was because he was looking after things, taking on a part of the burden without being asked. It was because he had listened to her.

Becky English, lying there in her bed, naked, with her sheet pulled up around her chin, studied her ceiling, so awfully aware that a woman could fall for a guy like him before she even knew what had happened to her.

CHAPTER SEVEN

THANKFULLY FOR BECKY, Drew Jordan had already warned her about guys like him.

"What does a confirmed bachelor know about canopy beds?" she said, keeping her gaze on the ceiling and her tone deliberately light. "No, never mind. I don't want to know. I think I'm still slightly discombobulated."

"Admit it."

She glanced over at him just as he grinned. His teeth were white and straight. He looked way too handsome. She returned her gaze to the ceiling. "I just did. I'm still slightly discombobulated."

"Not that! Admit it's brilliant."

She couldn't help but smile. And look at him again. "It is. It's brilliant. It will create that illusion of a room, and possibly provide some protection from the sun if we use fabric as a kind of ceiling. It has the potential to be exceedingly romantic, too. Which is why I'm surprised you came up with it."

"Hey, nobody is more surprised than me. Sadly, after traipsing all over the island this afternoon, I still haven't found a good site for the ceremony. But you might as well come see what's going on with the pavilion."

She should not appear too eager. But really? Pretending just felt like way too much effort. She would have to chalk it up to her near drowning and the other rattling events of the day. "Absolutely. Give me five minutes."

"Sure. I'll meet you on the front stairs."

Of course, it took Becky longer than five minutes. She had to shower off the remains of her adventure. She had sand in places she did not know sand could go. Her hair was destroyed. Her leg was a mess and she had to rewrap it after she was done. She had faint bruising appearing in the most unlikely places all over her body.

She put on her only pair of long pants—as uninspiring as they were in a lightweight grey tweed—and a long-sleeved shirt in a shade of hot pink that matched some of the flowers that bloomed in such abundance on this island. Her outfit covered the worst of the damage to her poor battered body, but there was nothing she could do about the emotional battering she was receiving. And it wasn't his fault. Drew Jordan was completely oblivious to the effect he was having on her.

Or accustomed to it!

Becky dabbed on a bit of makeup to try to hide the crescent moons from under her eyes. She looked exhausted. How was that possible after nearly twenty-four hours of sleep? At the last minute, she just touched a bit of gloss to her lips. It wasn't wrong to want him to look at them, but she hoped she would not be discombobulated enough to offer them to him again anytime in the near future.

"Or any future!" she told herself firmly.

She had pictured Drew waiting impatiently for her, but when she arrived at the front step, he had out a can of spray paint and was marking big X's on the grassy lawn in front of the castle.

Just when she was trying not to think of kisses anymore. What was this clumsy artwork on the lawn all about? An invitation? A declaration of love? A late Valentine?

"Marking where the posts should go," he told her, glancing toward her and then looking back at what he was doing. "Can you come stand right here and hold the tape measure?"

So much for a declaration of love! Good grief. She had always harbored this secret and very unrealistic side. She thought Jerry had cured her of her more fantastic romantic notions, but no, some were like little seeds inside her, waiting for the first hint of water and sun to sprout into full-fledged fairy tales. Being rescued from certain death by a very good-looking and extremely competent man who had so willingly put his own life on the line for her had obviously triggered her most fanciful longings.

She just needed to swat herself up the side of the head with the facts. She and Drew Jordan barely knew one another, and before she was swept off the rock they had been destined to butt heads.

She had to amend that: she barely knew Drew Jordan, but he knew her better than he should because she had blurted out her whole life story in a moment of terrible weakness. It was just more evidence that she must have hit her head somewhere in that debacle. Except for the fact she was useful for holding the tape measure, he hardly seemed aware that she was there.

Finally, he rolled up the tape measure. "What do you think?"

His X's formed a large rectangle. She could picture it already with a silken canopy and the posts swathed in fabric. She could picture the tables and the candles, and music and a beautiful bride and groom.

"I think it's going to be perfect," she breathed. And for the first time since she had taken on this job, she felt like maybe it would be.

How much of that had to do with the man who was, however reluctantly, helping her make it happen?

"Don't get your hopes up too high," he said. "Perfection is harder to achieve than you think. And we still have the evening tropical breezes to contend with. And I haven't found a ceremony site. It could go sideways yet."

"Especially if you talk to your brother?"

He rolled his shoulders. "There doesn't seem to be much chance of that happening. But there are a lot of things that could go sideways before the big day."

Yes, she had seen in recent history how quickly things could go sideways. In fact, when she looked at him, she was pretty sure Drew Jordan was the kind of man who could make your whole life go sideways with no effort on his part at all.

"Let's go see if we can find a place for the ceremony."

She *had* to go with him. It was her job. But tropical breezes seemed to be the least of her problems at the moment.

"I should be getting danger pay," she muttered to herself.

"Don't worry, I won't be letting you anywhere near any rocks."

No sense clarifying with him that was not where the danger she was worried about was coming from. Not at all.

They were almost at the edge of the lawn when a voice stopped them.

"Miss Becky. Mr. Drew."

They turned to see Tandu struggling across the lawn with a huge wicker basket. "So sorry, no good with blood. Take you to place for wedding vow now."

"Oh, did you tell him we were looking for a new ceremony site?" Becky asked. "That was smart."

"Naturally, I would like to take credit for being smart, but I didn't tell him. They must do weddings here all the time. He's used to this."

"Follow, follow," Tandu ordered.

They fell into step behind him, leaving the lawn and entering the deep, vibrant green of the jungle forest. Birds chattered and the breeze lifting huge leaves made a sound, too.

"Actually, the owner of the island told me they had hosted some huge events here, but never a wedding," Becky told Drew. "He's the music mogul, Bart Lung. He's a friend of Allie's. He's away on business but he'll be back for the wedding. He's very excited about it."

"Are you excited about meeting him?"

"I guess I hadn't really thought about it. We better catch up to Tandu, he's way ahead of us."

Drew contemplated what had just happened with a trace of self-loathing.

Are you excited about meeting him? As bad as asking the question was how much he had liked her answer. She genuinely seemed not to have given a thought to meeting Bart Lung.

But what had motivated Drew to ask such a question? Surely he hadn't been feeling a bit threatened about

Becky meeting the famously single and fabulously wealthy record broker? He couldn't possibly have felt the faintest little prickle of...jealousy.

He never felt jealous. He'd had women he had dated who had tried to make him jealous, and he'd been annoyed by how juvenile that felt. But at the heart of it, he knew they had wanted him to show what he couldn't: that he cared.

But he'd known from the moment she had instigated that kiss that Becky English was different from what his brother liked to call the rotating door of women in his life. The chemistry between them had been unexpected, but Drew had had chemistry before. He wasn't sure exactly what it was about the cheerleader-turned-event-planner that intrigued him, but he knew he had to get away from it.

Which was exactly why he had marched up to her room. He had two reasons, and two reasons only, to interact with her: the pavilion and the ceremony site. He'd promised his brother and Becky his help, and once the planning for his assigned tasks was solidly in place, he could minimize his interactions with her. He was about to get very busy with construction. That would leave much less time for contemplating the lovely Miss English.

"I hate to say it," he told Becky, looking at Tandu's back disappearing down a twisting path in front of them, "but I've already been over this stretch of the island. There is no—"

"This way, please." Tandu had stopped and was holding back thick jungle fronds. "Path overgrown a bit. I will tell gardening staff. Important for all to be ready for big day, eh?"

It was just a short walk, and the path opened onto a beautiful crescent of beach. Drew studied it from a construction point of view. He could see the high tide line, and it would be perfect for building a small pavilion and setting up chairs for the two hundred guests. Three large palms grew out of the center of the beach, their huge leathery leaves shading almost the entire area.

Becky, he could see, was looking at it from a far less practical standpoint than he was. She turned to look at him. Her eyes were shiny with delight, and those little plump lips were curved upward in the nicest smile.

Task completed! Drew told himself sternly. Pavilion, check. Wedding location, check. Missing brother...well, that had nothing to do with her. He had to get away from her—and her plump little lips—and *stay* away from her.

"It's perfect," he said. "Do you agree?"

She turned those shining eyes to him. "Agree?" she said softly. "Have you ever seen such a magical place in your whole life?"

He looked around with magic in mind rather than construction. He was not much of a magic kind of person, but he supposed he had not seen a place quite like this before. The whole beach was ringed with thick shrubs with dark green foliage. Tucked in amongst the foliage was an abundance of pale yellow and white flowers the size of cantaloupes. The flowers seemed to be emitting a perfume that was sweet and spicy at the same time. Unfortunately, that made him think of her lips again.

He glared at the sand, which was pure white and finer than sugar. They were in a cove of a small bay, and the water was striped in aqua shades of turquoise, all the way out to a reef, where the water turned dark navy blue, and the waves broke, white-capped, over rocks.

"Well," he said, "I'll just head back."

"Do you ever just answer a question?"

"Sit, sit," Tandu said from behind them.

Drew swung around to look at him. While he had been looking out toward the sea, Tandu had emptied the wicker basket he carried. There was a blanket set up in the sand, and laid out on it was a bottle of wine, beaded with sweat, two wineglasses and two plates. There was a platter of blackened chicken, fresh fruit and golden, steaming croissants.

"What the hell?" Drew asked.

"Sit, sit—amens...amens."

"I'm not following," Drew said. He saw that Becky had had no trouble whatsoever plopping herself down on the blanket. Had she forgotten she'd lost a whole day? She had to be seriously behind schedule.

"I make amens," Tandu said quietly, "for not doing first aid."

"Oh, *amends*," Drew said uncomfortably. "Really, it's not necessary at all. I have a ton of stuff to do. I'm not very hungry." This was a complete lie, though he had not realized quite how hungry he was until the food had *magically* appeared.

Tandu looked dejected that his offer was being refused.

"You very irritated with me," Tandu said sadly.

Becky caught his eye, lifted her shoulder—*come on, be a sport*—and patted the blanket. With a resigned shake of his head, Drew lowered himself onto the blanket. He bet if he ate one bite of this food that had been set out the spell would be complete.

"Look, I wasn't exactly irritated." This was as much a lie as the one about how he wasn't hungry, and he had a feeling Tandu was not easily fooled. "I was just a little surprised by a first aid man who doesn't like blood."

"Oh, yes," Tandu said happily. "Sit, sit, I fix."

"I am sitting. There's to nothing to fix." Except that Sainte Simone needed a new first aid attendant—before two hundred people descended on it would be good—but Drew found he did not have the heart to tell Tandu that.

Maybe the place was as magical as it looked, because he found himself unable to resist sitting beside Becky on the picnic blanket, though he told himself he had complied only because he did not want to disappoint Tandu, who had obviously misinterpreted his level of annoyance.

"I am not a first aid man," Tandu said. "Uh, how you say, medicine man? My family are healers. We see things."

"See things?" Drew asked. "I'm not following."

"Like a seer or a shaman?" Becky asked. She sounded thrilled.

Drew shot her a look. *Don't encourage him.* She ignored him. "Like what kind of things? Like the future?"

Drew groaned.

"Well, how did he know we needed a wedding site?" she challenged him.

"Because two hundred people are descending on this little piece of paradise for a marriage?"

She actually stuck one of her pointy little elbows in his ribs as if it was rude of him to point out the obvious.

"Yes, yes, like future," Tandu said, very pleased,

missing or ignoring Drew's skepticism and not seeing Becky's dig in his ribs. "See things."

"So what do you see for the wedding?" Becky asked eagerly, leaning forward, as if she was going to put a great deal of stock in the answer.

Tandu looked off into the distance. He suddenly did not look like a smiling servant in a white shirt. Not at all. His expression was intense, and when he turned his gaze back to them, his liquid brown eyes did not seem soft or merry anymore.

"Unexpected things," he said softly. "Lots of surprises. Very happy, very happy wedding. Everybody happy. Babies. Many, many babies in the future."

Becky clapped her hands with delight. "Drew, you're going to be an uncle."

"How very terrifying," he said drily. "Since you can see things, Tandu, when is my brother arriving?"

"Not when you expect," Tandu said, without hesitation.

"Thanks. Tell me something I don't know."

Tandu appeared to take that as a challenge. He gazed off into the distance again. Finally he spoke.

"Broken hearts mended," Tandu said with satisfaction.

"Whose broken hearts?" Becky asked, her eyes wide. "The bride? The groom?"

"For Pete's sake," Drew snapped.

Tandu did not look at him, but gazed steadily and silently at Becky.

"Oh," Becky said, embarrassed. "I don't have a broken heart."

Tandu cocked his head, considering. Drew found himself listening with uncomfortable intentness.

"You left your brokenness in the water," Tandu told Becky. "What you thought was true never was."

She gasped softly, then turned faintly accusing eyes to Drew. "Did you tell him what I said about Jerry?"

He was amazed how much it stung that she thought he would break her confidence. That accusing look in her eyes should be a good thing—it might cool the sparks that had leaped up between them.

But he couldn't leave well enough alone. "Of course not," he said.

"Well, then how did he know?"

"He's a seer," Drew reminded her with a certain amount of satisfaction.

Tandu seemed to have not heard one word of this conversation.

"But you need to swim," he told Becky. "Not be afraid of water. Water here very, very good swimming. Safe. Best swimming beach right here."

"Oh, that's a good idea," she said, turning her head to look at the inviting water, "but I'm not prepared."

"Prepared?" Tandu said, surprised. "What to prepare?"

"I don't have a swimming suit," Becky told him.

"At all?" Drew asked, despite himself. "Who comes to the Caribbean without a swimming suit?"

"I'm not here to play," she said with a stern toss of her head.

"God forbid," he said, but he could not help but feel she was a woman who seemed to take life way too seriously. Which, of course, was not his problem.

"I don't actually own a swimming suit," she said. "The nearest pool is a long way from Moose Run. We aren't close to a lake."

"Ha. Born with swimming suit," Tandu told her seriously. "Skin waterproof."

Drew watched with deep pleasure as the crimson crept up her neck to her cheeks. "Ha-ha," he said in an undertone, "that's what you get for encouraging him."

"You swim," Tandu told her. "Eat first, then swim. Mr. Drew help you."

"Naked swimming," Drew said. "Happy to help when I can. Tandu, do you see skinny-dipping in my future?"

There was that pointy little elbow in his ribs again, quite a bit harder than it had been the last time.

But before he could enjoy Becky's discomfort too much, suddenly Drew found himself pinned in Tandu's intense gaze. "The heart that is broken is yours, Mr. Drew?"

CHAPTER EIGHT

DREW JORDAN ORDERED himself to say no. No to magic. No to the light in Becky's eyes. And especially no to Tandu's highly invasive question. But instead of saying no, he found he couldn't speak at all, as if his throat was closing and his tongue was stuck to the roof of his mouth.

"They say a man is not given more than he can take, eh?" Tandu said.

If there was an expression on the face of the earth that Drew hated with his whole heart and soul it was that one, but he still found he could say nothing.

"But you were," Tandu said softly. "You were given more than you could take. You are a strong man. But not that strong, eh, Mr. Drew?"

His chest felt heavy. His throat felt as if it was closing. There was a weird stinging behind his eyes, as if he was allergic to the overwhelming scent of those flowers.

Without warning, he was back there.

He was seventeen years old. He was standing at the door of his house. It was the middle of the night. His feet and chest were bare and he had on pajama bottoms. He was blinking away sleep, trying to comprehend the stranger at the door of his house. The policeman said, "I'm sorry, son." And then Drew found out he wasn't anyone's son, not anymore.

Drew shook his head and looked at Tandu, fiercely.

"You heal now," Tandu said, not intimidated, as if it was an order. "You heal." And then suddenly Tandu was himself again, the easygoing grin on his face, his teeth impossibly perfect and white against the golden brown of his skin. His eyes were gentle and warm. "Eat, eat. Then swim. Then sunset."

And then he was gone.

"What was that about?" Becky asked him.

"I don't have a clue," he said. His voice sounded strange to him, choked and hoarse. "Creepy weirdness."

Becky was watching him as if she knew it was a lie. When had he become such a liar? He'd better give it up, he was terrible at it. He poured two glasses of wine, handed her one and tossed back the other. He set down the glass carefully.

"There. I've toasted the wedding spot. I'm going to go now." He didn't move.

"Have you?" she asked.

"Have I what? Toasted the wedding spot?"

"Had a heartbreak?" she asked softly, with concern.

And he felt, suddenly, as alone with his burdens as he had ever felt. He felt as if he could lay it all at her feet. He looked at the warmth and loveliness of her brushed-suede eyes. *You heal now.*

He reeled back from the invitation in her eyes. He was the most pragmatic of men. He was not under the enchantment of this beach, or Tandu's words, or her.

Not yet, an inner voice informed him cheerfully.

Not ever, he informed the inner voice with no cheer

at all. He was not touching that food with its potential to weaken him even further. And no more wine.

"People like me," he said, forcing a cavalier ease into his voice.

She leaned toward him.

"We don't have hearts to break. I'm leaving now." Still, he did not move.

She looked as if she wanted to argue with that, but she took one look at his face and very wisely turned her attention to the chicken. "Is this burned?" she asked, poking one of the pieces gingerly with her fingertip.

"I think it's jerked, a very famous way of cooking on these islands." It felt like a relief to focus on the chicken instead of what was going on inside himself.

She took a piece and nibbled it. Her expression changed to one of complete awe. "You have to try it," she insisted. "You have to try it and tell me if it isn't the best thing you have ever tasted. Just one bite before you go."

Despite knowing this food probably had a spell woven right into it, he threw caution to the wind, picked up a leg of chicken and chomped into it. Just a few hours ago it definitely would have been the best thing he had ever tasted. But now that he was under a spell, he saw things differently.

Because the blackened jerk chicken quite possibly might have been the best thing he'd ever tasted, if he hadn't very foolishly sampled her lips when she had offered them yesterday afternoon.

"You might as well stay and eat," she said. She reached over and refilled his empty wineglass. "It would be a shame to let it go to waste."

He was not staying here, eating enchanted food in

an enchanted cove with a woman who was clearly putting a spell on him. On the other hand, she was right. It would be a shame to let the food go to waste.

There was no such thing as spells, anyway. He picked up his second piece of chicken. He watched her delicately lick her fingertips.

"We don't have this kind of food in Moose Run," she said. "More's the pity."

"What kind of food do you have?" He was just being polite, he told himself, before he left her. He frowned. That second glass of wine could not be gone.

"We have two restaurants. We have the Main Street Diner which specializes in half-pound hamburgers and claims to have the best chocolate milk shake in all of Michigan."

"Claims?"

"I haven't tried all the chocolate milk shakes in Michigan," she said. "But believe me, I'm working on it."

He felt something relax within him. He should not be relaxing. He needed to keep his guard up. Still, he laughed at her earnest expression.

"And then we have Mr. Wang's All-You-Can-Eat Spectacular Smorgasbord."

"So, two restaurants. What else do you do for fun?"

She looked uncomfortable. It was none of his business, he told himself firmly. Why did he care if it was just as he'd suspected? She did not have nearly enough fun going on in her life. Not that it was any concern of his.

"Is there a movie theater?" he coaxed her.

"Yes. And don't forget the church picnic."

"And dancing on the grass," he supplied.

"I'm not much for the church socials, actually. I don't really like dancing."

"So what do you like?"

She hesitated, and then met his eyes. "I'm sure you are going to think I am the world's most boring person, but you know what I really do for fun?"

He felt as if he was holding his breath for some reason. Crazy to hope the answer was going to involve kissing. Not that anyone would consider that boring, would they? Was his wineglass full again? He took a sip.

"I read," she said, in a hushed whisper, as if she was in a confessional. She sighed. "I love to read."

What a relief! Reading, not kissing! It should have seemed faintly pathetic, but somehow, just like the rest of her, it seemed real. In an amusement park world where everyone was demanding to be entertained constantly, by bigger things and better amusements and wilder rides and greater spectacles, by things that stretched the bounds of what humans were intended to do, it seemed lovely that Becky had her own way of being in the world, and that something so simple as opening a book could make someone contented.

She was bracing herself, as if she expected him to be scornful. It made him wonder if the ex-beau had been one of those put-down kind of guys.

"I can actually picture you out in a hammock on a sunny afternoon," he said. "It sounds surprisingly nice."

"At this time of year, it's a favorite chair. On my front porch. We still have front porches in Moose Run."

He could picture a deeply shaded porch, and a sleepy street, and hear the sound of birds. This, too, struck him as deliciously simple in a complicated world. "What's your favorite book?" he asked.

"I have to pick one?" she asked with mock horror.

"Let me put it differently. If you had to recommend a book to someone who hardly ever reads, which one would it be?"

And somehow it was that easy. The food was disappearing and so was the wine, and she was telling him about her favorite books and authors, and he was telling her about surfing the big waves and riding his motorbike on the Pacific Coast Highway between LA and San Francisco.

The fight seemed to ease out of him, and the wariness. The urgent need to be somewhere else seemed silly. Drew felt himself relaxing. Why not enjoy it? It was no big deal. Tomorrow his crew would be here. He would immerse himself in his work. He could enjoy this last evening with Becky before that happened, couldn't he?

Who would have ever guessed it would be so easy to be with a man like this? Becky thought. The conversation was comfortable between them. There was so much work that needed to be done on Allie's wedding, and she had already lost a precious day. Still, she had never felt less inclined to do work.

But as comfortable as it all was, she could feel a little nudge of disappointment. How could they go from that electrifying kiss, to this?

Not that she wanted the danger of that kiss again, but she certainly didn't want him to think she was a dull small-town girl whose idea of an exciting evening was sitting out on her front porch reading until the fireflies came out.

Dinner was done. The wine bottle was lying on its

side, empty. All that was left of the chicken was bones, and all that was left of the croissants were a few golden crumbs. As she watched, Drew picked one of those up on his fingertip and popped it in his mouth.

How could such a small thing be so darned sexy?

In her long pants and long-sleeved shirt, Becky was suddenly aware of feeling way too warm. And overdressed. She was aware of being caught in the enchantment of Sainte Simone and this beautiful beach. She longed to be free of encumbrances.

Like clothing? she asked herself, appalled, but not appalled enough to stop the next words that came out of her mouth.

"Let's go for that swim after all," she said. She tried to sound casual, but her heart felt as if she had just finished running a marathon.

"I really need to go." He said it without any kind of conviction. "Are you going to swim in nature's bathing suit?"

"Don't be a pervert!"

"I'm not. Tandu suggested it. One-hundred-percent waterproof."

"Don't look," she said.

"Sure. I'll stop breathing while I'm at it."

What was she doing? she asked herself.

For once in her life, she was acting on a whim, that's what she was doing. For once in her life she was being bold, that's what she was doing. For once in her life, she was throwing convention to the wind, she was doing what she wanted to do. She was not leaving him with the impression she was a dull small-town girl who had spent her whole life with her nose buried in a book. Even if she had been!

She didn't want that to be the whole truth about her anymore, and not just because of him, either. Because the incident in the water yesterday, that moment when she had looked her own death in the face and somehow been spared, had left her with a longing for second chances.

She stood up and turned her back to him. Becky took a deep breath and peeled her shirt over her head, then unbuckled her slacks and stepped out of them. She had on her luxurious Rembrandt's Drawing brand underwear. The underwear was a matching set, a deep shade of turquoise not that different from the water. It was as fashionable as most bathing suits, and certainly more expensive.

She glanced over her shoulder, and his expression—stunned, appreciative, approving—made her run for the water. She splashed in up to her knees, and then threw herself in. The water closed over her head, and unlike yesterday afternoon, it felt wonderful in the heat of the early evening, cool and silky as a caress on her nearly naked skin.

She surfaced, then paddled out and found her footing when she was up to her neck in water, her underwear hidden from him. She turned to look at where he was still sitting on the blanket. Even from here, she could see the heat in his eyes.

Oh, girlfriend, she thought, *you do not know what you are playing with.* But the thing about letting a bolder side out was that it was very hard to stuff it back in, like trying to get a jack-in-the-box back in its container.

"Come in," she called. "It's glorious."

He stood up slowly and peeled his shirt off. She held

her breath. It was her turn to be stunned, appreciative and approving.

She had seen him without his shirt already when he had sacrificed it to doctor her leg. But this was different. She wasn't in shock, or in pain, or bleeding all over the place.

Becky was aware, as she had been when she had first laid eyes on him, that he was the most beautifully made of men. Broad shouldered and deep chested, muscular without being muscle-bound. He could be an actor or a model, because he had that mysterious something that made her—and probably every other woman on earth—feel as if she could look at him endlessly, drink in his masculine perfection as if he was a long, cool drink of water and she was dying of thirst.

Was he going to take off his shorts? She was aware she was holding her breath. But no, he kicked off his shoes and, with the khaki shorts safely in place, ran toward the water. Like she had done, he ran in up to about his thighs and then she watched as he dived beneath the surface.

"I didn't peg you for shy," she told him when he surfaced close to her.

He lifted an eyebrow at her.

"I've seen men's underwear before. I'm from Moose Run, not the convent."

"You've mentioned you weren't a nun once before," he said. "What's with the fascination with nuns?"

"You just seem to think because I'm small town I'm prim and proper. You didn't have to get your shorts all wet to save my sensibilities."

"I don't wear underwear."

Her mouth fell open. She could feel herself turning crimson. He laughed, delighted at her discomfort.

"How are your sensibilities doing now?" he asked her.

"Fine," she squeaked. But they both knew it was a lie, and he laughed.

"Come on," he said, shaking the droplets of water from his hair. "I'll race you to those rocks."

"That's ridiculous. I don't have a hope of winning."

"I know," he said fiendishly.

"I get a head start."

"All right."

"A big one."

"Okay, you tell me when I can go."

She paddled her way toward the rocks. When it seemed there was no chance he could catch her, she called, "Okay, go."

She could hear him coming up behind her. She paddled harder. He grabbed her foot!

"Hey!" She went under the water. He let go of her foot, and when she surfaced, he had surged by her and was touching the rock.

"You cheater," she said indignantly.

"You're the cheater. What kind of head start was that?"

"Watch who you are calling a cheater." She reached back her arm and splashed him, hard. He splashed her back. The war was on.

Tandu had been so right. She needed to leave whatever fear she had remaining in the water.

And looking at Drew's face, she realized, her fear was not about drowning. It was about caring for someone else, as if pain was an inherent ingredient to that.

Becky could see that if she had not let go enough in

life, neither had he. Seeing him like this, playful, his face alight with laugher and mischief, she realized he did carry some burden, like a weight, just as Tandu had suggested. Drew had put down his burden for a bit, out here in the water, and she was glad she had encouraged him to come swim with her.

She wondered what his terrible burden was. Could he really have been given more than he thought he could handle? He seemed so unbelievably strong. But then again, wasn't that what made strength, being challenged to your outer limits? She wondered if he would ever confide in her, but then he splashed her in the face and took off away from her, and she took chase, and the serious thoughts were gone.

A half hour later, exhausted, they dragged themselves up on the beach. Just as he had promised, the trades came up, and it was surprisingly chilly on her wet skin and underwear. She tried to pull her clothes over her wet underwear, but it was more difficult than she thought. Finally, with her clothes clinging to her uncomfortably, she turned to him.

He had pulled his shirt back on over his wet chest and was putting the picnic things back in the basket.

"We have to go," she said. "I feel guilty."

"Tut-tut," he said. "There's that nun thing again. But I have to go, too. My crew is arriving first thing in the morning. I'd like to have things set up so we can get right to work. You're a terrible influence on me, Sister English."

"Sister Simone, to you."

He didn't appear to be leaving, and neither did she.

"I am so far behind in what I need to get done," Becky said. "I didn't expect to be here this long. If I go to work right now, I can still make a few phone calls. What time do you think it is in New York?"

"Look what I just found."

Did he ever just answer the question?

He had been rummaging in the picnic basket and he held up two small mason jars that looked as if they were filled with whipped cream and strawberries.

"What is that?" Knowing the time in New York suddenly didn't seem important at all.

"I think it's dessert."

She licked her lips. He stared at them, before looking away.

"I guess a little dessert wouldn't hurt," she said. Her voice sounded funny, low and seductive, as if she had said something faintly naughty.

"Just sit in the sand," he suggested. "We'll wrap the picnic blanket over our shoulders. We might as well eat dessert and watch the sun go down. What's another half hour now?"

They were going to sit shoulder to shoulder under a blanket eating dessert and watching the sun go down? It was better than any book she had ever read! The time in New York—and all her other responsibilities—did a slow fade-out, as if it was the end of a movie.

CHAPTER NINE

BECKY PLUNKED HERSELF down like a dog at obedience class who was eager for a treat. Drew picked up the blanket and placed it carefully over her shoulders, then sat down in the sand beside her and pulled part of the blanket over his own shoulders. His shoulder felt warm and strong where her skin was touching it. The chill left her almost instantly.

He pried the lid off one of the jars and handed it to her with a spoon.

"Have you ever been to Hawaii?" He took the lid off the other jar.

"No, I'm sorry to say I haven't been. Have you?"

"I've done jobs there. It's very much like this, the climate, the foliage, the breathtaking beauty. Everything stops at sunset. Even if you're still working against an impossible deadline, you just stop and face the sun. It's like every single person stops and every single thing stops. This stillness comes over everything. It's like the deepest form of gratitude I've ever experienced. It's this thank-you to life."

"I feel that right now," she said, with soft reverence. "Maybe because I nearly drowned, I feel so intensely alive and so intensely grateful."

No need to mention sharing this evening with him might have something to do with feeling so intensely alive.

"Me, too," he said softly.

Was it because of her he felt this way? She could feel the heat of his shoulder where it was touching hers. She desperately wanted to kiss him again. She gobbled up strawberries and cream instead. It just made her long, even more intensely, for the sweetness of his lips.

"I am going to hell in a handbasket," she muttered, but still she snuggled under the blanket and looked at where the sun, now a huge orb of gold, was hovering over the ocean.

He shot her a look. "Why would you say that?"

Because she was enjoying him so much, when she, of all people, was so well versed in all the dangers of romance.

"Because I am sitting here watching the sun go down when I should be getting to work," she clarified with a half-truth. "I knew Allie's faith in me was misplaced."

"Why would you say that?"

"I'm just an unlikely choice for such a huge undertaking."

"So, why did she pick you, then?"

"I hadn't seen her, or even had a note from her, since she moved away from Moose Run." Becky sighed and pulled the blanket tighter around her shoulders. "Everyone in Moose Run claims to have been friends with Allison Anderson *before* she became Allie Ambrosia the movie star, but really they weren't. Allison was lonely and different, and many of those people who now claim to have been friends with her were actually exceptionally intolerant of her eccentricities.

"Her mom must have been one of the first internet daters. She came to Moose Run and moved in with Pierce Clemens, which anybody could have told her was a bad bet. Allie, with her body piercings and colorful hair and hippie skirts, was just way too exotic for Moose Run. She only lived there for two years, and she and I only had a nodding acquaintance for most of that time. We were in the same grade, but I was in advanced classes."

"That's a surprise," he teased drily.

"You could have knocked me over with a feather when I got an out-of-the-blue phone call from her a couple of weeks ago and she outlined her ambitious plans. She told me she was putting together a guest list of two hundred people and that she wanted it to be so much more than a wedding. She wants her guests to have an *experience*. The island was hers for an entire week after the wedding, and she wanted all the guests to stay and have fun, either relaxing or joining in on organized activities.

"You know what she suggested for activities? Volleyball tournaments and wienie roasts around a campfire at night, maybe fireworks! You're from there. Does that strike you as Hollywood?"

"No," he said. "Not at all. Hollywood would be Jet Skis during the day and designer dresses at night. It would be entertainment by Cirque and Shania and wine tasting and spa treatments on the beach."

"That's what I thought. But she was adamant about what she wanted. I couldn't help but think that Allie's ideas of fun, despite this exotic island setting, are those of a girl who had been largely excluded from the teen cliques who went together to the Fourth of July activities. She seems, talking to her, to be more in sync with the small-town tastes of Moose Run than with lifestyles of the rich and famous."

"It actually makes me like her more," he said reluctantly.

"I asked her if what she wanted was like summer camp for adults, to make sure I was getting it right. She said—" Becky imitated the famous actress's voice "—'Exactly! I knew I could count on you to get it right.'"

Drew chuckled at Becky's imitation of Allie, which encouraged her to be even more foolish. She did both voices, as if she was reading for several parts in a play.

"Allie, I'm not sure I'm up to this. My event company has become the go-to company for local weddings and anniversaries, but— 'Of course you are up to it, do you think I don't do my homework? You did that great party for the lawyer's kid. Ponies!'

"She said *ponies* with the same enthusiasm she said *fireworks* with," Becky told Drew ruefully. "I think she actually wanted ponies. So I said, 'Um…it would be hard to get ponies to an island—and how did you know that? About the party for Mr. Williams's son?' And she said, 'I do my research. I'm not quite as flaky as the roles I get might make you think.' Of course, I told her I never thought she was flaky, but she cut me off and told me she was sending a deposit. I tried to talk her out of it. I said a six-week timeline was way too short to throw together a wedding for two hundred people. I told her I would have to delegate all my current contracts to take it on. She just insisted. She said she would make it worth my while. I told her I just wasn't sure, and she said she was, and that I was perfect for the job."

"You were trying to get out of the opportunity of a lifetime?" Drew weighed in, amused.

"Was I ever. But then her lighthearted delivery kind of changed and she said I was the only reason she survived Moose Run at all. She asked me if I remembered the day we became friends."

"Did you?"

"Pretty hard to forget. A nasty group of boys had her backed into the corner in that horrid place at the high school where we used to all go to smoke.

"I mean, I didn't go there to smoke. I was Moose Run High's official Goody Two-shoes."

"No kidding," he said drily. "Do not elbow my ribs again. They are seriously bruised."

They sat there in companionable silence for a few minutes. The sun demanded their stillness and their silence. The sunset was at its most glorious now, painting the sky around it in shades of orange and pink that were reflecting on a band on the ocean, that seemed to lead a pathway of light right to them. Then the sun was gone, leaving only an amazing pastel palette staining the sky.

"Go on," he said.

Becky thought she was talking too much. Had they really drunk that whole bottle of wine between the two of them? Still, it felt nice to have someone to talk to, someone to listen.

"I was taking a shortcut to the library—"

"Naturally," he said with dry amusement.

"And I came across Bram Butler and his gang tormenting poor Allie. I told them to cut it out.

"Allie remembers me really giving it to them. She told me that for a long time she has always thought of me as having the spirit of a gladiator."

"I'll attest to that," he said. "I have the bruises on my ribs to prove it." And then his tone grew more serious. "And you never gave up in the water yesterday, either."

"That was because of you. Believe me, I am the little bookworm I told you I was earlier. I do not have the spirit of a gladiator."

Though she did have some kind of unexpected spirit of boldness that had made her, very uncharacteristically, rip off her clothes and go into the water.

"How many guys were there?"

"Hmm, it was years ago, but I think maybe four. No, five."

"What were they doing?"

"They kind of had her backed up against a wall. She was quite frightened. I think that stupid Bram was trying to kiss her. He's always been a jerk. He's my second cousin."

"And you just waded right in there, with five high school guys being jerks? That seems brave."

She could not allow herself to bask in his admiration, particularly since it was undeserved.

"I didn't exactly wade right in there. I used the Moose Run magic words."

"Which were?"

"Bram Butler, you stop it right now or I'll tell your mother."

He burst out laughing, and then so did she. She noticed that it had gotten quite dark. The wind had died. Already stars were rising in the sky.

"Allie and I hung out a bit after that," she said. "She was really interesting. At that time, she wanted to be a clothing designer. We used to hole up in my room and draw dresses."

"What kind of dresses?"

"Oh, you know. Prom. Evening. That kind of thing. Allie and her mom moved away shortly after that. She said we would keep in touch—that she would send me her new address and phone number—but she never did."

"You and Allie drew wedding dresses, didn't you?"

"What would make you say that?" Becky could feel a blush rising, but why should she have to apologize for her younger self?

"I'm trying to figure out if she has some kind of wedding fantasy that my brother just happened into."

"Lots of young women have romantic fantasies. And then someone comes along to disillusion them."

"Like your Jerry," he said. "Tell me about that."

"So little to tell," she said wryly. "We lived down the street from one another, we started the first grade together. When we were seventeen he asked me to go to the Fourth of July celebrations with him. He held my hand. We kissed. And there you have it, my whole future mapped out for me. We were just together after that. I wanted exactly what I grew up with, until my dad left. Up until then my family had been one of those solid, dull families that makes the world feel so, so safe.

"An illusion," she said sadly. "It all ended up being such an illusion, but I felt determined to prove it could be real. Jerry went away to college and I started my own business, and it just unraveled, bit by bit. It's quite humiliating to have a major breakup in a small town."

"I bet."

"When I think about it, the humiliation actually might have been a lot harder to handle than the fact that I was not going to share my life with Jerry. It was like a second blow. I had just barely gotten over being on the receiving end of the pitying looks over my dad's scandal."

"Are you okay with your dad's relationship now?"

"I wish I was. But they still live in Moose Run, and I have an adorable little sister who I am pathetically jealous of. They seem so happy. My mom is still a mess. Aside from working in the hardware store, she'd never even had a job."

"And you rushed in to become the family breadwinner," he said.

"It's not a bad thing, is it?"

"An admirable thing. And kind of sad."

His hand found hers and he gave it a squeeze. He didn't let go again.

"Were you thinking of Jerry when you were drawing those dresses?" he finally asked softly.

"No," she said slowly, "I don't think I was."

She suddenly remembered one dress in particular that Allie had drawn. *This is your wedding dress*, she had proclaimed, giving it to Becky.

It had been a confection, sweetheart neckline, fitted bodice, layers and layers and layers of filmy fabric flowing out in that full skirt with an impossible train. The dress had been the epitome of her every romantic notion. Becky had been able to picture herself in that dress, swirling in front of a mirror, giggling. But she had never, not even once, pictured herself in that dress walking down an aisle toward Jerry.

When Jerry had broken it to her that her "business was changing her"—in other words, he could not handle her success—and he wanted his ring back, she had never taken that drawing from where it was tucked in the back of one of her dresser drawers.

"I've talked too much," she said. "It must have been the wine."

"I don't think you talked too much."

"I usually don't confide in people so readily." She suddenly felt embarrassed. "Your name should be a clue."

"To?"

"You *drew* my secrets right out of me."

"Ah."

"We have to go now," she said.

"Yes, we do," he said.

"Before something happens," she said softly.

"Especially before that," he agreed just as softly.

Her hand was still in his. Their shoulders were touching. The breeze was lifting the leathery fronds of the palm trees and they were whispering songs without words. The sky was now almost completely black, and finding their way back was not going to be easy.

"Really," Becky said. "We need to go."

"Really," he agreed. "We do.

Neither of them moved.

CHAPTER TEN

DREW ORDERED HIMSELF to get up and leave this beach. But it was one of those completely irresistible moments: the stars winking on in the sky, their shoulders touching, the taste of strawberries and cream on his lips, the gentle lap of the waves against the shore, her small hand resting within the sanctuary of his larger one.

He turned slightly to look at her. She was turning to look at him.

It seemed like the most natural thing in the world to drop his head over hers, to taste her lips again.

Her arms came up and twined around his neck. Her lips were soft and pliant and welcoming.

He could taste everything she was in that kiss. She was bookish. And she was bold. She was simple, and she was complex. She was, above all else, a forever kind of girl.

It was that knowledge that made him untangle her hands from around his neck, to force his lips away from the soft promise of hers.

You heal now.

He swore under his breath, scrambled to his feet. "I'm sorry," he said.

"Are you?"

Well, not really. "Look, Becky, we have known each other for a shockingly short period of time. Obviously circumstances have made us feel things about each other a little too quickly."

She looked unconvinced.

"I mean, in Moose Run, you probably have a date or two before you kiss like that."

"What about in LA?"

He thought about how fast things could go in Los Angeles and how superficial that was, and how he was probably never going to be satisfied with it again. Less than forty-eight hours, and Becky English, bookworm, was changing everything in his world.

What was his world going to look like in two weeks if this kept up?

The answer was obvious. This could not keep up.

"Look, Becky, I obviously like you. And find you extremely attractive."

Did she look pleased? He did not want her to look pleased!

"There is obviously some kind of chemistry going on between us."

She looked even more pleased.

"But both of us have jobs to do. We have very little time to do those jobs in. We can't afford a, um, complication like this."

She stared at him, uncomprehending.

"It's not professional, Becky," he said gruffly. "Kissing on the job is not professional."

She looked as if he had slapped her. And then she just looked crushed.

"Oh," she stammered. "Of course, you're right."

He felt a terrible kind of self-loathing that she was taking it on, as if it were her fault.

She pulled herself together and jumped up, doing what he suspected she always did. Trying to fix the whole world. Her clothes were still wet. Her pink blouse looked as though red roses were blooming on it where it was clinging to that delectable set of underwear that he should never have seen, and was probably never going to be able to get out of his mind.

"I don't know what's gotten into me. It must still be the aftereffects of this afternoon. And the wine. I want you to know I don't usually rip my clothes off around men. In fact, that's extremely uncharacteristic. And I'm usually not such a blabbermouth. Not at all."

Her voice was wobbling terribly.

"No, it's not you," he rushed to tell her. "It's not. It's me, I—"

"I've given you the impression I'm—what did you call it earlier—wanton!"

"I told you at the time I was overstating it. I told you that was the wrong word."

She held up her hand, stopping him. "No, I take responsibility. You don't know how sorry I am."

And then she rushed by him, found the path through the darkened jungle and disappeared.

Perfect, he thought. He'd gotten rid of her before things got dangerously out of control. But it didn't feel perfect. He felt like a bigger jerk than the chicken they had eaten for supper.

She had fled up that path—away from him—with extreme haste, probably hoping to keep the truth from him. That she was crying.

But that's what I am, Drew told himself. He was a

jerk. Just ask his brother, who not only wasn't arriving on the island, but who also was not taking his phone calls.

The truth was, Drew Jordan sucked at relationships. It was good Becky had run off like that, for her own protection, and his. It would have been better if he could have thought of a way to make her believe it was his fault instead of hers, though.

Sitting there, alone, in the sand, nearly choking on his own self-loathing, Drew thought of his mother. He could picture her: the smile, the way she had made him feel, that way she had of cocking her head and listening so intently when he was telling her something. He realized the scent he had detected earlier had reminded him of her perfume.

The truth was, he was shocked to be thinking of her. Since that day he had become both parents to his younger brother, he had tried not to think of his mom and dad. It was just too painful. Losing them—everything, really, his whole world—was what life had given him that was too much to bear.

But the tears in Becky's eyes that she had been holding back so valiantly, and the scent in the air, made him think of his mother. Only in his mind, his mother wasn't cocking her head, listening intently to him with that soft look of wonder that only a mother can have for her offspring.

No, it felt as if his mother was somehow near him, but that her hands were on her hips and she was looking at him with total exasperation.

His mother, he knew, would never have approved of the fact he had made that decent, wholesome young woman from Moose Run, Michigan, cry. She would be really angry with him if he excused his behavior by saying, *But it was for her own good.* His mother, if she was here, would remind him of all the hurt that Becky had already suffered at the hands of men.

She would show him Becky, trying to keep her head up as her father pushed a stroller down the main street of Moose Run, as news got out that the wedding planner's own wedding was a bust.

Sitting there in the sand with the stars coming out over him, Drew felt he was facing some hard truths about himself. Would his mother even approve of the man he had become? Work-obsessed, so emotionally unavailable he had driven his brother right out of his life and into the first pair of soft arms that offered comfort. His mother wouldn't like it one bit that not only was he failing to protect his brother from certain disaster, his brother would not even talk to him.

"So," he asked out loud, "what would you have me do?"

Be a better man.

It wasn't her voice. It was just the gentle breeze stirring the palm fronds. It was just the waves lapping onshore. It was just the call of the night birds.

But is that what her voice had become? Everything? Was his mother's grace and goodness now in everything? Including him?

Drew scrambled out of the sand. He picked up the picnic basket and the blanket and began to run.

"Becky! Becky!"

When he caught up with her, he was breathless. She was walking fast, her head down.

"Becky," he said, and then softly, "Please."

She spun around. She stuck her chin up in the air.

But she could not hide the fact that he was right. She had been crying.

"I didn't mean to hurt your feelings," he said. "I'm the one in the wrong here, not you."

"Thank you," she said icily. "That is very chivalrous of you. However the facts speak for themselves."

Chivalrous. Who used that in a sentence? And why did it make him feel as if he wanted to set down the picnic basket, gather her in his arms and hold her hard?

"Facts?"

"Yes, facts," she said in that clipped tone of voice. "They speak for themselves."

"They do?"

She nodded earnestly. "It seems to me I've just dragged you along with my *wanton* behavior, kissing you, tearing off my clothes. You were correct. It is not professional. And it won't be happening again."

He knew that it not happening again was a good thing, so why did he feel such a sense of loss?

"Becky, I handled that badly."

"There's a good way to handle 'keep your lips off me'?"

He had made her feel rejected. He had done to her what every other man in her life had done to her: given her the message that somehow she didn't measure up, she wasn't good enough.

He rushed to try to repair the damage.

"It's not that I don't want your lips on me," he said. "I do. I mean I don't. I mean we can't. I mean I won't."

She cocked her head, and looked askance at him.

"Do I sound like an idiot?" he said.

"Yes," she said, unforgivingly.

"What I'm trying to say, Becky, is I'm not used to women like you."

"What kind of women are you used to?"

"Guess," he said in a low voice.

She did not appear to want to guess.

He raked his hand through his hair, trying desperately to think of a way to make her get it that would somehow erase those tearstains from her cheeks.

"I'm scared I'll hurt you," he said, his voice gravelly in his own ears. "I don't think it's a good idea to move this fast. Let's back up a step or two. Let's just be friends. First."

He had no idea where that *first* had come from. It implied there would be something following the friendship. But really, that was impossible. And he just had to get through what remained of two weeks without hurting her any more than he already had. He could play at being the better man for eleven damn days. He was almost sure of it.

"Do you ever answer a question?" she asked. "What kind of women are you used to?"

"Ones who are as shallow as me," he said.

"You aren't shallow!"

"You don't know that about me."

"I do," she said firmly.

He sucked in his breath and tried again. Why was she insisting on seeing him as a better man when he did not deserve that? "Ones who don't expect happily-ever-after."

"Oh."

"You see, Becky, my parents died when I was seventeen." *Shut up*, he ordered himself. *Stop it.* "It broke something in me. The sense of loss was just as Tandu said this afternoon. It was too great to bear. When I've had relationships, and it's true, I have, they have been deliberately superficial."

Becky went very still. Her eyes looked wide and beautiful in the starlight that filtered through the thick leaves of the jungle. She took a step toward him. And she reached up and laid the palm of her hand on his cheek.

Her touch was extraordinary. He had to shut his eyes against his reaction to the tenderness in it. In some ways it was more intimate than the kisses they had shared.

"Because you cannot handle one more loss," she guessed softly.

Drew opened his eyes and stared at Becky. It felt as if she could see his soul and was not the least frightened by what she saw there.

This was going sideways! He was not going to answer that. He could not. If he answered that, he would want to lay his head on her shoulder and feel her hand in his hair. He would want to suck up her tenderness like a dry sponge sucking up moisture. If he answered that he would become weak, instead of what he needed to be most.

He needed to be strong. Since he'd been seventeen years old, he had needed to be strong. And it wasn't until just this minute he was seeing that as a burden he wanted to lay down.

"I agree," she said softly, dropping her hand away from his cheek. "We just need to be friends."

His relief was abject. She got it. He was too damaged to be any good for a girl like her.

Only then she went and spoiled his relief by standing on her tiptoes and kissing him on the cheek where her hand had lay with such tender healing. She whispered something in his ear.

And he was pretty sure it was the word *first*.

And then she turned and scampered across the moon-lit lawn to the castle door and disappeared inside it.

And he had to struggle not to touch his cheek, where the tenderness of her kiss lingered like a promise.

You heal now.

But he couldn't. He knew that. He could do his best to honor the man his mother had raised him to be, to not cause Becky any more harm, but he knew that his own salvation was beyond what he could hope for.

Because really in the end, for a man like him, wasn't hope the most dangerous thing of all?

CHAPTER ELEVEN

BECKY LISTENED TO the sound of hammers, the steady *ratta-tat-tat* riding the breeze through the open window of her office. When had that sound become like music to her?

She told herself, sternly, she could not give in to the temptation, but it was useless. It was as if a cord circled her waist and tugged her toward the window.

This morning, Drew's crew had arrived, but not his brother. They had arrived ready to work, and in hours the wedding pavilion was taking shape on the emerald green expanse of the front lawn. They'd dug holes and poured the cement they had mixed by hand out of bags. Then they had set the posts—which had arrived by helicopter—into those holes.

She had heard helicopters delivering supplies all morning. It sounded like a MASH unit around here.

Now she peeped out the window. In all that activity, her eyes sought him. Her heart went to her throat. Drew, facing the ocean, was straddling a beam. He had to be fifteen feet off the ground, his legs hanging into nothingness. He had a baseball cap on backward and his shirt off.

His skin was sun-kissed and perfect, his back broad

and powerful. He was a picture of male strength and confidence.

She could barely breathe he was so amazing to look at. It was also wonderful to be able to look at him without his being aware of it! She could study the sleek lines of his naked back at her leisure.

"You have work to do," she told herself. Drew, as if he sensed someone watching, turned and glanced over his shoulder, directly at her window. She drew back into the shadows, embarrassed, and pleased, too. Was he looking to glimpse her? Did it fill him with this same sense of delight? Anticipation? Longing?

Reluctantly, she turned her back to the scene, but only long enough to try to drag her desk over to the window. She could multitask. The desk was very heavy. She grunted with exertion.

"Miss Becky?" Tandu was standing in the doorway with a tray. "Why you miss lunch?"

"Oh, I—" For some reason she had felt shy about lunch, knowing that Drew and his crew would be eating in the dining room. Despite their agreement last night to be friends, her heart raced out of control when she thought of his rescue of her, and eating dinner with him on the picnic blanket last night, and swimming with him. But mostly, she thought of how their lips had met. Twice.

How was she going to choke down a sandwich around him? How was she going to behave appropriately with his crew looking on? Anybody with a heartbeat would take one look at her—them—and know that something primal was sizzling in the air between them.

This was what she had missed by being with Jerry

for so long. She had missed all the years when she should have been learning the delicate nuances of how to conduct a relationship with a member of the opposite sex.

Not that it was going to be a relationship. A friendship. She thought of Drew's lips. She wondered how a friendship was going to be possible.

There must be a happy medium between wanton and so shy she couldn't even eat lunch with him!

"What you doing?" Tandu asked, looking at the desk she had managed to move about three feet across the room.

"The breeze!" she said, too emphatically. "I thought I might get a better breeze if I moved the desk."

Tandu set down the lunch tray. With his help it was easier to wrestle the big piece of furniture into its new location.

He looked out the window. "Nice view," he said with wicked amusement. "Eat lunch, enjoy the view. Then you are needed at helicopter pad. Cargo arriving. Many, many boxes."

"I have a checklist. I'll be down shortly. And Tandu, could you think of a few places for wedding photographs? I mean, the beaches are lovely, but if I could preview a few places for the photographer, that would be wonderful."

"Know exactly the place," he said delightedly. "Waterfall."

"Yes!" she said.

"I'll draw you a map."

"Thank you. A waterfall!"

"Now eat. Enjoy the view."

She did eat, and she did enjoy the view. It was actually much easier to get to work when she could just glance up and watch Drew, rather than making a special trip away from her desk and to the window.

Later that afternoon, she headed down to the helicopter loading dock with her checklist and began sorting through the boxes and muttering to herself.

"Candles? Check. Centerpieces? Check."

"Hi there." She swung around.

Drew was watching her, a little smile playing across his handsome features.

"Hello." Oh, God, did she have to sound so formal and geeky?

"Do you always catch your tongue between your teeth like that when you are lost in thought?"

She hadn't been aware she was doing it, and pulled her tongue back into her mouth. He laughed. She blushed.

"The pavilion is looking great," she said, trying to think of something—anything—to say. She was as tongue-tied as if she were a teenager meeting her secret crush unexpectedly at the supermarket!

"Yeah, my guys are pretty amazing, aren't they?"

She had not really spared a glance to any of the other guys. "Amazing," she agreed.

"I just thought I'd check and see if the fabric for draping the pavilion has arrived. I need to come up with a method for hanging it."

"I'll look."

But he was already sorting through boxes, tossing them with easy strength. "This might be it. It's from a fabric store. There's quite a few boxes here." He took a box cutter out of his shirt pocket and slit open one of the boxes. "Come see."

She sidled over to him. She could feel the heat radiating off him as they stood side by side.

"Yes, that's it."

He hefted up one of the boxes onto his shoulder. "I'll send one of the guys over for the rest."

She stood there. That was going to be the whole encounter. *Very professional*, she congratulated herself.

"You want to come weigh in on how to put it up?" he called over his shoulder.

And she threw professionalism to the wind and scampered after him like a puppy who had been given a second chance at affection.

"Hey, guys," he called. "Team meeting. Fabric's here."

His guys, four of them, gathered around.

"Becky, Jared, Jason, Josh and Jimmy."

"The J series," one of them announced. "Brothers. I'm the good-looking one, Josh." He gave a little bow.

"But I'm the strong one," Jimmy announced.

"And I'm the smart one."

"I'm the romantic," Jared said, and stepped forward, picked up her hand and kissed it, to groans from his brothers. "You are a beauty, me lady. Do you happen to be available? I see no rings, so—"

"That's enough," Drew said.

His tone had no snap to it, at all, only firmness, but Becky did not miss how quickly Jared stepped back from her, or the surprised looks exchanged between the brothers.

She liked seeing Drew in this environment. It was obvious his crew of brothers didn't just respect him, they adored him. She soon saw why.

"Let's see what we have here," Drew said. He opened

a box and yards and yards of filmy white material spilled out onto the ground.

He was a natural leader, listening to all the brothers' suggestions about how to attach and drape the fabric to the pavilion poles they had worked all morning installing.

"How about you, Becky?" Drew asked her.

She was flattered that her opinion mattered, too. "I think you should put some kind of bar on those side beams. Long bars, like towel bars, and then thread the fabric through them."

"We have a winner," one of the guys shouted, and they all clapped and went back to work.

"I'll hang the first piece and you can see if it works," Drew said.

With amazing ingenuity he had fabricated a bar in no time. And then he shinnied up a ladder that was leaning on a post and attached the first bar to the beam. And then he did the same on the other side.

"The moment of truth," he called from up on the wall.

She opened the box and he leaned way down to take the fabric from her outstretched hand. Once he had it, he threaded it through the first bar, then came down from the ladder, trailing a line of wide fabric behind him. He went up the ladder on the other side of what would soon look like a pavilion, and threaded the fabric through there. The panel was about three feet wide and dozens of feet long. He came down to the ground and passed her the fabric end.

"You do it," he said.

She tugged on it until the fabric lifted toward the sky, and then began to tighten. Finally, the first panel was in place. The light, filmy, pure-white fabric formed a dreamy roof above them, floating walls on either side of them. Only it was better than walls and a roof because of the way the light was diffused through it, and the way it moved like a living thing in the most gentle of breezes.

"Just like a canopy bed," he told her with satisfaction.

"You know way too much about that," she teased him.

"Actually," he said, frowning at the fabric, "come to think of it, it doesn't really look like a canopy bed. It looks like—"

He snatched up the hem of fabric and draped it over his shoulder. "It looks like a toga."

She burst out laughing.

He struck a pose. "'To be or not to be...'" he said.

"I don't want to be a geek..." she began.

"Oh, go ahead—be a geek. It comes naturally to you."

That stung, but even with it stinging, she couldn't let *To be or not to be* go unchallenged. "'To be or not to be' is Shakespeare," she told him. "Not Nero."

"Well, hell," he said, "that's what makes it really hard for a dumb carpenter to go out with a smart girl."

She stared at him. "Are we going out?" she whispered.

"No! I just was pointing out more evidence of our incompatibility."

That stung even worse than being called a geek. "At least you got part of it right," she told him.

"Which part? The geek part?"

"I am not a geek!"

He shook his head sadly.

"That line? 'To be or not to be.' It's from a soliloquy in the play *Hamlet*. It's from a scene in the nunnery."

"The nunnery?" he said with satisfaction. "Don't *you* have a fascination?"

"No! You *think* I have a fascination. You are incorrect, just as you are incorrect about me being a geek."

"Yes, and being able to quote Shakespeare, chapter and verse, certainly made that point."

She giggled, and unraveled the fabric from around him.

"Hey! Give me back my toga. I already told you I don't wear underwear!

But it was her turn to play with the gauzy fabric. She inserted herself in the middle of it and twirled until she had made it into a long dress. Then she swathed some around her head, until only her eyes showed. Throwing inhibition to the wind, she swiveled her hips and did some things with her hands.

"Guess who I am?" she purred.

He frowned at her. "A bride?"

The thing he liked least!

"No, I'm not a bride," she snapped.

"A hula girl!"

"No."

"I give up. Stop doing that."

"I'm Mata Hari."

"Who? I asked you to stop."

"Why?"

"It's a little too sexy for the job site."

"A perfect imitation of Mata Hari, then," she said with glee. And she did not stop doing it. She was rather enjoying the look on his face.

"Who?"

"She was a spy. And a dancer."

He burst out laughing as if that was the most improbable thing he had ever heard. "How well versed was she in her Shakespeare?"

"She didn't have to be." Becky began to do a slow writhe with her hips. He didn't seem to think it was funny anymore.

In fact, the ease they had been enjoying—that sense of being a team and working together—evaporated.

He stepped back from her, as if he thought she was going to try kissing him again. She blushed.

"I have so much to do," she squeaked, suddenly feeling silly, and at the very same time, not silly at all.

"Me, too," he said.

But neither of them moved.

"Uh, boss, is this a bad time?"

Mata Hari dropped her veil with a little shriek of embarrassment.

"The guys were thinking maybe we could have a break? It's f—"

Drew stopped his worker with a look.

"It's flipping hot out here. We thought maybe we could go swimming and start again when it's not so hot out."

"Great idea," Drew said. "We all need cooling off, particularly Mata Hari here. You coming swimming, Becky?"

She knew she should say no. She had to say no. She didn't even have a proper bathing suit. Instead she unraveled herself from the yards of fabric, called, "Race you," ran down to the water and flung herself in completely clothed.

Drew's crew crashed into the water around her,

following her lead and just jumping in in shorts and T-shirts. They played a raucous game of tag in the water, and she was fully included, though she was very aware of Drew sending out a silent warning that no lines were to be crossed. And none were. It was like having five brothers.

And wouldn't that be the safest thing? Wasn't that what she and Drew had vowed they were going to do? Hadn't they both agreed they were going to retreat into a platonic relationship after the crazy-making sensation of those shared kisses?

What had she been thinking, playing Mata Hari? What kind of craziness was it that she wanted him to not see her exactly as she was: not a spy and dancer who could coax secrets out of unsuspecting men, but a book-loving girl from a small town in America?

After that frolic in the water, the J brothers included her as one of them. Over the next few days, whenever they broke from work to go swimming, one of them came and pounded on her office door and invited her to come.

Today, Josh knocked on the door.

"Swim time," he said.

"I just can't. I have to tie bows on two hundred chairs. And find a cool place to store three thousand potted lavender plants. And—"

Without a word, Josh came in, picked her up and tossed her over his shoulder like a sack of potatoes.

"Stop it. This is my good dress!" She pounded on his back, but of course, with her laughing so hard, he did not take her seriously. She was carried, kicking and screaming and pounding on his back, to the water, where she was unceremoniously dumped in.

"Hey, what the hell are you doing?" Drew demanded, arriving at the water's edge and fishing her out.

The fact that she was screaming with laughter had softened the protective look on his face.

Josh had lifted a big shoulder. "Boss, you said don't take no for an answer."

"No means no, boss," she inserted, barely able to breathe she was laughing so hard.

Drew gave them both an exasperated look, and turned away. Then he turned back, picked her up, raced out into the surf and dumped her again!

She rose from the water sputtering, still holding on to his neck, both their bodies sleek with salt water, her good dress completely ruined.

Gazing into the mischief-filled face of Drew Jordan, Becky was not certain she had ever felt so completely happy.

CHAPTER TWELVE

AFTER THAT BECKY was "in." She and the J's and Drew became a family. They took their meals together and they played together. Becky soon discovered this crew worked hard, and they played harder.

At every break and after work, the football came out. Or the Frisbee. Both games were played with rough-and-tumble delight at the water's edge. She wasn't sure how they could have any energy left, but they did.

The first few times she played, the brothers howled hysterically at both her efforts to throw and catch balls and Frisbees. They good-naturedly nicknamed her Barnside.

"Barnside?" she protested. "That's awful. I demand a new nickname. That is not flattering!"

"You have to earn a new nickname," Jimmy informed her seriously.

"Time to go back to work," Drew told them, after one coffee-break Frisbee session when poor Josh had to climb a palm tree to retrieve a Frisbee she'd thrown. He caught her arm as she turned to leave. "Not you."

"What?" she said.

"Have you heard anything from Allie recently?" he asked.

"The last I heard from her was a few days ago, when she okayed potted lavender instead of tulips." She scanned his face. "You still haven't heard from Joe?"

He shrugged. "It's no big deal."

But she could tell it was. "I'm sorry."

He obviously did not want to talk about his distress over his brother. Becky was aware that she felt disappointed. He was okay with their relationship—with being "friends" on a very light level.

Did he not trust her with his deeper issues?

Apparently not. Drew said, "It's time you learned how to throw a Frisbee. I consider it an essential life skill."

"How could I have missed that?" she asked drily. As much as she wanted to talk to him about his brother, having fun with him was just too tempting. Besides, maybe the lighthearted friendship growing between them would develop some depth, and some trust on his part, if she just gave it time.

"I'm not sure how you could have missed this important life skill," he said, "but it's time to lose 'Barnside.' They are calling you that because you could not hit the side of a barn with a Frisbee at twenty feet."

"At twenty feet? I could!"

"No," Drew informed her with a sad shake of his head, "you couldn't. You've now tossed two Frisbees out to sea, and Josh risked his life to rescue the other one out of the palm tree today. We can't be running out of Frisbees."

"That would be a crisis," she agreed, deadpan.

"I'm glad you understand the seriousness of it. Now, come here."

He placed her in front of him. He gave her a Frisbee. "Don't throw it. Not yet."

He wrapped his arms around her from behind, drawing her back into the powerful support of his chest. He laid his arm along her arm. "It's in the wrist, not the arm. Flick it, don't pitch it." He guided her throw.

Becky actually cackled with delight when it flew true, instead of her normal flub. Soon, he released her to try on her own, and then set up targets for her to throw at. The troubled look that had been on his face since he mentioned his brother evaporated.

Finally, he high-fived her, gave her a little kiss on the nose and headed back to his crew. She watched him go and then looked at the Frisbee in her hand.

How could such a small thing make it feel as if a whole new world was opening up to her? Of course, it wasn't the Frisbee, it was him.

It was being with him and being with his crew.

It occurred to Becky she felt the sense of belonging she had craved since the disintegration of her own family. They were all becoming a team. Drew and his crew were a building machine. The pavilion went up, and they designed and began to build the dance floor. And Becky loved the moments when she and Drew found themselves alone. It was so easy to talk to each other.

The conversation flowed between them so easily. And the laughter.

The hands-off policy had been a good one, even if it was making the tension build almost unbearably between them. It was like going on a diet that had an end date. Not that they had named an end date, but some kind of anticipation was building between them.

And meanwhile, her admiration for him did nothing but grow. He was a natural leader. He was funny. He was smart. She found herself making all kinds of excuses to be around him. She was pretty sure he was doing the same thing to be around her.

The days flew by until there were only three days until the wedding. The details were falling into place seamlessly, not just for the wedding but for the week following. The pagoda and dance floor were done, the wedding gazebo was almost completed, though it still had to be painted.

Usually when she did an event, as the day grew closer her excitement grew, too. But this time she had mixed feelings. In a way, Becky wished the wedding would never come. She had never loved her life as much as she did right now.

Today she was at the helipad looking at the latest shipment of goods. Again, there was a sense of things falling into place: candles in a large box, glass vases for the centerpieces made up of single white roses. She made a note as she instructed the staff member who had been assigned to help her where to put the boxes. Candles would need to be unwrapped and put in candle holders, glass vases cleaned to sparkling. The flowers—accompanied by their own florist—would arrive the evening before the wedding to guarantee freshness.

Then one large, rectangular box with a designer name on it caught her eye. It was the wedding dress. She had not been expecting it. She had assumed it would arrive with Allie.

And yet it made sense that it would need to be hung.

Becky plucked it from all the other boxes and, with some last-minute instructions, walked back to the castle with it. She brought it up to the suite that Allie would inhabit by herself the day before the wedding, and with her new husband after that.

The suite was amazing, so softly romantic it took Becky's breath away. She had a checklist for this room, too. It would be fully supplied with very expensive toiletries, plus fresh flowers would abound. She had chosen the linens from the castle supply room herself.

Becky set the box on the bed. A sticker in red caught her eye. They were instructions stating that the dress should be unpacked, taken out of its plastic protective bag and hung immediately upon arrival. And so Becky opened the box and lifted it out. She unzipped the bag, and carefully lifted the dress out.

Her hands gathered up a sea of white foam. The fabric was silk, so sensuous under her fingertips that Becky could feel the enchantment sewn right into the dress. There was a tall coatrack next to the mirror, and Becky hung the silk-wrapped hanger on a peg and stood back from it.

She could not believe what she was seeing. That long-ago dress that Allie had drawn and given to her, that drawing still living in the back of Becky's dresser drawer, had been brought to life.

The moment was enough to make a girl who had given up on magic believe in it all over again.

Except that's not what it did. Looking at the dress made Becky feel as though she was being stabbed with the shards of her own broken dreams. The dress shimmered with a future she had been robbed of. In every winking pearl, there seemed to be a promise: of someone to share life with, of laughter, of companionship, of passion, of "many babies," fat babies chortling and clapping their hands with glee.

Becky shook herself, as if she was trying to break free of the spell the dress was weaving around her. She wanted to tell herself that she was wrong. That this was not the dress that Allie had drawn on that afternoon of girlish delight all those years ago, not the drawing she had handed to her and said, *This is your wedding dress.*

But she still had that drawing. She had studied it too often now not to know every line of that breathtakingly romantic dress. She had dreamed of herself walking down the aisle in that dress one too many times. There was simply no mistaking which dress it was. Surely, Allie was not being deliberately cruel?

No, Allie had not kept a drawing of the dress. She had given the only existing drawing to Becky. Allie must have remembered it at a subliminal level. Why wouldn't she? The dress was exactly what every single girl dreamed of having one day.

But Becky still felt the tiniest niggle of doubt. What if Drew's cynicism was not misplaced? What if his brother was making a mistake? What if this whole wedding was some kind of publicity stunt orchestrated by Allie? The timing was perfect: Allie was just finishing filming one movie, and another was going to be released in theaters within weeks.

With trembling hands, Becky touched the fabric of the dress one more time. Then she turned and scurried from the room. She felt as if she was going to burst into tears, as if her every secret hope and dream had been shoved into her face and mocked. And then she bumped right into Drew and did what she least wanted to do. She burst into tears.

"Hey!" Drew eased Becky away from him. She was crying! If there was something worse than her laughing and being joyful and carefree, it was this. "What's the matter?"

"Nothing," she said. "I'm just tired. There's so much to do and—"

But he could tell she wasn't just tired. And from working with her for the past week, he could tell there was hardly anything she liked more than having a lot to do. Her strength was organizing, putting her formidable mind to problems that needed to be solved. No, something had upset her. How had he come to be able to read Becky English so accurately?

She was swiping at those tears, lifting her chin to him with fierce pride, backing away from a shoulder to cry on.

The wisest thing would be to let her. Let her go her own way and have a good cry about whatever, and not involve himself any more than he already had.

Who was he kidding? Just himself. He'd noticed his crew sending him sideways looks every time she was around. He'd noticed Tandu putting them together. He was already involved. Spending the past days with her had cemented that.

"You want to be upset together?" he asked her.

"I told you I'm not upset."

"Uh-huh."

"What are you upset about?"

He lifted a shoulder. "You're not telling, I'm not telling."

"Fine."

"Tandu asked me to give you this."

"How could Tandu have possibly known you were going to bump into me?" Becky asked, taking the paper from him.

"I don't know. The man's spooky. He seems to know things."

Becky squinted at the paper. "Sheesh."

"What?"

"It's a map. He promised it to me over a week ago. Apparently there's a waterfall that would make a great backdrop for wedding pictures. Can you figure out this drawing?"

She handed the map back to him. It looked like a child's map for a pirate's treasure. Drew looked at a big arrow, and the words, *Be careful this rock. Do not fall in water, please.*

"I'll come with you," he decided.

"Thank you," she said. "That's unnecessary." She snatched the map back and looked at it. "Which way is north?"

"I'll come."

The fight went out of her. "Do you ever get tired of being the big brother?"

He thought of how tired he was of leaving Joe messages to call him. He looked at her lips. He thought of how tired he was getting of this friendship between them.

"Suck it up, buttercup," he muttered to himself.

She sighed heavily. "If you have a fault, do you know what it is?"

"Please don't break it to me that I have a fault. Not right now."

"What happened?"

"I said I'm not talking about it, if you're not talking about it."

"Your fault is that you don't answer questions."

"Your fault is—" What was he going to say? Her

fault was that she made him think the kind of thoughts he had vowed he was never going to think? "Never mind. Let's go find that waterfall."

"I don't know," Becky said dubiously, after they had been walking twenty minutes. "This seems like kind of a tough walk at any time. I'm in a T-shirt and shorts and I'm overheating. What would it be like in a wedding dress?"

Drew glanced at her. Had she flinched when she said *wedding dress*?

"Maybe her royal highness, the princess Allie is expecting to be delivered to her photo op on a litter carried by two manservants," Drew grumbled. "I hope I'm not going to be one of them."

Becky laughed and took the hand he held back to her to help her scramble over a large boulder.

"Technically, that would be a sedan chair," she said, puffing.

"Huh?"

"A seat that two manservants can carry is sedan chair. Anything bigger is a litter."

He contemplated her. "How do you know this stuff?" he asked.

"That's what a lifetime of reading gets you, a brain teeming with useless information." She contemplated the rock. "Maybe we should just stop here. There's no way Allie can scramble over this rock in a wedding dress."

He contemplated the map. "I think it's only a few more steps. I'm pretty sure I can hear the falls. We might as well see it, even if Allie never will."

And he was right. Only a few steps more and they

pushed their way through a gateway of heavy leaves, as big and as wrinkled as elephant ears, and stood in an enchanted grotto.

"Oh, my," Becky breathed.

A frothing fountain of water poured over a twenty-foot cliff and dropped into a pool of pure green water. The pond was surrounded on all sides by lush green ferns and flowers. A large flat rock jutted out into the middle of it, like a platform.

"Perfect for pictures," she thought out loud. "But how are we going to get them here?"

"Wow," Drew said, apparently not the least bit interested in pictures. In a blink, he had stripped off his shirt and dived into the pond. He surfaced and shook his head. Diamonds of water flew. "It's wonderful," he called over the roar of the falls. "Get in."

Once again, there was the small problem of not having bathing attire.

And once again, she was caught in the spell of the island. She didn't care that she didn't have a bathing suit. She wanted to be unencumbered, not just by clothing, but by every single thought that had ever held her prisoner.

CHAPTER THIRTEEN

So AWARE OF the look on Drew's face as he watched her, Becky undid the buttons of her blouse, shrugged it off and then stepped out of her skirt.

When she saw the look on Drew's face, she congratulated herself on her investment in the ultra-sexy and exclusive Rembrandt's Drawing brand underwear. Today, her matching bra and panties were white with tiny red hearts all over them.

And then she stepped into the water. She wanted to dive like him, but because she was not that great a swimmer, she waded in up to her ankles first. The rocks were slipperier than she had expected. Her arms began to windmill.

And she fell, with a wonderful splash, into where he was waiting to catch her.

"The water is fantastic," Becky said, blinking up at him.

"Yes, it is."

She knew neither of them were talking about the water. He set her, it seemed with just a bit of reluctance, on her feet. She splashed him.

"Is that any way to thank me for rescuing you?"

"That is to let you know I did not need to be rescued!"

"Oh," he said. "You planned to fall in the water."

She giggled. "Yes, I did."

"Don't take up poker."

She splashed him again. He got a look on his face. She giggled and bolted away. He was after her in a flash. Soon the grotto was filled with the magic of their splashing and laughter. The days of playing with him—of feeling that sense of belonging—all seemed to have been leading to this. Becky had never felt so free, so wondrous, so aware as she did then.

Finally, exhausted, they hauled themselves out onto the warmth of the large, flat rock, and lay there on their stomachs, side-by-side, panting to catch their breaths.

"I'm indecent," she decided, without a touch of remorse.

"I prefer to think of it as wanton."

She laughed. The sun was coming through the greenery, dappled on his face. His eyelashes were tangled with water. She laid her hand—wantonly—on the firmness of his naked back. She could feel the warmth of him seeping into her hand. He closed his eyes, as if her touch had soothed something in him. His breathing slowed and deepened.

And then so did hers.

When she awoke, her hand was still on his back. He stirred and opened his eyes, looked at her and smiled.

She shivered with a longing so primal it shook her to the core. Drew's smile disappeared, and he found his feet in one catlike motion. As she sat up and hugged herself, chilled now, he retrieved his T-shirt. He came back and slid it over her head. Then he sat behind her, pulled her between the wedge of his legs and wrapped his arms around her until she stopped shivering.

The light was changing in the grotto and the magic deepened all around them.

"What were you upset about earlier?" he asked softly.

She sighed. "I unpacked Allie's wedding dress."

He sucked in his breath. "And what? You wished it was yours?"

"It was mine," she whispered. "It was the dress she drew for me one of those afternoons all those years ago."

"What? The very same dress? Maybe you're just remembering it wrong."

Was there any way to tell him she had kept that picture without seeming hopelessly pathetic?

"No," she said firmly. "It was that dress."

"Representing all your hopes and dreams," he said. "No wonder you were crying."

She felt a surge of tenderness for him that there was no mockery in his tone, but instead, a lovely empathy.

"It was just a shock. I am hoping it is just a weird coincidence. But I'm worried. I didn't know Allie that well when we were teenagers. I don't know her at all now. What if it's all some gigantic game? What if she's playing with everyone?"

"Exactly the same thing I was upset about," Drew confessed to her. "My brother was supposed to be here. He's not. I've called him twice a day, every day, since I got here to find out why. He won't return my calls. That isn't like him."

"Tell me what *is* like him," Becky said gently.

And suddenly he just wanted to unburden himself. He felt as if he had carried it all alone for so long, and he was not sure he could go one more step with the weight of it all. It felt as if it was crushing him.

He was not sure he had ever felt this relaxed or this at ease with another person. Drew had a deep sense of being able to trust this woman in front of him. It felt as if every day before this one—all those laughter-filled days of getting to know one another, of splashing and playing, and throwing Frisbees—had been leading to this.

He needed to think about that: that this wholesome woman, with her girl-next-door look, was really a Mata Hari, a temptress who could pull secrets from an unwilling man. But he didn't heed the warning that was flashing in the back of his brain like a red light telling of a train coming.

Drew just started to talk, and it felt as if a rock had been removed from a dam that had held back tons of water for years. Now it was all flowing toward that opening, trying to get out.

"When my parents died, I was seventeen. I wasn't even a mature seventeen. I was a superficial surfer dude, riding a wave through life."

Something happened to Becky's face. A softness came to it that was so real it almost stole the breath out of his chest. It was so different than the puffy-lipped coos of sympathy that he had received from women in the past when he'd made the mistake of sharing even small parts of his story.

This felt as if he could go lay his head on Becky's slender, naked shoulder, and rest there for a long, long time.

"I'm so sorry," she said quietly, "about the death of your parents. Both of them died at the same time?"

"It was a car accident." He could stop right there, but no, he just kept going. All those words he had never spoken felt as if they were now rushing to escape a building on fire, jostling with each other in their eagerness to be out.

"They had gone out to celebrate the anniversary of some friends. They never came home. A policeman arrived at the door and told me what had happened. Not their fault at all, a drunk driver..."

"Drew," she breathed softly. Somehow her hand found his, and the dam within him was even more compromised.

"You have never met a person more totally unqualified for the job of raising a seven-year-old brother than the seventeen-year-old me."

She squeezed his hand, as if she believed in the younger him, making him want to go on, to somehow dissuade this faith in him.

He cleared his throat. "It was me or foster care, so—" He rolled his shoulders.

"I think that's the bravest thing I ever heard," she said.

"No, it wasn't," he said fiercely. "Brave is when you have a choice. I didn't have any choice."

"You did," she insisted, as fierce as him. "You did have a choice and you chose love."

That word inserted into any conversation between them should have stopped it cold. But it didn't. In fact, it felt as if more of the wall around everything he held inside crumbled, as if her words were a wrecking ball seeking the weakest point in that dam.

"I love my brother," he said. "I just don't know if he knows how much I do."

"He can't be that big a fool," Becky said.

"I managed to finish out my year in high school and

then I found a job on a construction crew. I was tired all the time. And I never seemed to be able to make enough money. Joe sure wasn't wearing the designer clothes the rest of the kids had. I got mad if he asked. That's why he probably doesn't have a clue how I feel about him."

Becky's hand was squeezing his with unbelievable strength. It was as if her strength—who could have ever guessed this tiny woman beside him held so much strength?—was passing between them, right through the skin of her hand into his, entering his bloodstream.

"I put one foot in front of the other," Drew told her. "I did my best to raise my brother. But I was so scared of messing up that I think I was way too strict with him. I thought if I let him know how much I cared about him he would perceive it as weakness and I would lose control. Of him. Of life.

"I'd already seen what happened when I was not in control."

"Did you feel responsible for the death of your parents?" she asked. He could hear that she was startled by the question.

"I guess I asked myself, over and over, what I could have done. And the answer seemed to be, 'Never let anyone you love out of your sight. Never let go.' Most days, I felt as if I was hanging on by a thread.

"When he was a teen? I was not affectionate. I was like Genghis Khan, riding roughshod over the troops. The default answer to almost everything he wanted to do was *no*. When I did loosen the reins a bit, he had to check in with me. He had a curfew. I sucked, and he let me know it."

"Sucked?" she said, indignant.

"Yeah, we both agreed on that. Not that I let him know I agreed with him in the you-suck department."

"Then you were both wrong. What you did was noble," she said quietly. "The fact that you think you did it imperfectly does not make it less noble."

"Noble!" he snapped, wanting to show only annoyance and not vulnerability. "There's nothing noble about acting on necessity."

But she was having none of it. "It's even noble that you saw it as a necessity, not a choice."

"Whatever," he said. He suddenly disliked himself. He felt as if he was a small dog yapping and yapping and yapping at the postman. He sat up. She sat up, too. He folded his arms over his chest, a shield.

"Given that early struggle, you seem to have done well for yourself."

"A man I worked for gave me a break," Drew admitted, even though he had ordered himself to stop talking. "He was a developer. He told me I could have a lot in one of his subdivisions and put up a house on spec. I didn't have to pay for the lot until the house sold. It was the beginning of an amazing journey, but looking back, I think my drive to succeed also made me emotionally unavailable to my brother."

"You feel totally responsible for him, still."

Drew sighed, dragged a hand through his sun-dried hair. "I'm sure it's because of how I raised him that we are in this predicament we're in now, him marrying a girl I know nothing about, who may be using him. And you. And all of us."

"I don't see that as your fault."

"If I worked my ass off, I could feed him," he heard himself volunteering. "I could keep the roof over his head. I could get his books for school. I even managed to get him through college. But—"

"But what?"

"I could not teach him about finding a good relationship." Drew's voice dropped to a hoarse whisper. It felt as if every single word he had said had been circling around this essential truth.

"I missed them so much, my mom and dad. They could have showed him what he should be looking for. They were so stable. My mom was a teacher, my dad was a postal worker. Ordinary people, and yet they elevated the ordinary.

"I didn't know what I had when I had it. I didn't know what it was to wake up to my dad downstairs, making coffee for my mom, delivering it to her every morning. He sang a song while he delivered it. An old Irish folk song. They were always laughing and teasing each other. We were never rich but our house was full. The smell of cookies, the sound of them arguing good-naturedly about where to put the Christmas tree, my mom reading stories. I loved those stories way after I was too old for them. I used to find some excuse to hang out when she was reading to Joe at night. How could I hope to give any of that kind of love to my poor orphaned baby brother? When even thinking about all we had lost felt as if it would undermine the little bit of control that I was holding over my world? Instead, the environment I raised Joe in was so devoid of affection that he's gotten involved with Allie out of his sheer desperation to be loved."

"Maybe he longs for your family as much as you do."

"It's not that I didn't love him," Drew admitted gruffly. "I just didn't know how to say that to him."

"Maybe that's the area where he's going to teach you," she said softly.

Something shivered up and down Drew's spine, a tingle of pure warning, like a man might feel seconds before the cougar pounced from behind, or the plane began to lose altitude, or the earth began to shake. The remainder of the dam wall felt as if it tumbled down inside him.

"You can say that, even after finding the dress? When neither of us is sure about Allie or what her true motives are?"

"I'm going to make a decision to believe love is going to win. No matter what."

He stared at her. There should have been a choice involved here. There should have been a choice to get up and run.

But if there was that choice? He was helpless to make it.

Instead he went into her open arms like a warrior who had fought too many battles, like a warrior who had thought he would never see the lights of familiar fires again. He laid his head upon her breast and felt her hand, tender, on the nape of his neck.

He sighed against her, like a warrior who unexpectedly found himself in the place he had given up on. That place was home.

"You did your best," she said softly. "You can forgive yourself if you weren't perfect."

She began to hum softly. And then she began to sing. Her voice was clear and beautiful and it raised the hair on the back of his neck. It was as if it affirmed that love was the greatest force of all, and that it survived everything, even death.

Because of the millions of songs in the world, how was it possible Becky was gently singing this one, in her soft, true voice?

It was the same song his father had sung to his mother, every day as he brought her coffee.

Drew's surrender was complete. He had thought his story spilling out of him, like water out of a dam that had been compromised, would make him feel weak, and as though he had lost control.

Instead, he felt connected to Becky in a way he had not allowed himself to feel connected to another human being in a long, long time.

Instead, he realized how alone he had been in the world, and how good it felt not to be alone.

Instead, listening to her voice soar above the roar of the waterfall and feeling it tingle along his spine, it felt as though the ice was melting from around his heart. He felt the way he had felt diving into the water to save her all those days ago. He felt brave. Only this time, he felt as if he might be saving himself.

Drew realized he felt as brave as he ever had. He contemplated the irony that a complete surrender would make him feel the depth of his own courage.

You heal now.

And impossibly, beautifully, he was.

CHAPTER FOURTEEN

NIGHT HAD FALLEN by the time they left the waterfall and found their way back to the castle grounds. He left her with his T-shirt and walked beside her bare-chested, happy to give her the small protection of his clothing. He walked her to her bedroom door, and they stood there, looking at each other, drinking each other in like people who had been dying of thirst and had found a spring.

He touched the plumpness of her lip with his thumb, and her tongue darted out and tasted him.

She sighed her surrender, and he made a guttural, groaning sound of pure need. He did what he had been wanting to do all this time.

He planted his hands, tenderly, on either side of her head, and dropped his lips over hers. He kissed her thoroughly, exploring the tenderness of her lips with his own lips, and his tongue, probing the cool grotto of her mouth.

He had thought Becky, his little bookworm, would be shy, but she had always had that surprising side, and she surprised him now.

That gentle kiss of recognition, of welcome, that sigh of surrender, deepened quickly into something else.

It was need and it was desire. It was passion and it

was hunger. It was nature singing its ancient song of wanting life to have victory over the cycle of death.

That was what was in this kiss: everything it was to be human. Instinct and intuition, power and surrender, pleasure that bordered on pain it was so intense. He dragged his lips from hers and anointed her earlobes and her eyelids, her cheeks and the tip of her nose. He kissed the hollow of her throat, and then she pulled him back to her lips.

Her hands were all over him, touching, exploring, celebrating the hard strength in the muscles that gloried at the touch of her questing fingertips.

Finally, rational thought pushed through his primal reaction to her, calling a stern *no*. But it took every ounce of Drew's substantial strength to peel back from her. She stood there, quivering with need, panting, her eyes wide on his face.

His rational mind was gaining a foothold now that he had managed to step back from her. She had never looked more beautiful, even though her hair was a mess, and any makeup she had been wearing had washed off long ago. She had never looked more beautiful, even though she was standing there in a T-shirt that was way too large for her.

But nothing could hide the light shining from her. It was the purity of that light that reminded Drew that Becky was not the kind of girl you tangled with lightly. She required his intentions to be very clear.

In the past few days, he had felt his mother's spirit around him in a way he had not experienced since her death. It was the kind of idea he might have scoffed at two short weeks ago.

And yet this island, with its magic, and Becky with

her own enchantment, made things that had seemed impossible before feel entirely possible now.

Drew knew his mother would be expecting him to be a decent man, expecting him to rise to what she would have wanted him to be if she had lived.

She knew what he had forgotten about himself: that he was a man of courage and decency. Drew took another step back from Becky. He saw the sense of loss and confusion in her face.

"I have to go," he said, his voice hoarse.

"Please, don't."

Her voice was hoarse, too, and she stepped toward him. She took the waistband of his shorts and pulled her to him with surprising strength.

"Don't go," she said fiercely.

"You don't know what you're asking."

"Yes, I do."

For a moment he was so torn, but then his need to be decent won out. If things were going to go places with this girl—and he knew they were—it would require him to be a better man than he had been with women in the past.

It would require him to do the honorable thing.

"I have to make a phone call tonight, before it's too late." It was a poor excuse, but it was the only one he could think of. With great reluctance, he untangled her hands from where they held him, and once again stepped back from her.

If she asked again, he was not going to be able to refuse. A man's strengths had limits, after all.

But she accepted his decision. She raked a hand through her hair and looked disgruntled, but pulled herself together and tilted her chin at him.

"I have a phone call to make, too," she said. She was, just like that, his little bookworm spelling-bee contestant again, prim and sensible, and pulling back from the wild side she had just shown him.

She took a step back from him.

Go, he ordered himself. But he didn't. He stepped back toward her. He kissed her again, quickly, and then he tore himself away from her and went to his own quarters.

Rattled by what he was feeling, he took a deep breath. He wandered to the window and looked at the moon, and listened to the lap of the water on the beach. He felt as alive as he had ever felt.

He glanced at the time, swore softly, took out his cell phone and stabbed in Joe's number.

There was, predictably, no answer. He needed to tell Joe what he had learned of love tonight. It might save Joe from imminent disaster. But, of course, there was no answer, and you could hardly leave a message saying somehow you had stumbled on the secret of life and you needed to share that *right now*.

Joe would think his coolheaded, hard-hearted brother had lost his mind. So, that conversation would have to wait until tomorrow.

According to the information Becky had, Joe and Allie were supposed to arrive only on the morning of the wedding day. This was apparently to slip under the radar of the press.

Tomorrow, the guests would begin arriving, in a co-ordinated effort that involved planes and boats landing on Sainte Simone all day.

Two hundred people. It was going to be controlled chaos. And then Joe and Allie would arrive the next day, just hours before the wedding. How was he going to get Joe alone? Drew was aware that he *had* to get his brother alone, that he *had* to figure out what the hell was really going on between him and Allie.

And he was aware that he absolutely *had* to protect Becky. He thought of her tears over that dress that Allie had had specially made, and he felt fury building in him. In fact, all the fury of his powerlessness over Joe's situation seemed to be coming to a head.

"Look, Joe," he said, after that annoying beep that made him want to pick up the chair beside his bed and throw it against the wall, "I don't know what your fiancée is up to, but you give her a message from me. You tell your betrothed if she does anything to hurt Becky English—anything—I will not rest until I've tracked her to the ends of the earth and dealt with it. You know me well enough to know I mean it. I'm done begging you to call me. But I don't think you have a clue what you're getting mixed up in."

Drew disconnected the call, annoyed with himself. He had lost control, and probably reduced his chances of getting his brother to meet with him alone.

Becky went to her room and shut the door, leaning against it. Her knees felt wobbly. She felt breathless. She touched her lips, as if she could still feel the warmth of his fire claiming her. She hugged herself. She could not believe she had invited Drew Jordan into her room. She was not that kind of girl!

Thank goodness his good sense had prevailed, but what did that mean? That he was not feeling things quite as intensely as she was?

She sank down on her bed. It was as if the world had

gone completely silent, and into that silence flowed a frightening truth.

She had fallen for Drew Jordan. She loved him. She had never felt anything like what she was feeling right now: tingling with aliveness, excited about the future, aware that life had the potential to hold the most miraculous surprises. She, Becky English, who had sworn off it, had still fallen under its spell. She was in love. It wasn't just the seduction of this wildly romantic setting. It wasn't.

She loved him so much.

It didn't make any sense. It was too quick, wasn't it?

But, in retrospect, her relationship with Jerry had made perfect sense, and had unfolded with respectable slowness.

And there had been nothing real about it. She had been chasing security. She had settled for safety. Salt and pepper. Good grief, she had almost made herself a prisoner of a dull and ordinary life.

But now she knew how life was supposed to feel. And she felt so alive and grateful and on fire with all the potential the days ahead held. They didn't feel safe at all. They felt like they were loaded with unpredictable forces and choices. It felt as if she was plunging into the great unknown, and she was astonished to find she *loved* how the great adventure that was life and love was making her feel.

And following on the heels of her awareness of how much she loved Drew, and how much that love was going to make her life change, Becky felt a sudden fury with his brother. How could he treat Drew like this? Surely Joe was not so stupid that he could not see his brother had sacrificed everything for him?

Drew's whole life had become about making a life for his brother, about holding everything together. He had tried so hard and done so much, and now Joe would not even return his phone calls?

It was wrong. It was just plain old wrong.

Becky's fingers were shaking when she dialed Allie's number. She didn't care that it was late in Spain. She didn't care at all. Of course, after six rings she got Allie's voice commanding her to leave a message.

"Allie, it's Becky English. I need you to get an urgent message to Joe. He needs to call his brother. He needs to call Drew right now. Tomorrow morning at the latest." There, that was good enough. But her voice went on, shaking with emotion. "It's unconscionable that he would be ignoring Drew's attempts to call him after all Drew has done for him. I know you will both be arriving here early on the morning of the wedding, but he needs to talk to Drew before that. As soon as you get this message he needs to call."

There. She didn't need to say one other thing. And yet somehow she was still talking.

"You tell him if he doesn't call his brother immediately he'll be..." She thought and then said, "Dealing with me!"

She disconnected her phone. Then snickered. She had just used a terrible, demanding tone of voice on the most prosperous client she had ever had. She didn't care. What was so funny was her saying Drew's brother would be dealing with her, as if that was any kind of threat.

And yet she felt more powerful right now than she had ever felt in her entire life. It did feel as if she could whip that disrespectful young pup into shape!

That's what love did, she supposed. It didn't take away power, it gave it.

Becky allowed herself to feel the shock of that. She had somehow, someway, fallen in love with Drew Jordan. And not just a little bit in love: irrevocably, crazily, impossibly, feverishly in love.

It was nothing at all like what she had thought was love with Jerry. Nothing. That had felt safe and solid and secure, even though it had turned out to be none of those things. This was the most exciting thing that she had ever felt. It felt as if she was on the very crest of the world's highest roller coaster, waiting for that stomach-dropping swoop downward, her heart in her throat, both terrified and exhilarated by the pathway ahead. And just like that roller coaster, it felt as if somehow she had fully committed before she knew exactly where it was all leading. It felt like now she had no choice but to hang on tight and enjoy the wildest ride of her life.

In a trance of delight at the unexpected turn in her life, Becky pulled off Drew's T-shirt and put on her pajamas. And then she rolled up the T-shirt, and even though it was still slightly damp, she used it as her pillow and drifted off to sleep with the scent of him lulling her like a boat rocking on gentle waves.

She awoke the next morning to the steady *wop-wop-wop* of helicopter blades slicing the air. At first, she lay in bed, hugging Drew's T-shirt, listening and feeling content. Waking up to the sound of helicopters was not unusual on Sainte Simone. It was the primary way that supplies were delivered, and with the wedding just one day away, all kinds of things would be arriving today. Fresh flowers. The cake. The photographer.

Two hundred people would also be arriving over

the course of the day, on boats and by small commercial jets.

There was no time for lollygagging, Becky told herself sternly. She cast back the covers, gave the T-shirt one final hug before putting it under her pillow and then got up and went to the window.

One day, she thought, looking at the helicopters buzzing above her. She had to focus. She had to shake off this dazed, delicious feeling that she was in love and that was all that mattered.

And then it slowly penetrated her bliss that something was amiss. Her mouth fell open. She should have realized from the noise levels that something was dreadfully wrong, but she had not.

There was not one helicopter in the skies above Sainte Simone. From her place at the window, she could count half a dozen. It looked like an invasion force, but with none of the helicopters even attempting to land. They were hovering and dipping and swooping.

She could see a cameraman leaning precariously out one open door! There were so many helicopters in the tiny patch of sky above the island that it was amazing they were managing not to crash into each other.

As she watched, one of the aircraft swooped down over the pavilion. The beautiful white gauze panels began to whip around as though they had been caught in a hurricane. One ripped away, and was swept on air currents out to the ocean, where it floated down in the water, looking for all the world like a bridal veil.

A man—Josh, she thought—raced out into the surf and grabbed the fabric, then shook his fist at the helicopter. The helicopter swooped toward him, the cameraman leaning way out to get that shot.

Becky turned from the window, got dressed quickly and hurried down the stairs and out the main door onto the lawn. The staff were all out there—even the chef in his tall hat—staring in amazement at the frenzied sky dance above them.

Josh came and thrust the wet ball of fabric at her.

"Sorry," he muttered. Tandu turned and looked at her sadly. "It's on the news this morning. That the wedding is here, tomorrow. I have satellite. It's on every single channel."

She felt Drew's presence before she saw him. She felt him walk up beside her and she turned to him, and scanned his familiar face, wanting him to show her how to handle this and what to do.

He put his hand on her shoulder, and she nestled into the weight of it. This is what it meant to not be alone. Life could throw things at you, but you didn't have to handle it all by yourself. The weight of the catastrophe could be divided between them.

Couldn't it? She turned to him. "What are we going to do?"

He looked at her blankly, and she realized he was trying to read her lips. There was no way he could have heard her. She repeated her question, louder.

"I don't know," he said.

He didn't know? She felt a faint shiver of disappointment.

"How could we hold a wedding under these circumstances?" she shouted. "No one will be able to hear anything. The fabric is already tearing away from the pavilion. What about Allie's dress? And veil? What about dinner and candles and..." Her voice fell away.

"I don't think there's going to be a wedding," he said.

Her sense of her whole world shifting intensified. He could not save the day. Believing that he could would only lead to disillusionment. Believing in another person could only lead to heartache.

How on earth had she been so swept away that she had forgotten that?

She shot him a look. He sounded sorry, but was there something else in his voice? She studied Drew more carefully. He had his handsome head tilted to look at the helicopters, his arms folded over his chest.

Did he look grimly satisfied that there was a very good possibility that there was going to be no wedding?

CHAPTER FIFTEEN

BECKY FELT HER heart plummet, and it was not totally because the wedding she had worked so hard on now seemed to be in serious danger of being canceled.

Who, more than any other person on the face of the earth, did not want this wedding to happen?

Drew took his eyes from the sky and looked at her. He frowned. "Why are you looking at me like that?"

"I was just wondering about that phone call you were all fired up to make last night," she said. She could hear the stiffness in her own voice, and she saw that her tone registered with him.

"I recall being all fired up," he said, "but not about a phone call."

How dare he throw that in her face right now? That she had invited him in. He saw it as being all fired up. She saw, foolishly, that she had put her absolute trust in him.

"Is this why you didn't come in?" she said, trying to keep her tone low and be heard above the helicopters at the same time.

"Say what?"

"You didn't give in to my wanton invitation because you already knew you were planning this, didn't you?"

"Planning this?" he echoed, his brow furrowing. "Planning what, exactly?"

Becky sucked in a deep breath. "You let it out, didn't you?"

"What?"

"Don't play the innocent with me! You let it out on purpose, to stop the wedding. To stop your brother and Allie from getting married, to buy yourself a little more time to convince him not to do it."

He didn't deny it. Something glittered in his eyes, hard and cold, that she had never seen before. She reminded herself, bitterly, that there were many things about him she had never seen before. She had only known him two weeks. How could she, who of all people should be well versed in the treachery of the human heart, have let her guard down?

"That's why you had to rush to the phone last night," she decided. "Maybe you even thought you were protecting me. I should have never told you about the wedding dress."

"There are a lot of things we should have never told each other," he bit out.

She stared at him and realized the awful truth. It had all happened too fast between them. It was a reminder to her that they didn't know each other at all. She had been susceptible to the whole notion of love. Because the island was so romantic, because of that dress, because of those crazy moments when she had wanted to feel unencumbered, she had thrown herself on the altar of love with reckless abandon.

She'd been unencumbered all right! Every ounce of good sense she'd possessed had fled her!

But really, hadn't she known this all along? That love

was that roller coaster ride, thrilling and dangerous? And that every now and then it went right off the tracks?

She shot him an accusing look. He met her gaze unflinchingly.

A plane circled overhead and began to prepare to land through the minefield of helicopters. Over his shoulder, she could see a passenger barge plowing through seas made rough by the wind coming off those blades.

"Guess what?" she said wearily. "That will be the first of the guests arriving. All those people are expecting a wedding."

He lifted a shoulder negligently. What all those people were expecting didn't matter one iota to him. And neither did all her hard work. Or what this disaster could mean to her career. He didn't care about her at all.

But if he thought she was going to take this lying down, he was mistaken.

"I'm going to call Allie's publicity people," she said, with fierce determination. "Maybe they can make this disaster stop. Maybe they can call off the hounds if they are offered something in exchange."

"Good luck with that," Drew said coolly. "My experience with hounds, limited as it might be, is once they've caught the scent, there is no calling them off."

"I'm sure if Allie offers to do a photo shoot just for them, after the wedding, they will stop this. I'm sure of it!"

Of course, she was no such thing.

He gazed at her. "Forever hopeful," he said. She heard the coldness in his tone, as if being hopeful was a bad thing.

And it was! She had allowed herself to hope she could love this man. And now she saw it was impossible. Now, when it was too late. When she could have none of the glory and all of the pain.

Drew could not let Becky see how her words hit him, like a sword cleaving him in two. Last night he had taken the biggest chance he had ever taken. He had trusted her with everything. He had been wide-open.

Love.

Sheesh. He, of all people, should know better than that. Joe had not called him back. That's what love really was. Leaving yourself wide-open, all right, wide-open to pain. And rejection. Leaving yourself open to the fact that the people you loved most of all could misinterpret everything you did, run it through their own filter and come to their own conclusions, as wrong as those might be. He, of all people, should know that better than anyone else.

How could she think that he would do this to her? How could she trust him so little? He felt furious with her, and fury felt safe. Because when his fury with Becky died down, he knew what would remain. What always remained when love was gone. Pain. An emptiness so vast it felt as though it could swallow a man whole.

And he, knowing that truth as intimately as any man could know it, had still left himself wide-open to revisiting that pain. What did that mean?

"That I'm stupid," he told himself nastily. "Just plain old garden-variety stupid."

Becky felt as if she was in a trance. Numb. But it didn't matter what she was feeling. She'd agreed to do a job, and right now her job was welcoming the first of the wedding guests to the island and trying to hide it from them all that the wedding of the century was quickly turning into the fiasco of the century.

She stood with a smile fixed on her face as the door of the plane opened and the first passenger stepped down onto the steps.

In a large purple hat, and a larger purple dress, was Mrs. Barchkin, her now retired high school social sciences teacher.

"Why, Becky English!" Mrs. Barchkin said cheerily. "What on earth are you doing here?"

Her orders had been to keep the wedding secret. She had not told one person in her small town she was coming here.

Her smile clenched in place, she said, "No, what on earth are you doing here?"

Mrs. Barchkin was clutching a rumpled card in a sweaty hand. She passed it to Becky. Despite the fact people were piling up behind Mrs. Barchkin, Becky smoothed out the card and read, "In appreciation of your kindness, I ask you to be my guest at a celebration of love." There were all the details promising a limousine pickup and the adventure of a lifetime.

"Pack for a week and plan to have fun!" And all this was followed with Allie Ambrosia's flowing signature, both the small *i*'s dotted with hearts.

"Isn't this all too exciting?" Mrs. Barchkin said.

"Too exciting," Becky agreed woodenly. "If you just go over there, that golf cart will take you to your accommodations. Don't worry about your luggage."

Don't worry. Such good advice. But Becky's sense of worry grew as she greeted the rest of the guests coming down the steps of the plane. There was a poor-looking young woman in a cheaply made dress, holding a baby who looked ill. There was a man and a wife and their three kids chattering about the excitement of their first plane ride. There was a minister. At least he *might* be here to conduct the ceremony.

Not a single passenger who got off that plane was what you would expect of Hollywood's A-list. And neither, Becky realized an hour later, was anyone who got off the passenger barge. In fact, most everyone seemed to be the most ordinary of people, people who would have fit right in on Main Street in Moose Run.

They were all awed by the island and the unexpected delight of an invitation to the wedding of one of the most famous people in the world. But none of them—not a single person of the dozens that were now descending on the island—actually seem to know Allie Ambrosia or Joe Jordan.

Becky had a deepening conviction that somehow they were all pawns in Allie's big game. Maybe, just maybe, Drew had not been so wrong in doing everything he could to stop the wedding.

But why had he played with her? Why had he made it seem as if he was going along with getting a wedding ready if he was going to sabotage it? Probably, this— the never-ending storm of helicopters hovering overhead—had been a last-ditch effort to stop things when his every effort to reach his brother had been frustrated.

Still, the fact was she had trusted him. She was not going to make excuses for him! She was determined to not even think about him.

As each boat and plane delivered its guests and departed, Becky's unease grew. Her increasingly frantic texts and messages to Allie and members of Allie's staff were not being answered. In fact, Allie's voice mailbox was now full.

Becky crawled into bed that night, exhausted. The wedding was less than twenty-four hours away. If they were going to cancel it, they needed to do that now.

Though one good thing about all the excitement was that she had not had time to give a thought to Drew. But now she did.

And lying there in her bed, staring at the ceiling, she burst into tears. And the next morning she was thankful she had used up every one of her tears, because a private jet landed at precisely 7:00 a.m.

The door opened.

And absolutely nothing happened. Eventually, the crew got off. A steward told her, cheerfully, they were going to layover here. He showed her the same invitation she had seen at least a dozen times. The one that read, "In appreciation of your kindness, I ask you to be my guest at a celebration of love."

Becky had to resist the impulse to tear that invitation from his hands and rip it into a million pieces. Because now she knew the plane was empty. And Allie and Joe had not gotten off it.

Of course, it could be part of the elaborate subterfuge that was necessary to avoid the paparazzi, but the helicopters overhead were plenty of evidence they had already failed at that.

How could she, Becky asked herself with a shake of her head, still hope? How could she still hope they were coming, and still hope that love really was worth celebrating?

She quit resisting the impulse. She took the invitation from the crew member, tore it into a dozen pieces and threw them to the wind. Despite the surprised looks she received, it felt amazingly good to do that!

She turned and walked away. No more hoping. No more trying to fill in the blanks with optimistic fiction. She was going to have to find Tandu and cancel everything. She was going to have to figure out the logistics of how to get all those disappointed people back out of here.

Her head hurt thinking about it.

So Drew had won the headache competition after all. And by a country mile at that.

CHAPTER SIXTEEN

DREW PULLED HIMSELF from the ocean and flung himself onto the beach. His crew had just finished the gazebo and had departed, sending him looks that let him know he'd been way too hard on them. He'd had them up at dawn, putting the final touches of paint on the gazebo, making sure the dance floor was ready.

What did they expect? There was supposed to be a wedding here in a few hours. Of course he had been hard on them.

Maybe a little too hard, since it now seemed almost everyone on the island, except maybe the happy guests, had figured out the bride and groom were missing.

Drew knew his foul mood had nothing to do with the missing bride and groom, or the possibility, growing more real by the second, that there wasn't going to be a wedding. He had driven his crew to perfection anyway, unreasonably.

He had tried to swim it off, but now, lying in the sand, he was aware he had not. The helicopter that buzzed him to see if he was anyone interesting did not help his extremely foul mood.

How could Becky possibly think he had called the

press? After all they had shared together, how could she not know who he really was?

It penetrated his morose that his phone, lying underneath his shirt, up the beach, was ringing. And then he froze. The ring tone was the one he had assigned for Joe!

He got up and sprinted across the sand.

"Hello?"

"Hi, bro."

It felt like a shock to hear his brother's voice. Even in those two small syllables, Drew was sure he detected something. Sheepishness?

"How are you, Drew?"

"Cut the crap."

Silence. He thought Joe might have hung up on him, but he heard him breathing.

"Where the hell have you been? Why haven't you been answering my calls? Are you on your way here?"

"Drew, I have something to tell you."

Drew was aware he was holding his breath.

"Allie and I got married an hour ago."

"What?"

"The whole island thing was just a ruse. Allie leaked it to the press yesterday morning that we were going to get married there to divert them away from where we really are."

"You lied to me?" He could hear the disbelief and disappointment in his own voice.

"I feel terrible about that. I'm sorry."

"But why?"

Inside he was thinking, *How could you get married without me to stand beside you? I might have made mistakes, but I'm the one who has your back. Who has always had your back.*

"It's complicated," Joe said.

"Let me get this straight. You aren't coming here at all?"

"No."

Poor Allie, Drew thought.

"We got married an hour ago, just Allie and me and a justice of the peace. We're in Topeka, Kansas. Who would ever think to look there, huh?"

"Topeka, Kansas," he repeated dully.

His brother took it as a question. "You don't have to be a resident of the state to get married here. There's a three-day waiting period for the license, but I went down and applied for it a month ago."

"You've been planning this for a month?" Drew felt the pain of it. He had been excluded from one of the most important events of his brother's life. And it was his own fault.

"I'm sorry," he said.

"For what?" Joe sounded astounded.

"That I could never tell you what you needed to hear."

"I'm not following."

"That I loved you and cared about you and would have fought alligators for you."

"Drew! You think I don't know that?"

"I guess if you know it, I don't understand any of this."

"It's kind of all part of a larger plan. I'll fill you in soon. I promise. Meanwhile, Allie's got her people on it right now. In a few hours the press will know we aren't there, and whatever's going on there will die down. They'll leave you guys alone."

"Leave us alone? You think I'm going to stay here?"

"Why not? It's a party. That's all the invitations ever said. That it was a party to celebrate love."

"Who are all these people arriving here?"

And when Joe told him, Drew could feel himself, ever so reluctantly, letting go of the anger.

Even his anger at Becky felt as if it was dissipating.

He understood, suddenly, exactly why she had jumped at the first opportunity to see him in a bad light. That girl was terrified of love. She'd been betrayed by it at too many turns. She was terrified of what she was feeling for him.

"Joe? Tell Allie not to call Becky about the wedding not happening. I'll look after it. I'll tell her myself."

There was a long silence. And then Joe said softly, "All part of a larger plan."

"Yeah, whatever." He wanted to tell his brother congratulations, but somehow he couldn't. Who was this woman that Joe had married? It seemed as if she was just playing with all their strings as if they were her puppets.

Drew threw on his shirt and took the now familiar path back toward the castle. What remained of his anger at Becky for not trusting him was completely gone.

All he wanted to do was protect her from one more devastating betrayal. He understood, suddenly, what love was. With startling clarity he saw that it was the ability to see that it was not all about him. To be able to put her needs ahead of his own and not be a baby because his feelings had been hurt.

As he got closer to the castle, he could see there were awestruck people everywhere prowling the grounds. He spotted Tandu in the crowd, talking to a tall, distinguished-looking man in a casual white suit and bare feet.

"Mr. Drew Jordan, have you met Mr. Lung?" Tandu asked him.

"Pleasure," Drew said absently. "Tandu, can I talk to you for a minute?"

Tandu stepped to the side with him. "Have you seen Becky?" he asked, with some urgency.

"A few minutes ago. She told me to cancel everything."

So, she already knew, or thought she did. She was carrying the burden of it by herself.

"Impossible to cancel," Tandu said. "The wedding must go on!"

"Tandu, there is not going to be a wedding. I just spoke to my brother."

"Ah," he said. "Oh, well, we celebrate love anyway, hmm?" And then he gave Drew a look that was particularly piercing, and disappeared into the crowd.

"How are you enjoying my island?" Bart Lung was on his elbow.

"It's a beautiful place," Drew said, scanning the crowd for Becky. "Uh, look, Mr. Lung—"

"Bart, please."

"Bart, I think you need to have a qualified first aid person on the island to host this many guests."

"I have an excellent first aid attendant. That was him who just introduced us. Don't be fooled by the tray of canapés."

"Look, Tandu is a nice guy. Stellar. I just don't think being afraid of blood is a great trait for a first aid attendant."

"Tandu? Afraid of blood? Who told you that?"

Before Drew could answer that Tandu himself had told him that, Bart went on.

"Tandu is from this island, but don't be fooled by that island boy accent or the white shirt or the tray of canapés. He's a medical student at Oxford. He comes back in the summers to help out." Bart chortled. "Afraid of blood! I saw him once when he was the first responder to a shark attack. I have never seen so much blood and I have never seen such cool under pressure."

Drew felt a shiver run up and down the whole length of his spine.

And then he saw Becky. She was talking to someone who was obviously a member of the flight crew, and she was waving her arms around expressively.

"Excuse me. I have an urgent matter I need to take care of."

"Of course."

"Becky!"

She turned and looked at him, and for a moment, everything she felt was naked in her face.

And everything she was.

Drew realized fully that her lack of trust was a legacy from her past, and that to be the man she needed, the man worthy of her love, he needed to not hurt her more, but to understand her fears and vulnerabilities and to help her heal them.

Just as she had, without even knowing that was what she was doing, helped him heal his own fears and vulnerabilities.

"We need to talk," he said. "In private."

She looked at him, and then looked away. "Now? I don't see that there is any way they are coming. I was just asking about the chances of getting some flight schedules changed."

Despite the fact she *knew* Allie and Joe weren't coming, despite the fact that she had asked Tandu about canceling, despite the fact that she was trying to figure out how to get rid of all these people, he saw it, just for a second, wink behind her bright eyes.

Hope.

Against all odds, his beautiful, funny, bookish, spunky Becky was still hoping for a happy ending.

"We need to talk," Drew told her.

She hesitated, scanned the sky for an incoming jet and then sighed. "Yes, all right," she said.

He led her away from the crowded front lawn and front terrace.

"I just talked to Joe," he said in a low voice.

"And? Is everything okay? Between you?"

This was who she really was: despite it all, despite thinking that he had betrayed her trust, she was worried about him and his troubled relationship with his brother, first. And the wedding second.

"I guess time will tell."

"You didn't patch things up," she said sadly.

"He didn't phone to patch things up. Becky, he gave me some bad news."

"Is he all right?" There it was again, a boundless compassion for others. "What?" she whispered.

"There isn't going to be a wedding."

It was then that he knew she had been holding her breath, waiting for a miracle, because the air whooshed out of her and her shoulders sagged.

"Because of the press finding out?" she said.

"No, Becky, there was never going to be a wedding."

She looked at him with disbelief.

"Apparently this whole thing—" he swept his arm to indicate the whole thing "—was just a giant ruse planned out in every detail by Allie. She sent the press here, yesterday morning, on a wild-goose chase."

"It wasn't you," she whispered. Her skin turned so pale he wondered if she was going to faint.

"Of course it wasn't me."

She began to tremble. "But how are you ever going to forgive me for thinking it was you?"

"I don't believe," he said softly, "that you ever did believe that. Not in your heart."

"Why did she do that?" Becky wailed.

"So that she and my brother could sneak away and get married in peace. Which they did. An hour ago. In Topeka, Kansas, of all places."

Her hand was on his arm. She was looking at him searchingly. "Your brother got married without you?"

He lifted a shoulder.

"Oh! That is absolutely unforgivable!"

"It's not your problem."

"Oh, my God! Here I am saying what is unforgivable in other people, and what I did was unforgivable. I accused you of alerting the press!"

"Is it possible," he asked her softly, "that you wanted to be mad at me? Is it possible it was just one last-ditch effort to protect yourself from falling in love with me?"

She was doing now what she had not done when he told her there would be no wedding. She was crying.

"I'm so sorry," she said.

"Is it true then? Are you in love with me?"

"Yes, I'm afraid it is. It's true."

"It's true for me, too. I'm in love with you, Becky. I am so in love with you. And I'm as terrified as you are. I'm afraid of loving. I'm afraid of loss. I'm afraid I can't be the man you need me to be. I'm afraid…"

She stopped him with her lips. She stopped him by twining her hands around his neck and pulling him close to her.

And when she did that, he wasn't afraid of anything anymore.

CHAPTER SEVENTEEN

"Why did she do all this?" Becky asked.

"Joe told me that she never told any of these people they were coming to a wedding."

"She didn't! That's true. She told them in appreciation for their kindness they were being invited to a celebration of love. I saw some of the invitations today. It doesn't really answer *why* she did all this, does it? All this tremendous expense for a ruse? There are a million things that would have been easier and cheaper to send the press in the wrong direction so they could get married in private."

"Joe told me why she did it."

"And?"

"Joe told me that people would look at her humble beginnings and share personal stories about themselves. And so she sent invitations to the ones with the most compelling personal stories, a comeback from cancer, a bankruptcy, surviving the death of a child.

"Joe says she has thought of nothing else for months—that she did her homework. That she chose the ones who rose above their personal circumstances and still gave back to others.

"He said those are the ones they want to celebrate

love with them. He said Allie wants her story to bring hope to lives where too many bad things had occurred. He says she's determined to make miracles happen."

"Wow," Becky said softly. "It almost makes me not want to be mad at her."

"Regretfully, me, too."

They laughed softly together.

"It's quite beautiful, isn't it?" Becky said quietly.

He wanted to harrumph it. He wanted to say it was impossibly naive and downright dumb. He wanted to say his future sister-in-law—no, make that his current sister-in-law—was showing signs of being extraordinarily clever about manipulating others.

He wanted to say all that, but somehow he couldn't.

Because here he was, the beneficiary of one of the miracles that Allie Ambrosia had been so determined to make happen.

You heal now, Tandu had said to him. And somehow his poor wounded heart had healed, just enough to let this woman beside him past his defenses. Now, he found himself hoping they would have the rest of their lives to heal each other, to get better and better.

"You know, Becky, all those people are expecting a wedding. Tandu said it's impossible to put a hold on the food now."

"It's harder to reschedule those exit flights than you might think."

"The minister is already here. And so is the photographer."

"What of it?"

"I think any wedding that is a true expression of love will honor why we are all here."

"What are you suggesting?"

"I don't think she ever had that dress made to hurt you."

"Oh, my God." Becky's fist flew to her mouth, and tears shone behind her eyes.

"And I've been thinking about this. There is no way my brother would ever get married without me. Not unless he thought it was for my own good."

"They put us together deliberately!"

"I'm afraid that's what I'm thinking."

"It's maddening."

"Yes."

"It's a terrible manipulation."

"Yes."

"It's like a blind date on steroids."

"Yes."

"Are you angry?"

"No."

"Me, neither."

"Because it worked. If they would have just introduced us over dinner somewhere, it would have never worked out like this."

"I know. You would have seen me as a girl from Moose Run, one breath away from becoming a nun."

"You would have seen me as superficial and arrogant and easily bored."

"You would have never given me a second chance."

"You wouldn't have wanted one."

They were silent for a long time, contemplating how things could have gone, and how they did.

"What time is the wedding?" he asked her.

"It's supposed to be at three."

"That means you have one hour and fifteen minutes to make up your mind."

"I've made up my mind," Becky whispered.

"You should put on that dress and we should go to that gazebo I built, and in the incredible energy of two hundred people who have been hand-chosen for the bigness of their hearts, we should get married."

"It won't be real," she whispered. "I mean, not legal. It will be like we're playing roles."

"Well, I won't be playing a role, and I don't think you're capable of it. We'll go to Kansas when it's all over. In three days we'll have a license."

"Are you asking me to marry you? For real? Not as part of Allie's amazing pretend world?"

"Absolutely, 100 percent for real."

She stared at him. She began to laugh, and then cry. She threw her arms around his neck. "Yes! Yes! Yes!" she said.

All the helicopters had gone away. The world was perfect and silent and sacred.

Despite the fact they were using up a great deal of that one hour and fifteen minutes, they talked. They talked about children. And where they would live. And what they would do. They talked about how Tandu seemed as if he was a bit of a matchmaker, too, leaving Drew to doctor Becky's leg when he had been more than capable of doing it himself, of delivering them to the best and most romantic places on the island, of "seeing" the future.

Finally, as the clock ticked down, they parted ways with a kiss.

Tandu was waiting for her when she arrived back at the castle. He took in her radiant face with satisfaction.

"You need my help to be best bride ever?"

"How do you know these things?" she asked him.

"I see."

"I know you're a medical student at Oxford."

He chuckled happily. "That is when *seeing* is the most helpful."

Tandu accompanied her up the stairs, but when she went to go to her room, Tandu nudged her in a different direction. "Take the bridal suite."

Becky stared at him suspiciously. "Have you been in on this all along?"

He smiled. "Allie has been to Sainte Simone before. I count her as my friend. I will go let the guests know there has been a slight change in plan and arrange some helpers. I will look after everything."

She could not argue with him. All her life she had never been able to accept good things happening to her, but she was willing to change. She was willing to embrace each gift as it was delivered.

Had she not been delivered a husband out of a storybook? Why not believe? She went to the bridal suite, and stood before the dress that she had hung up days before. She touched it, and it felt not unlike she had been a princess sleeping, who was now waking up.

Tandu had assembled some lovely women helpers and she was treated like a princess. Given that the time until the wedding was so brief, Becky was pampered shamelessly. Her hair was done, her makeup was applied.

And then the beautiful dress was delivered to her. She closed her eyes. Becky let her old self drop away with each stich of her clothing. The dress, and every dream that had been sewn right into the incredible fabric, skimmed over her naked skin. She heard the zipper whisper up.

"Look now," one of her shy helpers instructed.

Becky opened her eyes. Her mouth fell open. The most beautiful princess stood in front of her, her hair piled up on top of her head, with little tendrils kissing the sides of her face. Her eyes, expertly made-up, looked wide and gorgeous. Her cheekbones looked unbelievable. Her lips, pink glossed and slightly turned up in an almost secretive smile, looked sensual.

Her eyes strayed down the elegant curve of her neck to the full enchantment of the dress. The vision in the mirror wobbled like a mirage as her eyes filled with tears.

The dress was a confection, with its sweetheart neckline and fitted bodice, and layers and layers and layers of filmy fabric flowing out in that full skirt with an impossible train. It made her waist look as if a man could span it with his two hands.

Shoes were brought to her, and they looked, fantastically, like the glass slippers in fairy tales.

All those years ago this dress had been the epitome of her every romantic notion. Becky had been able to picture herself in it, but she had never been able to picture it being Jerry that she walked toward.

Because she had never felt like she felt in this moment.

She was so aware that the bride's beauty was not created by the dress. The dress only accentuated what was going on inside, that bubbling fountain of life that love had built within her.

"No crying! You'll ruin your makeup."

But everyone else in the room was crying, all of them feeling the absolute sanctity of this moment, when someone who has been a girl realizes she is ready to be a woman. When someone who has never known the reality of love steps fully into its light.

A beautiful bouquet of island flowers was placed in her hands.

"This way."

Still in a dream, she moved down the castle stairs and out the door. The grounds that had been such a beehive of activity were strangely deserted. A golf cart waited for her and it whisked her silently down the wide path, through the lushness of the tropical growth, to the beach.

She walked down that narrow green-shaded trail to where it opened at the beach. The chairs were all full. If anyone was disappointed that it was not Allie who appeared at the edge of the jungle, it did not show on a single face.

If she had to choose one word to explain the spirit she walked in and toward it would be *joy*.

Bart Lung bowed to her and offered her his arm. She kicked off the glass slippers and felt her feet sink into the sand. She was so aware that she felt as if she could feel every single grain squish up between her toes.

A four-piece ensemble began to play the traditional wedding march.

She dared to look at the gazebo. If this weren't true, this was the part where she would wake up. In her nightmares the gazebo would be empty.

But it was not empty. The minister that she had welcomed on the first plane stood there in purple cleric's robes, beaming at her.

And then Drew turned around.

Becky's breath caught in her throat. She faltered, but the light that burned in his eyes picked her up and made her strong. She moved across the space between them unerringly, her eyes never leaving his, her sense of wonder making it hard to breathe.

She was marrying this man. She was marrying this strong, funny, thrillingly handsome man who would protect those he loved with his life. She was the luckiest woman in the world and she knew it.

Bart let go of her arm at the bottom of the stairs, and Becky went to Drew like an arrow aimed straight for his heart.

She went to him like someone who had been lost in the wilderness catching sight of the way home.

She went to him with his children already being born inside her.

She repeated the vows, those age-old vows, feeling as if each word had a deep meaning she had missed before.

And then came these words:

"I now pronounce you husband and wife."

And before the minister could say anything more, Becky turned and cast her beautiful bouquet at the gathering and went into his arms and claimed his lips.

And then he picked her up and carried her down the steps and out into the ocean, and with the crowd cheering madly, he kissed her again, before he wrapped his arms tightly around her and they both collapsed into the embrace of a turquoise sea.

When they came up for air, they were laughing and sputtering, her perfect hair was ruined, her makeup was running down her face and her dress was clinging to her in wet ribbons.

"This has been the best day of my entire life," she told him. "There will never be another day as good as this one."

And Drew said to her, "No, that's not quite right. This day is just the beginning of the best days of our lives."

And he kissed her again, and the crowd went wild, but her world felt like a grotto of silence and peace, a place cut out of a busy world, just for them. A place created by love.

EPILOGUE

"WHO AGREED TO this insanity?" Drew demanded of his wife.

"You did," Becky told him. She handed him a crying baby and scooped the other one out of the car seat that had been deposited on their living room floor.

Drew frowned at the baby and held it at arm's length. "Does he stink?"

"Probably. I don't think that's he. I think it's she. Pink ribbon in hair."

Drew squinted at the pink ribbon. It would not be beyond his brother to put the ribbon in Sam's hair instead of Sally's.

"I've changed my mind," Drew declared over the howling of the smelly baby. "I am not ready for this. I am not even close to being ready for this."

"Well, it's too late. Your brother and Allie are gone to Sainte Simone. They never had a honeymoon, and if ever a couple needed one, they do."

"I'm not responsible for their choices," he groused, but he was aware it was good-naturedly. His sister-in-law, Allie, was exasperating. And flaky. She was completely out of touch with reality, and her career choice of pretending to be other people had made that quality even more aggravating in her. She believed, with a childlike enthusiasm, in the fairy tales she acted out, and was a huge proponent of happily-ever-after.

And yet…and yet, could you ask for anyone more genuinely good-hearted than her? Or generous? Or kind? Or devoted to her family in general, and his brother in particular?

There was no arguing that Joe, his sweet, shy brother, had blossomed into a confident and happy man under the influence of his choice of a life partner.

In that Hollywood world where a marriage could be gone up in smoke in weeks, Allie and Joe seemed imminently solid. They had found what they both longed for most: that place called home. And they were not throwing it away.

"Mommy gone? Daddy gone?"

Drew juggled the baby, and stared down at one more little face looking up at him. It occurred to him now would be a bad time to let his panic show.

"Yes, Andrew," he said quietly, "You're staying with Uncle Drew and Aunt Becky for a few days."

"Don't want to," Andrew announced.

That makes two of us.

Joe and Allie had adopted Andrew from an orphanage in Brazil not six months after they had married. The fact that the little boy was missing a leg only seemed to make them love him more. He'd only been home with them for about a month when they had found out they were pregnant. The fact that they had been pregnant with twins had been a surprise until just a few weeks before Sam and Sally had been born.

But the young couple had handled it with aplomb.

Drew could see what he had never seen before: that

Joe longed for that sense of family they had both lost even more than he himself had. Joe had chosen Allie, out of some instinct that Drew did not completely understand, as the woman who could give him what he longed for.

So, Joe and Allie were celebrating their second anniversary with a honeymoon away from their three children.

And Drew and Becky would celebrate their second anniversary, one day behind Joe and Allie, with a pack of children, because Allie had announced they were the only people she would trust with her precious offspring.

"I wish I had considered the smell when I agreed to this," he said. "How are we going to have a romantic anniversary now?"

"Ah, we'll think of something," Becky said with that little wink of hers that could turn his blood to liquid lava. "They have to sleep sometime."

"Are you sure?"

"It will be good practice for us," she said. She said it very casually. Too casually. She shot him a look over the tousled dandelion-fluff hair of the baby she was holding.

He went very still. He moved the baby from the crook of one arm to the crook of the other. He stared at his wife, and took in the radiant smile on her face as she looked away from him and gazed at the baby in her arms.

"Good practice for us?"

Andrew punched him in the leg. "I hate you," he decided. "Where's my daddy?"

Becky threw back her head and laughed.

And he saw it then. He wondered how he had missed

it, he who thought he knew every single nuance of his wife's looks and personality and moods.

He saw that she was different. Becky was absolutely glowing, softly and beautifully radiant.

"Yes," she said softly. "Good practice for us."

Andrew kicked him again. Drew looked down at him. Soon, sooner than he could ever have prepared for, he was going to have a little boy like this. A boy who would miss him terribly when he went somewhere. Who would look to him for guidance and direction. Who would think he got up early in the morning and put out the sun for him.

Or maybe he would have a little girl like the one in his arms, howling and stinky, and so, so precious it could steal a man's breath away. A little girl who would need him to show her how to throw a baseball so that the boys wouldn't make her think less of herself. And who would one day, God forbid, need him to sort through all the boys who wanted to date her to find one that might be suitable.

How could a man be ready for that?

He looked again into his wife's face. She was watching him with a soft, knowing smile playing across the fullness of her lips.

That's how he could be ready.

Because love made a man what he could never hope to be on his own. Once, because of the loss of those he had loved the most, he'd thought it was the force that could take a man's strength completely.

Now he saw that all love wove itself into the person a man eventually became. His parents were with him. Becky's love shaped him every day.

And made him ready for whatever was going to happen next.

Andrew punched him again. Juggling the baby, he bent down and scooped Andrew up in his other arm.

"I know," he said. "I know you miss your daddy."

Andrew wailed his assent and buried his head in Drew's neck. The stinky baby started to cry. Becky laughed again. He leaned over and kissed her nose.

And it felt as if in a life full of perfect moments, none had been more perfect than this one.

Daddy. He was going to be a daddy.

It was just as he had said to her the day they had gotten married. It wasn't the best day of their lives. All that was best was still in front of him, in a future that shone bright in the light of love. That love flowed over him from the look in her eyes. It flowed over him and drenched him and all of those days that were yet to come in its shimmering light.

* * * * *

THE PRINCE AND THE WEDDING PLANNER

JENNIFER FAYE

PROLOGUE

February, Tuscany, Italy

THIS WAS A living nightmare.

Bianca creaked open the door to her parents' bedroom. She peered inside, just like she used to do when she was a little girl. She paused as though waiting to be bid entrance. That would never happen.

Bianca tentatively stepped into the room, her gaze hungrily taking in her surroundings. The bed was made just as her mother left it each morning. There was still an indentation on her father's pillow as though his head had just been there—as though he would return to it that evening.

But that wasn't to be the case.

Her parents had died. The acknowledgment made her heart clench. One minute they'd been vibrant and active. In the next moment, they'd died in a horrific vehicle accident.

They hadn't been going anywhere special. It hadn't been a special day. It had been a perfectly ordinary day on a perfectly ordinary ride to the city to do some ordinary shopping. And yet it had ended with extraordinarily horrific results.

The backs of Bianca's eyes burned with unshed tears. She blinked repeatedly and sniffled. She had to pull herself together. Falling apart now wouldn't help anyone.

The funeral had just concluded and the will was to be read shortly. Everything was being pushed into fast forward as the vineyard had to be maintained. Springtime would soon be here and work would kick into high gear. Without someone in charge, the Barto Vineyard would suffer—her father's legacy would languish. His precious prize-winning grapes would wither on the vine.

The family's attorney thought with the vineyard at stake, it was reason enough to push her and her two siblings to read the will today of all days—while she was still wearing her black dress from the funeral, while the estate was still filled with mourners that had come to pay their respects.

All Bianca wanted to do that day was remember her parents—to bask in the love that lived within the walls of this vast villa. She pushed the door closed before stepping further into the bedroom. It was here, within her parents' suite of rooms, she felt closest to them.

It was here that her mother showed her how to put on makeup for the first time. It was here that her father had told her she could go away to university in the UK. Bianca walked around the spacious room, running her fingers over her mother's elaborately carved dresser with the huge mirror suspended above it.

She picked up her mother's silver hairbrush and noticed the few long dark strands of hair tangled around the bristles. The last of her mother. Tears clouded Bianca's vision as she thought of never seeing her parents ever again. It still seemed so utterly inconceivable.

She kept walking around the room, her fingers tracing over all the things, that until just days ago, her parents had touched—had used. The thought tugged on her heart strings. How could they be here one moment and then gone the next?

Bianca pressed a shaky hand to her mouth, holding back a wave of emotion that threatened to drown her in unbearable sorrow. She struggled to make sense of it. Why had they been stolen away when they were still so vital—still so needed? When she still didn't have their approval—their blessing for the choice she'd made about her path in life.

Knock. Knock.

"Bianca, are you in there?" It was her brother's voice.

"Yes." She'd been found too soon.

The door creaked open and Enzo's somber face met hers. Thankfully, he didn't ask what she was doing in their parents' room. She didn't want to explain how she was grasping at anything that would make her feel close to them once more.

"Everyone is waiting for us downstairs in father's study."

The moment was at hand. Her parents' final wishes would be known. And then the estate would be divvied up between her, her older brother and her younger sister. It would be so—so final. Her parents' absence from their lives would be undeniable.

"I... I'll be there." She turned her back to him, not wanting him to see the unshed tears shimmering in her eyes. She could be strong like him. She could get through this agonizing day without crumbling into a million pieces.

She needed to think about anything but the hollow spot in her heart. She lifted her head and her gaze came to land on the old photos on the wall. It was a collage of her grandparents, her parents' wedding and herself and her two siblings. They'd all looked so happy—

"Bianca, they loved you." And then her brother exited the room, closing the door softly.

It was like her brother to cut through everything to get to the heart of the problem. Did her parents love her like they'd loved her siblings? She had her doubts.

Bianca paused next to her mother's nightstand. It was there that she noticed her mother's journal. She recalled coming across it as a child and her mother shooing her away. She'd asked her mother what she wrote in her journal and her mother said it was a way to vent or a chance to mark something memorable. Her mother didn't write in it often. Her mother had said she liked to reflect upon where she'd come from, so she knew where she was going.

As a teenager, Bianca had tried keeping a journal of her own, but with two nosey siblings close to her own age, it didn't go well. And when her little sister announced one evening at dinner that Alfio Costa had kissed Bianca after school, she had burned her journal and vowed never to write in one again.

She so desperately longed to hear the gentle lilt of her mother's voice but she couldn't recall it. It was like her mind had erased the memory. How could that be? If she was already forgetting her mother's voice, how soon until she forgot what she looked like and their moments together?

She knew that she was being overly dramatic, but her emotions at the moment felt amplified. She didn't know how to calm them. She picked up her mother's journal. Her fingers traced over the buttery soft binding. Inside were her mother's final words.

Her fingertip traced down over the gold gilded pages. Part of her wanted to open the cover and let her mother's voice speak to her. And another part of her said not to do it. Whatever was written within those pages was none of her business. The struggle raged within her.

At last, she convinced herself a fair compromise was just to read a little bit. Just enough to hear her mother's voice once more. One page. That was all. And then she'd put it away.

She let the book fall open to a random page. There was her mother's very distinctive handwriting. Bianca would recognize it anywhere.

Her gaze hungrily took in every word. Once more, she could hear the lilt of her mother's voice. It was as though she were there in the room with her. Her mother was speaking about her upcoming wedding anniversary. There was mention of a gap growing between Bianca's parents and how her mother wanted to do something that would draw them back together again.

Bianca read the last lines of the page.

Has the past come back to haunt us? Has he truly forgiven me? Or does he blame me and my child...

Blame her? And one of her children? For what?

Not even pausing to consider the right and the wrong of it, Bianca flipped the page.

...for the affair.

Bianca's breath lodged in her throat. Her mother had had an affair? How could that be? Her parents always seemed so much in love. How could this have happened?

Bianca dropped onto the edge of the bed, her legs no longer able to hold her up. Her mind grappled to understand the ramifications of this.

Knock. Knock.

The door opened and her younger sister stepped inside. "Hey, Enzo said you were up here. Everyone is waiting for you. The attorney is looking a bit impatient...okay, a lot impatient."

Bianca didn't care about the attorney. This news altered everything she thought she knew about her parents—everything she believed about them—everything about her not living up to their expectations.

"Bianca, what is it?" Her sister moved across the room, stopping in front of her. "I know this is hard for you. It's hard on all of us—"

"It's not that." She didn't know if she should say something to her sister about the affair. Maybe it was best she just left it alone. Was that even possible? This was a bombshell. And it would blow apart her family—

"Hey," Gia grabbed the journal out of her hands, "this is Mamma's journal. What are you doing with it?"

Guilt washed over Bianca. "I... I just needed to hear her voice—to feel like she was still here."

"And so you thought you'd read her private thoughts."

"It was only one page and then..." Bianca stopped herself. Should she share what she'd learned? How could she not? This changed everything.

"And then what?"

Bianca shook her head. She didn't want her sister to endure further pain. "Nothing."

Her sister studied her for a moment. "It was something all right." Gia lifted the still open journal and read the page. By the bottom line, her mouth gaped and her eyes were rounded. "Seriously?"

Bianca shrugged her shoulders. She wasn't sure what to say. At least she wasn't the only one who didn't know about this affair.

Knock. Knock.

Enzo opened the door. "What's going on with you two? Everyone is waiting downstairs for us?"

Gia motioned for him to come in. "Close the door."

He did as she asked. When he stopped in front of them, he asked, "Why are you reading Mamma's journal? You need to put it back. It's none of your business."

When he went to reach for the journal, Gia was too fast for him. She leaned back on the bed, out of his reach.

Bianca spoke up. "It was only going to be one page. Just enough to feel like Mamma wasn't totally gone. And then—"

"Then we discovered something. Something big."

Enzo shook his head. "Whatever it is. It's none of our business."

"Did you know Mamma had an affair?" Gia blurted out.

"What? No. That can't be right. She wouldn't do something like that." He shook his head as though to chase away the troubling thought. He stepped back from them, distancing himself from the world-shattering news.

Gia scooted back on the big bed, crossed her legs and focused on the journal. She started to read their mother's troubling words. Bianca's gaze stayed on her brother, watching him as the wave of emotions washed over him. It was obvious that he hadn't known about this affair. And the journal didn't say when it'd taken place.

Gia turned the page.

He said that he still loved me and forgave me for what happened, but when we fight, when the distance looms between us, I wonder if he remembers that bad time in our marriage when we separated.

I was so sure that he was never coming back. That we would end up divorced. Days turned to weeks and then to months. I was weak and let a handsome man sweet-talk me into his bed. I've never regretted anything so much in my life. And then the worst happened...

"Stop," Enzo said. "This is wrong."

"I can't stop," Gia said. "This affects us all."

Enzo shook his head. "I don't want to know." Then his gaze narrowed and his voice shook with anger. "Isn't it enough that we lost both of them? Do we have to do this today?"

He might not need to know but Bianca couldn't live with the not knowing. What could be worse than her mother cheating on her father? Bianca needed answers as much as she needed oxygen.

As her sister argued with their brother, Bianca grabbed the journal from her. Her siblings' voices faded into the background as she took in her mother's words.

And then the worst happened. I became pregnant. Aldo said he'd forgiven me and would accept the baby as his own...

Wait. What? One of the three siblings wasn't a true Bartolini? Bianca's gaze hungrily sought out the next words, anxious to know that the family she'd known all her life was truly hers—that she wasn't an outsider.

...but now I wonder if he meant it or if he just accepted the baby because our families were pressuring both of us to get back together.

Am I overthinking his words? Maybe he just spoke in the heat of the moment. Tonight, when he comes in from the vineyard, we'll talk. It's the only way to fix things.

Who? Who isn't a Bartolini? Frustration, anger and sorrow churned in her stomach, making her nauseated. The journal was jerked out of her grasp before she could turn the page.

Enzo held the journal. Anger sparked in his eyes. "Stop! We're not doing this. We have a will to read. We have our parents to mourn. The past must stay in the past."

"What are you going to do with the journal?" Gia asked.

"I'm taking it downstairs and burning it in the fireplace—"

"No." Bianca jumped off the bed. "You can't do that."

"Why not?"

"Because one of us isn't a Bartolini. And that's the only key to the past."

CHAPTER ONE

Six weeks later, Bartolini Villa

HE NEEDED THIS EXCURSION.

He wished it could last longer—much longer.

Crown Prince Leopold stood in the lush garden of an Italian villa. He was surrounded by a group of lavishly dressed people. They all wanted a word with him. Why did he think coming to Tuscany would be any different than attending a social occasion in his homeland?

But in that moment, everyone's attention gravitated from him to a woman who'd joined their group. Her bold makeup and flamboyant hot pink outfit matched her personality. He was grateful the woman enjoyed being the center of attention. All he wanted to be was just another person in the crowd. What was it about people always wanting what they didn't have?

Just as his sister, the Princess of Patazonia, wanted a wedding that reflected her personality instead of a traditional royal wedding. But the queen insisted that tradition must rule above all else. Just as his father had said to him, right before he died:

Traditions are the bedrock of this kingdom.

Leo gave himself a mental shake. Now wasn't the time to get caught in the past—in the regrets—in the what-ifs.

Right now, he had his hands full with his feuding mother and sister. The battles between the two headstrong women was a daily occurrence. So when he was invited to this wedding of a childhood friend, he'd ordered up the family jet. Since he was of no help back at the palace, he figured he might as well wish his friend the very best.

Leo moved away from the flamboyant woman. He could take her high pitched, nasally voice only in small doses. Truth be told, there was another woman that had caught his attention. Her hair was dark and her skin glowed a warm tan. He noticed that she spoke when addressed but for the most part she was quiet. And when she did speak, her voice was soft.

He caught himself staring at her more than once. Maybe it was because she didn't make a point of walking up to him and introducing herself like so many of the other people. In fact, she acted as though she didn't even know he was royalty. Could that be possible?

Regardless, his interest in the beautiful woman increased. It'd been a while since he'd enjoyed a woman's company. With his pending engagement and marriage—a necessity in order to ascend to the throne—he wasn't in a position to start anything. But for the moment, he was still a free man.

He noticed how the other men stared at this woman—even the men that were in committed relationships discreetly turned their heads when she walked by. He couldn't blame them. She was stunning. He had to know more about her.

Noticing that she didn't have anything to drink, he snagged two flutes of champagne. He weaved his way through the crowd, dodging attempts at conversation, on his mission to meet the mystery woman. She was difficult to catch up with as she didn't stop to talk to any person for more than a second or two.

At last, he came up behind her. "Excuse me. I believe this is yours."

The woman turned to him. He held the glass out to her. Her brown eyes were filled with confusion. "But I didn't have any champagne."

"I noticed. That's why I retrieved this for you."

She accepted the glass, but he noticed she didn't drink any of it. "Are you enjoying the wedding?"

"I am. The setting is well done. And the gelato treats are unique."

"That was the bride's idea to help keep guests cool."

"You know her—the bride that is?"

"I do now."

"Ah, so you're a friend of the groom."

"I am now." She smiled.

He was confused. Was this beautiful woman some sort of wedding crasher? Was that why she was quiet? He quickly dismissed the idea. There was nothing about her that said she was anything but cultured.

"I'm confused," he said. "Are you a guest of the bride or the groom?"

"Neither. I'm their wedding planner, Bianca Bartolini."

He hadn't expected that response. He must be slipping. He was usually very good at reading people. It probably had something to do with the turmoil back at the palace. By the time he turned in at day's end, he usually had a headache that kept him up until late into the night.

He needed to do something to bring peace back to the palace. If he couldn't do that for his family, how would he ever keep peace over the nation?

He turned his attention back to his beautiful acquaintance. "It's a pleasure to meet you. I'm Pr…erm… Leo."

"It's an honor to meet you."

"You've done a lovely job with the wedding. The groom seems quite pleased."

"Thankfully."

He hesitated. "You say that like there was a chance he wouldn't be happy."

"I only had six weeks to plan this wedding. Six weeks. Do you know how short that is in wedding time?"

Before he could reply, Bianca was called away by the

waitstaff. With a curtsy and an apology, she was gone and he found himself disappointed to see her go.

A prince.

A real live, sexy-as-sin, bona fide prince.

And he'd been talking to her. Her heart fluttered. It was all Bianca could do not to spill the drink he'd so kindly gotten for her. But she didn't dare drink it. She had to maintain all her senses throughout the ceremony and reception. Everything had to go perfectly. Her future was riding on it.

Still, no one, including the bride and groom, had told her that the prince, whose face graced every gossip magazine, would be in attendance. Someone should have told her. She would have gone to great pains to make sure he had everything he needed.

Instead she'd stood there trying to keep her knees from shaking. And she had absolutely no idea what she'd said to him. She'd been so nervous. She'd probably made a complete fool of herself. And that curtsy. Did people still curtsy to royalty? She wasn't up on her royal etiquette.

Her rambling thoughts and precious memories of meeting the dashing prince would have to wait until later. Right now, she had a job to do.

She approached the bride, who was waiting to walk down the aisle. "Camilla, is everything all right? What do you need?"

Camilla looked flustered. "I forgot my gift for the groom." She paced around the study. "I don't know how I could forget the watch. It took forever to pick out the right one. And I had it engraved."

"Don't worry. Everything is going to be all right."

The bride's eyes shimmered with unshed tears. "No. It's not. This is an omen. Our marriage is doomed."

Bianca reached out, taking the bride's ice-cold hands in her own. "I just need you to breathe. Can you do that?"

"But—"

"No but's. Just breathe. Inhale. Deeply." Bianca demonstrated, hoping the bride would follow her example.

Camilla nodded. Her chest visibly expanded.

"And now breathe out." When the bride did as instructed, Bianca said, "Again."

Once the bride was looking a bit calmer, Bianca said, "You keep taking those deep breaths, and I'll be right back. This is all going to work out. I promise."

Bianca let go of the bride's hands and rushed out of the study, closing the door behind her. The ceremony was already a few minutes late. She walked calmly outside to the string octet and asked them to keep playing, entertaining the guests.

As she headed inside, her brother caught up with her. "What's wrong? Does the bride have cold feet?"

"No." Bianca said it firmly. "I just have to take care of one thing."

She dashed past her brother and headed up the stairs to the second floor. Her high heels didn't slow her down as she headed for the bridal suite. Bianca was certain everything would be all right. This was far from her first wedding—but it was her first wedding all on her own.

Using a master key that each of the Bartolini siblings had, she let herself into the bride's room. The bed was unmade, pillows were tossed about and there were heaps of clothes strewn everywhere. She'd known three-year-old's who kept their rooms tidier. She'd send one of the staff up here to tidy things up before the couple turned in for the night.

It took Bianca longer than she'd have liked to locate the bride's luggage. She searched through the carry-on first, knowing the bride wouldn't want the expensive watch to be far from her during her flight. It was on the third try that she found what she'd come for.

With the watch in hand, she raced out of the room and down the steps. She rushed into the study where Camilla once more looked like she was just about to have a meltdown.

"Here it is." Bianca placed the watch in the bride's hand.

"You found it. But how? Where?"

"None of it matters. All that matters is that your groom is waiting for you. He's starting to wonder if you're going to walk down the aisle."

"Oh, no! Please go reassure him that I want to marry him more than anything in the world."

Bianca didn't want to ask, but she felt obligated. "Are you sure you want to get married? It's okay if you've changed your mind. I know you were worried about omens—"

Camilla brushed aside Bianca's words. "I was just panicking. Everything is right now." She glanced down at the box containing the watch. "Thanks to you."

Bianca pressed a hand to her chest. "Me?"

"Yes. You've done everything to keep this wedding on track even though it was short notice, and I know I haven't been the easiest bride. I just want to thank you."

"You're welcome. And now I just want to get you down the aisle."

The bride smiled and nodded. "Let's do this." When Bianca turned for the door, the bride followed her. "Oh, here." She held out the watch. "Could you put this in our room for later?"

"Certainly." Bianca smiled and took the box. "You're a beautiful bride."

And with that Bianca headed out the door. She set the watch in a safe spot inside a buffet until she could get to it after the ceremony. And then she rushed out the back where all the wedding guests were looking a bit anxious.

A number of people turned her way as though wondering what she was doing and why the wedding had yet to start.

The groom paced in front of the minister and the groom's younger brother. He stopped when he spotted Bianca.

He rushed up to her. "What's going on? Where's Camilla?"

"Don't worry. She'd misplaced something. But it's been located and now the bride is ready. Shall I have the orchestra play the wedding march?"

"Yes, please. I was so worried she'd changed her mind."

Bianca reached out and squeezed his forearm. "She loves you with all of her heart."

"Thanks."

As Bianca turned away, her gaze caught that of the prince's. He didn't make any pretense to act as though he wasn't watching her. His stare was direct and observant. It made her heart skip a beat.

But she couldn't stop now and talk to him—as much as she wanted. She moved to the orchestra and the wedding music started. Bianca moved toward the French doors that were now open. This was where the bride was to make her grand entrance. The bride's father was standing outside waiting to escort his daughter down the aisle.

When Bianca saw the bride make her entrance, she backed away. She was no longer needed. All her work was done. Now she could take a seat at the back and watch the nuptials. It didn't matter how many weddings she attended, they never became any less romantic.

And it helped that the prince was in her line of sight. She was drawn to him. His bronze skin, dark hair and mysterious eyes were so attractive. A soft sigh passed her lips. If only she could get to know him. But that would never happen.

CHAPTER TWO

WEDDINGS WERE NOT his favorite events.

But Prince Leo had to admit, if only to himself, that the element of *will-they-or-won't-they?* made this particular wedding interesting. He had been leaning toward *they won't*. And by the worried look that had been on the groom's face, he had been leaning the same way.

And then the calm and unflappable wedding planner had made her entrance. She'd spoken softly to the groom and immediately put him at ease. Leo couldn't help but watch her as she took control of the situation. Her demeanor was casual. If she'd been worried about this event reaching its happy conclusion, she hadn't let on.

When he had to get married, he'd want someone like her to organize it. She seemed to roll with the punches as though she'd been through it a million times and knew that all would work out in the end. His sister probably wished she had a wedding planner like Miss Bartolini too.

Right now, the woman organizing the wedding was the same one who had planned his parents' wedding. His sister had tried bringing in her own wedding planner from the nation's capital, but the woman had caved when opposed by the queen and her crony. So his sister's most important day was about to be his mother's vision of how things should be without the bride's input. Leo had tried to help, but he'd been at a disadvantage, not knowing anything about weddings.

He'd known most of his life that when he married, it would be an arranged marriage—a logical, beneficial union. The fact that his parents had planned to have him betrothed as a teenager still soured his stomach. It'd been the last thing he fought about with his father before he'd died suddenly.

It'd taken Leo years to accept that he would marry and have children with a woman he did not love. And so he'd told himself that when he married, it wasn't going to be a big deal to him. It would be done out of duty and obligation—one more thing to tick off the royal duty list.

Love was intended for other people, like his sister. Giselle had found the love of her life and Leo couldn't be happier for her. And that was why her wedding was so important to him. One of them deserved to be truly happy.

"Looks like you have the weight of the world on your shoulders."

Leo turned to find the groom at his side. He smiled, happy for his childhood friend. "Not the entire world, just the weight of Patazonia."

Benito arched a brow. "Problems at home? I hadn't heard anything."

"Oh. You will. Pretty soon my mother and sister are going to have a nuclear meltdown over the upcoming wedding."

Benito laughed. "I can see that happening. Those are two really strong-minded women. You have my sympathies. I'm lucky. Even though our wedding was spontaneous, we had the perfect wedding planner. She took on the big things, including Camilla's parents, and let us enjoy our short engagement. Maybe you should hire her."

Leo was about to dismiss the idea when he realized this might actually work. "You were that impressed by this woman?"

Benito nodded. "Bianca is amazing. She interned with one of the greatest wedding planners in Venice. And now she has returned to her childhood home to start up her own wedding business."

His friend wasn't one to say things he didn't mean. So

for him to speak so highly of this Bianca, it meant a lot. If he were to consider hiring her for his sister's wedding, she would report to him. He would at last have some control over this event that was spiraling out of control—and causing a rift between the bride and groom. Best of all, Miss Bartolini wouldn't be a subject of the queen. Therefore, she wouldn't be under her thumb.

The more he thought about hiring his sister a wedding planner, the more he warmed to the idea. And the fact that Bianca was beautiful as well as composed was just a bonus.

"Have you met her?" Benito asked.

Before Leo could respond, Benito was off seeking out the woman who just might be the answer to his problems. The woman who might bring peace back to the nation. And quiet the gossip floating through the media of unrest in the royal household.

And with that in mind, he didn't try to stop his friend. He was looking forward to doing business with the wedding planner. If this all worked out, he could get back to his search for a bride. And soon he would become king.

A contest.

Not just any contest but one that pitted sibling against sibling.

Bianca still couldn't believe her parents' will had spelled out a competition between her and her siblings to decide who would end up inheriting the vast Bartolini estate. It included the villa, the vineyard, the stables with its award-winning stallions and mares as well as hundreds of fertile acres. It was a paradise of luxury and tranquility.

The siblings who didn't win the contest would lose their childhood home in exchange for an equivalent amount of investments and cash. The money didn't interest Bianca. It was cold and impersonal.

All three of the Bartolini siblings had been raised to appreciate the beauty of this land. And within the walls of this vast villa were all of their childhood memories. And for Bianca, it was crucial to succeed and win this contest.

For it was here in the lush, rolling hills of Tuscany that she intended to establish a destination wedding-planning service. And she was off to a mighty fine start.

Bianca glanced around at the mingling guests. And there was her brother, all dressed up in his finest suit and tie. He definitely didn't look like he spent his days out in the fields tending to the grape vines. In actuality, he cleaned up really well.

After the reading of their parents' will, tensions between the normally civil siblings was running high. It took a bit but the siblings all agreed that they would go with their strengths. Gia would run the boutique hotel, aka their family's sprawling villa. Enzo would oversee the vineyard with its world-renowned Chianti wine. And Bianca had agreed to coordinate weddings at the villa—talk about a romantic backdrop.

An outside accounting firm would be hired to tally their net incomes. Everything was to be aboveboard. And the family's attorney would oversee the contest. Nothing would be left to question. Everything would be certified and final. It seemed so cold—so final.

Enzo smiled at the beautiful young woman next to him. It was then that Bianca realized it was the first time she'd seen Enzo smile since the journal with their parents' devastating secret had been discovered. It had rocked the very foundation of this family—leaving their relationships vulnerable and strained.

Her gaze moved across the garden area, searching for her sister. Gia hadn't wanted to attend the wedding even though she managed the hotel. Bianca had pushed until she'd agreed. Bianca wanted the Bartolini estate well represented to the influential guest list. She was hoping for new clients—for all of them.

All her life she'd felt as though she didn't fit in. She was different than her siblings. While her brother and sister had enjoyed horses and grapes, she enjoyed the finer things in life. Her father used to get aggravated with her reluctance to get dirty.

And when she was pushed out of the nest, just like her siblings, so they could go off and seek their own path in life, she'd ended up in the UK where she'd worked her way through school. Once her education was completed, she moved to Venice. It was there that she followed her passion with a career in wedding planning. And when she landed a prestigious position as assistant to a world-renowned wedding planner, she thought her wishes had come true.

At first, that had been the case. Things went amazingly well. It was later, when Bianca was ready to put what she'd learned into practice that she realized she was terrible at following directions exactly as they'd been told to her.

She had a penchant for embellishing and taking the bride's ideas into consideration instead of convincing the bride that the wedding planner's methods were the best. Her mentor couldn't deny that Bianca had a flair for wedding planning, even if it wasn't quite the way she'd been instructed.

But now as the bride and groom were surrounded by their guests enjoying the afterglow of the ceremony, Bianca was able to take her first easy breath. Striking out on her own had been the right decision. Things were looking up—

"Bianca, there you are." Benito rushed up to her. "I've been looking everywhere for you."

Immediately she assumed her wedding planner persona. She stood a little taller and straightened her shoulders, prepared to deal with the latest developments. "What's wrong? Whatever it is, we'll deal with it."

Benito shook his head and smiled. "Nothing is wrong. In fact, something is right. Come with me."

He motioned for her to follow and then began walking away without any further explanation. She fell in step behind him, wondering what the normally quiet groom had on his mind.

When he stopped, she stepped up next to him. Her gaze met that of the man standing across from them, Prince Leopold. His eyes were a warm golden-brown that made her empty stomach suddenly feel as though a swarm of butterflies had invaded it.

She didn't know how long she stood there, caught up in his gaze. But when Benito cleared his throat, breaking the connection, heat swirled in her chest, rushing up her neck and setting her cheeks ablaze.

"Bianca Bartolini, I'd like to introduce you to His Royal Highness, Crown Prince Leopold of Patazonia."

Once again, Bianca curtsied. She willed her face to cool down, but it only succeeded in making her warmer. Goodness. What was he going to think of her? First, she was openly staring at him. And now her face must look like a roasted beet—all red and steamy. Not good. Not good at all.

"You've put on a splendid wedding," the prince said. "I've quite enjoyed it."

"Th...thank you, Your Highness."

"The prince is searching for a wedding planner," Benito said. "And I was telling him what a great job you did with our wedding."

"You did?" Then catching herself, she said, "I mean, thank you." She'd wondered after the wristwatch delay if Benito would still be happy with her services. "I'm sorry for the slight delay."

"Don't worry about it. Camilla told me what happened. Thank you for helping her and calming her down."

Bianca's eyes widened. "She told you all of that?"

"She did. I told her that she just wanted to keep me guessing for as long as she could."

Bianca wasn't used to brides standing up for her. Usually she took the blame, even for something that she had no control over. And when something stunning happened, the bride would take the credit. But every once in a while there were brides that were considerate and kind. Camilla was both of those.

"Anyway, Prince Leopold might be in need of your services. I'll let you two talk." And with that Benito made his way toward his bride.

Bianca's gaze moved to the prince. Her mouth suddenly went dry and she wasn't sure what to say.

What does one say to royalty? Hi? How are you? Beautiful day?

A nervous giggle welled up within her. She stifled it. What was wrong with her? She wasn't the nervous type. She'd worked with the very rich and the very famous. In the end, they were all just people. As her mother used to say, they put their pants on one leg at a time, just like everyone else.

But this man standing before her was most definitely not just another person. When he stared at her, like he was doing now, her pulse raced. Her insides shivered with a nervous energy. Her whole body reacted in the most unnerving ways.

She attempted to compartmentalize all these new and exciting sensations.

Focus on business.

If he had a job for her, it must be something big, something important. And it might be what she needed to launch a successful wedding business.

Coming to her senses, Bianca said, "If I may be of service to you, Your Highness, please let me know."

"There's going to be a wedding. And I think you might be just the right person to help plan it."

He wants me to plan his wedding? Me...planning a prince's wedding?

The honor of such a position was quite apparent to her. To plan such a wedding would mean she would have her choice of weddings going forward. She wouldn't have to search for prestigious clients, they would seek her out.

It would be sad that such a handsome and intriguing man would soon be off the market—not that she was in any position to be courted by anyone—most especially not a prince. With her heredity in question, it was best to keep to herself. But it didn't hurt to daydream.

"Um...thank you, Your Highness. I'm honored to be considered for such a role. Please let me know what I can do to help you."

He didn't say anything for a moment. "Do you have references?"

She nodded. "I can forward them to you."

"I will need to know more about you before I hire you for this very important position."

"Understood."

His expression gave nothing away. "How old are you?"

"Twenty-nine." What did that have to do with anything? But she didn't know the ways of the royals so she kept her questions to herself.

His dark brows drew together as he studied her. "Do you have much experience?"

"I've been working in the wedding industry since I was eighteen."

A brief flicker of skepticism showed in his eyes but in a blink, it was gone. "That's mighty young."

She nodded. "I started interning with a wedding planner when I was at university. My parents didn't believe in coddling their children. When my siblings and I became adults, we were expected to find our own way."

"But this estate is your family's, is it not?"

"It is. But our parents wanted us to rely on ourselves and not our birthright. Even now..." She stopped herself. The wound of her parents' deaths was still too new—too raw—to discuss, not even to gain the wedding of a lifetime.

"Interesting." He held out his hand. "May I have your phone."

She pulled it from the hidden pocket in the folds of her blue satin skirt. When she handed it over, their fingers touched. A tingly sensation raced up her arm and settled in her chest, setting her heart aflutter.

He took her phone and ran his finger over the touch screen. "I have given you my contact information. I trust that you will not share it with anyone."

"You have my word."

He nodded and then returned the phone to her. "Very good. Forward me your references as soon as possible."

She took her phone and moved her fingers over the same touch screen where his long, lean fingers had just been. And in no time, she had completed her task.

His phone chimed and he withdrew it from his pocket. She subdued a smile when his eyes widened as he read his phone. "You have forwarded me the information already?"

She nodded. "I like to be prepared. I keep relevant information on a cloud account."

"Thank you. I will be in touch." And then he turned and walked away.

She wanted to rush after him and ask when he would be in touch. This week? This month? This year? How was she supposed to plan anything when there was a real possibility of working for the Prince of Patazonia?

Or was it nothing more than a fantasy? Would a prince who could hire the best of the best want to hire a no-name like herself? Sure, she'd worked on the biggest and best weddings, but it hadn't been her name associated with those weddings, it had been her boss's. Bianca was still working to make her name known in the wedding world. So thinking a prince would hire her, well, it was nothing more than a fairy tale.

CHAPTER THREE

HE LIKED HER.

He liked her style. He liked her lack of pushiness. He liked her confidence.

And most of all, he liked the thought of her bringing peace to his home.

As the wedding reception wound down, Leo decided to make his move. His assistant had run a preliminary background check on Miss Bianca Bartolini and as for the references, each and every person had nothing but glowing compliments for Bianca and her capabilities.

He'd been observing Bianca. She was not a loud woman, not by any stretch. When the buffet table had run out of pastries, she'd quietly reminded the young woman to refill the tray. No matter what came up, she was on top of it. And had he not been keenly observing her, he wouldn't have noticed that she was constantly working to make the event seamless.

And now he was armed with the information he needed to put his plan into action. He approached Bianca, who currently had her back to him. It gave him a moment to notice the gentle curls of her dark hair with its half up and half down hairdo. The curls settled on the exposed nape of her neck before falling partway down her back. Her narrow waist was accentuated by the sash of her dress.

He followed the dress down over the curve of her hips to where the hemline stopped just a couple inches above her knees. He shouldn't be checking her out, especially not when he was about to hire her. Still, his gaze did its own thing, continuing to the end, where he found she wore a pair of silver stiletto heels.

She was a knockout. So much different from the very prim, very proper wedding planner that his mother preferred to work with. But if he was about to become king, then it was time everyone in the kingdom, including his mother, learned that traditions have their time and place but the future of their nation relied upon their ability to stay current and evolve with the times in order to remain relevant. And Miss Bartolini was going to be his first statement to his mother and the staff.

Next, he'd have to announce his choice for a bride. And he didn't have much time to make this monumental decision. By the end of the year, he would be married. The happily part was doubtful.

The ridiculous requirement in the country's charter about him being married in order to become ruler—talk about your archaic notions. Try as he might to get around that sticking point, it was law. One of his ancestors had written it into the country's charter and now he must abide by it, if he were to step up and be the king that people needed. It was something he intended to change once he was king.

Though he'd dragged his feet about taking on the position, he'd grown a lot in recent years. He'd gotten involved in politics and government, finding that he had a real head for these things. And then he'd gone out in disguise amongst his people and seen how the decisions made by government affected everyday citizens. And he wanted to be a part of that—he wanted to help the people of Patazonia.

But first, he had to see to his sister's happiness.

As though Bianca sensed his presence behind her, she turned. "Your Highness." She dipped her chin. "Is there something I can do for you?"

Just then the orchestra started to play a new song. It'd been a while since he'd danced and from what he'd observed, Bianca hadn't let up on her duties long enough to enjoy the evening. It was wrong for her to miss out on such a marvelous evening.

With the lanterns sending a warm cast over the patio area, he asked, "Would you care to dance?"

Her expressive eyes widened before she resumed her neutral expression. "Thank you. But I shouldn't be seen dancing. I have work to do."

He was surprised by her refusal. He couldn't recall the last time he'd been rebuffed. This just made him all the more determined to get her out on the dance floor.

"You've worked so hard to make this the perfect evening for my friend and his bride. You should take a moment to enjoy the fruits of your labor."

She smiled but didn't say anything.

"Why are you smiling?"

Immediately the smile slipped from her lips. "It's just the way you say some things. It's different."

"Ah, I see. I was taught by older scholars who believed formal speech is befitting a king. Or a king in the making."

"And what do you believe?"

"I believe a good king can speak any way he wants. It's what's in his heart that matters most. And now that I've indulged your curiosity, it's time you indulge mine as well." He held his arm out to her. "Shall we?"

She glanced around as though checking to see if she was needed. And when there was no one around clamoring for her attention, she placed her hand in the crook of his arm. "Lead the way."

That's exactly what he did. Once among the other couples, he clasped her one hand with his own and wrapped his other arm around her waist. Leaving a modest distance between them, they began dancing.

"It was so nice of you to attend the wedding," Bianca said. "Benito must be a really good friend."

"He's a very old friend. I'm happy he found his soul mate."

Her finely plucked brows lifted, but again she didn't say anything.

He couldn't help but be curious about her reaction. "Are you surprised that I'm happy for the couple?"

She shook her head. "I'm just surprised you believe in soul mates."

Perhaps he should watch his wording with her going forward. He didn't like explaining himself, especially about such a sensitive subject. "I do believe in love and soul mates. I just don't believe everyone has one." He noticed the frown on her face. "Has your heart been broken?"

The thought of it didn't sit well with him. He didn't know how a man lucky enough to win her heart could turn around and break it. If it was him—

He halted his thoughts. He didn't even know where that thought had come from. He wasn't looking for love. He was looking for a princess. They were two mutually exclusive things.

"No, it wasn't my heart. Not directly."

Talk about your cryptic answers. But before he could delve further into the subject, the music ended and a round of applause filled the air.

"If you'll excuse me," Bianca said, "I have things to attend to."

His phone chimed. He didn't have to look at it to know his car was out front, waiting to escort him to his hotel room in Florence. But he had one more thing to do.

"Bianca, I would like to offer you the job."

Her lush lips gaped. It took her a second to regain her composure. "Really? I mean, that was so fast. Are you sure?"

He smiled at her shocked reaction. "Would you like that I change my mind?"

She shook her head as she smiled. "No, I wouldn't."

"I have some business in Florence. Will you be ready to go in two days' time?"

"Two days? Boy, you don't give a girl much warning, do you?"

He hadn't considered that she might have another wedding. "I could definitely make this worth your time?"

Her eyes were like windows to the wheels turning in her mind. If her request for her services was within reason, he would grant it. And then the wedding planner would be all his for the next seven weeks.

"Where are you going? You can't just leave now."

Bianca stopped packing and turned to her sister who was standing in the doorway. She didn't know why Gia cared if she left. All they'd been doing was fighting. And that broke Bianca's heart. She was starting to worry that they'd never be a real family again.

"I have to go. It's for the best," Bianca said, calmly and emotionless. Tensions were so high that she didn't know what would set off one of her siblings.

"So that's it," her brother chimed in. "What about the estate?"

Bianca looked at Gia, then at Enzo. "I'm leaving because all of this fighting isn't good for us. It's tearing us apart."

Gia crossed her arms and glared at her sister. "You're bailing on us. And leaving me to fight it out with Enzo."

"That's the reason I'm leaving. I don't want to fight anymore. It's exhausting. And it hurts too much." Bianca placed her makeup bag in her suitcase and then crossed it off her packing list. At this point, she had three suitcases. And, according to her lists, everything she would need was packed. It might look like a lot, but she would be working for a prince and she had no idea what she'd need to wear.

"I agree," Gia said.

Bianca closed her full suitcase and then turned to her sister. "You agree with what? That we shouldn't argue anymore? Or that I should leave?"

Gia sighed. "Really? You honestly think I want you to go?"

Bianca shrugged. "I don't know. So much has been said. And…and what if I'm not a real Bartolini. What happens then?"

Gia pressed her hands to her hips. "What if I'm not a Bartolini?"

Bianca didn't know what words to say to her sister. She couldn't think of any words that would make this situation any better for any of them. They just had to wait it out.

"We'll know soon." Enzo started to pace.

Her brother was referring to the DNA tests they'd submitted last week. But they'd been warned it would be a while until they heard back. Until then, they would have to find a way to deal with the unknown.

"Not soon enough," Bianca muttered.

Gia stepped up next to her sister. "Don't give up on being a part of this family."

"I won't. You either."

"I won't." And then they hugged. When they pulled back, Gia asked, "Do you want help getting these suitcases downstairs?"

"Sure—"

"Hey." Enzo stopped in front of the window. "There's a car here." His gaze moved to the luggage. "I guess it's for you."

She was having the most trouble with him. Everything she said struck him the wrong way. She hoped the distance would help their relationship.

"Enzo, don't just stand there," Gia said. "Grab a suitcase." She gestured to the largest piece.

He hesitated. Then with a sigh, he did as instructed. On

the way downstairs, he said, "I don't think you're doing the right thing."

"You never do." Bianca moved to the front door, stopped and turned to face her siblings.

"I can't believe you're giving up on the estate," Gia said.

"She won't have any worries," Enzo said quickly. "She's working for a prince. She'll be paid a fortune."

Gia's lips formed an O. "I didn't think of that. This DNA stuff has me so distracted."

The thing they didn't know was that she was being paid very little. She'd negotiated for something more important—a national marketing campaign for her destination wedding service.

A heated discussion of the ramifications of Bianca's actions on the contest ensued. Should the money she earned for the royal wedding be counted toward her total? Bianca settled the argument by voluntarily excluding the profit from the royal wedding.

But that wasn't enough to bring peace to the family. The heated debate segued to the subject of whether the sibling without Bartolini blood should inherit. Bianca's stomach turned. She was certain they were talking about her.

It all fit. The way she wasn't like her siblings and taking part in the heritage laid out for them by their parents. She'd always felt like a square peg in a round hole—never measuring up in her parents' eyes and always a mystery to her siblings.

Not able to stand the pain in their eyes, she said, "I can't do this! This fighting, it's not us. We never used to fight."

Her brother and sister looked as though they'd been about to say something, but then lowered their gazes and nodded in agreement. It was then that she felt she had to say something—something important.

"I've got to go," Bianca said, "but before I do, I want you both to know that no matter how this contest turns out or what the DNA says, we're family. We're all the family we have left. And…" Her voice faltered. She wasn't used to talking about her feelings to her siblings. "I love you both."

"Aww…" Gia's eyes misted.

And the next thing she knew Gia pulled both her and a reluctant Enzo into a group hug. The closeness didn't last all that long, but it was enough to assure them that they could face these challenges and get through them together.

When they pulled apart, Bianca regretted having to leave, but she'd already given her word and signed a contract. "I can't miss my flight. But I'll be back soon."

"Aren't you flying on a private jet?" Enzo asked.

"The prince's jet?" Gia's eyes were wide with amazement.

A smiled pulled at Bianca's lips as she nodded. And then she was out the door, promising to keep Gia informed about the upcoming royal wedding.

CHAPTER FOUR

HE'D AGREED.

Inwardly, she squealed with delight.

She'd asked for the moon and she'd been given not only it but the stars too.

Bianca sat in the leather seat of the prince's jet as they neared Patazonia. She couldn't believe she was about to become the prince's wedding planner. He'd still not told her the details of his upcoming nuptials. Since she'd boarded the plane, he'd been busy either on the phone or working with his assistant on what she surmised was a very big export deal.

It gave her time to update her day planner as well as make phone calls. Even if she was out of town, it didn't mean she couldn't book weddings at the Tuscany estate. The truth of the matter was she didn't have any other weddings booked, just a handful of people making inquiries.

The reason she'd landed Camilla and Benito's posh wedding had been a fluke. The original wedding planner was pregnant and when complications ensued, she was ordered on bedrest for the remainder of her pregnancy. And taking an immediate liking to Bianca when their paths had crossed in Venice, she'd recommended her services.

Bianca was anxious to get to work on the royal wedding, but the prince kept putting her off. She'd already made an extensive list of questions for him.

As she stared out the window at a passing white puffy cloud, she recalled their dance at the wedding. There had been some sort of connection between them. She'd felt it in his touch and the way his gaze had lingered on her longer than necessary.

Was it wrong that she wanted the prince to notice her as a woman as well as a wedding planner? After all, she was here to plan his wedding—his wedding. Her shoulders sank. Here she was worrying over a man who was taken. What was wrong with her?

Those moments on the dance floor, they must have all been in her imagination. After all, he was so invested in his wedding that he'd taken it upon himself to go out and find a wedding planner instead of leaving all the details up to the bride.

Just then the pilot came over the intercom to let everyone know they would soon be on the ground of Patazonia. It was a small kingdom just off the French border.

In the time since the prince had proposed the job to her, Bianca had been online researching customs and weddings within this foreign land. The problem was there wasn't much detailed information about Patazonian matrimonial traditions.

"See anything you like?"

She turned to find prince Leo now in the seat next to hers. "I was thinking the land looks so lush. I'm hoping to have a chance to explore the area just a little." And then realizing how that sounded, she rushed to say, "But not before I have all of the wedding preparations in place. Don't worry. The wedding will be my top priority."

"I have no doubt or I would not have hired you. This wedding must go off without a hitch. I am counting on you."

"And the bride, she'll be meeting with us when we land?" She pulled out her notebook. "I have a whole list of questions for her."

The hint of a smile played at his lips. "I doubt she'll meet us at the airport, but she'll be at the palace."

"Good. Good." Nervous energy flooded Bianca's system. She felt like an athlete preparing for their biggest event. She was ready to spring out of the gate and get as much done as fast as she could—all the while paying attention to the details. Because like it or not, as her mentor used to say, the devil is in the details.

"You seem anxious to get started."

"I am."

"I didn't anticipate you would want to start today after traveling."

"There's no time to waste. The wedding will be here in no time." And she'd never done a royal wedding. It would be daunting compared to the garden wedding where she'd met the prince.

Her stomach churned with nerves. What if she had taken on too big of a task? She should have hired an assistant. Maybe she could hire one in Patazonia. In fact, that might work out better. This person would have a full working knowledge of the local traditions.

"Bianca, is everything all right?" The prince's deep, smooth voice drew her from her thoughts.

"Yes. Why do you ask?"

"You looked worried."

She bestowed upon him her brightest smile. "Not worried at all."

And if he believed that she had a Christmas elf to introduce him to. But she was a professional. She could do this. She kept telling herself that as the plane touched down on the tarmac.

Had he made a mistake?

He didn't care what Bianca said. She was worried.

As a dark sedan moved them from the airport to the palace, Leo couldn't tell what it was about this trip that bothered her. And he had yet to tell her about the tension between his mother and sister. Perhaps he should have, but he hadn't wanted to scare her off. He'd already had all the qualified wedding planners in Patazonia turn him down when they realized the queen already had her own planner.

He needed someone on his sister's side. And Bianca was that person. He was pretty adept at reading people. She may be apprehensive now, but he'd seen her in action. He knew when she was in planner mode that nothing ruffled her.

Maybe he should warn her about the exact details of this wedding. He didn't want her totally blindsided—

"I will need an assistant," Bianca said.

"Don't you already have one?"

Her gaze didn't quite meet his. "I thought by hiring one here, they would be able to help with the local customs."

He had to admit it did make sense. "I'll have my assistant provide you with a list for you to choose from."

"Thank you." She glanced down at her list. "And I assume I'll have an office. I mean I could work out of my room, but that would be crowded and awkward—"

"Yes, I'll see that you have a set of private offices."

Bianca rattled off a couple of other items on her list and he was able to appease her. Nothing she'd asked for had been outrageous or over-the-top and by the time she'd checked off everything on her list, they'd pulled up to the palace. His explanation of how things would work would have to wait.

When he'd spoken to Giselle last, he'd told her he had a big surprise for her. He knew how much his sister loved surprises. Even though she was now in her twenties, she was still the first one up on Christmas morning, eager to find out what was in the garishly wrapped packages under the tree.

When the car pulled to a stop, the doors were opened by the staff. Leo stepped out of the car into the late afternoon sun. It didn't matter how many times he traveled, returning home always felt amazing. This place was in his blood—it was a part of him. He couldn't imagine wanting to live anywhere else.

He rounded the back of the car and stopped next to Bianca as she craned her neck, staring up at the palace. "What do you think?"

She continued to take in the enormity of the very old structure with its detailed stonework and its soaring turrets. He stared up at the palace, trying to see it as she did. The gray stone with the ivy climbing up it against the blue sky with the sun's rays peeking out was portrait worthy. Along the border were flowering shrubs. The fuchsia pink blooms added softness to the hard stone. The grounds were perfectly manicured in distinct designs. This place looked the same as it had when his father was alive. Leo couldn't decide if the lack of change was good or bad.

The enormous wooden doors to the palace swung open. The rest of the staff, in black-and-white formal attire, rushed out to greet them.

Leo stopped just outside the doorway next to one of the maids. "Bianca, this is Zola. She will see to anything you need during your visit."

The young woman briefly curtsied.

"Thank you."

Just then his sister came rushing to the doorway. Her long golden-brown hair fell over her shoulders. Her face lit up at the sight of him. He didn't know whether to be flattered that he was missed or concerned that yet again, something was amiss with the wedding.

"You're home." Giselle hugged him, as was her nature.

When they pulled apart, Leo said, "I wasn't gone that long."

"Long enough." His sister frowned. "You should hear what they want to do for the wedding now—"

"Not now, Giselle." Leo's voice was low but firm. "We have a guest."

It was only then that Giselle's blue gaze met Bianca's. The friendly smile returned to his sister's face. She moved to stand in front of Bianca. "Welcome. Leo didn't say he was bringing home company. He can be forgetful that way."

Forgetful? He took exception to that comment. He had a lot on his mind at the moment. And he didn't want his mother to know about Bianca until he'd had a chance to speak with her.

"It's so nice to meet you." Bianca curtsied. "I can't believe I'm here. This place, it's amazing."

Giselle's smile broadened as she moved next to Leo. "She's marvelous. Where did you find her?"

"At a wedding."

Giselle's brows rose. "Really? And you went there voluntarily?"

Leo shrugged off the question. "I've hired Miss Bartolini to plan the wedding."

"And I'm quite honored," Bianca said, punctuating her words with a smile. "But we don't have much time so if you two could sit down with me and tell me what you have in mind for your big day, we can get started."

"We?" Giselle's fingers moved between her and Leo. Her eyes glittered with amusement. "You think *we* are getting married?"

When Bianca turned a questioning gaze in his direction, Leo cleared his throat. "I suppose I was rather light on the details. My apologies. You will not be planning my wedding. You are here to plan my sister, Giselle's, wedding."

Bianca's gaze moved back and forth between the two siblings. "I... I'm sorry."

"It's okay," Giselle said. "It's like my brother to leave out the most important bits of information." Then she turned to Leo. "I can't believe you hired a wedding planner. Mother is going to have a fit."

"If you'll let me, I can be a big help to you with planning your big day," Bianca uttered. "I have a lot of experience with big weddings, famous weddings and difficult weddings."

That bit of spunk was why he'd hired her. He just hoped Bianca didn't back down when it came to dealing with his mother. Only time would tell.

Giselle's wary gaze turned to Bianca. "How well do you cope with difficult people?"

"Giselle," Leo said, "let's not scare her off before she's even started."

His sister shrugged. "Fair enough. Bianca, once you're settled, we can go over the plans that have been made so far."

Bianca smiled. "I'll be ready."

"I'll show you to your room," Leo said.

"That's okay. I've got this." Giselle moved to Bianca's side. "It'll give us a chance to get acquainted while you go speak to Mother."

Leo had been looking forward to spending more time with Bianca, but arguing with his sister would only arouse his sister's suspicions about his intentions with Bianca. And that was the very last thing he needed at this point.

He nodded. "I'll see you both at dinner."

His gaze briefly connected with Bianca's. It was long enough for his heart to pick up its pace. They'd been together for hours on the trip here and yet they'd barely had a chance to say more than a few words to each other. He deeply regretted it. And now he had to walk away. Why did dinner have to be so far off?

Disappointment shrouded her in its murky grayness. She really had been hoping to talk to him—to get to know him better. There was an air of mystery that surrounded him.

Prince Leopold was different. And it wasn't just that he was royalty, though that was definitely enough to set him apart from anyone else she'd ever known. But there was this invisible yet impenetrable wall that he kept himself cloaked in at all times, much like a body of armor.

As she watched him walk away, she noticed his broad shoulders were pulled back in a straight line. He held his head high as he took long, sure steps. She couldn't help but wonder about the man behind the facade. He might have all the physical things one could want, plus some, but what had happened to him to keep him segregated from the rest of the world?

Once he was out of sight, it gave her a chance to look around. She wasn't sure what she expected to find inside. It wasn't like she'd ever been in a palace before, but this place, it was enormous. The foyer was larger than the flat she'd had in Venice.

From the gleaming marble floors to the sparkling crystal chandelier, she realized this place was ripped out of the pages of a fairy tale. In that very moment, the enormity of the task before her became crystal clear. Not even the biggest, most star-studded wedding could compare to this affair. Her stomach knotted with nervous tension. This wedding would come with challenges, which she couldn't even comprehend at this point.

But she couldn't let Leo or Giselle see her insecurities. She stilled her rambling thoughts. She focused her gaze on her newest client.

"This way." Giselle's sweet voice drew Bianca from her wandering thoughts.

Bianca glanced around for her luggage but didn't see it.

"Don't worry. Your bags are already in your room. Come on." She headed for the grand staircase in the middle of the great foyer.

As they climbed the staircase with a royal red runner up the center, the princess said, "You must be very good at your job for my brother to hire you."

"I am." The admission might sound like bragging. It wasn't. It was the truth.

Bianca might be a train wreck in other areas of her life, but when it came to planning weddings and looking after the details, she was in her zone. Lists were her friends. Her digital calendar ran her life, from a reminder to get up in the morning to the reminder to wind down for the night.

At the top of the steps, the princess paused and turned to her. "I don't know if you know this, but my brother does not make spur of the moment decisions often." The princess's expression was quite serious. Her gaze searched Bianca as though hunting for answers to unspoken questions. "When he does, it has to be for a very special reason."

She didn't want Giselle to think ill of her. "I can assure you that I did nothing to sway your brother's decision. I didn't even know of your wedding until he brought it to my attention."

For a long tenuous moment, Giselle didn't react. Then as though mulling over Bianca's response, she smiled. "I'm glad he hired you because this wedding needs help." She turned and began walking once more. "And if my brother believes in your skills, then so will I."

"Thank you. I won't let you down."

Giselle led her down a wide carpeted hallway with so much expensive artwork that it felt as though they were visiting a museum. They stopped before an open door and Giselle turned to her.

"Here we are. Your things should already be in your room."

Bianca glanced in the sunny room. It was no less stunning than the other parts of the palace. "Would you like to come in? We could start going over details for the wedding."

Giselle shook her head. "I have to meet with William, my fiancé. But we can speak after dinner." She turned to walk away but then turned back. "Did my brother tell you about dinner?"

"No." She had to wonder what was special about dinner.

"It's sharply at seven. Don't be late. It will be in the formal dining room and dress appropriately. There will be guests."

She was hoping for something more casual, more conducive to work. But when in the palace, do as they do. "I'll see you then."

"One more thing. Did my brother mention our mother?"

"The queen? No." Bianca had a feeling he'd left a lot out and she couldn't wait to speak with him.

"You should know that my mother has very definite ideas of how the wedding should go."

Bianca relaxed a bit. "Most mothers do."

"But my mother is different. She's used to getting her way. But this is my wedding—my day. I want some say in it."

"I'm sure compromises can be made. I'll do my best to incorporate both of your ideas, if that's what you'd like."

"It is. As long as it's more my ideas and less hers."

Bianca smiled. "I understand. I will keep that in mind."

Just then a phone buzzed, and it wasn't Bianca's.

"That's William." Giselle's face lit up. "I must go. I'll see you later," she called over her shoulder as she rushed away.

Bianca smiled at the young woman's excitement over seeing her fiancé. A deep, abiding love was something special to witness. And that meant Bianca didn't have time to rest before dinner. She stepped into her spacious room and the first thing to draw her attention was a crystal chandelier. It caught the sun's rays shining in through the French doors and sent a cascade of colors across the walls. She'd never stayed in a place so fancy that chandeliers were placed in bedrooms.

But this was far from a bedroom. The beige-and-cream

room had a spacious bed with a quilted velvet headboard and footboard, but it also had a full-size couch, two chairs and a fireplace. Her gaze moved slowly around the room. There was just so much to take in, from the intricacies on the ceiling and wall, all the way down to the oriental rug.

Next to the French doors was a small table and chairs. She had a feeling she would be spending countless hours sitting there strategizing particulars for the wedding. She knew that the prince had assured her of having an office, but her working hours never fit into a normal business day. Ideas would strike at all hours of the day and night. And with the high importance of this wedding, she knew her mind would be on business 24/7.

And then there was the prince. A soft sigh escaped her lips as she pictured him. She definitely wanted to impress him—for more than one reason.

CHAPTER FIVE

"I won't stand for this!"

The queen's harsh words echoed in Leo's mind. He knew she wasn't going to take well to his interference in the royal wedding plans, but it was time his mother realized her time as regent—of steamrolling over everyone—was almost at an end. By the end of the year he would be king.

As his mother glared at him, he couldn't help but wonder if part of her hostility was due to the part he played in his father's death. Ever since that horrific day, his relationship with his mother had been strained.

Or it could be that she resented having to step in as regent. Though if that were the case, why had she given him so much freedom up until now? If it weren't for public pressure, would she have pushed him to marry—to step into his birthright?

He had a lot of questions, but he couldn't bring himself to dredge up the past—the most painful period of his life. Because even though he and his father disagreed on certain things, Leo had looked up to his father like some kids idolized sports figures and actors. His father had been his role model.

"Mother, I know you love Giselle, but if you keep interfering with her wedding, you're going to drive a permanent wedge between the two of you."

The queen's eyes flared with anger. "And you think bringing in some stranger that knows nothing of our customs is the solution?"

"I do." He made sure to keep his voice calm. "Bianca is quite capable—"

"Bianca?" His mother crossed her arms as she continued to frown at him. "You're on a first name basis with this woman?"

There was no point in denying it. "Yes, we are on a first name basis. It is not uncommon to call people by their first names."

"And this woman, is she beautiful?"

His jaw tightened in frustration, but he immediately released the tension. He didn't want his very astute mother to get a whiff of his discomfort. She would take it and turn it on him.

"She's a wedding planner. I did not notice her looks." He was lying, but his mother didn't need to know everything.

The queen arched a penciled brow. "I do not believe you."

"This isn't about me or for that matter Bianca. This is about stopping the fighting between you and Giselle. Her wedding is supposed to be a happy time for her—"

"Her wedding is a duty—an obligation—just as yours will be. It's about forging an alliance with another country. It's about the future of Patazonia."

Leave it to his mother to remove the emotions and go straight for business. Many outsiders thought being part of the royal family was all about sitting back and letting everyone wait on them. But there were things that an outsider didn't know or stop to consider.

As a prince, he was raised to consider how his choices would affect the future of Patazonia. Everything he did was scrutinized by the press—most of the time their headlines were erroneous. But it didn't diminish his need to make careful decisions.

Just like now when there was a growing divide between the royal family and its citizens. The woman he married needed to bridge the gap between the palace and the commoners. It was imperative.

His mother had picked up right where the king had left

off with the old-school philosophies. She preferred to remain on her side of the palace wall and rule while the citizens were to remain disconnected on the other side.

When he became king, things were going to change. He wanted to be a king of the people, not a distant, cold ruler. He could do better. This whole dynasty could step up their game by being more interactive and breaking down some of the traditions that had kept them locked in their ivy tower.

He met his mother's angry gaze. "Does the future of this country include fighting?"

His mother gasped. "We were not fighting. We do not fight."

"Then what would you call the slamming of doors and the yelling that has disrupted the entire household?"

His mother's gaze lowered. "Your sister might have gotten a bit emotional over some points with the wedding."

"Some?"

"She wants to throw away everything traditional. But she's a princess. A princess must adhere to certain protocols."

"And was that how it was for you?"

"I don't know what you mean?" His mother glanced away.

This was his opportunity to ask her a question he'd wondered about for a long time. "Did you love my father? Or was it all about obligation?"

The queen, who always prided herself on maintaining her composure, looked at him slack-jawed. Was what he'd asked really that out of line? He supposed. Still, he needed to know the truth.

"This isn't about me or your father." The queen's voice was strained. Her face had noticeably paled.

"It might not have been but it is now—"

"No. It's not." Her firm tone let him know that he'd most definitely crossed a line. "Mrs. Schmidt knows what's best for your sister's wedding. After all, she's been planning royal weddings for nearly fifty years. She helped plan your father's and mine."

"And therein lies the problem, Mother. Giselle is young and times have changed. She doesn't want the same things that a bride of fifty years ago would want." When his mother went to argue, he held up a hand stopping her. "And, as the soon-to-be king, I believe the bride should have a say in her wedding."

"But she'll ruin everything."

"I highly doubt it. I believe a compromise can be reached, marrying some of the old traditions with some of the current trends. And before you resist, remember your future relationship with your daughter is at stake."

His mother huffed. "You're exaggerating."

"Am I?" He'd soothed his sister's tears. He'd listened to her vent about moving away from Patazonia—away from his mother—and moving to her groom's country. Leo knew it wasn't all talk. There was some serious consideration going on.

His mother didn't speak for a moment. At last he'd gotten through to her. "You really believe she's that upset over this?"

"I do. And you need to be careful how you handle things going forward."

"And you just want me to trust this stranger—this outsider?"

"I do. I think if you give Bianca a chance, you'll like her. She's a people person and well organized. Giselle has already met her and they've hit it off." Now that he was finally getting through to his mother, he didn't want to walk away without an understanding. "So will you give this a chance? Let Bianca try to bring peace to this family?"

His mother stirred her tea and then removed the silver spoon, setting it on the fine bone chine saucer. Even standing halfway across the room, he could see the wheels of her mind turning. This wasn't going to be the easy agreement that he'd been hoping for.

Oh, well. So be it. He'd been negotiating with his mother since his father had died. He told himself it was just training for his future as king.

The queen took a sip of tea. Returning the cup to the saucer, she turned her full attention to him. "I'll give your wedding planner a chance, if you'll do something in return."

And there she went with her negotiations, just as he'd predicted. At this point, he was willing to do most anything for some peace in his own home. And most of all, he wanted his younger sister to have the wedding of her dreams with the man she loved.

But he'd been down this road before. To have a party with his friends after graduation, it had cost him. He'd had to wear a suit and tie all summer as he'd visited country after country throughout Europe as part of a goodwill campaign. He couldn't even imagine what this wedding would cost him.

He stifled the resigned sigh. "What do you want?"

A slight smile lifted the queen's lips ever so briefly. "I want you to announce your engagement the day after your sister's wedding."

The day after? As in just a matter of a couple months? Seven weeks, give or take a day?

Leo swallowed hard. He struggled to maintain his composure. His gaze never wavered from his mother's. He didn't want her to detect any weakness. He knew his engagement must be announced soon if he were to be king by the New Year, but this felt so sudden—so final.

The queen held up a finger. "There's one more caveat."

Acid swirled in the pit of his stomach. "I'm listening."

"If you don't choose an appropriate wife by your sister's reception, I'll choose one for you."

He schooled his features as he'd practiced since he was a child. Because a future king could not be emotional. His tutors had drilled that into him since he was just out of diapers.

He intended to tell his mother that horses would fly before he'd allow her to pick his wife, but instead he uttered, "It's a deal."

That little smile on his mother's face bloomed into a full-fledged grin. She got to her feet and approached him. "This is for the best. You'll see."

He highly doubted it. "And you will play nice with the wedding planner?"

It was his mother's turn to sigh. "I will do my best—"

"Mother?"

Her lips pressed into a firm line. "I will hear her out."

"No." He shook his head. "I will receive regular updates and I'll hear everything. I will also have the final decision on the details of the wedding."

"What?" His mother looked horrified. "But you know nothing about weddings."

"I guess it's my caveat. Now, do we have an agreement?"

"You drive a hard bargain." His mother gave him an appraising look. "You're so much like your father. He would be proud of you."

"No one can ever replace him, but I try to do what I think he'd want of me."

"Like the wedding." The queen glanced away. "He would not approve of the bickering. Therefore, I will agree to your plan. However, you must keep in mind that this will be a state wedding with dignitaries in attendance."

"Yes, Mother. But it's also a personal, deeply touching moment for Giselle."

"Agreed. Since we're speaking of your father, you should know that he would not approve of you putting off your destiny for so long."

"I know." The weight of her words had been pressing on him for some time. It's why he was willing to go along with his mother's bargain. At least Giselle would end up happy. "I will take the throne by the New Year."

His mother turned back to the table. "I have a list of appropriate women for you to consider for your queen."

He'd already been introduced to some women his mother deemed "appropriate." His mother's ideal woman was quiet, meek and dare he say it—boring. He needed a strong woman who spoke her own mind and had a sense of humor so he wouldn't bore of her too quickly.

Sadly, he'd squandered his time to find a wife on his own terms. Now he was left to choose from his mother's preapproved candidates. And his mother knew she had the upper hand. If he had any doubts, the Cheshire smile on her face said it all.

He needed a bit of time to accept what was about to happen—he was going to marry a woman of his mother's choosing. "I must go check on our guest and make sure she has settled in."

His mother turned back to him. "But I'll see you at dinner?"

"I would not miss the kickoff to your birthday celebrations." This was a milestone for his mother. She would turn sixty and a lengthy celebration would ensue over the next few weeks. "We'll both be there."

"Very well."

And with their agreement in place, he departed. His mother wasn't quite herself. Sure, she was one to cling to traditions, but behind closed doors she normally relaxed a bit. That was not the case lately. This wedding had everyone on edge. He was really hoping Bianca would help bring his family back together again.

Speaking of Bianca, he should check on her before dinner, just to make sure she'd settled in without any problems.

At least that's what he told himself. Because the truth was that the flight home hadn't gone the way he'd planned. One problem after another kept creeping up and stealing away his time.

But no more. He took the steps two at a time, anxious to see Bianca once more. He wanted to show her around the palace and help her get her bearings as she launched into the wedding preparations.

He stopped outside her door and knocked. "Bianca? It's Leo."

Nothing.

He should probably just walk away and leave well enough alone, but he couldn't resist trying once more.

This time he knocked harder. Louder. "Bianca?"

With a resigned sigh, he turned toward his own private set of rooms. He'd taken no more than three steps when he heard her door swing open.

"Were you looking for me?"

He turned. "I was."

"Sorry. I was out on the balcony, enjoying what's left of this beautiful day."

He retraced his steps. "Your room, is it to your liking?"

"Yes, it is. I think it's the most beautiful room I've ever stayed in."

"That's good." That's good? Was that the best he could do?

But the thing was that every time he was within Bianca's gravitational pull, it messed with his thinking. His thoughts got tangled and his words seemed to lack substance.

It wasn't like him to be caught up in a beautiful woman. Yes, he'd admired many attractive women and he'd definitely enjoyed their time. But none of them had ever driven him to go out of his way to know more about them.

"I was just working on some preliminary plans for the wedding," Bianca said, interrupting his thoughts. "Well, it's more like a list of questions." Her glittering brown eyes lifted until their gazes met. "Perhaps you'd care to help me."

"Yes." What was he saying? He knew next to nothing about weddings. And that was being generous.

But if this gave him more of an opportunity to spend time with Bianca, then he was all for it. He stepped into the room, closing the door behind him. It was then that he inhaled the gentlest scent of wildflowers. It wasn't the first time he'd come across the unique scent.

As he followed Bianca to the balcony, he realized it was her. She was the one who smelled like sweet blossoms. He didn't think he'd ever come across a field of wildflowers without thinking of her.

When she came to a sudden stop, he nearly ran into her. As it was, his hands reached out for her tiny waist, his fingers wrapping around her so as not to bump her into the table.

She turned in his hands. "Sorry." Their gazes met once more. This time he was holding her and he didn't want to let go.

The breath hitched in his throat. His gaze dipped to her berry-red lips. They looked so full, so succulent. What would she do if he were to draw her to him and pluck a deep, long kiss?

He could have his choice of women. There was even a stack of biographies from available, eager women waiting for him on his desk. So why was he drawn to this quiet wedding planner?

Though Bianca was beautiful with her long loose curls, a golden complexion and dark lashes that framed her eyes, which were the mirrors to her soul, she was not from Patazonia. She was not royal. She was not even the daughter of an influential businessman. In his mother's eyes, Bianca was a nobody.

But to him, she was intriguing. She was tempting. And the more time he spent with her, the more captivated he became.

As though Bianca could read his thoughts, she moved out of his grasp. "I... I meant to offer you some coffee. I just brewed a pot."

He raked his fingers through his hair. A cup of coffee would be good. It would give his hands something to do besides finding their way back to her. Because if he were to pull her close again, he couldn't guarantee that things wouldn't move from a business relationship to something much more intimate.

"That sounds good." He took a seat at the small table on the balcony.

A minute later, Bianca returned with a full cup. "I forgot to ask what you take in your coffee."

"Black is fine." Right now, he wasn't sure he would actually notice what he was drinking. As Bianca took a seat next to him, his full attention returned to her. "How may I help with the wedding?"

She opened her laptop and moved her cursor to the top of a form. "Do you know approximately how many guests to expect?"

While the sun began its slow descent toward the horizon, he answered as many of her questions as he could. He surprised himself by how many details he'd picked up on by listening to his sister and mother argue.

He knew things about his sister's dress. Whether the ceremony would be ultraformal. And he knew where the reception was being held. Even the number of courses to be served for dinner.

"I'd like to do something for my sister on her wedding day," he said. "She's making a lot of concessions to please my mother and go along with tradition, but I think she needs a chance to let down her hair and live it up on her big day. Do you have any ideas?"

Bianca stopped typing and thought for a moment. "Since the wedding is early in the day, you could do an after-party."

"An after-party." He mulled this over. "Does this mean we could have a select list of guests?"

"Certainly. You could exclude some of the guests from the ceremony and include some others that were not fortunate enough to receive a ceremony invite. The after-party can be as formal or informal as you'd like."

This appealed to him. He knew his sister and her fiancé had a lot of friends—friends that had to be overlooked for invitations to the ceremony in order to invite heads of state and dignitaries from all over Europe and beyond. This would be a way for his sister to have everyone she cared about around her on her big day.

"I like it," he said. "But for the moment, let's just keep this between us. I'll have a list of guests for you by the end of the week."

"That's good because we don't have much time to plan something like this." She hesitated.

"What's bothering you?"

Her gaze lifted to meet his. "With it being so close to the wedding, a lot of people might have other obligations already?"

"Let me worry about it. You pick out an appropriate invite and I'll put together the list."

"What about the venue?"

"That's the easiest part. We will have it at the Hampstead estate next to the lake. It's about fifteen kilometers from here. Far enough that it won't bother my mother with the loud music."

Bianca's eyes widened. "You were serious about letting your hair down."

"Definitely. I just wish I'd have thought of it."

"Why? I don't mind sharing ideas with you. After all, it's my job."

He shook his head. "It's not that. If I'd have had this idea a lot sooner, I could have booked some headline bands. As it is, they are probably all booked."

They continued to talk about bands. He named the ones he'd heard his sister mention. Then he inquired about Bianca's favorite band and in turn, he told her his. For a moment, it wasn't work. It was like they were two friends getting to know each other.

"Thank you." Bianca finished her list of potential bands. "I'll do the best I can to get someone your sister will approve of."

"And my mother doesn't need to know about any of this for now. Speaking of which, it is time to dress for dinner." He got to his feet. And then he realized he needed to make something else perfectly clear. "You will be reporting to me on this wedding. I know my mother likes to think she's in control, but I would like to have dinner with you each evening to go over everything—to make sure we're on track."

Bianca nodded. "Understood. And we can discuss my promotional campaign."

He couldn't help but smile. "I won't forget. I already have my people working on some preliminary mockups. I'll have them for you to approve shortly."

Her face lit up with excitement. "Thank you."

"I'll stop back and walk you to dinner." And with that he left.

CHAPTER SIX

IT WASN'T A QUESTION.

It wasn't an invite.

It was a declaration. Prince Leopold would be escorting her to dinner.

As Bianca stared into the mirror, she became distracted. Try as she might, she couldn't forget the turmoil back in Tuscany. Her attention focused on her face. She searched for signs that she was a Bartolini. Her nose—was it too small? She turned this way and that way.

Her eyes—were they too close together? Were they the same size and shape as her father's? She struggled to conjure up the exact details of her father's face. The more she struggled to recall, the more frustrated she became.

As she continued to stare at her reflection, she remembered people commenting on how much she resembled her mother. Was that a clue? Did she look like her mother because her father wasn't truly her father?

And if she wasn't a Bartolini, who was she?

The questions tumbled through her mind. They weighed on her, putting everything she thought she knew about herself into question.

Tears of frustration pricked the backs of her eyes. She blinked repeatedly. How long were those DNA tests going to take? The wait was agonizing.

But right now, she had an important dinner with the royal family. She put on diamond stud earrings followed by diamond dangle earrings. She may be a poor pauper compared to the wealth of this royal family, but back in her own world, the Bartolini's had made a name for themselves.

She gazed down at the navy-and-silver dress she'd selected for this evening. It was formfitting and hugged her curves. As she stared in the mirror, she sucked in her breath, pulling in her stomach. Maybe this wasn't the right dress to wear for meeting the queen for the first time. But when she checked the time, it was a quarter to seven. Too late to change now. She expected Leo to arrive any minute.

Bianca slipped on the silver rhinestone–studded stilettos. Still, she was stuck on the fact that a prince—a sexy, gorgeous prince—would be her escort for dinner. Who cared if he was a bit presumptuous? She knew how to put him in his place if he got obnoxious. Though she just couldn't imagine Leo being an overbearing jerk.

As she finished with the delicate strap on her shoe, her attention focused on her nails. She'd had them done for the wedding at the vineyard. She lifted her hands to her face and inspected them. Other than a slight tremor, they looked good. The French manicure was holding up nicely. The last thing she wanted was to greet the queen looking anything other than her best.

The nervous tremor that had started in her hands moved to her stomach. She was meeting a queen. Who did that? People with a much higher social status than her. She didn't even know what to say to the woman. Her mouth grew dry. Her brain drew a blank.

Don't think about it. Think about something else.

She wanted someone to share this moment with. Her thoughts turned to her sister. She knew Gia would be in awe over this just as she was. And she had promised to let her siblings know when she'd arrived safely.

She reached for her phone. As she went to pull up her sisters' number, she paused. The last time she'd seen them, there had been a big argument. She didn't want to go there again. Perhaps a text message would be best.

Arrived safely.

Immediately a response pinged on her phone.

Exciting! What's it like?

Amazing!

And the prince?

Bianca thought for a moment. Scads of adjectives raced to the front of her mind.

Amazing!

#jealous Tell me more.

Knock. Knock.
"Coming," Bianca called out.

Can't now. My prince...

Bianca groaned. *Erase. Erase.*

Can't now. The prince has arrived for dinner.

#exciting Don't forget. Details. Lots of details.

LOL. Talk soon.

Bianca smiled as she set aside her phone. Things were starting to seem normal between her and her sister. Perhaps she'd had the right idea about putting a little distance between them. Because during this whole thing of losing her parents and the mess with the will, she could really use her friend—her sister.
Knock. Knock.

"Bianca, are you ready?"

"Yes. I'll be right there." She glanced in the mirror. She adjusted a stray hair and then smoothed the makeup under her left eye. It was as good as it was going to get.

She moved to the door and swung it open. She didn't know it was possible for Leo to look any better than she'd seen him so far. But she'd been wrong.

His short dark hair was still damp from his shower. The sides were clipped close to his head while the curls on top were short but just long enough for them to do their own things. And what they did made Bianca want to reach out and run her fingers through the damp curls.

Her gaze met his smiling eyes. Her heart raced. His face was clean-shaven. She paused to inhale, imagining the slightest hint of a spicy aftershave. Mmm… She longed to take a step forward and lean into him for a real whiff.

"You look beautiful." His voice drew her from her meandering thoughts.

"Th-thank you." She needed to calm herself.

Otherwise she was likely to make a fool of herself in front of the queen. If she did that, she'd end up fired before she even began her job. And she didn't want to think of the negative consequences to her business.

"Are you ready to go?"

She glanced back at the room just to make sure she hadn't forgotten anything. She leveled her shoulders and turned back to him. "I'm ready."

He arched a brow. "Are you sure?"

"Positive."

In true princely fashion, he held his arm out to her. "Then let's go."

She stepped out, pulled the door shut behind her and then placed her hand in the crook of his arm. The heat of his body radiated into her skin, warming her cell by cell, bone by bone. Did he have any idea what he did to her heart rate?

She hoped not. As it was, she had to concentrate on walking. She didn't want to trip over her own two feet. How embarrassing would that be?

She swallowed hard, trying to put on a calm exterior. "What's your mother like?"

"Hmm... How long do you have?"

"Oh, boy."

A soft deep laugh rumbled in his chest. "Relax. I'll be there with you."

That was of little comfort considering she didn't rely on others to fight her battles. It was one of the lessons her father had instilled in her and her siblings. To make it in this world you have to be strong with a kind heart.

"How do I address her?"

"Don't address her unless she speaks to you first. And then you may refer to her as Your Majesty."

"Oh, my. That formal, huh?" This definitely wasn't like any other time where she'd gone to meet a boyfriend's mother. Far from it.

Leo nodded. "My mother is a stickler for titles, duty and tradition."

"What do you call her?"

"Mother, in private."

"And in public?"

"Your Majesty."

It took a second for Bianca to realize that her mouth was agape. She couldn't even begin to imagine what it was like to grow up the way he had.

Sooner than she was prepared for, they arrived just outside the dining room. Leo turned to her. "Are you ready?"

Bianca nodded.

With her stomach twisted in a nervous knot, she entered. She found Giselle standing by a tall handsome man who must be her fiancé, by the way she was looking at him.

Next to them stood another couple. They were older.

The man looked quite distinguished and though he didn't smile that often, his wife beamed as she made small talk with Giselle.

And then Bianca's attention moved to an older woman with silver hair. It was cut short into a neat bob. That she presumed was the queen. Her stomach shivered with anxiety. Surely that queen couldn't be as intimidating as she was imagining. Could she?

Leo came to a stop near the group and waited for a pause in the conversation. "Mother," he waited until she turned her attention to them, "I'd like to introduce Bianca Bartolini of Tuscany, Italy." And then he turned to Bianca. "Bianca, I'd like to introduce the Queen of Patazonia."

Bianca's mouth went dry but her brain worked just enough for her to remember to curtsy to the queen. She hoped that was right. When she straightened, the queen was staring at her with a hawk-like stare. Bianca's breath stilled in her lungs.

She felt so out of place—so out of her realm. But she couldn't falter. She had to stay strong for Leo, for Giselle, for herself. Without this account, the future of her wedding business looked uncertain. She needed her business as her touchstone. Without it she'd be adrift.

Leo had warned her not to speak until spoken too. And yet she felt compelled to say something—anything to break this awkward silence.

"It's so nice to meet you, ma'am. I'm honored to be here. Your palace, it's quite extraordinary."

A penciled brow rose. "Perhaps if my son isn't too busy, he can give you a tour of the gardens before you leave. They were my husband's passion."

"Thank you but…" Just then Leo gave a slight shake of his head. Bianca adjusted what she was about to say. "I will definitely make a point of visiting the gardens."

"Very well. Shall we eat?" The queen started for the head of the table.

The queen acted as though she were there just for the evening. Did the woman not know that she was the wedding planner? Had Leo failed to tell her?

Bianca glanced over at Leo who was making conversation with a gentleman who had such a sour expression that it looked as though he'd just sucked on a lemon. She had no idea who the man was but he obviously didn't have a very optimistic view of life.

Thankfully she'd been seated near Giselle. She really liked the young woman. She was warm and vivacious, unlike her mother. Bianca also noticed that the bride-to-be mentioned the wedding only once in passing. She found that odd. Most of the brides she'd worked with were quite excited for the big day and would talk about the preparations almost nonstop. Perhaps the rift between mother and daughter was the reason for the quietness on the subject.

The queen made a point of talking to each person at the table except Bianca. It was as though she were invisible. It wasn't an ideal way to begin a working relationship, but at least she hadn't been banished. That had to count for something. Right?

When the queen mentioned the gardens once more to her guests, Bianca seized the opportunity. "I'm very anxious to see the gardens. It would be a beautiful backdrop for the wedding. In fact, I just hosted a garden wedding at my family's estate. It's where I met L...erm...the prince."

"Is that so?" The queen turned to her son.

"Yes. I attended Benito's wedding."

"I see. Now I understand why you feel like an expert on the subject."

The seconds ticked away as mother and son stared at each other. A war of wills quietly ensued. Bianca felt bad for Leo. He was only trying to help his sister have a happy wedding. This wasn't his fight but he was taking it on for his sister's sake. Bianca's respect for him escalated.

"I hope to be able to make this wedding a very memorable and happy occasion for everyone," Bianca said, trying to diffuse the situation.

The queen turned to her. "This is not your typical wedding. Giselle is a princess and certain obligations go along with that title—even if she doesn't like it."

She's the mother of the bride. Just the mother of the bride.

Bianca lowered her hand to her lap where no one could see its slight tremble. And then she pasted on a bright smile. "I'm eager to learn of your traditions."

The queen arched a disbelieving brow. "Are you? Because I already have a wedding planner that knows everything about planning a royal wedding."

"And I'm looking forward to working with her. I think we'll be able to make room for your traditions and for Giselle's wishes." Bianca could now understand why Leo had brought in reinforcements. The queen was very determined to have her way, no matter how unhappy it made her daughter.

And that was it. The conversation ended as the queen turned to the female guest to her right.

CHAPTER SEVEN

HER CONCENTRATION WAS AMISS.

It might have something to do with a very handsome prince staring across the table at her.

Every time Bianca's gaze met his, he would glance away. Was it possible the prince was interested in her? Or was it a case of wishful thinking?

She didn't know how she did it, but she made it through the seven-course dinner without spilling her water, dribbling her wine or dropping her fork, even though her hands insisted on trembling. Giselle included her in a friendly conversation, but Leo for the most part was quiet. He paid attention to the conversations around him, but he didn't participate unless someone directly addressed him.

When dinner was concluded, the queen, the prince and Giselle's fiancé spoke with their guests about a matter of government while Giselle pulled Bianca aside. They walked to the terrace, which overlooked the gardens that were highlighted by a vast array of soft lights. They were huge and looked exactly like a maze. Her inner child was anxious to go explore.

"I think you impressed my mother," Giselle said. "But she would never let on. She isn't used to someone standing up to her."

Bianca worried that she'd said too much. "I hope I didn't offend her. That was not my intention."

"My mother does not respect many people. And certainly not the ones she can easily walk over. That's why my brother is the perfect person to be king. He stands up to our mother and calls her out on things when she goes too far."

"And what about you?" It would be helpful to get more

information about the dynamic between the bride and her mother.

Giselle shrugged. "Before the wedding, my mother and I never had much of a reason to clash because I was never interested in the inner workings of the country. There were always enough people handling affairs of state, allowing me to concentrate on my own life. But this wedding, it went from being my marriage to William to being world-wide publicity for our country. There are news networks bidding for strategic camera placements within the cathedral." There was a tone of disbelief and disgust in her voice. "Can you imagine?"

Actually, she could. She once did a wedding for two American movie stars. The paparazzi was everywhere. And the first photo of the newlywed couple sold for millions. But that wouldn't do anything to soothe this bride's nerves.

"I'll handle the press. That's not for you to worry about."

Giselle studied her for a moment as though trying to figure out if she should trust her. "You've dealt with big weddings before?"

"Yes. I've worked for some very famous people. Some of them had huge weddings and others preferred privacy. Every wedding is different. Just as every bride is different."

"My brother must really like you." Giselle smiled like she knew a secret.

Bianca glanced around, afraid someone might overhear them. Luckily there wasn't anyone too close to them. "I think he likes the way I do my job."

Giselle's smile broadened. "He's never brought home a woman before."

Heat engulfed Bianca's face. "It's only work."

"Uh-huh." But the look in Giselle's eyes said that she didn't believe her.

"We're working on your wedding and—" She caught

herself, not sure if Leo would mind if she shared their arrangement.

"And what?" Giselle drew out the words with a definite note of interest. "Do tell."

"It's no big deal." That was a lie. It was a huge deal to her. "In exchange for me planning your wedding, he has agreed to sponsor an advertising campaign to draw people to my family's vineyard in Italy for my wedding planning business."

Giselle didn't even attempt to hide her gaping mouth. It took her a couple of seconds to speak. "My brother is doing all of that?"

"Yes. For you. To give you the wedding of your dreams."

"My brother isn't the kind to go out of his way for just anyone. Trust me. He likes you."

"It's not for me. It's for you."

"Uh-huh." Her eyes said that she didn't believe her.

Bianca's stomach fluttered as though it'd been invaded by a swarm of butterflies. Giselle had to be wrong. Leo wasn't interested in her—

"There you are." Leo's voice came from behind them.

Both Bianca and Giselle turned. When Bianca's gaze met his, her heart beat wildly. And this was all Giselle's fault for putting these wildly inappropriate thoughts into her mind.

Giselle glanced around. "Where's William?"

"He's waiting inside for you. Everyone has called it an evening."

Giselle turned to Bianca. "I'm glad you're here. I like you. And I think together, we'll plan a great wedding. Can we meet first thing tomorrow to go over details?"

Bianca nodded. "That would be perfect."

"I'll see you then." Giselle headed back inside. She paused next to her brother. "You have good taste. Just don't go and scare her off."

Leo arched a brow at his sister but didn't say a word. Giselle giggled as she headed inside, leaving them alone in the moonlight.

He approached her. "You did well at dinner. My mother is not an easy woman."

"But I don't think she likes me."

"I'll let you in on a secret—I don't think she likes many people. But give her time. She won't be able to resist liking you."

His words warmed a spot in Bianca's chest. That warmth radiated up her neck and once again set her cheeks ablaze. She wasn't one that normally blushed but there was something about being here—talking with Leo—being so close to him.

"I think you're trying to put me at ease, but I know dealing with your mother over this wedding is not going to be easy. She has her thoughts and they aren't easily going to be swayed, but I intend to do my best. I can at least run interference for your sister. Your mother can yell at me—"

"My mother rarely raises her voice. It's more along the lines of looks that could kill as well as a warning tone in her voice that makes people quiver."

"Quiver, huh? Are you trying to get rid of me?"

"Not a chance. Instead, I came out here to see if you'd like to stroll through the gardens with me." He once again held his arm out to her. "Shall we?"

She loved his gentlemanly ways. The guys she'd dated didn't do things like offer their arm, get her chair for her or open her car door. But Leo, he was definitely different.

She placed her hand in the crook of his arm and walked with him as they moved to the sweeping stone steps that led to the gardens. As they moved along the cobblestone walkway, she inhaled a sweet floral scent. It was delightful.

"This is beautiful. How big is it?"

"Every year, they expand it. I don't know exactly how

big it is. I just know that when I was little, it was fun to play in. But the head gardener wasn't so happy when we veered off the path and trampled the plants."

The thought of Leo as a young boy made her smile. "I bet he wasn't that upset with you."

"Oh, I think he was, but there wasn't much he could do since I was a prince. And so we kept playing out here and getting in more trouble."

"I can't blame you. When I was young, my brother and sister would play with me among the grapevines at the vineyard. But it was nowhere near as fun as this winding garden path. There are so many hiding places."

"There's a lot more to Patazonia than the royal gardens. I hope to show you around while you're here." He stopped and turned to her. "You haven't changed your mind about the wedding, have you?"

She shook her head. With him gazing into her eyes, her heart had leaped into her throat. Was that desire reflected in his eyes? The prince desired her? Her heart tumbled in her chest.

She didn't know how long they stood there staring into each other's eyes. It was like Leo had a gravitational force around him and she was being drawn in. Though she knew letting anything happen between them would be a mistake—compounding all of the other uncertainties in her life—she remained rooted to the spot in front of him.

Her heart raced as she found herself getting lost in his dark gaze. Her fingers tingled with the urge to reach out to him—

Someone cleared their throat. Loudly. Annoyingly.

And in that second, the connection dissipated. Bianca blinked and glanced away. Heat returned to her face. She was grateful she didn't have to speak because she didn't trust her tongue to work correctly.

Leo cleared his throat. "Yes, Michael. What is it?"

"You are needed, sir. The call from Canada."

Leo sighed. "I'll be right there." Once the man moved on, Leo turned his full attention to her. "I'm sorry. I've been expecting this call all day."

"I understand. You have important business to attend to."

Reality had come crashing in on them. And none too soon. He was a royal prince. She was a wedding planner with an uncertain heritage. They did not belong together.

"About this…" As his voice trailed off, he looked at her with confusion reflected in his eyes.

He wasn't the only one to be confused. Her heart had betrayed her mind in wanting what it could not have. And now that her feet were once again planted firmly on the ground, she couldn't forget that she was here to do a job. That needed to be her focus. Not getting swept up in some fairy tale.

"It's okay," she said. "You have important work to do."

"You're not upset about ending the evening so soon?"

She shook her head. "Not at all. I understand that business must come first."

As he escorted her back to the palace, he didn't offer her his arm. And she made sure to keep a reasonable distance between them. Because as much as nothing had happened between them, something most definitely had almost happened.

For a brief moment awareness had passed between them. It had been something genuine. Something not quite tangible but utterly unique. But for both their sakes, it was best neither of them examined it too closely.

CHAPTER EIGHT

HE'D ALMOST KISSED the wedding planner.

And the only thing he regretted was that they'd been interrupted.

A hectic week had flown by since that very memorable moment and Bianca filled every nook and crevice of Leo's thoughts. He sighed. He was playing with fire. He was supposed to be choosing a wife in order to announce his engagement after his sister's wedding, not indulging in a fleeting desire. But, oh, what a desire.

"What are you smiling about?"

Immediately Leo cleared his facial expression. His sister stood in front of his desk studying him. How long had she been there? He'd been so caught up in his thoughts that he hadn't heard her enter his office.

He leaned back in his chair. "Good morning, Giselle."

"From the look on your face you must have had a good night too."

He frowned at her, warning her off the subject. But his sister wasn't good with warnings. She dared to tread where most people would veer away.

"If you must know, I worked late into the night. And it was a very successful meeting."

Giselle crossed her arms. "If that's what you need to tell yourself, then go ahead. But I think it was something far more personal that had you smiling."

He cleared his throat. "Did you need something?"

"You didn't show up at breakfast—"

"I was working."

"And Bianca wondered where you might be."

He leaned forward and straightened the papers on the

desk. "I thought you would be working with her this morning and going over all of the relevant details for the wedding."

"We are. I'm just waiting for her to grab her things and then we're off." He could feel her gaze on him the whole time she spoke. "I just stopped by to see if you would want to accompany us."

His gaze moved to the stack of bios of potential wives for him to choose from. He'd been dragging his feet long enough. The time had come. It wasn't just his mother who was pushing for him to move into the role of king. It was the cabinet too. And, truth be told, he'd been allowed his freedom to be young and a bit adventurous. Now, it was time for him to assume his responsibilities. Even if marrying for duty wasn't something he relished.

He stared blindly down at the papers on his desk. "Thanks. But I have a lot of work to catch up on."

He'd used the excuse of urgent business to cancel his daily meetings with Bianca. Though he really did have pressing matters, he needed the time and distance to regain a certain level of detachment where the alluring wedding planner was concerned.

"You're sure? You and Bianca seem to enjoy each other's company."

His sister was right, but he wasn't going to encourage her. "I'll catch up on the wedding plans this evening."

Now that Bianca had had a chance to settle in, it was time she filled him in on the progress with the wedding. If there were problems, he wanted them addressed straight away. Nothing would ruin this event for his sister.

Giselle turned to leave but then turned back to him. "How did you get Mother to go along with this plan?"

His gaze met hers. "It's not for you to worry about. I told you I would work this out so that you could enjoy your wedding and I've done just that."

Giselle rushed around the desk, wrapped her arms around him and pressed a feathery kiss to his cheek. "You really are a great brother. And someday I'll pay you back for all you've done for me."

"I didn't do it for payback."

Giselle pulled away. "I know. You did it because you love me." She moved to the other side of the desk. "I'm your favorite sister."

"You're my only sister. Now go before I disown you." He sent her a teasing smile.

She smiled back at him. "I'll tell Bianca you're sorry you were detained, but you're eager to see her this evening—"

"Giselle—"

She scurried out of the office, giggling the whole time.

He shook his head. His sister had a good heart, but she could be relentless at times. He just hoped when he did pick a wife that she would be friends with his sister. It'd be nice to finally have some family harmony.

At last, he'd run out of excuses to resume his search for a wife. As the queen had reminded him that morning in the hallway, only six weeks remained until Giselle's wedding followed by his official engagement announcement. And there was no way he would allow his mother to choose his wife. He inwardly shuddered at the thought.

He reached for the first bio on the rather large stack. As he started to read the page, he found himself comparing the woman to Bianca. He stopped, trying to clear Bianca's beautiful image from his thoughts. He started to read again. This candidate's photo had short hair unlike Bianca's long hair—he stopped again. This was going to take a long, long time.

Was he avoiding her?

Had that moment of attraction unsettled him?

Those were the questions that snuck into Bianca's

thoughts as their dinner meetings had been cancelled night after night. She'd scarcely seen him since that moment in the gardens.

She tried to tell herself that he was a prince and therefore very busy. And that had worked the first day. But she couldn't lie to herself any longer. Leo was avoiding her. It hurt.

And for that reason, Bianca had kept herself busy from first thing in the morning until she'd passed out from utter exhaustion late at night. Planning a national event was not for the faint of heart.

This morning, Giselle was giving her a tour of the cathedral. Its soaring arched roof was jaw-dropping. The stained-glass windows were stunning works of art. And the suspended lanterns were absolutely charming. This church would provide the most stunning backdrop for the wedding. Bianca made a list of items she'd like to address later, after she'd given them some thought.

At lunch in the nearby village, Bianca tried her best to catch everything Giselle said. However, the princess was the opposite of her brother. Where he was reserved and spoke only when he had something substantial to say, Giselle rambled on about this, that and another thing.

The princess was like a sunny ball of energy. And Bianca could easily imagine them being lifelong friends. Not that it was possible. When the wedding was completed, her time in Patazonia would also be completed.

But would Leo avoid her until then?

"What's the matter?" Giselle asked as the chauffeured car whisked them back to the palace earlier than expected.

"Um…nothing." Bianca lied. There was no way she was discussing Leo with his sister. If Giselle didn't approve of the match, she would fire Bianca on the spot. And if she did like them together, she would just make the whole situation even more awkward.

"That frown on your face says you have something on your mind," Giselle said. "You can talk to me."

"I was just thinking about the wedding." She needed a diversion. "You've told me what you want for the wedding and now I have to speak to your mother and her planner to find out what they expect."

"Do you have to?" Giselle's voice carried with it a slight whine.

"My goal is to give you the best day of your life. A day you can look back on and smile. If you're fighting with your mother throughout the whole ordeal, you aren't going to enjoy your big day and you definitely won't want to re-member it."

"You're right." Giselle looked down at her skirt and picked a piece of lint from it. "You know, William and I have even talked about eloping. But please don't tell my brother and certainly not my mother. She would explode and then lock me in the tower until the wedding."

"My lips are sealed. But is that what you really want to do?"

Giselle shrugged her slim shoulders. "It's better than fighting about everything, even down to the table linens."

"Then it's a good thing I'm here. You don't have to fight anymore. I'll be your go-between."

"Thank you. I feel so much better with you here." The car pulled to a stop at a side entrance to the palace. "Now, let's get you back to your office."

"That would be nice. I have so much to do."

"And I believe someone will be waiting for you."

Bianca's heart raced with anticipation. She couldn't wait. Her steps were quick through the maze of hallways until Giselle stopped outside the door. "I won't keep you any longer."

"Thank you for everything. I won't let you down."

"I know you won't. I can see why my brother hired you on the spot."

Bianca sent her a reassuring smile. "I'll send you the questionnaire I use for the details of the ceremony. If you could get that back to me right away, it would be helpful."

"I will." Giselle took a few steps down the hallway before pausing and turning back. "You know this is the first time I've been truly excited about the wedding. I just know with you here it's going to be extra special."

Once Giselle was gone, Bianca opened the office door fully expecting to find Leo waiting for her. Instead, standing behind an oversized dark wood desk was a beautiful young woman.

"Hi." The young woman straightened. "You must be Bianca." She moved from behind the desk. "I'm Sylvie. I'm your assistant for the wedding."

The young woman appeared to be about her age and she had the friendliest smile. "It's nice to meet you, Sylvie. Have you ever arranged a wedding before?"

She nodded her head. "I work for a wedding planner in town. The prince—" just the mention of him had the young woman blushing "—hired me to help you."

"I hope he didn't take you away from anything important."

Sylvie vehemently shook her head. And then with a perfectly serious expression, she said, "Nothing could be nearly as important as the royal wedding. I just can't believe I was chosen over all of the other more experienced people."

Bianca couldn't help but smile at Sylvie's sense of awe. "I'll tell you a secret. I was surprised too when the prince hired me."

"You were?"

Bianca nodded. "I've done a lot of big weddings but nothing this big and not on my own."

"You aren't alone. You've got me."

"And together, you and I will give Giselle and her fiancé the wedding of the century."

"Let's do it."

They sat down and went over what Bianca had sorted out so far. They made lists because nothing got done in Bianca's world without detailed lists. Sometimes she even made lists of lists. But her curiosity of when she'd see Leo again was a constant distraction.

CHAPTER NINE

BEING A PRINCE did have its drawbacks.

From marrying out of duty to his lack of anonymity.

Leo might have grown up in the spotlight but that didn't mean he'd grown accustomed to always standing out in a crowd. Instead, he found ways of creating his own privacy. One such way was moving into his own private apartment right here in the palace.

He made his bed every morning. He picked up around the apartment. He liked a neat space. He cooked for himself regularly during the week. He had to admit that cleaning wasn't his thing and so he did let the staff go through the apartment once a week vacuuming, dusting and tidying everything.

But when it came to cooking, he found, to his mother's horror, that he enjoyed it. He had taken many lessons from the palace chef over the years. Not that he was an expert now, but he could make a number of reasonably easy dishes. Tonight's menu included a tossed salad followed by fettuccine Alfredo.

He set the small table on the balcony. It was simple but cozy. He assured himself that it was nothing more than he would do for a friend. Then again, maybe not just any friend—

Knock. Knock.

He gave the table one last glance and then headed for the door. When he swung it open and found Bianca standing there, he told himself that his racing heart was due to rushing around to get ready for the evening. It had absolutely nothing to do with how beautiful Bianca looked that evening.

She was wearing a black dress that dipped at the neckline, giving a hint of her cleavage. The straps over her shoulders left her arms bare. A belt showed off her delicate waist. The skirt stopped a couple inches above her knees. And on her feet were black sandals.

She was a knockout. He swallowed hard, hoping his voice didn't fail him. "You look amazing."

Suddenly his dark-wash jeans and white oxford shirt seemed quite underwhelming. "I should have told you tonight would be casual. My apologies." He moved to the side. "Come in."

She stepped inside and looked around. "Is this your place?"

"It is."

As she stepped to the center of the living room, she said, "It's like a home within a home."

"It's my private space. It's where I can unwind and be myself."

"It's very nice. And much more modern than the other parts of the palace."

"How is your office? Is it to your liking?"

"Yes, thank you. I like it a lot."

Things between them took on a nervous tension. He wondered if she was remembering their moment in the gardens. If they hadn't been interrupted, things definitely would have escalated. Not wanting to make this evening more awkward, he pushed aside the thoughts.

He cleared his throat. "I apologize for being detained the last couple of days. Something urgent came up and it took all of my time."

"No need to apologize. As a prince, your time must be constantly in high demand. And I was busy getting caught up on wedding details."

He nodded in understanding. He was grateful she'd let him off the hook so easily. Though he was busy catching up on matters of state, as well as busy searching for a wife, he'd needed the time to gather his senses where Bianca was concerned. She was the wedding planner—nothing more.

"And thank you for hiring Sylvie." Bianca's voice interrupted his thoughts. "I think we're going to work well together." Then Bianca frowned. "Will she be joining us this evening? Should I have waited for her?"

"No. This dinner meeting is just for us. I think you have some information to share with me and I have some to share with you."

"It sounds like this is going to be a very productive meal."

"I hope so."

He poured her a glass of white wine. He'd had two cases of each type of wine shipped from the Barto Vineyard. He wondered if she'd notice.

This had to be a dream.

A cozy dinner for two. Just her and a prince. A gorgeous, handsome, dashing prince. Definitely a dream.

And there was music playing in the background. There was the distinct moan of a saxophone floating ever so softly through the dimly lit room. If she were to close her eyes, it'd be so easy to imagine this was a date. A smile lifted her lips.

But this wasn't a date. Far from it. Bianca's eyes opened. This was a business dinner. She couldn't let herself forget it. Just like she'd forgotten what they'd been talking about.

Her gaze met his expectant one. She glanced down, remembering the glass of wine in her hand. Oh, yes, she was supposed to sample the wine.

First, she swirled the wine, inhaling its fruity fragrance. And then she sipped it. Immediately a moan escaped her lips.

Her gaze moved to meet his. "How did you know?"

"Know what?"

"That this is my favorite wine."

"I didn't. But I recalled you drinking it after the wedding at the villa."

"You're a very observant man."

"I try. I hope you're equally as impressed with the dinner."

"It certainly smells good." She reached for her tablet. "Before we eat—"

"No work before dinner. It'll ruin your appetite."

"But we have so much to go over and not much time until the wedding."

"There will be time tonight. I promise. But first, we eat."

He led her to a private balcony. The view of the lush manicured lawn stretched out before her. This place, it was amazing. It was like something written in a storybook. And yet it was real. She wondered what it must have been like to grow up in a place like this.

"This is beautiful. I just love what I've seen of Patazonia."

Leo stepped up next to her. "I get so busy that I rarely stop to appreciate the view."

Was he saying that he didn't regularly have romantic dinners here? The thought of him sharing this kind of moment with another woman soured her mood. She gave herself a mental shake. Where had that thought come from? It wasn't like she had a claim on him.

When she went to turn, she realized just how close he was standing. Her heart pounded in her chest. When she inhaled, she breathed in the light scent of his spicy aftershave mingled with his manly scent. It was quite an intoxicating combination.

He didn't move. He stood there right in front of her. All she had to do in that moment was to lift up on her tiptoes. Her gaze dipped to his mouth—his very kissable mouth. And then she could press her lips to his.

The temptation was more than she could take. After all,

he was the one to set up this very intimate dinner. Surely, he expected more to happen than business. Right?

With him staring into her eyes, she lifted up on her tiptoes. The common sense in her head was drowned out by the pounding of her heart. His hands reached out to her, wrapping around her waist, drawing her closer.

She leaned forward—

Beep. Beep. Beep.

As though the spell had been lifted, Bianca pulled back.

Beep. Beep. Beep.

Leo inhaled an unsteady breath. "Sorry. It's the kitchen timer."

He turned and headed inside. Bianca paused on the balcony, trying to slow the pounding of her heart. What in the world had gotten into her?

Well, he was amazingly handsome. He was available— sort of. He was, after all, a prince. And she didn't have a drop of royal blood—at least not that she knew of. And then the memory of her mother's journal entry came rushing back to her.

The uncertainty cast over her and her siblings brought her feet back to the ground. What was she going to do if she wasn't a blood Bartolini? Would her siblings look at her differently?

She pushed the troubling thoughts to the back of her mind. There was nothing she could do about her siblings and the fallout from their parents' deaths now. The only thing she could control was giving Giselle the very best wedding and growing her business as a result.

This meal was going to be a challenge. How was she supposed to sit there as the last rays of the sun disappeared and the stars twinkled overhead and stare across the table at the most handsome man and keep her thoughts focused on work?

She walked to the galley kitchen. "Can I help?"

"Would you mind grabbing that basket of bread?"

She turned to the counter and found the bread. "Anything else?"

He shook his head. In his hands were two plates of pasta. "I already put the salad on the table."

She didn't miss how amazing this dinner smelled. Her stomach rumbled its approval. "Did you make all of this?"

He set the food on the table. "Not the bread. I cheated and stole it from the palace kitchen. No one can beat their fresh bread."

He pulled out a chair for her and she sat down. She was tempted to ask if he went to all this trouble for every business meeting but didn't want to ruin this moment. She knew later, when she was alone in her room, that she would replay this evening in vivid detail.

Dinner was quiet without the constant interruption of his phone—or hers for that matter. She knew why hers was quiet—she'd totally muted it. It was a habit she'd gotten into before important meetings. There was nothing worse than a creative and productive meeting halted for a phone call that could wait until another time. In the time it took to answer the call, ideas may have been lost, enthusiasm for a more daring, more bold idea may have waned. And the thing Bianca disliked the most was letting a good idea slip away.

But right now, her ideas had strayed from flower arrangements and quartets to something far more daring—far bolder. As the prince ran the fine linen napkin over his lips one last time, she couldn't help but stare. She wondered what would have happened if they hadn't been interrupted out on the balcony.

In this very intimate setting with no guards, no family—absolutely no one to interrupt them—would they have even made it to dinner? Or would they be enjoying something far more delicious—

"What is it?" The prince's deep voice rumbled across the table, drawing her from her thoughts.

Did he know what she'd been thinking? No. Impossible. It was best to move things along to the business of the wedding. It would focus her thoughts. And once they wrapped things up, she'd be on her way before her thoughts had another chance to stray again.

She swallowed hard. "Thank you for dinner. It was delicious."

He shook his head. "You don't have to say that."

Was he serious? He doubted his skills in the kitchen? Was it possible a prince could have normal insecurities like everybody else in the world? "You're a talented cook."

Was it possible he was blushing? He moved so quickly to clear the dishes from the table that she wasn't able to get a good look at his face. Perhaps it was a figment of her imagination.

Then realizing she was just sitting there with the prince waiting on her, she jumped to her feet. "Let me help."

"I've got it."

"It's the least I can do after that amazing dinner." She followed him to the kitchen with the near-empty breadbasket.

He placed the plates in the sink and then he turned, almost bumping into her. "I can take that." He placed the basket on the counter. "Would you like some more wine?"

She shook her head. "No. I mean, I would but I still have work to do."

"Oh, yes. The wedding. Let's go to the living room and you can tell me your thoughts."

Her gaze strayed to the sink. "I should help you wash the dishes."

"There's no need because as much as I like to pretend that this apartment is my space to maintain, there's a staff that periodically puts everything to rights."

"Must be nice."

He smiled and set her heart pounding. "There are some advantages to being the crown prince."

"Talk about a charmed life," she teased.

The smile slipped from his face. "There's a lot more to it than most people know. There are expectations and demands. Sometimes your life is not your own."

"Sorry. I didn't mean anything by the comment."

He shook his head. "It's okay. How about we work on the wedding plans?"

Together they moved to the couch. Leo cleared off the coffee table and Bianca spread out her stuff. She wasn't exactly sure how this was to work. The truth was this evening was feeling more like a date than a business meeting.

A nervous giggle bubbled up in the back of her throat. She choked it down. She had to keep her composure, even if she was a jittery ball of nerves on the inside. What was it about this man that had her losing her calm, collected demeanor?

CHAPTER TEN

TWO LIT CANDLES.

Two wine glasses.

And this wasn't a date?

Bianca turned a questioning gaze to Leo, finding him sitting closer than she'd anticipated. When his dark, probing gaze met hers, her mouth grew dry. Did he have any idea how his close proximity made her heart pound? What exactly did he have in mind for this evening? Was she going to be dessert?

"Did you have a question for me?" Leo asked.

Act professional. Don't let him see how he gets to me.

She swallowed, hoping her voice didn't betray her. "Um, yes, I'm not sure how this is going to work. Are you planning to have input into the wedding? Or are you just looking for an overview?"

"An overview."

Thank goodness. There were already enough people fighting to have their way with the wedding. "Would you like an overview of everything? Or is there a specific area you're interested in? Such as the disagreements between the queen and the princess?"

His eyes widened with her last question. "I would be most interested in the differing opinions."

Bianca nodded. "Will you make the final decision in those cases?"

A thoughtful look came over his face. "Am I to take it that you would prefer if I were to take on a more active role?"

Bianca resisted the urge to shrug her shoulders. Though the prince had taken on a friendly persona with her, she realized their relationship was still grounded in business. And as a professional, she tried to maintain certain standards that left out shrugging.

She swallowed. "I believe if you were to take on such a role it would help alleviate some of the tension flowing between mother and daughter."

He nodded. "Then I will do it. Anything to bring some peace back to the palace."

"Great." She picked up her tablet. Her finger moved over the screen, searching for the photos she'd taken earlier. "The first disagreement is about the setting for the ceremony."

The prince sighed.

Bianca paused and turned to him. "Have you changed your mind about being the deciding voice?"

"No. Continue."

"Your sister is interested in having a small, intimate ceremony. The queen says she has a long list of relatives and dignitaries that must be allowed to attend without insulting anyone. I can see both points of view."

Frown lines bracketed his eyes. "I really want my sister to have the wedding of her dreams, but I know there are a lot of influential people that will expect an invitation."

"Would you mind if I made a suggestion?"

"Please do."

"What if we were to have the ceremony in the cathedral as your mother wants, but in order to create a cozy intimate ceremony, we can dim the stained-glass windows with curtains and we could use candles to illuminate the aisle and the front of the church. The focus then would be on the happy couple and the wedding party."

Prince Leo paused as though considering all sides of the scenario. And then he looked at her. "I like it. Do it."

"Your mother might not like it—"

"Leave her to me. Make the arrangements. Now, what else is there?"

They went over the guest list, trying to trim it back to the size to fit in the cathedral. The princess and the queen couldn't agree on who should be cut on the list so the formal invitations could be sent out. Surprisingly, Leo was able to glance down over the list and cut the necessary names.

"And how about my sister's dress?"

Bianca struggled to hide a smile. "She has that under control. No one is to see the dress. It is under lock and key in her suite of rooms. Only her and the dressmaker have access to it."

"My mother must be having a fit."

"I couldn't say. But your sister appears quite pleased with her selection. She said it's a real head turner."

"Oh, no. I'm afraid to imagine."

"Your mother said she won't stand for anything inappropriate so she's having her bridal gown resized for the princess."

Leo didn't bother hiding the fact that he rolled his eyes. "Those two are so stubborn. Should I be worried about my sister's selection?"

"I can't honestly say. I haven't seen the dress. But your sister seems reasonable to me."

"That's what I was hoping you'd say."

Now was the time for her to inquire about her compensation for planning the wedding, but how did one ask a prince if he'd followed through with what he'd promised her?

Hey, did you get a chance to call anyone? Um...do you want me to give you ideas—?

"It's my turn." Leo got up and moved to the desk in the next room, which looked to be his study. He returned with a laptop. "As soon as we came to an agreement, I had my people start on preliminary campaigns for your wedding business."

"Wow. You are very efficient." The words were already out of her mouth by the time she realized she wasn't talking to just anyone. Heat rushed to her cheeks. Leo was a prince, the crown prince. Soon he would be ruling a nation. Of course, he would be on top of things.

"I have five different approaches for you to consider." He acted as though she hadn't just stuck her shimmery heels in her mouth. It made her like him even more.

They went over the different themes. First, flowers everywhere. Second, location shots of her family's estate. Third, following an actual wedding. Fourth, a modern approach with romantic words for art. And last, her as the spokesperson and model.

The proposal was quite involved, more so than she'd ever imagined. "These are all so impressive. Would you mind if I took the night to consider them all?"

"Not at all. Take as long as you need."

"It won't take me long. It's just that the busy day is catching up with me."

"Of course. And I have some phone calls to return before I can call it a night."

She gathered her things. His fingers brushed over hers as he attempted to help her. His touch was like a jolt of static electricity. The sensation raced up her arm and settled in her chest where her heart beat wildly. She'd never experienced anything like it before.

She didn't remember moving to the door, but suddenly she was standing there. When she paused and turned back, Leo was standing right there next to her—closer than two business acquaintances and yet too far away for the perfect ending to an intimate dinner.

He didn't say anything.

She stood perfectly still.

And then his gaze lowered to her mouth. Was he going to kiss her? Her heart tumbled in her chest. This moment was surreal. She, Bianca Bartolini, standing in a palace with a dashingly handsome prince standing before her. Not only had he prepared her dinner but now he might actually kiss her.

If this was a dream, she didn't want to wake up. She was quite content to live the rest of her days in this delicious fantasy.

With her eyes, she willed him to her—like casting a spell over him. She knew it was ridiculous. Of course, it couldn't work—

But then he was there. His lips pressing to hers. Her heart suspended its pounding in utter shock. Could this be happening? Was Prince Leo really kissing her?

But as his lips moved over hers, as his hands wrapped around her waist, as her body was instinctively drawn to his, as her feet felt as though they were floating, she knew that this moment was real. This moment—this kiss—it was something that she would remember for the rest of her life.

His kiss was gentle at first but as she opened herself up to him, he wanted more and so did she. As the blood warmed in her veins, her responses to him became bolder. A deep moan of ecstasy filled the air. Was that her? Or was it him? In that moment, it didn't matter. Each was getting lost in this exquisitely sweet moment—

Knock. Knock.

They jumped apart.

Leo looked at her with desire still smoldering in his eyes. He ran a hand over his disheveled hair. Had she done that? Things had certainly moved beyond a simple goodnight kiss.

Her fingers traced over her still-tingling lips. All the while, she couldn't bear to take her eyes off him.

He cleared his throat. "I need to get this."

She nodded in understanding and then stepped back out of the way of the door. Luckily for her, the door would shield her because she had no doubt that one look at her and whoever was on the other side of the door would know what she'd been up to—getting lost in the steamy kisses of the prince.

Leo swung the door open. "Oscar, I thought I'd left strict instructions that I wasn't to be disturbed this evening."

Bianca wondered how far he'd anticipated that good-night kiss going. Had it been a sudden flare of passion? Or had it been something he'd been planning, anticipating even?

The last thought doused the remaining embers of passion as well as the hope that once the door closed, they would pick up where they'd left off.

"Sir," Oscar said with a baritone voice, "my apologies. It's the princess—"

"Is something wrong with Giselle?"

"No, sir. It's just she's been searching for Miss Bartolini. When she didn't find her in her room, she started searching for her. And when she couldn't find her anywhere, she worried that she'd wandered off sightseeing and perhaps had gotten lost."

Bianca took a couple steps back. She couldn't help but smile at the older man's obvious discomfort of delivering this news to the crown prince. And the frown that covered Leo's face was cute.

"She's not lost," Leo ground out. "She's here. We were just finishing our meeting."

"Very good, sir. I will let the princess know."

"And Oscar?"

"Yes, sir. No more interruptions."

Leo closed the door with a firm thud. Then he turned to her. "I'm sorry about that. Leave it to my sister to jump to farfetched conclusions."

"I should go." Thankfully it was Giselle searching for her, but it could have been the queen. Bianca didn't have to wonder what the queen would think of her lip-locking with the prince. The queen would have her on the first flight out of Patazonia.

"You don't have to." His eyes pleaded with her. "Not yet."

It was so tempting to stay—to find out where that kiss would lead them. But then again, she didn't have to stay to learn the answer to that question. She already knew if she were to stay that they were going to cross over a line they couldn't come back from. And that wasn't something she was ready to do. Not even for a strikingly handsome prince.

And now she had to leave before the little bit of common sense failed her. Because when she stared into his mesmerizing eyes, like she was doing right now, it was so easy to lose herself.

She glanced away. She had to stay focused on her job. It was important. Kissing the prince was not on any of her lists. The lists would get her what she wanted—her successful business, her security. She had to focus on her lists and not on how his enchanting kisses could cast the most delightful spell over her.

"I should be going," she said, glancing down at her hands.

"Are you sure I can't tempt you to stay a little longer? I still have some more of your favorite wine and I have some moonlight I can show you out on the veranda."

Did he have to make this so hard? It was as though she had a devil on one shoulder, telling her to live in the moment, and an angel on the other, telling her to march out that door. To say she was torn between her desires and her common sense was an understatement.

"As tempting as the offer is, if I don't go to the princess and find out what she needs, I'm pretty certain Oscar will be back. And I feel bad for him—being caught in between you and your sister."

"My sister can't possibly need anything important at this hour. Whatever it is can wait until morning."

"With the wedding so close, it might be urgent."

He rubbed the back of his neck. "Very well. We will meet again tomorrow evening."

Bianca nodded. "As per our agreement."

He opened the door for her. She moved past him, leaving a wide berth between them.

"Good night," she said.

"Till tomorrow."

His words sent a wave of excitement fluttering through her chest. Was that some sort of promise of more delicious kisses to come?

She kept moving down the hallway, not trusting herself to slow down and have one last backward glance. Because she'd been listening for the door to close behind her and it hadn't. Leo was standing there, watching her walk away.

It wasn't until she turned the corner that she stopped for a moment to gather herself. Had that really happened? She touched a finger to her well-kissed lips. Oh, yes, it had.

The moment though sweet and spicy must be a thing of the past. It was a memory she would hold dear. But now that she could once again think straight, she knew the knock had been her saving grace. Because to have a fling with the prince was to risk her entire future, which had enough uncertainty already. It was best that it ended here.

CHAPTER ELEVEN

HE'D BARELY SLEPT.

And he had no appetite.

In the two weeks since that earth-shifting kiss, Leo had taken every precaution not to be alone with Bianca. What was wrong with him? He'd never had a woman get under his skin the way Bianca had done. When he was around her, he longed to pull her into his embrace.

And that's exactly why they didn't dine alone again. They'd had their business dinners in the village a few nights, another night he'd invited Giselle and William to accompany them. Yet another night they'd had a working dinner with Sylvie. He'd even considered dining with his mother just so they wouldn't be alone, but he wasn't quite that desperate—yet.

Now, he sat alone in his office with two stacks of paper in front of him. They were the bios of candidates for his future wife. He'd been through the pages countless times. With his sister's wedding now only four weeks away, he had to get serious about his search. With a large portion of bios cast into the not-a-chance pile, it was time to meet the remaining women face-to-face.

A frown pulled at his lips. Why had he agreed to this? Oh, yes, so his mother would go along with his plan to let Bianca coordinate his sister's wedding. And now he had to hold up his end of the agreement.

The task left a sour feeling in the pit of his stomach. No wonder he'd skipped breakfast. Who could eat when they had to pick a marriage partner from a stack of biographies of strangers? Well, that wasn't entirely true. Some of the women he'd met on formal occasions. However, he hadn't dated any of them. He knew if he were ever to indicate a liking for someone his mother deemed appropriate, he would be formally engaged by the end of the day.

Maybe that would have been better than sitting here playing Russian roulette with his future. But there was something he'd rather be doing. He'd rather see how the wedding plans were progressing. Judging by the glance he'd had at dinner of Bianca's to-do list, she was hard at work.

He'd never met a person who ran their life by lists. He wouldn't be surprised if Bianca had lists for her lists. He had a lot of things to do as the next King of Patazonia, but even he left room for the unexpected—for a chance to enjoy life. He wondered if Bianca ever let herself enjoy spontaneous moments.

"Sir, your lunch date is here," Oscar said, standing in the open doorway of his office.

He checked the time. She was a half hour early. Normally he appreciated a visitor being prompt, even a few minutes early, but thirty minutes early. That was too much.

"Please tell Miss Ferrara that I'll be with her shortly. I have a few things I must finish up."

"Very well, sir." Oscar nodded and then backed into the hallway and walked away.

He liked Oscar. The older man was very good about keeping his thoughts to himself, unless Leo pushed for an answer. Other than that, the man did what was asked of him without causing any problems. The queen could take a few lessons from him.

"What are you doing in here?" came a familiar voice from the hallway.

He glanced up as his mother strode into his office. She didn't smile, but then again, she rarely smiled so that wasn't unusual. But by the etched lines across her forehead, she did have something on her mind.

"Mother, this is where I work."

"But you have a guest."

He arched a brow. "How would you know?"

She sighed. "Leopold, I thought you'd realized I know everything that goes on within these palace walls. Just like I know you've been spending far too much time with that... that person."

"I believe you mean with the wedding planner. And her name is—"

"I know what her name is. My question is what are you doing having intimate dinners with her?"

Leo refused to let his mother see that her question had poked him the wrong way. He met her gaze straight on. "They aren't intimate." Not anymore. "They are working dinners. Every evening, she dines with me and gives me a status report on the plans for the wedding."

His mother crossed her arms. "You expect me to believe you're really that interested in your sister's wedding? It's just an excuse to spend more time with that woman."

"Bianca is her name. And I'd appreciate you using her name instead of calling her that woman—"

"See, I was right. She's here because you're interested in her."

"She's here because you won't let Giselle have a hand in planning her own wedding and I don't have the patience nor the time to babysit the two of you."

His mother huffed. "Well, your dinner tonight will have to be cancelled."

"And why would that be?"

"Because I've invited the Duke of Lamar and his daughter to dinner. You will be there and you will spend some time with her."

"So this isn't a state dinner, it's a matchmaking ploy."

"Call it what you will, but you can't put off this marriage much longer. The press is already running negative stories about the royal family and your sister's wedding isn't enough to sway the growing discontent with the citizens.

They believe you have no interest in governing this nation. And frankly, I'm starting to think they might be right."

Leo stood. "If you believe that then you don't know me at all."

His mother arched a penciled brow. "Then I will see you at dinner."

He didn't want to go. He wanted to dine with Bianca. He'd been looking forward to that dinner—to, um, hearing about the latest wedding plans.

"I'll be there."

Without a word, his mother turned toward the door. "Don't keep your visitor waiting."

And with that his mother was gone.

His jaw tightened. He hated when his mother started throwing her weight around. He knew he'd started it by hiring Bianca without discussing it with the queen. But he knew she would have vetoed the idea. So he figured it was better to hire Bianca and hope for understanding than to mention it first and then go against his mother's wishes.

When he'd hired Bianca, he'd never imagined she'd be such good company. He wondered what she was doing now. He grabbed his phone to text her.

Are you busy?

He waited. No response.

Can't make dinner. Sorry. Something came up.

With a sigh, he placed his phone in his pocket. He'd put off meeting with—he glanced at his calendar—Jasmine Ferrara long enough. This was going to be more of a business interview than a date because he didn't have any interest in romance.

His thoughts returned to Bianca. He hoped cancelling

dinner wouldn't cause any problems. From what he could see so far, Bianca was quite capable of making sensible decisions concerning the wedding. She didn't need him looking over her shoulder, but he wasn't willing to let go of their connection. He needed to be on top of things should his mother decide to cause trouble.

Or at least that's what he told himself was the reason for insisting on dining with Bianca each evening. It had absolutely nothing to do with that unforgettable kiss. After all, he was supposed to be interviewing for a wife. He didn't have the right to kiss Bianca—even if it had been the best kiss ever.

How could the day be over already?

Where had the time gone?

Bianca made her way back to her office within the palace walls. She had so many notes. It was going to take her hours to sort through everything. But she was supremely pleased with how much she'd accomplished.

The ceremony, as well as the extensive security, had been planned down to the finest detail. And though it'd been a heated meeting with the queen and her wedding planner, they'd finally struck an agreement where the queen would get to keep her extensive guest list while the princess got to have a sense of intimacy with lots of candles and curtains that would be lowered over the stained-glass windows just as the ceremony was about to begin.

Bianca smiled as she entered the office.

"There you are." Sylvie glanced up. "I've been trying to reach you."

Bianca pulled out her suspiciously quiet phone. The battery was dead. No wonder she hadn't gotten any responses to her inquiries from that morning.

Nor had she heard from Leo. Not that there was any particular reason she should hear from him, but that hadn't kept her from hoping. Just the thought of him had heat rushing to her face.

"What has you blushing?" Sylvie asked.

Bianca swallowed hard. No one could know about the stolen kiss. Not even Sylvie, who was quickly becoming a good friend. The kiss had been a mistake. A moment of passion.

"I'm just warm," she said, hoping Sylvie would believe her and let the subject drop. "I was doing a lot of rushing around. For some reason, I imagined a palace would always be cold and drafty but that isn't the case here. Perhaps I should have packed more summer clothes."

"There are some great shops in the village. I could write down their names."

She didn't have time for shopping. It wasn't on her list of things to do. And she had something to do every minute of every day. The wedding was so close and there were still so many details to take care of, including the after-party.

Still, Bianca didn't want to be rude. "Sure. If you could jot those down for me that would be great."

Sylvie smiled. "I'll do that."

Bianca glanced at the time on the wall. "It's getting late. I'm surprised to find you still here."

"I didn't want to go home before you got back. You know, in case you had something that needed done ASAP."

Bianca glanced down at the stack of work she'd placed on her desk. "I do have a lot that needs done, but not tonight."

"Are you sure? I don't have any plans."

"I'm sure," Bianca said. "I need a chance to sort through my notes. I'll have a list for you in the morning."

"Okay. As long as you're sure."

"I am." The truth was she was so accustomed to working on her own that it was taking her some time to get used to having an assistant. "Go get some rest and I'll see you in the morning."

Sylvie grabbed her things and headed for the door. She paused and turned back. "I hope you have a nice dinner with the prince."

There was a look in her eyes like she knew what had gone down between Bianca and Leo. Was it possible rumors had started?

"I don't know what you've heard?"

"Heard?" A look of confusion came over Sylvie's face. "I haven't heard anything. Oh, gosh. I'm sorry. I didn't mean to imply anything. I just—I meant that I hoped everything goes well."

"Oh. Yes. Me too." She felt so ridiculous for thinking her secret had gotten out. She was going to have to be calmer going forward. "I think the prince will be impressed with what I was able to negotiate between the princess and her mother."

"I know that I am. I'm really enjoying working with you. I will see you in the morning. Good night."

"Good night."

Sylvie closed the door behind her. Bianca moved to sit down at her desk. She'd put an extra charger cord in her desk. She'd been meaning to replace her battery as it didn't last nearly as long as it once had. But one thing after another kept her from going into the village to buy one. She supposed she could order it online and have it delivered to the palace. Yes, that sounded like the best idea.

She plugged in her phone but it was so dead that it didn't immediately turn on. She set it aside to do its thing. But she didn't want to be late for dinner. Leo did have a thing for punctuality.

They hadn't discussed what time dinner would be tonight. If it was to be at the same time as usual she had to get moving. She didn't even have time to stop at her room and change clothes.

Bianca checked her makeup with her compact. She powdered her nose before reapplying her shimmery lip gloss. One final glance in the mirror and she decided it would have to do. It wasn't like she was going on a date. Right?

She stood up and checked her phone. It still had that blasted flashing red checkmark on the screen that let her know it was charging, but it wasn't ready to be used, just yet. And so she left it behind.

Thankfully she was good with directions because the palace was full of small staircases tucked discreetly in walls at the most unexpected places. When she reached the knight wearing the palace's coat of arms, she turned and headed up the carpeted steps. They were modest and absolutely nothing like the grand staircase in the front of the palace. If you didn't know about the steps, you might very well miss them.

At the top of the steps, she turned to the left. The prince's apartment was at the end of the hallway. It was very private. In fact, as she glanced around, she realized it was the only doorway. And considering Bianca hadn't passed anyone on her way here, she assumed not many people were welcome in this part of the palace. The fact that she'd been invited into this part of the prince's world made her feel special. A smile pulled at her lips.

She paused outside the apartment door. It was the first time she'd allowed herself to imagine how this evening might go. She envisioned another candlelight dinner with the prince flirting with her. Would it be proper to flirt back? Oh, who cared about proper? This was a fantasy.

Part of her said that she needed to stay focused on business, but the womanly part of her said that she was crazy to pass up a moment in Leo's arms. After all, what were the chances that another handsome prince would cross her path?

She halted her thoughts. She couldn't believe she was having this debate. It wasn't like the kiss would happen again. It was a fluke. A one-time thing.

With the internal conflict resolved, she leveled her shoulders and lifted her chin. It was time to do business. She inhaled a deep breath, hoping to slow her heartbeat. She raised her hand and knocked.

No response.

Perhaps she hadn't knocked loud enough. She tried again. Still nothing.

She turned and retraced her steps. At the bottom of the steps, she came across Oscar.

"Good evening, ma'am."

"Hi. Would you happen to know where the prince might be?"

"I just passed him heading into the gardens. But he—"

"Thank you. I'm late." She rushed off.

The gardens were down another floor. But when she got to the window, she saw Leo was already outside. Had he planned on having dinner in the gardens? The thought of such a beautiful romantic setting set her heart aflutter.

She started moving again, anxious to catch up with him. But when she reached the main floor and made her way out to the patio area, Leo was nowhere in sight. She set off down one of the paths but the shrubs and trees acted as walls, making the gardens more like a maze.

And then she spotted Leo just up ahead. She was about to call out to him when she noticed he wasn't alone. Bianca moved forward just enough to catch sight of a young woman smiling up at him. From that distance, Bianca couldn't make out what he was saying but whatever it was had his female companion thoroughly enthralled.

But then again, with his deep, rich voice he could be reading the information on the back of a medicine bottle and make it sound engaging. An uneasy feeling settled in the pit of her stomach.

Bianca took a step back. She didn't want them to see her lurking. Her foot landed on a fallen twig. The sound of cracking wood was much louder than she would have expected. Knowing it would draw attention, she jumped behind a bush. Her white heels sunk in the freshly watered dirt.

Tears stung the backs of her eyes. She told herself it was her being upset over ruining her cloth pumps and not the fact that Leo had gone from kissing her like she was the only woman in the world to romancing some other woman in the gardens instead of having dinner with her.

The murmur of voices faded away. They must have moved on. It was then that Bianca glanced around the bush, praying no one was around to witness her most embarrassing moment. To her relief, she was alone.

She stepped back upon the stone walkway. In the waning sunlight, she glanced down at her shoes. They were ruined—along with her daydream that the prince thought she was special. She was just another woman in his long list of admirers.

Avoiding the palace staff, she made her way back to her office where she retrieved her phone and a stack of work. She headed to her bedroom, skipping dinner altogether. She had no appetite.

Once in her room with the door closed, she looked at her phone. Now, it was charged and there were a couple of text messages. The first was from Sylvie. The second was from Leo, cancelling their dinner plans. And that was it. No explanation. No nothing.

She wanted to be angry with him, but she knew that wasn't logical. It wasn't like they were seeing each other. The kiss had been a mistake. They had a business relationship. Nothing more.

She would do well to remember that.

She needed to focus on her work. It was the only thing she could count on—the only thing in her life that she felt as though she had any control over.

CHAPTER TWELVE

SHE WAS TIRED of the games.

The prince could not kiss her one evening and then share moonlight walks with someone else another night. It didn't work that way. It didn't matter that he was a prince or that her heart raced every time they were in the same room. She had her standards.

And that's why for the next ten days, she'd reduced their meetings to daily status emails. It was much more efficient. And so much safer for her heart.

However, when she glanced up from her desk to find Leo standing in the doorway of her office, she was caught off guard.

She swallowed hard. "Your Highness, I wasn't expecting you. Can I do something for you?"

"Your Highness?" He frowned at her. "We're back to using titles?"

She gave a slight shrug before saving the current document on her laptop. She had a feeling the prince's visit would take a bit of time.

"Today is the final day of the queen's *la fête*."

"La fête?"

"Yes. Technically it's my mother's sixtieth birthday but she refuses to celebrate her birthday. She says she's too old to have birthdays. So they call her celebration the queen's *la fête*."

"Oh, I see. I'll make sure to keep out of the way. Besides I have plenty of work to do—"

"No, you don't understand. You are invited."

Bianca pressed a hand to her chest. "Me. But I'm a nobody."

"You are my guest."

Her heart stuttered. Was he asking her to be his date? Wait. No. He must mean his guest as in a general invitation because he'd moved on to that woman in the gardens. Bianca's mood dampened a bit.

She shook her head. "I couldn't intrude. It should be a private family event."

"It's not private nor a family-only event. This will be a big state dinner with fireworks afterward."

"Fireworks?" Now that was her kind of party.

He smiled and nodded. "And there is a place at the table with your name on it."

"But what's the dress code?"

"Formal."

"As in black tie?"

He nodded. "If that is a problem—"

"I've got a formal gown, but I had planned to wear it to your sister's wedding."

"Then I will see that you get a new gown for the wedding."

"No, you can't. That would be too much."

"You are doing me the favor. It is the least I can do."

"How so?"

"Because these events are usually stuffy and can veer into matters of state. I would like to avoid that this evening. And with you there, it will make the evening more festive. Perhaps the politics can be avoided for one evening. Your attendance would be in honor of the queen."

When he put it that way, how could she say no?

"Okay. I'll go."

"Good. I can stop by your room on the way to the cocktail hour."

That would be too much like a date and she needed to make sure the boundaries were clear. She couldn't let herself get swept up in the evening. She was hired help. Nothing more.

"It's okay. I'll make my way."

His eyes reflected disappointment, but in a blink it was gone. "Very well. Cocktails are at six in the library."

"I'll see you there." Bianca turned back to her laptop. She had so much work to do.

But she couldn't stop thinking about the fact that the prince had given her a personal invitation to a very important dinner. The thought of spending the evening with Leo made her heart race.

She told herself not to get too excited about it because they would be surrounded by heads of state and dignitaries. And then there was the queen. Bianca didn't care how much she told herself otherwise, that woman made her nervous.

This was it.

This was as good as it got.

Bianca gave her coral gown with its ivory and silver embellishments one last glance in the mirror. Her stomach shivered with nerves. She had no idea if she was overdressed or underdressed. Perhaps she should have consulted Giselle. She most likely wouldn't have minded giving her some fashion tips. But it was too late for that now.

She ran a hand over her pulled-up hair. It was then that she noticed the slight tremor in her hands. How could she have gone to some of the biggest weddings in the world with Hollywood stars and politicians but this birthday party made her quake.

Bianca sucked in a deep breath. She had to get a grip. She checked the time on the delicate diamond-studded watch that her parents had given her on her sixteenth birthday. It was stunning and something she wore only on the most special of occasions. But when she wore it, no matter where she was in the world, it made her feel like her family was a little closer. And now with her parents both gone, that connection was more important to her than ever before.

Sometimes she felt like a leaf just tumbling in the wind. There was no true place where she fit in. Her brother knew it. Her sister wouldn't say it, but she couldn't deny it.

But if Bianca were to make her wedding business a success, she would have a sense of security. She couldn't control the outcome of the DNA tests, but she could control the success of this wedding—so long as she stayed on top of every detail.

Buzz. Buzz. Buzz.

Her cell phone vibrated against the white marble vanity. Knowing it could be about any number of things regarding the quickly approaching wedding, she rushed to grab it. When the caller ID showed her sister's name, worry consumed Bianca for an entirely different reason.

"Gia, are the test results in?"

"Well, hello to you too." Gia expelled an exasperated breath.

"Sorry. It's just all this waiting. It's getting to me." If anyone would understand, it was her sister.

"You don't have to worry."

"What's that supposed to mean?"

"It's obvious you're a Bartolini. You look just like Nonna when she was your age."

"You really think so?" Bianca once more glanced in the mirror. She didn't see it.

"I do. I'm the one who should be worried."

"No, you shouldn't. You were Papa's favorite. And you can't deny it."

There was a moment of silence before Gia said, "That leaves Enzo."

They both hurriedly agreed that it couldn't be him. Could it? Secretly Bianca wondered if it was him as he and their father used to butt heads—a lot.

She stifled a sigh. The guessing game was getting old. And it was getting them no closer to the answers they so desperately needed.

They talked for a few more minutes, catching up on each other's lives. Then Bianca had to go. She couldn't be late for the queen's celebration. She promised to speak to Gia soon.

Bianca headed out the door. Truth be told, she wasn't sure where she was going, but she'd been too proud to admit that to Leo. But she figured if she could make it to the main entrance that she could just fall in line with the other guests as they made their way to the library.

And that's exactly what she did. Security was everywhere in dark suits and wearing earpieces. Since she was a guest within the palace, she was able to pass through the checkpoint without any problems.

She wondered if security was always this heavy. And then she realized that it would be this intense for the wedding. She would have to make allowances for that in her plans. She reached for her phone to make a note and then realized she'd left it back in her room. She tucked the information in the back of her mind.

She followed two couples to the library. As she glanced around, she was relieved to find her dress would fit in. At last, she took a full breath.

She could do this.

The funny thing was that everyone thought she didn't get nervous or filled with anxiety before a big event she'd planned. That wasn't true, but she didn't tell them. The trick was to put on a confident smile and never let them see her perspire. And that's what she intended to do this evening.

As she stepped into the massive room, she immediately searched for Leo. He was tall, so she hoped he would stand out in this crowd, but she didn't see him. And before she had a chance to make the rounds, Giselle rushed up to her.

"There you are." Giselle slipped her arm in Bianca's. "I've been telling everyone how you are putting a fresh spin on the wedding."

Was that what she was doing? Who was she to argue with a client? Correction: a princess.

"Bianca, I'd like to introduce you to the Duchess of Lamar."

Not sure how to properly greet a duchess, she said, "It's a pleasure to meet you."

The wedding conversation took off from there. The duchess said that she would be recommending Bianca's services to her nieces. That made Bianca smile.

When they entered the grand dining hall, it was stunning. The table was unlike any she'd ever seen as it must have seated at least a hundred people. Wow! She couldn't even wrap her mind around the size of the long narrow room with purple trim and portraits of the royal family through the generations.

She was seated in the middle of the table. Nowhere close to the queen at the head of the table, which was fine with Bianca. And nowhere close to the prince at the foot of the table, which she found deeply disappointed her.

But she was delighted that throughout the eight-course meal, she was entertained by the Earl of Saskan. By the looks of him, he was only a few years her senior. He was a delightful man, who could easily carry on an entertaining conversation. And he wasn't too bad looking, but he had nothing on the prince.

"It's nice that they invited you to dinner," the earl said. "They have such a tight knit group of people for these events that it's rare for an outsider to be included. Not that you're an outsider, but you know, not one of the group—"

With each word he spoke, her insecurities came rushing to the surface. She was an outsider in this grand, historic palace. Nothing would change that. She even felt out of place in her own family, she thought sadly.

"It's okay." She placed her hand on his forearm to get his attention. When his rambling stopped, she said, "I understand. I'm a guest at the palace, I believe they felt it would be rude not to invite me."

She felt someone staring at her. Could it be the prince? And then realizing that it was probably inappropriate to be touching the earl, she quickly withdrew her hand. When she lifted her gaze, the prince turned his head to the person on his right. Why should he care who she spoke to?

The earl looked at her with relief written all over his flushed face. "Sometimes, well, a lot of times I say the wrong thing. I didn't mean anything by it."

"No offense taken." But it was definitely time to change the subject. "And how are you connected to the royal family?"

She didn't know it was such a loaded question but it kept the earl talking of his lineage through most of the meal. All she had to do was interject an acknowledgment in the appropriate pauses as he regaled her with a detailed history lesson.

Surprisingly, the dinner didn't last as long as she'd imagined with that many courses. The queen didn't chat abundantly and when she finished the course, she signaled for the dishes to be cleared. In fact, during the salad course, the earl had talked so much that he'd squeezed in only one bite before the dishes were whisked away.

When the meal was over, they were escorted to the grand ball room. And grand it was with its gold trim and enormous landscape murals on the walls. A crystal chandelier was the focal point of the room. Bianca had never seen a chandelier of that magnitude. It took in the light, making the thousands of crystals shimmer and then cast a rainbow of colors throughout the room.

As the music started, Giselle sought her out. "Are you having a good time?"

"I am. Thank you. But I had no idea there would be dancing."

"My mother, though she hasn't danced since my father passed on, does enjoy the music. You should dance."

Bianca shook her head. "I don't think so."

Giselle frowned. "Why not?"

"I really should go back to my room. I have so much work to do—"

"Not tonight. There will be no work. I insist you enjoy yourself." Just then the earl passed by them and Giselle stopped him. "Donatello, my guest doesn't have an escort, would you mind dancing with her?"

The earl's face lit up. He turned to Bianca. "May I have this dance?"

"I… I don't think it's a good idea." She was a wedding planner, not any part of the royal society. It was more than enough that she'd sat at the dining table, but now to kick up her heels—it didn't seem right.

"Go ahead," Giselle encouraged.

The earl turned to Bianca. "If you don't know how to dance, I can show you. Trust me, it's not that hard."

Heat rushed to Bianca's face. How was she supposed to turn him down now? He was such a nice man, but he didn't make her heart race or fill her with giddiness like… like Leo.

In that moment, she realized she had a crush on the prince. Maybe it shouldn't come as such a shock. Probably most of the single women and maybe even some of the married ladies in the room had a crush on him. What wasn't to like?

But she couldn't just stand around here waiting for Leo to ask her to dance. That wasn't going to happen. And the best way to forget about how Leo made her feel was to get on with her life. Just one dance and then she would quietly slip away to her room.

"I'd love to dance." Bianca slipped her hand in the crook of Donatello's arm.

As he led her to the full dance floor, her gaze strayed across Leo's. This time she didn't have to wonder if he was looking at her. He was staring right at her. There was a frown pulling at his kissable lips. And his normally warm brown eyes were dark and stormy.

As the earl took her into his arms, she had to turn away from Leo. What was he frowning about? Leo might have invited her to the dinner, but it wasn't like he was her date. In fact, he hadn't spoken so much as a single word to her all evening. He didn't earn the right to be upset with her. She hadn't done anything wrong.

The earl hadn't been exaggerating about his skill on the dance floor. She knew how to dance, but her moves weren't as smooth as his. As they moved around the floor, she searched for Leo, but she wasn't able to locate him.

Maybe he'd been upset about something else. Yes, that must be it. Someone must have said something he didn't like. Perhaps it was the queen that had him out of sorts. Because there was no way he cared who she danced with.

When the music stopped, Bianca said, "Thank you so much for the dance. I enjoyed it." It was the truth. "And you are quite a talented dancer."

"Thank you. We could go again, if you want."

"Thanks. But I think I'll sit this one out."

"Perhaps later."

She nodded. "Maybe."

And that was it. The earl moved on. Without anyone around that she knew, Bianca was left to her own devices. She made her way to the edge of the crowd. It was time to make a quick exit, but she was on the opposite side of the room from the door.

She stayed near the wall as she made her way around the crowded room. She neared the corner where there were floor-to-ceiling purple drapes with gold trim that framed the wall of windows overlooking the gardens. She paused for just a moment to admire the view.

When she turned to continued walking, someone reached out. A hand pushed against her mouth, muffling her scream. Another arm wrapped around her waist and she was yanked back into the curtains. It all happened so suddenly that she didn't have time to fight back.

CHAPTER THIRTEEN

The door slipped closed.

Darkness surrounded her.

Bianca's heart raced. She was alone in the pitch black with her kidnapper. Her palms grew moist. Her mouth was dry. She had to do something. Fast.

Having gained her wits, she used all her might and kicked the person behind her. There was the muttering of a male voice. Immediately he released her. She spun around, but she couldn't so much as see her hand in front of her face.

"What'd you go and do that for?"

She immediately recognized that voice. It was Leo. Leo? What was he doing grabbing her out of the ballroom into—whatever this room was?

"Leo? Is that you?"

"Who else did you think it'd be?" He sounded a bit exasperated.

"I don't know. Some kidnapper. Or worse."

"You are safe. It's just me."

Her gaze moved around the room. Even though her eyesight had adjusted to the darkness, she couldn't make out anything, including him. "Leo, what are you doing? Why did you kidnap me from the ballroom?"

"I didn't kidnap you."

"Really? Because it sure seemed like it to me." She turned around. Her hands stretched out in the darkness, searching for the door. "How do I get out of here?"

"Come with me."

"No. Now turn on the lights."

It took a couple of seconds but then a bare lightbulb lit

up. She glanced around, finding that they were in some sort of passageway. And she couldn't make out a door.

"Where's the door?"

He pointed to a spot on the wall. It looked like the rest of the wall. And there was no door handle. She moved to it and tried to push it open but it wouldn't budge.

"Bianca, stop." The agitation had drained from his voice. "Let me explain."

Having no success with opening the door, she whirled around to him. "Is there another way out of here?"

"Yes."

"Then let's go."

"Aren't you even going to let me explain?"

She was mad at him. She didn't think anything he had to say at the moment was going to change that fact. "No. Let's go."

He let out a frustrated sigh. "Follow me."

He led her through a tunnel. In places the tunnel narrowed and they had to pass through it sideways. In other places there were wooden stairs.

"What is all of this?" she asked.

"So you're speaking to me again?"

She huffed. If he thought that he was off the hook, he was wrong. She didn't bother answering him. He could come to his own conclusion.

Not pushing his luck, the prince said, "These are secret passages that weave their way through the palace."

"I've heard of palaces having secret passageways but I thought they were just works of fiction."

"Now you know differently."

"But how do you know where you're going? There are so many different ways to go." She stayed close to him so as not to get left behind.

"I learned these tunnels when I was a kid."

"How did you keep from getting lost?"

"I did get lost, but my father found me. He taught me how to navigate the tunnels so I never got lost again. Once you figure it out, it's no harder than walking through the halls of the palace."

"Uh-huh." She didn't believe him.

If she was in here alone, not only would she be scared, but she was certain she'd never find her way out. She'd become a ghost that haunted the palace.

And then a thought came to her. "Is this place haunted?"

"Haunted?"

"Uh-huh. You know, ghosts that got trapped in these passageways."

Leo stopped and turned to her. In the cramped space they ended up being much closer than she was prepared for. His gaze met hers, making her heart pound. That's all it took—a look—for her body to respond to him.

She was so tempted to lift up on her tiptoes and press her lips to his. She wondered how he would react. Would he pull her closer? Would he wrap his arms around her, crushing her soft curves to his very muscular chest?

But that wasn't part of her plan. She was supposed to ignore these unwanted feelings. After all, he had practically kidnapped her from the party. Still, it'd be so easy to just live in the moment—this very intimate and most unique set of circumstances.

As though Leo could sense her conflicted emotions, he leaned forward as though to tip the scales in his favor. The breath hitched in her throat. He was going to kiss her.

But she couldn't let him off the hook that easy. Her hands moved, pressing against his very firm chest. Surprise flashed in his eyes.

"Don't even think about it." As the stern warning passed over her lips, her heart sank in her chest.

"Are you saying the thought hadn't crossed your mind?"

She wasn't playing this game with him because she knew

that she would end up losing. "I'm saying that you aren't getting off the hook that easily. Shouldn't you be here with your girlfriend?"

His brows drew together. "What girlfriend? I have no girlfriend."

She desperately wanted to believe him, but she knew what she saw. "The woman you were walking with in the gardens the night you cancelled our dinner plans."

His eyes momentarily widened. "You saw us?"

"I did."

"And that's why you've been so distant?"

"I've been busy." She answered a little too quickly—a little too vehemently.

He nodded in understanding, though they both knew it was much more than work that kept Bianca away from him.

"The woman you saw me with is an old friend of the family. I'm not now nor was I ever interested in her for anything other than friendship. We went for a walk while her father and the queen talked business. That is all."

"Really?" She wanted to take back the question, but it was too late.

"Really."

He said all the right words, but this thing between them—it was like playing with fire. It'd be so easy to get caught up in the flames—and get burned.

And then realizing that she was still touching him—still absorbing his body heat through his white dress shirt—she yanked her hands back to her sides. But it was too late. His energy had been absorbed into her body and it coursed through her faster than the speed of light. It warmed her chest and melted her core into a puddle of need.

No. This isn't going to happen. He isn't going to take what he wants.

She thought of stepping back, allowing more space between them, but she didn't want him to read weakness in her movement. And so she stood there, rooted to the spot. Her determined gaze continued to hold his. She would not let him detect any weakness in her.

But she was starting to wonder how long she could keep this up. Because every fiber of her being craved him.

He stood there for a moment as though questioning her decision. But her determination was stronger than the way his dark eyes could make her knees turn to gelatin. Wasn't it?

Before she could answer that question, he turned and continued through the passageway. She followed him as they ascended a set of narrow steps with no handrail. Bianca pressed her hands to the cold stone walls to balance herself. They kept going up and up. Then there was a switchback and they ascended another flight of steps.

"Where are we going?"

"We're almost there."

That didn't really answer her question. But she would be grateful to get out of this secret passageway. She felt totally disoriented and utterly reliant on Leo—the man of mystery. She wondered what other secrets he had and if any of them were nearly as interesting as these passageways.

At last they reached a doorway, if it could be called that. It was more like a movable part of the wall. A faint bit of light lit the way.

As they stepped out of the wall, Bianca asked, "Where are we?"

There wasn't a voice to be heard. So they were a long way from the ballroom. And there weren't any other sounds. They were alone. All alone.

Stay focused.

But he's so cute. And what happens here would be our secret.

But he hasn't apologized. He can't just do what he wants without consequences.

Leo turned to her on what appeared to be some sort of landing. There was a set of stairs to his left and a single step that led to a wooden door on his right. The window let in the moonlight.

"We are in the east tower," he said.

Her heart pitter-pattered in her chest.

Why had he brought her here?

Now that he had her alone, he wasn't sure this was such a good idea. But it was too late to back out now.

"I wanted you to have the best vantage point. Come on." Leo took Bianca's hand and led her up the step and out the door.

"Vantage point for what?" She glanced around.

In the moonlight, the general layout was visible. Leo let go of her hand and lit some torches. A warm glow filled the space and highlighted the large daybed with a twin mattress and a dozen plush pillows.

"What is this place?" Bianca asked.

"It's my private spot. It's where I come when I have a lot on my mind. Sometimes I sleep out here."

He gazed into her eyes.

His heart pounded against his ribs. All he wanted to do was pull her into his arms and crush his lips against hers. He wanted to forget his duty—his obligations. In Bianca's arms, he was certain he would find the release he was seeking.

But when she gazed up at him like he hung the stars—like she was doing now—guilt assailed him.

He needed to be honest with her. She needed to know the real him. Because he wasn't the perfect prince that his mother portrayed to the world.

His thoughts drifted back to the week he'd spent on this very terrace, refusing to go back inside the palace. It had been the darkest point in his life—

"Leo, what's the matter?" Bianca's voice drew him from his troubled thoughts.

He shook his head. "Nothing."

"It's something. The pain is written all over your face. I'm a pretty good listener—that is if you want to talk about it."

He hadn't talked about it with anyone. Not even his mother. And she had been there—she'd gone through the nightmare, not exactly with him. They'd each gone through it in their own individual ways.

Leo turned and gazed into Bianca's eyes. "I don't want to ruin this night for you."

"You won't. I'd like to think we're friends and that we can confide in each other." She stared into his eyes as though she could see clear through to his soul. "Does it have something to do with your father?"

How did she do that? How did she know what he was thinking? Did she have some sort of special power? Or were his thoughts that transparent?

"How did you know?"

She shrugged. "It was just a guess. But you never talk about him. How come?"

Leo took her hand and led her over to the daybed. They perched on the edge of it. He was trying to find a place to start. He supposed the best place to start was the beginning.

"I'd looked up to my father all of my life. When I grew up, I wanted to be just like him. The problem was that I had no idea what that would entail."

"I can't even begin to imagine. And I thought I had it hard fitting into my family."

He shook his head. "Don't feel sorry for me. I'm not the good guy you think I am."

"Sure you are. Look at what you're doing for your sister. And how you took time out of your busy schedule to attend your friend's wedding. And then there's what you're doing for me—"

"Stop." He held up a hand as though blocking her compliments. "You don't understand. None of that can undo the past."

He recalled how his mother made him promise to never speak of his father's death. She wanted to sweep all the unsavory details under the rug, where no one would notice them. His mother wanted the picture-perfect family and the unblemished prince to ascend to the throne. She wanted to live a lie because none of those things existed in real life.

But he'd already lashed out at his father and it had cost his father his life. Leo couldn't lose his only remaining parent and so he did as the queen wanted. However, it came with a price. Every time he had to gloss over the details or leave out a fact, especially when talking to his own sister, it'd killed a little piece of him.

He'd been living with the secret for so long that it felt as though it was going to smother him unless he let it out. And Bianca was so easy to talk to. It was though he could tell her anything and she would understand. But would she look at him the same way once he told her his secret?

He drew in an unsteady breath. Peeling back the scabs hurt just like the nightmare had happened yesterday. But this wasn't about his comfort. It was about proving to Bianca that he wasn't worthy of her.

He stared straight ahead into the black sky. "I was sixteen. And I wanted to go on holiday with one of my friends to the lake. But my father told me I had responsibilities to attend to. I was a kid. I hated being in the spotlight. I hated being escorted by bodyguards everywhere. I hated being different."

"It must have been difficult. I think every kid just wants to fit in. I know I did."

Her words of comfort gave him the encouragement he

needed to continue. "When I told him I was going with my friends and nothing he said could stop me, my father grew angry and started yelling at me. He told me it was time I grew up. He had plans for me to attend a royal wedding in another country. He said I would meet an appropriate young woman."

Leo could still recall his outrage when he realized his father had already chosen the young woman he was to marry. He wasn't even an adult yet and his whole life had been planned without even consulting him.

"I told him I didn't want to date anyone. My father said this wasn't going to be a date. This young woman would be my future wife." The exact words of that horrific fight were a little lost on him. "My father suddenly grew quiet. I thought it meant he was giving in to my demands. Being a kid, I told him I quit being a prince. That my sister could be queen. By then he was perspiring and his face was a pasty color." Leo could still see his father's sickly image in his mind. "He strode up to me. I never saw him so angry. Ever." Leo's voice faltered. "He told me I couldn't quit. I was a prince by blood. It was an honor—a privilege. And…"

Bianca reached out and squeeze his hand. There was so much to that innocent touch. There was kindness, compassion. Both of which he didn't deserve.

He swallowed hard, hoping his voice wouldn't fail him. He had to get out this secret that he'd been keeping so deep within him. It was as though it was choking him. And the only way he could take a full breath was to get it all out in the open.

"I should have known that something was seriously wrong with him. He'd been sweating profusely and he'd looked awful, but I was only worried about myself and being with my friends. I wasn't giving up. I kept yelling at my father. I… I can't believe those angry, hurtful words were the last ones I said to him." Tears stung his eyes as emotion choked off his next words.

Bianca shifted closer to him as though letting him know that she was there to lean on. Then ever so softly, she said, "He knew you loved him."

"Did he? Because when he stopped yelling midsentence the look in his eyes was full of rage. And…and then he collapsed." He ran the back of his hand over his eyes. "I don't know how long I stood there like a complete and utter fool."

"You were in shock."

"But it was my father—the king. If I'd acted faster, maybe things would have been different."

"I don't think a few seconds would have changed things. It was out of your hands."

"You might be the only one who thinks that. Because when I finally came to my senses and started screaming for help, my mother entered the room. When she rushed over to my father, she asked me what had happened. I told her we'd been fighting and he'd collapsed. She looked at me as though it was all my fault. Then she made me promise not to mention a word of what had happened to anyone, including my sister."

"That's a huge secret for a kid to keep. Is that why there's a distance between you and your mother?"

He shrugged. "Everything was different after that. She had to become the regent and it was a position she didn't want, but she said that duty must be upheld. So I guess she holds that against me too."

Bianca placed a finger on the side of his jaw, encouraging him to meet her gaze. "And you've been blaming yourself all of this time?"

"It was my fault. If I hadn't been so insistent on having my way, things would have been different."

"Or they might have happened the same way. I don't think anything you said or did would have changed your father having a heart attack. And did you ever think your mother was trying to protect you? Maybe she struggled stepping into such an important role and by taking a firm line, it was her way of proving to everyone, including herself, that she was up to the challenge."

He paused, giving Bianca's words some serious thought. "I never thought of it that way. My mother always seemed so calm, so in control."

"Maybe you only saw what she wanted you to see."

His gaze searched Bianca's. "You really don't think I had any part in my father's death?"

"I don't. And I think if he was here, he'd tell you the same thing."

Those are the words that he'd longed to hear. He just hadn't known it. And having shared his deepest-held secret with Bianca, they now had a bond he knew would never be broken.

Her heart raced.

She'd never felt as close to anyone as she did in that moment—

A great big boom shook the ground.

Bianca instinctively reached out for Leo. Her fingers wrapped around his muscular bicep.

"Relax," he said. "Everything is okay."

Was it? Okay, that is. Because she was beginning to wonder if those passageways had taken them back in time and they were suddenly a couple hundred years in the past. The boom could be that of a canon aimed at the palace. When she was with Leo, it was easy to believe that anything was possible.

But then again, maybe she'd had one too many sips of champagne. As another softer boom filled the air, she braced herself for the palace to shake, but instead she saw the sky fill with light—colorful shades of pink and blue.

Fireworks. She breathed more easily. And then quickly withdrew her hand from Leo's arm. She moved to the stone wall at the edge of the tower. There wasn't a soul near them. They were so high up that it felt as though they were in the sky with millions of stars sparkling around them.

And then she felt Leo's presence just behind her. She waited for him to reach out and touch her. Her traitorous heart picked up its pace in anticipation.

When she turned her face to him, he said, "I'm sorry. I handled this night all wrong."

He looked at her like she should say something here, but if he was waiting for her to disagree with him, he'd be waiting a long time.

As the silence stretched between them, Leo cleared his throat. "It's just when I saw Donatello flirting with you and you enjoying it...it bothered me."

When his gaze lifted to meet hers, she searched his brown depths. Not finding the answer she was looking for, she asked, "Why did it bother you who I was talking to?"

He stepped closer to her, so close that they were practically touching. All the while the booms of the fireworks sounded in the background and the sky lit up with a rainbow of colors.

And then he reached out to her, caressing her cheek ever so gently. "Because every time you smiled, I wanted you to be smiling at me. And when you let out that contagious bubbly laugh of yours, I wanted it to be because I made you happy. And when you danced, I wanted it to be my arms wrapped around you, holding you close."

She lifted her chin ever so slightly. And then in a breathy voice, she asked, "You did?"

He gave a slight nod of his head. "I did. Do you know how hard I've been fighting my attraction to you?"

"I have some idea. I've been doing the same thing."

Desire reflected in his eyes. "I've wanted to do this since

the first moment I spotted you this evening." He lowered his head and caught her lips with his own.

The breath stilled in her lungs. There were a million reasons why this shouldn't be happening. And in that moment, those reasons dissipated into the starry night.

With the cascade of white-and-blue fireworks overhead, Leo's mouth pressed to hers. Her heart leaped into her throat. This was really happening. Leo was kissing her again.

In that moment, it didn't matter that he was a prince. To her, he was just Leo—the man who made her heart race with just a look. There was so much more to him than a fancy title. And she was anxious to continue peeling back the layers that made Leo such an exceptional man.

As his lips moved over hers, she let herself get wrapped up in the moment. The boom and crackle of the fireworks faded into the background. Right now, Leo was shooting off fireworks in her mind...and her heart.

Her arms, almost of their own volition, moved up his chest, over his broad shoulders and wrapped around his neck, drawing him closer. She wanted more. She needed more.

And yet, he took an agonizingly long time savoring her lips—refusing to rush the moment like she was apt to do.

She couldn't tell if it was the boom of the fireworks or the pounding of her heart that filled her ears. Not that it mattered. The only thing she cared about at the moment was that this kiss never ended. Because she knew deep in her heart that this moment was very precious. They were making a memory that she would cherish for the rest of her life.

When Leo pulled back all Bianca wanted to do was to draw him near once more—to feel his warm lips pressed to hers. She struggled to calm her rushed breaths.

"Bianca, if you want me to stop," his voice was raspy as he drew in one quick breath after the other, "tell me now."

Was he serious? "Don't stop."

"You're sure? Because I don't just want you for this moment—I want you to stay the night with me beneath the stars."

She glanced around. "Won't someone find us here?"

A deep laugh bubbled up from deep in his chest. "Trust me, they know better. When I'm up here, I want to be alone."

"And how many other women have you brought here?" She didn't know why she'd asked, but she knew the answer was important to her. The breath hitched in her throat as she waited.

"You, *ma chère*, are the first."

Knowing this was as special to him as it was to her warmed a spot in her chest. She took him by the hand and led him to the daybed. She sank down on the soft cushion as Leo joined her.

When she turned her head to him, he claimed her eager lips once more. Oh, yes, this was most definitely what she needed. He was what she needed…as much as her lungs needed oxygen.

That evening, she let go of all her worries about the DNA tests, the plans for the royal wedding and the future of her business. Lying there wrapped in Leo's very strong, capable arms, all she could think about was him, her, them.

All the problems could wait. Right now, there was a driving need to see where their star-studded night would take them.

CHAPTER FOURTEEN

LAST NIGHT HAD been amazing, spontaneous and unforgettable.

But in the light of day, she knew it had been a mistake.

Bianca groaned in frustration. Her heart said one thing while her mind said the opposite. All her insecurities floated to the surface.

She paced back and forth on the balcony of her room. What had she been thinking to let down her guard and make love to the prince? For a moment, the memory of the night before came rushing to her mind. Leo had been so gentle with her, so loving and thoughtful.

But it hadn't been all sweet and tender. There had been some heady passion that left her utterly breathless and begging for more. It was a night that she would never forget. But it couldn't happen again—no matter how much she wanted to relive it.

It had been a mistake.

She'd put everything she held dear in jeopardy for a man that was out of her reach. She wasn't royal. She didn't have an aristocrat cell in her body. And worst of all, she had the DNA test weighing over her. When it came back and proved she wasn't a Bartolini, who would she be?

She certainly wasn't going to ask Leo to go through this nightmare with her. It wasn't fair to him. This was her burden to carry on her own.

Bianca stopped pacing. She knew what needed to be done. The sooner, the better.

She headed out the door. She knew where to find Leo—in his royal office. On her way, she practiced what she'd say to him.

The clean-cut, always proper assistant stopped typing on his desktop and turned to her when she arrived. "May I help you?"

"I need to speak with the prince."

In total sincerity, Michael asked, "Do you have an appointment?"

In her rush, she hadn't thought of that. She didn't usually have to see Leo during business hours. "No, I don't. But this won't take long."

"I'm sorry. The prince has asked not to be disturbed."

She wondered what that was all about. Did it have something to do with what had happened between them last night? Or did he normally ask for privacy while he worked?

She wanted to ask but it was none of her business. Instead she said, "Thank you."

Just as she was about to turn away, Michael said, "I could give him a message."

She shook her head. This was something that needed to be said in person. "I'll speak with him later."

She moved to the doorway and started down the hallway when she heard her name called out. She paused and turned to find Leo standing there.

He rushed to catch up with her. "Did you need to speak to me?"

"I did."

"What did you need?" His voice and expression were neutral so she wasn't able to figure out what he was thinking.

She glanced around as people passed through the spacious hallway. Offices lined both sides of the hallway. There was absolutely no privacy. "Not here."

"Then come to my office."

In his office, it'd be easier to stick to the matter at hand. She wouldn't let herself get distracted with how good his lips felt pressed to hers—

She halted her meandering thoughts. This was what she feared would happen when they were together. She needed to make this meeting short and straight to the point.

"Let's go." Her stomach shivered with nerves, but that didn't stop her from leveling her shoulders and following him.

Once they were in his office with the door closed, she turned to him, finding that he was standing closer than she'd been expecting. She swallowed hard. "It's about last night—"

"I wanted to speak with you about that too."

"You did?" Her gaze met his.

He nodded. "Yes. But you go first."

This was it. All those practiced words fled her. And now she was left scrambling for a way to phrase this that would leave them in as good a place as possible.

Drawing upon the calm exterior she used for her wedding planner position, she lifted her chin just a bit. "Last night...it was a mistake."

"It was..."

Was that a question? Or was he in agreement? She wasn't able to discern his intent. Her heart raced, pumping her body with nervous energy.

"I shouldn't have let things get out of control," she said.

"You think we are better off sticking to our working relationship?"

"You do understand, don't you?"

He didn't say anything for a moment as though absorbing what she said. "So you would like to pretend like last night never happened?"

"Yes. Exactly."

There was some emotion reflected in his eyes, but before she could define it, he blinked and his feelings were locked behind a wall of indifference.

"We will forget it ever happened."

She held out her hand to him. "Then we have an agreement that our relationship will be nothing but business?"

His thumb stroked the back of her hand, sending tremors of yearning flooding her system. He looked at her with desire in those warm brown eyes.

"Be careful what you ask for," he said. "You might end up regretting it."

She was already regretting many things—none of which were spending those precious hours wrapped in his arms or tasting his addictive kisses. She was in trouble. Big trouble.

The week was getting away from him.

And nothing was going right.

First, the fact that his fling with Bianca was over before it'd really begun bothered him.

Second, his mother was on his case every chance she had, pushing him for the name of his chosen bride. There was little more than a week until his sister said "I do" and his engagement would be announced to the kingdom. His fate would be sealed.

And Leo was not ready. In the beginning, it'd appeared to be an easy enough task. Find a friendly woman whose goals aligned with his. They'd marry, he'd become king and the rest would hopefully fall into place. But somewhere along the way, the gravity of this decision had set in.

Maybe it was seeing how happy his sister was with William. Or maybe it was how happy he was in Bianca's company. Or perhaps it was that magical night beneath the fireworks. Whatever it was, he couldn't settle for mere tolerance of his wife. There had to be more...

His mind filled with the image of Bianca smiling and laughing. How it filled him with such warmth. He recalled their many meals together and though they'd started off discussing his sister's wedding, they'd eventually end up on a far more personal note. Those were the sort of experiences he wanted to share with his wife. Was that asking too much?

But if he didn't make a decision and soon, his mother would take the matter into her own hands. His hands clenched. This was an utterly impossible situation.

And he'd only compounded the matter by acting upon his growing feelings. How was he supposed to choose a wife when all he could think about was Bianca?

Leo frowned as it was now early Friday morning and he hadn't seen or spoken to Bianca since their business lunch yesterday. She'd kept her word about their relationship being all business. He didn't like it. He didn't like it at all. And that's why he'd planned something special for them this morning.

Knowing Bianca was an early riser, he went to find her. It took a bit but he finally tracked her down in the library with his mother. It definitely wasn't the ideal place to meet up with her, but he was determined to see her. His surprise couldn't wait.

The doors were open and he slowed as he heard his mother's voice.

"And why are we supposed to take your advice when you dress like—like that."

Without missing a beat, Bianca spoke up. "Pardon me, ma'am. But this isn't about my personal tastes. We're talking about the princess and what she would like for her wedding. And I must say your daughter has exceptional tastes. She must take after you."

"I, uh, thank you." There was a slight pause as though Bianca's compliment had knocked his mother off her game. But the queen was quick and she soon had the conversation back on track. "However, the princess will wear my wedding dress."

He recognized the stern tone of his mother's voice. She was in no mood to bend or be persuaded from her decision.

Leo stepped into the room. "There you are." His gaze settled upon Bianca just as her mouth was opening to argue with his mother. "We have a meeting."

"We do?"

"Yes."

"But—"

"Leopold, don't forget you are to have lunch with Elizabeth." The queen arched a penciled brow.

"I haven't forgotten. Plans have changed." He was tired of his mother's constant interference. Today, he was going to do what he wanted to do, not what he was expected to do. "Are you ready to go, Bianca?"

Bianca's confused gaze moved between mother and son. Her mouth opened but nothing came out. That was a first.

A smile pulled at Leo's lips. "We don't want to be late." He turned his attention to his mother. "Please excuse us."

His mother looked exasperated. She waved them off.

Once out in the hallway, Bianca stepped in front of him. She glared at him. "Why did you interrupt my meeting with your mother?"

"I was doing you a favor."

"A favor?" Her voice rose with agitation.

He took her hand in his. They moved swiftly down the hallway. It wasn't until they were out of earshot of his mother that he stopped. Bianca yanked her hand free as she shot him another angry glare.

"I'd appreciate if you would let me do my job," she said. "And we don't have any plans."

"That's where you would be wrong."

"No. I'm not." She reached for her phone and ran her finger over the screen. Then she turned the phone to him. "See, I don't have you on my calendar."

"Then your calendar must be wrong."

"My calendar is never wrong. It's what keeps my life, my business, on track."

He wasn't going to argue the point. He had more important matters in mind. "My car is waiting for us. This way."

"And if I refuse?"

"You'll regret it. I promise you're going to love this." He could tell by the widening of her eyes that she was hooked.

Did he have to interrupt her meeting with the queen?

She'd just started to make some headway.

Bianca admitted that she might have pushed the queen hard, but someone had to stand up to her. Otherwise the queen was about to roll right over her daughter. It was Bianca's job to make sure that didn't happen.

When she went to speak to Leo, she realized he was already walking away. She rushed to catch up with him. His long legs took lengthy strides and she had to take two steps for every one of his.

"Do you mind telling me where we're going?"

"Out." He stopped and opened the door for her.

She stepped out into the cool morning air. The sun was shining in the cyan blue sky. There wasn't a cloud in sight. It was going to be a beautiful day.

When Bianca lowered her gaze, she noticed a sleek black sports car sitting in the middle of the drive. It wasn't a new model. This car was a classic but in mint condition. The top was down, revealing its black leather bucket seats. It looked perfect for cruising around and taking in the sights. Not that she had time for sightseeing.

As though Leo had read her thoughts, he moved to the car and opened the passenger side door for her. Just then her phone vibrated in her hand. Her breath hitched as she wondered if it was a message about the DNA results. She glanced at the phone, willing the results to be in—so she'd at last know if she was a true Bartolini…or not.

However, the text message on her phone was from Sylvie. The replacement linens were to be delivered that afternoon. Though it was good news so far as the wedding, she was still left wondering about the DNA results and how they would change her life.

"Bianca? Hey Bianca?"

She glanced up to find Leo waving at her. She pressed her lips into a firm line as she sent off a quick text to her assistant, thanking her for following up on the order.

"Sorry. I have a lot going on right now."

"Exactly why you need a little break."

"You aren't going to let this go, are you?"

"Not until you come with me."

She climbed into the car. The leather seats were so soft it felt as though they'd been wrapped around her. After Leo climbed in the driver's seat, he fired up the powerful engine. It purred, but Bianca sensed the purr was deceptive. A little pressure on the accelerator and they roared off, down the driveway.

As he adjusted the rearview mirror, she asked. "Are you allowed to do this?" When he glanced at her with a questioning arc of his brow, she added, "You know, go off on your own. After all, you're the crown prince."

A smile lit up his face. Oh, my, was he handsome. Her heart swooned. The traitorous thing.

"It took a lot of negotiating but I've been allowed a certain bit of freedom."

"I bet the queen wasn't happy about that."

He laughed. The sound was warm and rich. "It's not the queen that I had to convince. It was Sir George."

"Who is Sir George?"

"He's the head of my security detail. In fact, he's the head of the royal protection for the palace and the family. But he personally oversees my protection and I've been a challenge to him over the years."

"And he agreed that you could go out driving by yourself?"

"Hardly. Behind us is a dark SUV filled with heavily armed guards. If anyone were to stop this vehicle, they would have an ex-military team to deal with. I can assure you, we are quite safe."

The low-set car clung to the road as they whipped around the mountainous curves. Bianca's hand tightened around the door handle. It'd been a long time since she had been in a sports car. She remembered not long after her brother started to drive that he would be given the task of driving her to visit with friends. He drove so fast, as though he were a race car driver, only he'd had a lot less experience at the time than Leo had now.

Still, Enzo had been a good sport. Without him, she wouldn't have been able to see her friends since they lived so far apart. And her parents were always busy. Her father with the winery and her mother with the horses and the gardening. None of which interested Bianca all that much.

But Enzo made sure she didn't get forgotten in the rush of everyday life. She smiled at the memory. Maybe the distance between them now was something that could be overcome. Maybe they could be close once more. She didn't realize until that moment that it was something she wanted, something she wanted as much as—no, more than—she wanted to win the contest.

"What are you thinking about?" Leo's voice interrupted her thoughts.

"My family. Actually, my brother."

"And that made you smile?"

"Yes, it did. Riding in this sports car reminded me of him when I was a kid and how he would drive me around so I could see my friends. I'd forgotten about it—about how we'd crank up the music and I would sing at the top of my lungs. He'd laugh and we, well, we just had fun."

"And you two don't have fun any longer?"

She glanced down at her hands. "We haven't in a lot

of years. We drifted apart when I was a teen. I was more worried about my hair and my clothes than hanging out with my family."

"Isn't that normal for a teenage girl?"

She shrugged. "Maybe. But once the distance was there, we were never able to overcome it."

"By the smile on your face when you thought of your brother, I don't think it'll be hard to repair your relationship."

"It might be harder than you're imagining." And then the story of finding her mother's diary and the fact that one of the three siblings was not a Bartolini by blood all came spilling out.

She didn't know why she'd confessed to Leo. She'd been intending to keep the secret until the DNA results proved what she already surmised—she wasn't a Bartolini. But it felt good to get it out—even if the results were not what she wanted for herself or either of her siblings.

Leo took his gaze off the road for a moment to glance at her. Sympathy reflected in his dark eyes before he focused back on the road. "You shouldn't assume you are not a Bartolini. It could be any one of you. Or maybe you misunderstood—"

"There was no misunderstanding." Bianca wrung her hands. "It makes sense that it's me." Her voice crackled with emotion. "I never lived up to my parents' expectations. I always marched to a different drummer. I wasn't like my brother or sister."

He reached out and took her hand in his. "It doesn't mean you aren't a Bartolini."

"If only that were the truth," she muttered under her breath.

Leo gave her hand one last reassuring squeeze. And then the car pulled to a stop.

She glanced around. "Where are we?"

"This is the best view of the palace and the surrounding area. I like to come up here just to get away from all the pressures. Though I don't get time to do that very often these days."

"I can see why you'd want to come up here. The view is stunning." She stared out at the land as the sun's early morning rays highlighted it. She reached for her phone and snapped a photo through the open window.

When she went to open her car door, he said, "Wait. I have an even better view for you."

"Better than this? Impossible."

"Trust me." He started driving again.

They moved further along the tree-lined road. The car climbed a gradual rise and at the top, a rainbow of color came into sight. It hovered there in all its big, bright brilliance. As the car moved closer, more color was revealed, and soon Bianca realized what she was looking at—a hot air balloon.

"Oh, look." She lightly clapped her hands together in excitement. "I just love hot air balloons. Do you think they'll fly it while we're here?"

Leo pulled the car to a stop. "We can ask."

"Do you know these people?"

He offered only a smile in response. What did that mean? Was he going to use his status as prince to get what he wanted?

As soon as the thought crossed her mind, she felt guilty. In all the time she'd known Leo, he'd never once abused his position as the crown prince. He was better than that.

Leo was a good man. No. He was a great man with a generous, caring heart. When it came time for him to take over the throne, the country of Patazonia would be very lucky.

Her door swung up, startling her from her thoughts. She glanced up to find Leo standing there.

"Are you coming?"

"Of course." She alighted from the car and walked beside Leo.

She thought they would be moving toward the edge of the mountainside for a view of the area, but Leo was headed for the hot air balloon. Suddenly she started to worry that he was doing this for her.

"Leo, we shouldn't interrupt them. They look busy."

"It'll be okay. I'm sure they won't mind letting us take an up-close look."

He took her hand in his. A rush of tingles started in her fingertips and worked their way up her arm. They settled in her chest and had her heart racing.

In that moment, her awareness of their bodies touching—of the smoothness of his palm brushing over hers—was all she could think about. Did he mean something by the touch? Did he need the connection of their laced fingers? Did he crave it like she did?

She felt like a girl once more with the biggest crush on the most popular guy in school. Only Leo was so much more than that—he was an intriguing puzzle of contradictions. And she wanted nothing more than to figure him out.

Leo released her hand to go and speak to the three-man crew filling the balloon. Two men, one on each side, held up the opening of the balloon, while the third man worked the controls. A blast of flames would shoot forth filling the balloon with hot air. It was marvelous to watch as the colorful material rippled and expanded. Up and up it went.

And then Leo was once more by her side, taking her hand in his. "Come on."

She walked with him. "Leo, are we allowed to get this close?"

"We are."

And the next thing she knew, she was being helped inside the basket. Her heart raced. This was the experience of a lifetime. She was never going to forget this—or the very special man sharing this experience with her.

CHAPTER FIFTEEN

THIS WAS DEFINITELY one of his better ideas.

Leo stood at the edge of the basket as Bianca filmed the lush landscape with her phone. The truth was that he hadn't noticed the passing scenery as he was entranced with the beautiful woman next to him.

Was it wrong that he was supposed to be looking for an appropriate wife and yet all he wanted to do was kiss Bianca? There was something about her—something that drew him to her. She filled his thoughts when he was supposed to be working, when he was supposed to be getting to know some young woman—he was always comparing them, and when he was alone at night, his thoughts were all about her.

He shoved aside his problems. Right now, all that mattered was making Bianca happy.

His gaze moved to her. The big smile on her face was brighter than the morning sun. And there was a gravitational pull to her that drew him close.

"Are you enjoying yourself?" he asked.

She lowered her phone. "I can't believe you did this." Her eyes glittered with happiness. "It's amazing. I love it. Thank you."

Oblivious to the pilot firing the flame to keep them aloft, Leo leaned toward Bianca and pressed his lips to hers. It was a quick kiss, but it had a big effect on the pounding of his heart.

If only they didn't have an audience, he would pull her into his arms and kiss her deeply and thoroughly. Her sweet, sweet kisses were addictive.

She pulled back and gazed up at him with her big round eyes. "What was that for?"

He shrugged, not sure what she was thinking. "Just seemed like the right thing to do in the moment."

A hint of smile pulled at her berry-red lips as she turned her head to the magnificent view. He gazed at the distant horizon, but all he could see in his mind's eye was Bianca.

All too soon the balloon lowered toward a large field not far from the palace grounds. The first touch-down was gentle. It was the second touch-down that jolted the basket and had Bianca reaching out to him to help steady her. He held on to the basket with one hand and placed an arm around her waist with the other arm. She melted into his side, her curves aligning with him as though they'd been made for each other. Her arm wrapped around him too as her other hand white-knuckled the edge of the basket.

When the basket came to a final rest, the relief was written all over Bianca's face. The chase vehicle hadn't caught up to them. Leo helped Bianca from the basket.

In the distance, they heard a vehicle approaching.

"That must be our ride," Leo said.

"You think of everything."

"I try." He sent her a smile, hoping she'd send one back. And she did.

There was no way he wanted this morning to end. And then a thought came to him. As soon as they got back to the palace, they could share a leisurely brunch. He liked that idea. Anything that kept Bianca close by appealed to him.

When he turned back, he noticed the vehicle rushing toward them wasn't a palace vehicle. And there were more vehicles behind it. When someone leaned out the passenger window and started yelling, Leo knew they were in trouble. Without his security team, they were in serious danger.

"Come with me." Leo took her hand in his and headed for the wooded area.

"Leo, what are you doing?"

"That's the paparazzi." At least that's who he hoped it was and not some anti-government group. "We have to go."

For several moments they ran, moving through the thick underbrush. He knew where he was going. He just hoped the paparazzi didn't know these woods.

"Leo?" Bianca called out in a breathy voice. "Leo, please stop."

He came to a complete halt and turned to her. "Are you okay?"

"I… I just need to catch my breath." She huffed and puffed. "I didn't know we were going for a morning run."

"I'm sorry." He felt terrible that their wonderful excursion was ruined. "I never meant for this to happen. Sometimes I forget that I'm a target for headlines."

"Do you think they got a photo of us?"

"I'm not sure. If they did, it was from a distance. Don't worry about it."

"And do you think they're following us?"

He didn't want to think that was true. But he knew that the paparazzi would go to great lengths to get a good photo or a juicy story.

"It's not far from here. Can you keep going?"

She nodded. "But could we slow down a little? The ground is uneven and there are roots sticking up."

He glanced around as he strained to hear any sign that they'd been followed. "I think we're good."

"Maybe you should call someone. Your security will be worried."

He pulled out his phone, but there was no reception out here in the middle of nowhere. "I can't call now, but I will as soon as we get back."

"Then we better get moving before the queen sends out every guard on the palace grounds."

They set off once more at a much more reasonable pace. He told himself he kept ahold of Bianca's hand to help her along the way.

Twenty or so minutes had passed when Leo came to a stop. He released Bianca's hand. She didn't say anything. He could tell she was tired and definitely not happy. The entire day had been ruined. And it was his fault for not doing a better job of planning ahead.

He knew there was an entrance around here somewhere. The problem was that it hadn't been used in so many years there was a significant amount of overgrowth.

He pulled on the vines and at last he found the bars over the entrance. "Here it is."

Bianca moved to his side. "What is it?"

"An entrance to the palace."

Bianca started to laugh. "You can't be serious. It looks like a drainage pipe."

"That's what it's supposed to look like."

"But I'm confused. Why would you want the entrance to the palace to look like a neglected drainage pipe?"

"Because it's a secret entrance."

He hunched down as he worked to release the lever that held the iron grate in place. There had been so many years of disuse and rain that it was rusty. Leo made a mental note to have someone come out here discreetly and make sure it was in better working order.

It took several minutes and all his might, but finally the latch gave way. And then he pulled the grate open.

He stepped inside and then turned back for Bianca. "Come on."

She shook her head. "I… I don't think so."

"Trust me. This a lot shorter than climbing the hillside to the palace."

"But there might be snakes or worse in there." She visibly shuddered.

"What's worse than a snake?"

Softly she uttered, "A spider."

He wanted to tease her, but he saw the genuine fear in her eyes. Instead he pressed a hand to his heart. "I swear upon my life that I will protect you from any snake or spider."

"You think I'm silly."

He shook his head. "Everyone is afraid of something."

"That's not true." Her gaze searched his. "You aren't afraid of anything."

Oh, there was something he feared. But it wasn't some eight-legged creature or the fangs of a reptile, no, what he feared went much deeper.

He feared having his heart broken again. He feared speaking too loudly—too harshly. The image of his father clutching his chest came to mind. If only he'd done what was asked of him—if he hadn't made waves—then maybe his father would still be here with them. Not wanting to delve further into the subject, Leo didn't correct her.

Using the flashlight app on his phone, he guided them through the tunnel until they came to a steel door with a keypad. He punched in the security code. The heavy door swung open with ease.

He stood aside and waved Bianca into the secure tunnel. He followed her, pausing to press the button for the door to swing shut behind them.

"We are safe now. No one can get in here." He took the lead, using his memory to lead them to the lower level of the palace—the old portion that no one bothered with anymore.

They walked in silence. After a series of turns and a few flights of steps, they'd reached the end. Leo released the catch on the secret movable wall panel. It took some effort, but he finally got it open.

He'd just stepped out into the hallway when he heard: "Leopold. There you are." He didn't have to turn to know it was the queen. And she was none too happy with him.

He inhaled a deep breath and then turned. "Mother."

It wasn't just the queen facing him. There were a half-dozen royal guards behind her. This was bad. Very bad.

The queen turned to the guards and dismissed them. Once they were gone, she turned back to him. Anger lit up her eyes like little bolts of lightning.

"What is the meaning of this?"

"How did you even know about this passageway?"

She arched a penciled brow. "Leopold, there isn't much around this palace that I don't know about. I've known about the secret passageways since your father took me through them when we were first married. Did you really think I didn't know about your adventures when you were a kid? I'd have thought you would have grown out of such things."

"I didn't have a choice today. The chase team was delayed and instead the paparazzi tracked us down. Do you really think it was a good idea to hang out and let them come up with whatever scandalous drivel sells their papers?"

"I suppose not. But did you stop to think about this before putting yourself in such a precarious position?" She didn't wait for him to answer. "Taking off on a hot air balloon ride of all things when there is work waiting for you. Not to mention—"

Bianca stepped out of the shadows of the secret passageway and stood next to him. The queen's gaze settled on Bianca as her frown grew deeper.

Leo cleared his throat. "I wanted to give Bianca a view of the land. And what better way than from above."

The queen crossed her arms, as though preparing for war.

Leo rushed on. "It was a beautiful morning. But I'm sure Bianca has to get back to work."

Bianca was spurred into motion. "I do. There's a gown fitting shortly. I should go and make sure everything is on track."

When Bianca went to move, the queen spoke up. "Not so fast. I would appreciate it if going forward you would curtail yourself to your work. That is what my son is paying you a fortune for, is it not?"

Leo considered telling his mother that technically he wasn't paying Bianca much, but then he decided that information might work against them. His mother might use it as an excuse to send Bianca packing.

"I assure you, ma'am, that everything for the wedding is on track," Bianca said before Leo could figure out the best way to placate his mother. "I have a checklist to keep us on a timely schedule."

"I hope that list doesn't include any fashions like that." The queen gestured to Bianca's white skinny capris and colorful top.

It wasn't the first time his mother pointed out that Bianca's fashion sense didn't align with hers. The truth was Leo enjoyed Bianca's colorful outfits. This palace certainly could stand to be brightened.

"I like Bianca's sense of style," Leo said, taking the heat off Bianca. "I'm hoping she'll add color to the wedding."

"Leopold—"

"Mother, not everything should be a shade of gray. Sometimes there needs to be bright oranges, pinks and purples. In fact, purple would suit you."

The queen remained quiet for a moment, not used to Leo getting in her face and disagreeing with her. The quietness didn't last for long. "Then maybe she should pay more attention to her color choices instead of taking up your time. You have other matters of great importance—"

"Bianca," he said, cutting off his mother because he

knew where this conversation was headed, "would you mind leaving my mother and me alone so we can talk?"

"No problem." Bianca nodded to the queen and then quietly escaped.

Lucky her. Leo wished he could follow her.

He turned his attention back to his mother. "I know you're frustrated with me but that's no reason to take it out on Bianca. She's doing a really good job with the wedding and Giselle is happy. Isn't that the important part?"

"You're falling for her."

"Bianca?" He shook his head. "No. I'm not."

It was just a passing attraction, nothing serious. When this wedding was over, she'd return to Italy. And he would get on with his royal duties. First, he would get married. And then he would ascend to the throne. It was all planned.

His mother's gaze searched his. "Do you really believe that?"

"Bianca is nice. And I enjoy her company, but that's all it is."

His mother sighed. "Then you are a fool. And I didn't raise a fool."

Without another word, she turned and walked away, leaving him alone with her words. Was she right? Did his feelings for Bianca go deeper than he allowed himself to believe?

CHAPTER SIXTEEN

L ast night had been the most boring date of his life.

And his lunch date wasn't faring much better.

Neither woman would do as his princess.

Leo set aside his now-empty coffee cup. When he glanced up, he found his luncheon companion staring at him. Immediately she smiled at him, like that was going to change things.

There was no spark between them. There wasn't even a fizzle. There was nothing. No chemistry. No anything.

Bridgette was the daughter of an earl of a small country in the Mediterranean. And though many had gone on about her beauty, all Leo could think was that she didn't hold a candle to Bianca's glittering eyes and her sparkling smile.

And then there was the fact that conversation between him and Bianca flowed easily. He didn't have to work to keep the conversation going like he did tonight. How was he supposed to marry someone when they had nothing to talk about?

Bridgette lit up with a smile. "This has been the most enjoyable evening."

She surely couldn't mean it. After all, they hadn't found one subject to talk about that they had in common.

"It was a nice meal. And I enjoyed your company." Was it wrong that in his mind he pretended he was speaking to Bianca?

"I've heard so much about your lovely gardens."

He followed her over to the glass doors that led out to the expansive patio on the edge of the famed gardens. All the while, he was thinking of how to get out of this. Because he knew as sure as he was standing there that they didn't have a chance for a future. There was no point in getting Bridgette's hopes up.

"Leo, there you are." Giselle rushed into the room. "I've been looking everywhere for you."

"Well, you've found me."

She glanced over at Bridgette. "There's a problem with the wedding."

"What sort of problem?"

Giselle shook her head. "I can't tell you. You have to come see."

"Now?" He knew his sister could get excited about things, but something felt off here.

"Yes, now. Right now—"

"We'd be happy to help," Bridgette interjected as though they were already a couple.

"Um, no. Sorry," Giselle said. "This is delicate and only my brother can handle it."

It was then that Leo glanced toward the interior doorway to find the butler waiting in the wings. His sister had planned this. And for once, he was grateful for his sister's schemes.

"Then let's go," he said. Before walking off, he turned to Bridgette. "It was lovely meeting you. Thank you so much for making the journey here. Oscar will see you out."

He turned and walked with his sister toward the door. They were just steps away from the hallway—

"Wait. That's it?" Bridgette called out from behind him. "I got all dressed up for this? We didn't even kiss. How are we supposed to get married if you won't even kiss me?"

Giselle grabbed his arm. "Don't you dare stop. If you saddle me with her as my sister-in-law, I will never speak to you again."

Leo smothered a hearty chuckle as they set off down the hallway, but he couldn't resist smiling. "So is there truly an emergency? Or did you simply feel sorry for me?"

Giselle shrugged once more. "There's only so much anguish I can watch my brother endure."

"You were watching us?"

"No. I mean I saw you through the doorway and then I inquired about your guest. When I found out it was Bridgette, I knew you were in trouble."

"You know her?"

Giselle shrugged. "We've met up before at various events. I know all I want to about her and trust me, she's not right for you."

"Maybe I should have you sort through my stack of possible brides."

Giselle stopped walking and frowned at him. "You're making a mistake."

"I'm not any happier about this than you are. But you know I have to marry in order to take the throne. They need to know there's a good possibility of an heir. I am doing what is expected of me. I've put it off as long as I can."

"You need to marry someone you love. Someone you trust. Someone who makes you smile."

He rubbed the back of his neck and glanced away. "That's a luxury I can't afford."

"It's a necessity you would be wise not to overlook."

"Since when did you become an expert on marriage? You haven't even said 'I do' yet." He regretted the words as soon as they slipped past his lips.

Pain reflected in his sister's eyes but in a blink, it was gone. "I have to go."

"Giselle, I'm sorry—"

"Forget it." She turned to walk away.

"What about the wedding?" he asked. "You know, the problem?"

"There isn't one."

And with that his sister marched off in the opposite direction. He knew she was upset with him and he would have to work on making it up to her.

His phone rang. He immediately answered it, hoping it was the news he'd been awaiting. And it was. By the time he disconnected the call, he had the perfect excuse to go see Bianca.

He set off with quick strides. With each step, his anticipation grew. He had a surprise for her. Something she was going to love.

"Come with me."

Bianca glanced over her shoulder to find Leo standing in the doorway of the palace's grand ballroom. Her fingers tightened around the stylus and her tablet. She was working on the setup for the reception—the best way to use the space available considering the large number of guests. They'd barely started.

"Hi." She couldn't help but smile. Every time he was around, a bubbly feeling sprang up inside her. "I can't leave now. We're working on some last-minute modifications to the layout of the reception."

He walked up to her and glanced at the tentative setup on her tablet. "Looks good. Let's go."

He grabbed her hand and started walking. Bianca dug in her heels, refusing to move. When he noticed her resistance, he stopped and turned back to her.

"What's wrong?" he asked.

"I told you I'm working."

"I know and I'm sorry, but this just can't wait." His eyes pleaded with her to follow him.

"Wait? What are you talking about?"

"Just come with me."

And then a worrisome thought came to mind. Was there some part of this royal wedding that she'd overlooked?

Her heart clenched with dread. There were so many

moving parts to this wedding that it was tough staying on top of anything. But in the end, if she could handle this wedding, she could handle any wedding. The trick was getting the princess down the aisle and then onto the dance floor. It was only then that Bianca would be able to take her first easy breath.

"Tell me," she said. "What's wrong?"

"Nothing is wrong." A smile pulled at the corner of his lips. "In fact, something is very right."

"But I need to finish here—"

"Sylvie," Leo called out.

Immediately, Sylvie dropped what she was doing and rushed over to them. She stopped in front of Leo with rounded eyes and a timid smile. She noticeably swallowed before gazing up at him as though he were some sort of god. "Yes, Your Royal Highness?"

Leo took the tablet from Bianca and handed it over to her assistant. "Could you continue to work on setting up the room?"

"I… I…uh…um…yes." Her eyes rounded like saucers. "Definitely. I'd be honored to, Your Highness."

"Thank you." Then he took Bianca by the hand and led her from the room.

"Leo, what are you doing?"

"We have to go. We don't have a lot of time."

"But I need to tell her what I have in mind for the changes."

At last, he stopped and turned to her. "Do you have it written down?"

"Yes—"

"Of course, you do." He turned and keeping his hand clasped around hers, he headed for the door. "I bet you have your entire life planned out in one big list."

She frowned at the back of his head. "Don't make fun of the lists. They keep everything organized and on time."

His pace didn't slow down. In fact, it might have sped up. "But where is the room for spontaneity and fun?"

She didn't respond at first. She'd been so busy proving herself to her parents and her siblings that even though she didn't have the same interests as them that she could still be a success.

When Leo stopped and turned a questioning look at her, she said, "Maybe I'm not the typical young person. So what if I don't live for Friday nights out on the town with my friends, hitting all of the hot spots. And maybe I didn't vacation in Monaco or sail the Mediterranean, but I've worked hard. I've accomplished a lot. If I hadn't, you wouldn't have hired me. Right?" When he didn't immediately respond, she asked again, "Right?"

He sighed. "Right."

"So then don't diss my lists. You might live your life without the need for organization—but being the crown prince, I can't see that lasting—but I need the lists. They make me feel like I have a handle on things. They make it possible for me not to stress out about everything."

Leo looked at her like he was seeing a whole new side of her. "You really enjoy those lists?"

"I know it might be strange for a lot of people, but yes, I like my lists. I need my lists. If I follow my lists, they'll get me where I need to go."

"Hmm... Perhaps you should start a list of fun things."

Now that was something she hadn't considered before. A list of restaurants she'd like to try out. A list of locations she'd like to visit. She already had a list of movies and television shows that she'd like to watch but as yet hadn't gotten around to them.

"So I'm forgiven?" Leo's voice drew her from her thoughts.

"Um...what?"

"You know, for dragging you away from your work?"

"I still don't even know why you drew my away."

"Can I show you?"

"Well, considering Sylvie looked excited to do anything that you asked, I wouldn't want to ruin it for her." And secretly she was curious to know what was so important to him. "Let's go."

Hand in hand, he led her out to a waiting car. The driver opened the door for them. Before Bianca climbed in, she looked back at Leo. "You aren't driving today?"

"I thought this would be easier."

"Easier? Easier for what?"

"You'll soon see." A big smile lifted the corners of his mouth and lit up his eyes.

Whatever he was up to had him very excited. In fact, she'd never seen him this excited. She wouldn't admit it, but his mood was contagious. After keeping her in suspense, he didn't deserve to see her smile. Two could play this game.

As the unmarked sedan moved out through the service entrance of the palace, no paparazzi noticed their exit. It was rather freeing after seeing how the press camped at the front gates and clambered over the official flagged cars as they emerged from the palace grounds.

Bianca wondered what it was like to live under a microscope. She glanced over at the prince. He didn't seem to let it get to him. But growing up in the spotlight must give him a different perspective versus someone like her who had lived a rather anonymous life.

A part of her felt sorry for him. Because not only were his greatest achievements on display for the whole world to see, but his failures and heartaches were all out there for people to criticize and dissect.

Maybe being a prince wasn't all it was hyped up to be, but as she leaned back against the buttery soft black leather seat and stared out the window at the passing greenery that was quickly giving way to more buildings, more cars, more people, there were definitely some pluses to this life as well.

Bianca questioned him a couple more times about their destination, but he wouldn't crack. And when the car pulled to a final stop and the driver got out to open their doors, she was confused. Leo donned a dark cap and sunglasses. He looked very mysterious.

She stepped out onto the asphalt, raised a hand to her forehead to block the bright sunlight and gazed around at big nondescript buildings.

She turned a questioning gaze to Leo. "You brought me to the warehouse district?"

He laughed. "Not exactly. Come with me and I'll show you the magic that lurks inside."

Magic and this place didn't seem to go together, but she had to admit he had her full attention now. "Leo, what are we doing here?" And then a worrisome thought came to her. "You don't want to move the princess's after-party here, do you?"

The deep rumble of laughter filled the air. "Bianca, do you trust me?"

"No. I mean… I guess—" She halted her rambling. Why did this man get to her and make her a blubbering mess?

When her gaze met his, she found that no harm had been done. He was still smiling.

They headed toward the side of the building. There was a nondescript door with a red light next to it. As they approached, the light went out.

Leo opened the door and stood aside for her to enter. It was darker inside and it took a moment for Bianca's vision to adjust. She let Leo take the lead. He quickly made his way to a group of people and bright lights.

"What is this?" she whispered while glancing up at the spotlights suspended from the ceiling. Then the cameras came into view. "A television station?"

"Close. It's a sound stage. And they are filming your advertisement for your business."

"What?" She slapped a hand over her mouth when her voice was a little too loud and heads turned in their direction.

Leo's smile lit up his eyes. "I told you I would take care of you. And soon this will be on the internet and network television."

"Quiet on the set," a man called out.

No one seemed to notice that beneath the dark baseball cap was the prince. She stood next to him and watched as a bride entered the scene carrying the biggest, most splendid bouquet of pink and white ranunculus and peonies. They were hands down Bianca's favorite flowers.

Leo guided her over to one of the monitors. It was there that they could see the background. In the distance were the green rolling hills of home. In the foreground was her courtyard. But how?

Her gaze moved to Leo. He sent her a knowing smile. That man was good, very good.

They stood quietly while lines were spoken, scenes and retakes were filmed. Bianca wasn't sure how much time passed as she was totally mesmerized by everything that was going on around her.

Leo had taken her marketing preferences and taken them a step further. As the reality of the situation sank in, it was getting harder and harder for her to stifle her excitement. She wanted to speak. She wanted to celebrate the moment.

This wasn't just any commercial. This was a chance to make her dream a reality. This was going to make her a household name in the wedding world. And it was all thanks to Leo.

She didn't know how to thank him, but she would figure out something special. She just had to think about it for a bit.

During a break, someone nudged the director and then pointed over his shoulder at them. Oops! They'd been spotted.

The director rushed toward them. The man made a big flourish of bowing to the prince. Leo stiffened ever so slightly. If she hadn't been standing so close to him, she never would have noticed. So, all of the pomp and circumstance didn't come so naturally to him. Interesting.

"Your Royal Highness, I didn't know you'd be stopping by today. I hope I haven't kept you waiting."

"Not at all." Leo smiled as though to put the man at ease. "We've enjoyed watching the filming."

"Thank you, sir. Is there anything I can do for you?"

"I would like you to meet Miss Bianca Bartolini. She is the woman behind BB Wedding Dreams."

Again, the man bowed. He took her hand and gave a feathery kiss to the back of it. "It's an honor. I hope when we are finished, you'll enjoy the image."

"I've already enjoyed what I've seen. When I see the film merged with the background, it's like I'm home once more."

"Your home, it's gorgeous. People are going to be clamoring to marry at your lovely villa."

"I hope you're right."

They talked for a few more minutes and then they left, leaving the crew alone to finish their work. Bianca couldn't quit smiling.

As soon as they stepped outside, she turned to Leo. "That was amazing. Thank you. It's more than I ever imagined."

His brows rose. "What were you expecting?"

She shrugged. "I don't know. But certainly nothing that elaborate. And you even filmed my villa."

"I thought it should show people exactly what they'd be missing by not getting married there."

Excitement and anticipation bubbled up in her and she acted without thinking by throwing her arms around Leo for a hug. It was when she leaned into him—when she breathed in his clean, masculine scent—that she realized she'd overstepped. His body remained stiff, as though she'd caught him off guard.

She quickly pulled back. "Sorry. I just lost my mind for a moment there."

"I take it you approve?"

She eagerly nodded her head. "I do."

And now the pressure was on her to do something extra special for him. She just had no idea what that might be. But she would think of something.

CHAPTER SEVENTEEN

BUZZ. BUZZ.

She didn't have time for phone calls.

Still, Bianca couldn't just ignore the call—not until she knew who was on the other end. She removed the phone from her purse. Her heart stilled in her chest when she saw the name of her family's attorney flash on the caller id.

There was no way this was anything but bad news. She'd been dreading this day for the longest time. And now it was here.

Maybe she should just ignore it. She could let it ring over to her voicemail. After all, today was the royal wedding. Giselle and Leo were counting on her to make this day go smoothly for everyone.

She had to bring her very best game today. She couldn't be upset. But she also couldn't be distracted wondering what the attorney wanted.

With great trepidation, she answered the call. "Hello. This is Bianca Bartolini."

As she said her name, she wondered how much longer she would have a right to it. When all was said and done, would everything about her life be a lie—even her name?

"Ms. Bartolini, this is Lando Caruso," the family's attorney said. "I've spoken with your brother and sister. They've informed me you're out of the country."

"That's correct. I'm working on a wedding."

"I see." His voice didn't give any hints as to what he was thinking. "The reason for my call is that the testing facility says they'll have the DNA result in a couple of days."

"Oh." Her heart was heavy and sank all the way down to her silver heels. Not wanting to have any witnesses to her utter meltdown, she said, "Can you give me the results over the phone?"

"No. The agreement with your siblings was that the results would be revealed when you were all in the same room."

"Right." She recalled making that agreement. It seemed like a lifetime ago.

"How soon will you be returning home? As you can understand, your siblings are quite anxious for the results."

She understood very well. "The wedding is today. I'll be able to fly home tomorrow or the next day."

"Very well. I will arrange to be at the villa on Tuesday. Will that give you enough time?"

"Y-yes." Her stomach shivered with nerves.

They ended the call and then Bianca stood there as though in a trance. This could very well be the end of her life as she knew it. With the results at hand, the stark reality of her future was daunting.

Knock. Knock.

Her future and the uncertainty of that future would have to wait for another time. She had a wedding to oversee. And absolutely nothing was going to go wrong today. She owed both Giselle and Leo her undivided attention.

There was another knock.

"Coming!" She glanced in the mirror to make sure she hadn't forgotten anything. She could do this. Because whether or not she was a Bartolini, she was a wedding planner. No one could take that away from her.

The bride was stunning.

The groom, eh, not too bad.

And the entire wedding had gone off without a hitch.

Leo knew who to thank for making his sister's big day so perfect—Bianca. She'd once again worked her magic. She'd smoothed out the rough edges, covered over the imperfections and highlighted the beauty of the day. The only thing that bothered him was that she'd been so busy he hadn't had a moment to so much as thank her.

But there was another part of this day that he dreaded. It meant the deadline for choosing a wife was at hand. It was like a ticking time bomb. And when it went off, life as he knew it would be over. How was he supposed to spend the rest of his days with someone he didn't love?

Because after spending time with Bianca, he'd realized how he longed to share his life with someone he cared about. Waking up in the morning, eager to see that person. Finding out something exciting and anxiously seeking out that person to share the news.

And then there were Giselle and William. They were so in love. They practically glowed when they were in the vicinity of each other. That's what he wanted for his life. Not a cold, heartless business deal—

"Come dance with me."

Leo turned to find the radiant bride next to him. "I'm not much of a dancer."

"We both know that's not true." She grasped his arm. "Come on."

With this being the formal reception, the music was more sedate. It made dancing and talking much easier, which didn't thrill Leo. His sister was good at reading his moods and he didn't want to get into what was on his mind at the moment. This was her wedding. A time for celebration. Not a time to dissect his life.

"You look beautiful," he said.

"Why thank you. You look pretty dashing yourself. Except for that frown on your face."

"What frown?" He didn't know he was frowning. He forced a smile to his lips. "Better?"

"You don't have to put on a show for me."

His muscles stiffened. "I don't know what you're talking about."

"Yes, you do. Mother gave you a deadline to find a wife and the time is up."

He stopped dancing and looked at his sister. "How do you know?"

She smiled and shrugged. "Mother isn't the only one with spies."

He shook his head. "You weren't supposed to know. This is your big day and it isn't your problem."

They started to dance again. "But I want to help."

"No one can help. At this point, I'm considering putting the names in a hat and pulling out one."

Giselle arched a brow. "You're joking, aren't you?"

Part of him was, the other part was seriously considering the option. "How do you choose a spouse that you don't care about?"

"Do you really need me to answer the question?" When he nodded, she said, "You don't."

"But I have to. I need a wife in order to become king. And I need to step into the role by the New Year. The nation is becoming restless." His gaze searched hers. "Who do you think I should marry?"

"I think the answer is right in front of you. All you have to do is open your eyes."

For a few minutes, they didn't speak. He knew his sister was referring to Bianca. He'd thought of her too. But she didn't fit into the mold of a princess. She was different from all the other prospective brides.

Still, he could see his future with Bianca. He could imagine waking up next to her each morning. He could see having a family with her—a happy family.

But he knew his mother would not approve. Not by a long shot.

"Stop fighting it," Giselle said, drawing him from his

thoughts. "You've fallen hard for her. Anyone can see it. Even Mother."

"Bianca is so easy to get along with. Everyone loves her—except Mother."

"Forget Mother for a second." Giselle stopped dancing and stared at him. "Do you love Bianca? Really love her?"

"I do." There was no hesitation. It was a fact that he hadn't been willing to acknowledge until now.

"Then stop standing here. Go get her."

That was easier said than done. He had no idea where she was and the reception was ending. But he would find her. He would tell her how he felt. And then he had to hope she felt the same way.

CHAPTER EIGHTEEN

THIS WAS IT.

The end.

Sadness assailed Bianca. It was the strangest reaction she'd ever had to the end of a wedding. Not just any wedding but a royal wedding that had received international attention. Her phone was ringing off the hook with people eager to have her plan their big days.

She should be thrilled. She should be out on the dance floor of the after-party celebrating, but instead she'd been busy ironing out small wrinkles in the background, from missing appetizers to a shortage of serving staff.

But now with the party in full swing and the prince's favorite band playing, she spotted him smiling and chatting with his sister and a group of guests. That was all the thanks she needed—

"Miss Bartolini, I'd like to have a word." The queen signaled for her to follow.

Once in the hallway, Bianca bowed her head. "Good evening, Your Majesty."

"It was a lovely day. And that in large part was due to you."

Bianca could hardly believe what she was hearing. The queen had just complimented her. After all the rows they'd had and how the queen was certain Bianca was going to make a disaster of everything.

"Thank you." Bianca didn't know what else to say.

"Perhaps my son should consider hiring you for his wedding." Apparently, Bianca failed to keep the surprise from showing on her face as the queen continued. "So, he didn't tell you that he will be announcing his engagement tomorrow. And his wedding will be later this year."

Bianca struggled to speak. "That's exciting news."

Inside she felt anything but excited. She felt sad. She felt as though she were losing the most special person from her life—not that he was ever hers to start with. Just the thought of Leo with another woman filled her with jealousy. She quickly reined in her rising emotions.

"Very exciting. Everything is working out." The queen beamed with happiness. "I've had my assistant forward you a bonus for your success tonight. And I know you must be anxious to get home to your villa so I've had my jet put on standby. It's yours tonight or tomorrow."

"Thank you. I really appreciate it."

"I won't keep you. Since this party isn't really my style, I'm going to call it a night and let the young people live it up. Goodbye, Miss Bartolini."

"Good night, ma'am." Bianca bowed her head once more.

She watched as the queen made her way to the door. There was nothing left for Bianca to do. Sylvie was seeing to any lingering details.

The thought of flying home tonight was tempting. It would be nice to get back to the villa while she was still a Bartolini—

"Bianca! There you are." Leo stepped out of the party, closing the door behind him. "I've been looking everywhere for you."

"Sorry. There were a lot of things to do today." Like saying goodbye to him. But she wasn't ready to do it. Not yet.

"You did a positively fabulous job. Not even my mother could find anything to complain about."

"I know. She gave me both a compliment and a bonus. Can you believe it?"

Leo's brown eyes widened. "You really impressed her.

I am not surprised. Everyone is calling it the perfect wedding. And it's all thanks to you."

She couldn't put on this "nice" show any longer. She had to know if it was true. Was Leo getting married? "And I heard about your engagement." Her voice wobbled. "Congratulations."

Confusion clouded his eyes. "How did you hear—wait, my mother, right?"

She nodded. "She's very excited."

"I didn't want you to find out this way."

"What way? The fact that I thought what we shared meant something and all of this time you were planning to marry someone else—"

"Bianca, stop." He reached out, gently grasping her upper arms. "It isn't like that."

She yanked free. Her gaze narrowed in on him. "How is it?"

"It's you."

"What's me?"

He rubbed the back of his neck. "This isn't how I meant for any of this to happen."

"You aren't making any sense. What about me?"

His gaze met hers. "It's you I want to marry."

She pressed a hand to her chest, feeling as though the air had been sucked from her lungs. "Marry me?"

Leo nodded.

She shook her head. This couldn't be happening. Leo wanted to marry her but she was a wedding planner, not a fitting wife for the crown prince. She was a nobody, a commoner. The prince must marry someone of noble birth.

"No." She took a step back. "You don't mean this. It would be a mistake."

"Bianca, I love you."

She took another step away from him. Her heart was

cracking and her vision blurred with unshed tears. "No, you don't."

He stepped up to her. His unwavering gaze met hers. "I don't know where all of this doubt is coming from, but if you're worried about my mother, don't be. I'll deal with her."

"It's not your mother."

"Good. Then what is it?"

"Will you still feel the same way about me if the DNA results reveal that I'm not a Bartolini? What happens if I don't know who my father is? For all I know, I could be the daughter of a criminal." Her voice wobbled. She blinked repeatedly, struggling to keep her emotions at bay. "I can't marry you with that hanging over our heads."

Silence filled the air between them.

The silence was more painful than acknowledging that everything she thought she knew about herself might be wrong. Because Leo's continued silence meant he agreed with her.

Unable to take the silence any longer, Bianca said, "My job is complete. Sylvie is inside and will oversee the cleanup. I need to go."

The door to the party opened. The blast of music echoed through the hallway. Giselle beamed at them and then yelled over the music. "Come on guys. Let's party." She moved over and latched her arm with Leo's. "I requested your favorite song."

Giselle motioned for Bianca to join them before disappearing inside. Bianca moved toward the door but remained in the hallway. She couldn't go back inside. She closed the door.

This was difficult enough. She just needed to get it over with. She needed to take the queen up on her offer and return to Tuscany as soon as possible.

Because if she loved Leo—and she did love him with all

her heart—she would be on that plane tonight. Leo needed to live the life he was destined for—the throne that he always wanted. He deserved to have a wife by his side that the people looked up to and respected.

And it wasn't her. She probably wasn't even a Bartolini. If she were to marry Leo and the press got ahold of the story it would ruin Leo. She would do anything to protect him, including sacrificing her heart.

The acknowledgment hurt Bianca more than she knew possible. She didn't fit in with her family. She didn't fit in Patazonia. Where did she belong?

CHAPTER NINETEEN

HE'D MESSED UP.

Big time.

Leo had taken time to think about what Bianca had said to him instead of following his heart. In his defense, he never expected her to turn down his marriage proposal. But that was becoming a thing with Bianca—not reacting the way he expected.

By the time he'd gotten his head screwed on straight, Bianca had left the party. He'd quietly slipped away, eager to find her. He had to convince her that they belonged together. Maybe theirs wouldn't be a fairy-tale marriage, but truth be told, he didn't believe in fairy tales.

He wanted a relationship that was real—a relationship that was strong, reliable and enduring. He could have all of that with Bianca. He firmly believed it. In fact, he couldn't imagine his life without her in it.

He demanded the keys to the SUV that his security detail had used to escort him to the reception. He was in no mood to be coddled by his team. He needed some space to himself. He tramped the accelerator. When he found the inside of the vehicle too constricting, he put down the windows and let the cool night air rush over his face as he raced back to the palace.

This can be fixed. It isn't too late.

He kept repeating the mantra the whole way home. It was as if he said it enough, it would be so.

The SUV's tires screeched to a halt in front of the palace. He raced inside. He could feel curious stares from the staff, wondering what had him in such a rush, but he didn't have the patience or the inclination to explain.

He took the stairs two at a time. He racewalked down the hallway. He rapped his knuckles on Bianca's door.

"Bianca?" He waited. No response. "Bianca, we need to talk."

The door opened but it wasn't Bianca on the other side. It was one of the staff.

"Where is Bianca?" he asked, not caring how anxious he might appear. He didn't have time to worry about appearances.

The young woman looked confused. "Miss Bartolini isn't here."

"Do you know where she is?"

"She left."

"Left?" That couldn't be. "As in left the palace? To go back to the party?"

The young woman looked flustered. "I don't know where she went. I was instructed to help her pack and then I started to straighten up. Was that a mistake?"

The mistake was all his. The weight of his error mounted with every passing moment.

Noticing the maid's worried look, he said, "You've done nothing wrong. Continue what you were doing."

He turned and strode away. She'd left already? The after-party hadn't even wound down.

He wasn't giving up yet. He could catch her at the airport. He'd do whatever it took.

Leo retraced his steps down the staircase, but at the bottom stood the queen. "Leopold, what is the meaning of this? You're racing up the driveway, screeching tires and running through the palace as though it's some sort of gymnasium."

He descended the stairs. "It's Bianca. I have to find her."

The queen's brows rose. "Is there a problem with the party?"

"No. It's fine." He raked his fingers through his hair. "There's something I have to discuss with her."

"Well, if that's all, you'll have to phone her because she's already in the air. I gave her my personal jet to return home."

"You did what?" He couldn't believe what he was hearing.

The queen frowned at him. "Come with me."

He followed her to her office, where most of the kingdom's decisions were made. It was where his ancestors including his grandfather, father and eventually he would rule from. This seemed like a fitting place to have this life-altering conversation.

"I've chosen a wife," he stated boldly. "If she'll have me."

His mother's frown lifted into a smile. "Very good. And I take it you'd like Bianca to plan the wedding. I will admit that she did a pretty good job with your sister's wedding, but you have to realize with you being in line for the crown, traditions must be strictly adhered to—"

"Mother, stop!"

She blinked as though surprised by his interruption. "Leopold, I'm not going to be as agreeable this time. Bianca cannot be your wedding planner."

"You're right. She's going to be my bride."

His mother's penciled brows rose high on her forehead. "Leopold, if you're trying to be funny—"

"I'm being perfectly serious. I want to marry Bianca. I want her to be my princess—"

"Stop! No." The queen vehemently shook her head. "It's not going to happen. I gave you a whole selection of very fine women to choose from. Just because you couldn't find your version of the ideal woman—"

"But I did. Bianca is everything I've ever wanted and more."

His mother shook her head again. "Leopold, you're missing the fact that she doesn't have noble blood. She isn't from a politically influential family. She brings nothing to the nation. She's…she's a wedding planner."

"She's the woman I love. And she loves me in spite of my faults—"

"Faults?" The queen's eyes narrowed. "This woman has convinced you that you are full of faults?"

"No, Mother," his voice filled with pent-up emotion. "You did that the day Father died." His mother's mouth opened but he didn't give her a chance to speak as he kept going. "When he died, you looked at me like it was all my fault. And you've been blaming me ever since."

"That's not true."

"It is true. Whether you admit it or not."

The composed look on her face crumbled. In its place were deep worry lines that aged his mother. She sat down on the window seat as though her legs would no longer hold her up. "I had no idea that's how you felt."

"How could I not when you sent me out of the room after father died as though you couldn't bear to look at me. And you made me promise not to tell anyone what had happened. Do you know what keeping that secret cost me? I couldn't even talk to Giselle."

For so long, he'd kept this torment of emotions locked up inside of him. But after confiding in Bianca, he realized the secret was destroying not only him but also his relationship with his family. He'd been distancing himself—avoiding conflicts. And it was no way to live life. It was no way to rule a country.

"But you told Bianca?" His mother's troubled gaze searched his.

"I did. I trust her. And I don't regret it."

"And she convinced you that I blamed you for your father's death?"

"On the contrary, she defended you." His mother's eyes widened. Maybe at last his mother would see that there was so much more to Bianca. "She suggested you might have been trying to protect me."

"I was." The queen's voice was soft as though all of the fight had gone out of her. "Our enemies will use anything to hurt us, even twisting innocent facts into something sinister."

He could barely allow himself to believe what he was hearing. "You never blamed me?"

She shook her head. "Your father had health issues."

"I never knew."

"Only four people knew of them. Two of them were your father and myself. A king must not look vulnerable."

Leo had a feeling his mother's last comment was aimed at his relationship with a commoner. "Bianca will not make me vulnerable. With her by my side, we can do great things together. I love her."

"But does she feel the same way?" The queen stood. "Maybe she doesn't love you and that's why she left so quickly."

"She left because I made a mistake. Now I need to make things up to her."

"You really love her, don't you?" When he nodded, his mother said, "There's a commercial flight tomorrow."

It was his turn to arch a brow. "You aren't going to try and stop me?"

"Maybe I should. But when it all comes down to it, I want my children to be happy. And Bianca makes you happier than I've ever seen you. So go get her. Make her your princess."

"Thank you." He hugged his mother, something they rarely did, but he had a feeling that was about to change. When he pulled back, he said, "You try to put on a crusty exterior but on the inside you're just a marshmallow."

She sent him a playful frown. "Go. Before I change my

mind." His mother turned and walked away. She called over her shoulder, "And have someone move that vehicle."

Now he had to wait through the night to get to his princess.

It was going to be the longest night of his life.

CHAPTER TWENTY

"You're back."

It was almost lunchtime when Bianca dragged herself to the main house. She glanced over at Gia as she entered the kitchen. Bianca smoothed a hand over her mussed-up ponytail. She'd forgotten that her sister had turned the place into a boutique hotel and that there might be guests lurking about. She peered past her sister, relieved to find her alone.

"I got in late last night."

Gia had already turned in by then, but Enzo had still been awake. He knew Bianca was upset but he hadn't pried. He just let her know he was there if she wanted to talk.

She turned her back to her sister to avoid questions about the shadows under her bloodshot eyes.

"I loved the photos you sent," Gia said. "Do you have some of the wedding?"

"Um… I do. But not on me." The last thing she wanted to discuss was the royal wedding. "I was so tired last night that I forgot to plug my phone in and now it's dead, kind of like me. Do you have some coffee you can spare?"

Gia made them both a cup and then joined Bianca at the kitchen island. "You don't look so good, considering you just planned the wedding of a lifetime."

And had my heart torn out and shredded.

"How am I supposed to look?"

Gia shrugged. "Like you're on top of the world. The phone has been ringing like crazy with people trying to reach you to plan their wedding."

"Sorry about that."

"Sorry?" Gia studied her. "Now I know something is

wrong. Bianca, what is it? Tell me what has you looking like you just lost your best friend."

Bianca needed someone to talk to and so she started at the beginning. She left out some of the steamy bits, some things weren't for sharing. And then the proposal—

"And you turned him down?" Gia's voice rose.

"Shh…" Bianca glanced at the doorway to assure herself that they were still alone. "I don't want anyone to know."

"I wouldn't want anyone to know you lost your mind either. I mean, it's obvious by the look on your face when you mention Leo that you love him. And he's a prince. What else do you need?"

"You don't understand. What happens when the DNA test says I'm not a Bartolini?"

"You're still you and he loves you."

Bianca shook her head. "He loves the idea of me. But when I pointed out about the DNA tests and that I could be anyone's daughter, including a criminal's, he went silent." It was only when her sister's face paled that Bianca realized she'd said too much. "Gia, I didn't mean that. I… I was just being thoughtless."

"It's okay." The look on her face said it was anything but okay. "It's the truth. We don't know anything about the biological father."

Not sure what to say, Bianca opted to distract her sister with her story about Leo. "Anyway, Leo didn't say a word and then he walked away. That was all the answer I needed."

Gia grabbed a tray of pastries and placed them in front of Bianca. "I think you're going to need these." When Bianca arched a questioning brow, Gia added, "You know, comfort food."

Bianca's gaze moved to the tray. "I'm going to need a lot more sweets than this. Do you have any chocolate?"

Before Gia could answer, sounds of a commotion came

from the front of the villa. What was that all about? Some rowdy guests?

"I'll be right back." Gia rushed out of the room.

Bianca browsed the cabinets for some chocolate. The voices in the front room grew louder and she could hear Gia's raised voice. Alarmed, Bianca pushed the cabinet door shut and rushed after her sister.

Bianca came to a halt when she spotted Leo.

Her heart leaped into her throat.

What was he doing here? Not that she should care. Whatever they'd shared was over.

"Go away."

Leo braced himself for a prickly reception. He just hadn't expected the hostility to come from Bianca's sister. It didn't surprise him. He'd handled things poorly with Bianca. He just needed a chance to make it up to her.

Luckily for him, the private jet had returned earlier than expected and he didn't have time to wait until noon for the commercial flight. It was refueled and ready to go early that morning. Still, it had taken him longer to get to the Bartolini estate than he'd planned because he had to make an important detour. It was a crucial part of his plan to win Bianca back. He hoped it would prove to her once and for all how much he cared about her...if only he could get past her brother and sister.

"I'm not leaving until I speak to Bianca," Leo said as Enzo continued to stand in front of him with his fists pressed into his sides.

"She doesn't want to see you," Enzo said while Gia agreed with him. "I don't care if you are a prince, you can't hurt my sister."

"You don't understand—"

"I understand that my sister was crying and that's all I need to know."

The fact he'd caused Bianca such pain weighed heavy on him. He had to make it up to her, if she'd let him. "I can fix this."

Gia stepped between the two men. She leveled her shoulders and tilted her chin upward. "If you've come to tell my sister that she's not good enough to be a royal, you can leave now."

That's what she thought? It couldn't be further from the truth. But he didn't want to explain himself to Bianca's siblings. The person he needed to explain things to was Bianca—

"Leo, you shouldn't be here." Bianca stepped into the room.

"Don't worry about him," Enzo said. "He was just leaving."

"No. I wasn't." Leo frowned at the man. And then he turned his attention to Bianca. "I need to speak with you. Alone."

"We have nothing left to discuss."

"Listen, I messed up and I'm sorry." He pulled a huge bouquet of red roses from behind his back. "These are for you."

Bianca's eyes paused on the flowers before meeting his gaze once more. He couldn't read her thoughts. It was as though she'd put up a protective wall and now he had to find a way to breach it.

"Please go, Leo. It's over. It was a mistake." She turned and walked away.

He desperately wanted to follow her—to tell her that nothing was over between them. They were just getting started, but her two protective siblings weren't about to let him get past them.

He placed the flowers on a stand by the door. "I'll be back."

He wasn't giving up. He loved Bianca. And she loved him too. She was afraid of the results of the DNA test and he had to prove to her that they didn't matter to him.

CHAPTER TWENTY-ONE

THE FLOWERS STARTED showing up the next day.

"I don't know where to put them all," Gia said. "It's starting to look like a florist shop in here." Gia looked at Bianca with sympathy in her eyes. "I know he screwed up, big time, but would it hurt to hear him out?"

Before Bianca could answer there was a knock at the door. She didn't have to wonder. She knew who was there—the florist. Again.

Bianca moved toward the door. "Don't worry. I'll have them take the flowers away."

She swung open the door, but the words lodged in her throat. There stood Leo.

"You can't be here," she said. "A guest might see you and it'll end up on social media."

"That's a risk I'm willing to take."

"Why are you making this so difficult?" Every time she saw him, the feeling of loss washed over her. How was she ever going to forget him—her very own Prince Charming?

"Just hear me out. That's all I'm asking. And then if you still want me to go, I will." He could see the indecision reflected in Bianca's eyes. "Please."

"Okay. We can go outside—"

"I have a car." When her eyes widened in surprise, he added, "It's getting late. I thought we could talk over dinner."

"I don't know."

"Go with him," Gia said. "Give him a chance. We don't have room for more flowers."

Maybe it was the best way to set things straight with

him. Bianca glanced down at her skinny jeans and purple top. "I should change."

"You look perfect," Leo said. "You're always beautiful."

Meanwhile, her sister stood to the side, urging them out the door.

Bianca said, "A quick dinner and then you'll leave?" When he nodded, she added, "And no more flowers?"

"I promise."

She grabbed her purse and shoes. Then they were out the door. She noticed him messaging someone as they headed toward the car. Then he slipped the phone in his pocket and opened the car door for her.

Why was he making this so difficult?

Bianca's heart ached.

There was nothing that could change things between them. Leo was royalty. She was not. And the DNA tests were delayed so it'd be another few days until they received the results.

Still, her body longed to fall into his strong arms— to rest her cheek against his muscular chest—to hear the steady pounding of his heart. It might have been a little more than twenty-four hours since she saw him last but she'd missed him dearly. How was she going to exist without seeing him again, except for on the front of a glossy magazine?

"We should talk now," she said as the car headed toward Florence.

"Not yet."

"Leo, nothing you say is going to change our circumstances."

"Just wait. We're almost there. And I'd like to be able to look at you when we talk instead of concentrating on the road."

The red sports car he'd rented slowed as they made their way into the city.

"There it is." Leo pulled into a parking spot.

Before she could get out, he'd rushed around the car and opened the door for her. As they started up the sidewalk, she noticed a group of photographers. They started snapping pictures as flashes repeatedly lit up the sky.

Bianca stopped walking. "Leo, we can't go in there."

"Sure we can."

"But the paparazzi—"

"It'll be okay."

"But how did they know you would be here?" She stared at him. Something was up, but what? "I didn't even know you'd be here."

"I told them," he said matter-of-factly.

"You did?" Her words got lost in the frenzy of questions volleyed at them from the reporters.

Leo took her hand and led her through the crowd. At last they were inside the restaurant. They were immediately seated—next to the window.

"Excuse me," Bianca said to the maître d'. "Can we have another table? Away from the window?"

"It's okay," Leo said. "I requested this table."

"You did?" She didn't understand. What was going on?

Leo took her hands in his as they stood next to the table. On the other side of the window flashes went off. But in that moment, as Leo stared into her eyes, he was all she could see. His voice was all she could hear.

"Bianca, I'm sorry about what happened back at the after-party. I didn't react the way I should have. When you started throwing out all those excuses of why we shouldn't be together, I got nervous. But now I want the entire world to know how I feel about you."

"Th-those weren't excuses. They are the truth. I'm not a part of your world. I don't even know what world I belong in. The DNA results—"

"I know where you belong. With me."

Tears stung the backs of her eyes. He was saying all the right things. "But what happens when the DNA results say I'm not a Bartolini? Those reporters out there will have a field day. It could threaten your position as king."

"It doesn't matter. Don't you know how much I love you?"

Her heart pounded in her chest. "But what about when you become king—?"

"I would step down from the throne if that's what it took for us to be together."

"You would?"

He nodded. "I would."

"But the queen—she'll never approve."

"I told her I love you and it took some convincing but she's coming around. I'm sure you can win her over."

How was it that he was overcoming all her objections? Her gaze searched his. "What are you trying to tell me?"

"Bianca, I love you and it doesn't matter about your heritage. I know you have the biggest, most caring heart." He removed a small black velvet box from his pocket and opened it. The camera flashes were now almost continuous. He held the biggest teardrop diamond ring out to her.

A tear of joy splashed onto her cheek. "Leo, what have you done?"

He dropped down on one knee. "Bianca Bartolini, I fell for you the day I saw you at the wedding at the villa. Since then I've come to love your company, your sense of humor and your warm smiles that light up my darkest days. No test is going to change my feelings for you. I love you with all my heart. And I just have one question for you: will you be my queen?"

Her heart pounded with love for this man. It was then that she realized exactly where she belonged—next to the man she loved.

"Yes. Yes, I will. I love you."

He pulled the ring from the box and slipped it on her trembling hand. And then he stood. He peered deeply into her eyes. "You're the most amazing woman. And the people of Patazonia are going to love you as much as I do."

And then he lowered his head and pressed his lips to hers as flashes lit up the entire room. Fairy tales really do come true.

* * * * *

MILLS & BOON MODERN IS
HAVING A MAKEOVER!

The same great stories you love,
a stylish new look!

Look out for our brand new look
COMING JUNE 2024

MILLS & BOON

LET'S TALK

Romance

For exclusive extracts, competitions and special offers, find us online:

f MillsandBoon

X @MillsandBoon

⊙ @MillsandBoonUK

♪ @MillsandBoonUK

Get in touch on 01413 063 232

afterglow BOOKS

Afterglow Books is a trend-led, trope-filled list of books with diverse, authentic and relatable characters, a wide array of voices and representations, plus real world trials and tribulations. Featuring all the tropes you could possibly want (think small-town settings, fake relationships, grumpy vs sunshine, enemies to lovers) and all with a generous dose of spice in every story.

♪ @millsandboonuk
⊙ @millsandboonuk
afterglowbooks.co.uk

#AfterglowBooks

For all the latest book news, exclusive content and giveaways scan the QR code below to sign up to the Afterglow newsletter:

SCAN ME

afterglow BOOKS

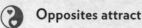
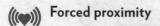
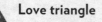

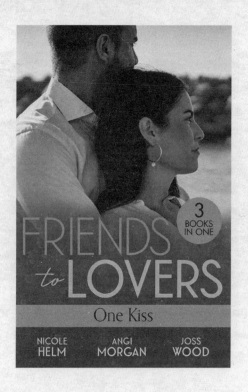

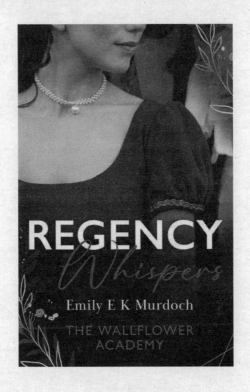

MILLS & BOON

THE HEART OF ROMANCE

A ROMANCE FOR EVERY READER

MODERN

Prepare to be swept off your feet by sophisticated, sexy and seductive heroes, in some of the world's most glamourous and romantic locations, where power and passion collide.

HISTORICAL

Escape with historical heroes from time gone by. Whether your passion is for wicked Regency Rakes, muscled Vikings or rugged Highlanders, awaken the romance of the past.

MEDICAL

Set your pulse racing with dedicated, delectable doctors in the high-pressure world of medicine, where emotions run high and passion, comfort and love are the best medicine.

True Love

Celebrate true love with tender stories of heartfelt romance, from the rush of falling in love to the joy a new baby can bring, and a focus on the emotional heart of a relationship.

HEROES

The excitement of a gripping thriller, with intense romance at its heart. Resourceful, true-to-life women and strong, fearless men face danger and desire - a killer combination!

From showing up to glowing up, these characters are on the path to leading their best lives and finding romance along the way – with plenty of sizzling spice!

To see which titles are coming soon, please visit

millsandboon.co.uk/nextmonth

GET YOUR ROMANCE FIX!

Get the latest romance news,
exclusive author interviews, story
extracts and much more!

blog.millsandboon.co.uk